THE **RED MOON**

The deadliest international secret of all . . .

THE **RED MOON**

A sensational thriller that ranks with the best . . .

THE **RED MOON**

Warren Murphy's latest web of intrigue, danger, and love will have you riveted until the last page is turned and you have discovered the secret known only as . . .

THE **RED MOON**

THE
RED MOON

WARREN MURPHY

FAWCETT GOLD MEDAL • NEW YORK

A Fawcett Gold Medal Book

Published by Ballantine Books

Copyright © 1982 by Davis/Panzer Productions
Published in association with Stan Corwin Productions

ISBN 0-449-14491-7

Manufactured in the United States of America

First Ballantine Books Edition: October 1982
10 9 8 7 6 5 4 3 2 1

For Maureen Baron,
editor and friend

Acknowledgements to: Gene Boffa, Jack Quigler, Dick Sapir, Steve Needham, Raquel Moran, Oscar Carballo, Brta Zurumay, Jose Soto, and John Adams Jr.

1943

The oil painting *Morning at Giverny* vanished from public view in 1943.

A world at war had little time to note its disappearance, and it would take the return of peace for people to wonder what had happened to the historic oil.

The canvas had been painted in the sleepy village of Giverny in France in 1880. The artist, Jean Renelle, was not well known. He had won no prizes, had been honored by no academies, and seemed content to labor in anonymity in his small studio on the top floor of the country inn at Giverny.

Morning at Giverny hung downstairs at the inn, over the fireplace. Few had seen it; fewer still had noted it. But one of those who had was the great French artist Claude Monet, who sat in the inn one long afternoon, studying the painting, marveling at its mass of color clusters that evoked morning by their brightness and light and life and not by the painting's representational values.

Monet never forgot the painting, and two years later he himself moved to Giverny. There he began a new series of major works—paintings that would help move French art further from the rigid strictures that constrained it to embrace, solidly, the Impressionist school that Monet had helped create and to exploit the freer forms that led the way to all twentieth-century painting.

By that time, Jean Renelle was dead and his painting gone, taken to Paris by the woman he had lived with. Eventually, she bartered it to a pharmacist in return for medicine and forty francs.

During the next half century, the painting was sold a half-dozen times, its value escalating as its role as one of Monet's inspirations became better known.

The last owner gladly paid five thousand times more for it than its first owner had received from the pharmacist. The new owner hung it in solitary splendor on a wall in his villa just outside Paris, receiving the homage paid it as his just due.

Then the Nazis came. France fell.

Morning at Giverny was among the looted art treasures shipped back to the Fatherland. It was a favorite of the fat comic-opera air force leader with the small avid eyes, and he hung it in a place of honor in his palace at Karinhall, in the forests north of Berlin, where he bestowed upon himself the title "Master of the German Hunt," while hiding from the war. He enjoyed gazing at the painting's lusty flamboyance before retiring to force himself on a young boy, during one of the orgies that were his primary contribution to the Nazi war effort.

In late 1943, however, the painting and three other paintings were taken from him. They were needed by Der Fuehrer for a more important purpose than providing pleasure to his Luftwaffe commander.

Carefully crated, they were taken by motorized armored car to Wilhelmshaven and loaded aboard U-505, one of Germany's newer submarines, along with a small, surprisingly heavy wooden box that took two sweating crewmen to carry. Easing from its moorings at dusk, the submarine started on its long journey out through the North Sea and over the top of the Orkney Islands. Then it veered south. Sailing on the surface at night, doing eighteen knots, and submerged during the day, traveling at seven knots, the U-505 plodded remorselessly southward, until it finally made its planned rendezvous off the eastern coast of Brazil, near the town of Fortaleza.

The paintings and the small heavy box were gingerly transferred aboard a small, aging tanker carrying Panamanian papers. They were awaited there by a stern-faced young man who wore his rumpled white suit as if it were the parade-ground finery of a French field marshal. The man was young, in his early twenties, but his blond hair was so white that, glinting in the sun, it looked gray. Yet his face was unlined, smooth with the internal glow of those who know their causes to be worthy of themselves.

The young blond man saluted the U-boat commander from the bridge of the tanker, automatically clicking his heels. He flushed at the dull thud from the rubber heels of his shabby brown shoes, then hurried to the captain's cabin to be with the wooden box and the crates containing the paintings.

The U-505, its fuel tanks replenished, turned back to the east, to prowl the coast of Africa. The tanker steamed slowly off toward the west, hugging the coastline. Days later, it slipped into a small Venezuelan port and moored at a rickety dock.

Morning at Giverny was about to be acquired by a new owner—a man who neither knew nor cared about art.

BOOK ONE

CHAPTER ONE

Ten years ago, Gus Griffin had gone hunting wild boar in the Tellico Plains along the Great Smokies in the southeastern corner of Tennessee, near its border with North Carolina. He had hit one of the bristly beasts with a single shot from his .38 caliber Smith & Wesson at forty yards. But the hit was not clean and the animal had squealed, changed direction, and plunged into some undergrowth beneath a stand of trees.

Griffin started after the boar.

"You can't go in there," his guide said. "Tuskers're crazy when they wounded."

"The hell I can't," Gus Griffin said. "Where I come from, you finish what you started."

It was hot afternoon, but in the tightly packed overhang of trees it was dark and cool. Gus was ten yards in when he heard a chilling hiss behind him. He wheeled, but before he could fire, a two-hundred-pound boar slammed its bomblike body into Gus's leg, knocking down the big Texan.

Though the Smith & Wesson flew from his hand, it did not occur to Griffin to yell for help. Instead, he reached for the knife on his belt.

The boar dug one of his tusks into Gus's face, and even as the man's fingers curled around the hilt of the knife, Gus knew that his right eye had been ripped out. It was a cold, emotionless thought, he would recall later, almost as if he had looked at the sky and commented to himself that it sure looked like it was going to be a nice day.

Gus felt the wild pig's hooves digging into his legs. He could smell the boar's hot breath, sickly-sweet with the aroma of decayed food. The beast's squealing resounded in his ears like the agonized shrieking of machinery that had gone too long without oil. As the boar reared up over Gus's prone body, the gray-haired man slammed upward with the tip of his razor-sharp knife. He felt it resist for a moment as it touched flesh, and he pressed harder, then ripped with all his strength to the left. The shrieking of the boar turned into a bubbling gurgle, and Griffin could feel the beast's weight sagging on the end of the knife. Gus rolled over and struggled to his knees, gripping the handle of the knife with both hands, tugging it from side to side, feeling the pulsing warm blood from the wild pig's throat spraying against his face.

Three minutes later when the guide arrived on the scene, Gus was standing over the dead boar. Its throat had been ripped out and its head seemed attached only by a handful of stringy tendons. Gus held his right hand over his eye, and blood ran down his face.

His left eye focused meanly on the guide, who reacted with horror.

"It's about time you got here, you dumb bastard," Griffin said. "You better get me to a hospital. And I want this frigging head."

Gus signed himself out of the Knoxville hospital six days later, wearing a patch over the empty socket of his right eye. Soon after, the head of the boar hung in his office over his long mahogany bar. When people asked him about the incident, Griffin said his only regret was that no one had been able to find his eyeball. "That goddam tusker must have mashed it underfoot," he said. "I wanted to mount it on the goddam plaque right over the bastard's head."

The story, surprisingly unembellished, was often repeated in Houston, Texas, as proof that Augustus—Gus—Griffin, the owner and chief operating officer of Griffin Oil, was the toughest old cocker who ever lived. And maybe a touch nuts.

Doyle Blaney thought about the story as he stood at the bar in Griffin's office on the top floor of the Griffin Oil Company building and looked up at the malevolent killing eyes of the wild pig. He poured a healthy shot of Jose Cuervo tequila into a water glass. He knew that if a similar tale were ever told about him, he would not

6

wind up being described as tough and charming and eccentric and lovable. He would be described as a mean goddam animal.

Blaney had been working for Gus Griffin for nine years, and while Griffin was accepted throughout all of Houston—in the oil community, which was one thing, and in the social community, which was quite another—Doyle Blaney was always an outsider, viewed with as much warmth as an insect that pops up from behind the sink in a hotel room. He consoled himself with the thought that he had thirty years on the seventy-five-year-old Griffin. He had time to make them all change their minds.

After he poured another drink, Blaney turned toward the large mahogany desk in the room. The two water glasses were dwarfed by his big hands, which jutted out from his sleeves, leaving the impression that the sleeves were too short on his good gabardine suit.

He handed one of the glasses to Griffin, who sat in shirt sleeves, his feet, encased in hand-tooled brown leather boots with decorative stitching across the toes, propped up on his desk.

It had taken a dozen years in Houston but Blaney had finally gotten used to the way oilmen dressed, even though he still thought it was comical. They all wanted to look like cowboys, but real cowboys dressed like farmhands, and nobody wanted to look like a farmhand. So oilmen compromised; they settled for dressing like cowboys in a movie musical. They wore boots and hand-stitched embroidered shirts and suits embellished with so much piping that a group of oilmen at lunch looked like the backup band at the Grand Ole Opry. It was how they showed they were Texans with money.

"Talk to Adam?" Blaney asked. He gestured toward Griffin with his glass in a casual toast, sipped his drink, then sat in the soft leather chair facing the desk.

"Not this week. Why?"

"You're going to have to do something about him. He's at me every day with facts and figures about how Griffin Oil could expand if we only got off the dime and took a few chances."

Griffin scratched under the leather patch covering his right eye. The corners of his mouth turned down in disgust.

7

"So what? He's been talking that way ever since he got out of Harvard. Just pat him on the head and ignore him. His day comes when I'm dead."

"He doesn't seem inclined to wait," Blaney said.

"I could drop dead next week."

"And you could live to the next century."

"Just between you and me and the smog out there, I damn well intend to."

"That's what Adam figures. Anyway, sometimes he makes sense. The company probably could take off. Especially if you expanded your money base."

"Don't you start too," Griffin said. "Share the profits. Sure. Bullshit. You share profits when you want to share risk. But there's no risk in this company. Why share anything? What the hell's Adam want, anyway? He's got all the money he can use."

"Power, Gus. Glory. He wants to see his name in *Business Week* and *The New York Times.* He wants *Fortune* to write an article about his hobbies. Most of all, he wants out from under your thumb to be his own man."

"Then let him get his own oil company." Griffin snorted. "He didn't build this company. I did. He can have it when I die. Until then, I run it my way." He tossed his drink down as if it somehow offended him, then slid the empty glass across the polished desk toward Blaney.

Blaney waited until he had finished his own drink, then stood up to make refills. "Whatever you say, Gus," he agreed casually. "But it's an irritation anyway. Bad for morale. Adam's going around talking to the managers, asking them what they could do to expand the company. Some of them like what he's saying. You might hear from them one day."

"The hell with them and the hell with Adam too. Maybe I made a mistake making him president. Maybe I ought to bounce him right out of that nice big office with the thick rug and that goddam im-ported furniture and tell him to find a real job for himself."

"Not worth the trouble," Blaney said, pouring more tequila. "He'd take you to court."

The old man frowned. "Adam? You think he'd have enough gumption? I almost wish I could believe it."

"You know your son better than I do, Gus. But people

8

change. Adam too. He's getting close to forty, and that's a big time in a man's life. He starts wondering if he's ever going to amount to anything. Some men get around it with women. But all Adam's got is the company."

Griffin slapped his hand on the desk in disgust. "Not quite and not ever," he said. "Christ, he's a strange one. I wonder how he ever got the nerve to ask Annie to marry him. Did I ever tell you about that girl in the typing pool, that Gonzalez?"

"She the one you always locked your door behind when she came up here?"

"How the hell'd you know that?"

"I wouldn't be much of a chief of security if I didn't know."

Griffin cleared his throat. "All right. Anyway, I told this little *puta* that I wanted her to get into Adam's office and put the make on him. I thought it might be good for him."

"And?"

"She came back and told me that he almost fainted when he realized what she was hinting at. He called her a harlot. For Christ's sakes, a *harlot*. I haven't heard that word in thirty years. I had to give her a raise just to make sure she wouldn't go spreading that story all over the building. It's hard to believe he's a Griffin."

Blaney handed the old man another drink. "He is, though. And he's got his wits and he's got his energy. That's why he keeps going to all those business meetings that you never bother to show up for. He's learning everything, making every contact he can. I think it's unhealthy. You ought to start paying him a little more mind. Throw him a bone once in a while."

"I don't need this," the old man snarled. "I got enough on my mind as it is. Keep an eye on him if you want to, but I ain't going to get worried about his pipe dreams."

"He had lunch with Sherry last week," Blaney said quietly.

Griffin looked at his aide in open surprise. "Adam and Sherry? Lunch? Hell, he can hardly choke down his food at the ranch when she's in the same room. What's that all about? And why didn't Sherry tell me about it?"

"Got me. I didn't hear about it until a couple of days

ago," Blaney said. "But it bothered me. Why would Adam have lunch with a stepmother he detests?"

"All right, Blaney," Gus said with finality. "You're sliding around to something. Why not just get it out in the open?"

"Okay, Gus. What would happen if Sherry voted her stock the way Adam wanted her to vote it?"

"I'd kill her."

Blaney shrugged and Griffin said, "Scratch that. I'd have you kill her while I was out of town."

Blaney smiled slightly. "You'd have to give me a raise. And then I'd have to think about it."

"We'll never have to find out," Griffin said. "Sherry wouldn't do that. She's too smart. She'd lose everything, and she knows it."

"Guess you're right," Blaney agreed politely.

"You know I'm right." Griffin looked at Blaney, but the tall man's face was impressively unconvinced. "All right. You can get somebody to start keeping an eye on her if you want, but make sure you trust him. I don't want some private detective who thinks he's Columbo finding her shacked up and thinking he can shake her down or make trouble."

"All right. Leave it with me," Blaney said.

"And keep an eye on Adam too while you're at it. Cozy up to him a little bit and figure out what's on his mind."

"Should be easy," Blaney said. "Adam's never been devious. If he's got something concrete in mind, he'll spill it."

"I know it," Griffin said, shaking his head in bafflement. "He's no boy of mine, that's for sure. He must take after somebody on his mother's side."

CHAPTER TWO

Adam Griffin looked at the beautiful blond woman with the mixed emotions of a born-again Christian being offered a rainy-night ride to a revival meeting by a prostitute—despising the woman but lusting after the ride.

His feelings were complicated further by the fact that though she was only two years older than he was, Sherry Griffin was technically his stepmother.

"It's a simple business proposition," he repeated with the patient tone of a kindergarten teacher. "It's really in your own best interests."

"No. I'll tell you what's in my own best interests. Staying alive. Gus would skin me if I did what you want. You don't have to live with your father. I do. You see him once or twice a week here at the office. I've got to put up with him seven days a week. I don't want to be killed."

"Dad can be difficult. I know that."

"Difficult? Nice word, Adam. But your father's not difficult. Your father is a raging homicidal maniac. You can shove difficult, I could deal with difficult. I can't deal with being a murder victim."

Adam Griffin looked pained.

"I'll buy it from you," he repeated desperately.

"Forget it. We went through all that a week ago at the lovely Burger King lunch you bought me. You can't afford it."

"Sherry, the stock's not worth anything if the company doesn't pay any dividends. And we're never going to, the way Dad keeps running things in the same old way. He collects his salary as chairman of the board and I collect my salary as president of the company and all you collect is a lot of wrinkles waiting for him to die."

Sherry looked at him with a faint smile on her face. "Don't try to dump that load on me, Adam. You'd turn cartwheels all the way to the cemetery if Gus dropped dead

11

today. But don't hold your breath. He's strong as an ox. He'll outlive us both."

She watched with amusement as Adam reddened. "Tha-that's not t-true," he stammered, reddening even more as his tongue betrayed his agitation. He took a deep breath, closed his eyes, and sat silently behind his desk for a moment. Then he looked again at his stepmother. "I hope Dad lives to be a hundred," he said. "But I'm tired of his treating this company like a private little piggy bank when it could become a major corporation. I own half of this company—almost half, dammit—and I have a right to w-w-want to see it grow."

"There, there, Adam, take it easy. Don't get so worked up. You want your ulcer to start acting up on you again?"

"Then don't ever say I want my father d-d-dead," he snapped. Standing up abruptly, he strode to the ceiling-to-floor window and looked blindly out at downtown Houston, sprawling smoggily out in front of him. The view revealed a series of clusters of tall buildings, all searching for a central core around which to build a city.

Sherry Griffin watched him from her chair. Adam was as tall as Gus Griffin and thirty pounds heavier, but on him it looked like thirty-eight-year-old baby fat. With his inexpensive dark-blue pin-striped suit and conservative black shoes, he looked more like a Wall Street bank clerk than the son and heir of craggy, weather-worn Gus Griffin, the oilfield roustabout who had made good.

She thought again of how little they seemed like father and son. Gus swore lustily, drank heavily, bore teenage tattoos on his arm and the scars of barroom brawls on his face, and loved all-night poker games for high stakes. His pudgy son lived quietly in a modest home, attended church regularly, confined his drinking to wine with meals, and seldom used even a mild curse.

"He wouldn't say crap if he had a mouthful of it," Gus had once told her, shaking his head scornfully.

Gus smoked cigars and occasionally chewed tobacco. Adam used to smoke an occasional filtered cigarette, but when he found himself up to five a day, he decided he was an addict, went to Smokenders, and gave them up. Sherry found herself amused that he had managed to father three prim and proper children by Anne, his prim and proper wife, and wondered to herself who had told Adam how.

Still, Adam could be cutting and mean. He had made it clear to Sherry when she had married Gus ten years ago that he regarded her as little better than a common prostitute who had taken advantage of his father in a moment of weakness. He had treated her with snubs and sarcasm, and their relationship had been cool to the point of frost.

Not that Sherry hadn't tried to change it. She was happy being Mrs. Gus Griffin and she went out of her way to try to improve her relationship with Adam and his family. She called Anne often to inquire about the health of the children. She offered herself up for baby-sitting services. She never forgot a birthday, always sending an expensive gift and a card with a personal note. But nothing seemed to work. Adam merely tolerated her efforts, and then he would tear it all down with one biting remark.

In the last six months, though, as Adam had become increasingly obsessed with the idea of assuming control over his father's small but independently owned oil firm, Sherry thought she had noticed some small softening in his attitude toward her. If she hadn't she would have instantly reported Adam's proposals to Gus and that would have been that. Instead, she had kept quiet and continued to meet with Adam and listened to him reel off his visions of expansion and diversification, of managing a huge conglomerate, of being treated as an equal by the mightiest forces in Houston and in New York and Washington.

Sherry held the key to his dreams, because her ten percent of the shares of Griffin Oil, added to Adam's forty-five percent, could give him voting control of the firm and free him from his father's tight control.

She had hoped that Adam's business interest in her might lead to a change in his personal animosity toward her. Even though Gus liked her to wear tight dresses and deep-cut blouses to show off her voluptuous figure, she dressed demurely, in tailored suits, for her meetings with Adam.

But nothing had changed. There had been no personal contact with Adam's family, no invitations to visit his home, and she finally realized that he regarded her as someone who had something he wanted, and as nothing more. Too bad, she thought; it was his loss.

13

Sherry interrupted his musing. "Adam, I've got to go. I've got some shopping I want to do, and I don't want to get caught in the traffic crush going back to the ranch."

Adam took a deep breath and turned back to the woman. She sat demurely in the chair, legs crossed at the ankle, wearing a beige silk suit. Her skin was healthily pink, without the suntanned leather look that so many rich Texas women seemed to favor. Her eyes were a cool blue, and they seemed to mock him.

"Unless you've got any more good reasons why I should let you vote my stock," she said.

"Just money," he said bluntly.

"That's not enough. I've got enough money, and Gus has tons more than you do."

"A hundred thousand for the right to vote your stock for two years. After that, it reverts to you and you'll be a multimillionaire."

"Well, that's twice as good as your last offer, but you're still a long way from home."

"I can do better once I've got the company moving," he said.

"Promises. All my life, people made me promises. Gus is one of the few who ever delivered."

"I can make you an officer of the firm. Vice-president if you want."

"And fire me if *you* want. No thanks." She stopped for a moment as she saw on his face a look of hopeless despair. She knew the look well. She had seen it in her own mirror in the years after she had first gone to Hollywood, when she found out that golden beauties from Nebraska and forty-nine other states were as common and as interchangeable as department-store coffee cups. She had first seen the look on her face then, and she had seen it with increasing frequency as she struggled to make a career as an actress. But each promising opportunity, each chance, somehow turned into a request for her to flop onto her back. And when the encounter was over, there was no job, there was no call, and the look of desperation grew. It grew even more with the bad marriage that left her with a baby, a thickened stomach, and not even a handful of good memories for solace. She knew what made it so desperate for

14

Adam. It had been awful for her because she had believed in herself, just as Adam believed in himself and what he planned to do with Griffin Oil. Setbacks were harder to take when they were illogical, when they failed to surrender to simple reason.

For a moment, she felt sorry for Adam, and impulsively she said, "You want a deal? A million dollars for an option. Five million if you exercise."

"A million dollars?" The expression on Adam's face changed from despair to disgust.

"Why not? Your father says I have million-dollar legs," she cooed. She smiled sweetly at Adam, her pearl-perfect teeth glinting in the bright sunlight that streamed through the office windows. She gestured as if to draw the hem of her skirt above her knees.

"Stop that," Adam snapped. "A million dollars. You must think I'm crazy."

Annoyed with herself for teasing him, Sherry stood up. "That's the way it is, Adam. Sorry. Gus gave that stock to me free and clear. I can do what I want with it."

"I'm sure you've earned it many times over," he said.

Sherry's face hardened. "There you go again. You just can't help being snotty, can you?"

"A million dollars," Adam repeated.

"You know, Adam, you're really a fool. You could have had that stock."

"For a million dollars?"

"For a song," she said. "You could have tried being nice to me. You could have invited me to dinner at your house. You could have stopped locking your kids up when I'm around. You could have stopped being snotty when you talked to me. You could have told Anne to smile at me once in a while. Was that too much to ask?" Belatedly, she realized that it sounded like a plea, and she was angered with herself for weakening enough to utter it.

"I don't know," Adam said. His face told Sherry that he had never considered the idea, never even thought of it. "I never pictured you as the grandmotherly type."

"The idea might grow on you," she said. She watched him, but his face was impassive. He said nothing. Disconsolately, she realized that her price was more than he was

15

willing to pay, and she walked toward the door. "It's tough dealing with stockholders, Adam. Maybe you're not cut out for the work. Toodle-ooo."

After the door closed behind her, Adam turned back to his desk, his thin lips pressed tightly together in his stolid face. He picked up the phone and dialed a number. When the telephone was answered, he said simply: "Get the bitch."

As Sherry left the elevator, she stopped at the lobby counter for a pack of cigarettes. The counterman recognized her and refused to take her money. She lit one of the cigarettes, then stepped out of the cool office building. The noonday Texas heat hit her almost like a blow. She glanced up and down the small access street, looking for her Cadillac limousine, but it was not there. Instead Doyle Blaney drove up in his car and electrically lowered the curbside window.

He leaned across the seat. "Gus sent your driver on an errand. He told me to take you where you wanted to go."

"No thanks, I'll walk."

"Come on. Don't get me into trouble," he said.

"All right," she said after a pause. "You can drop me at Nieman-Marcus."

She got into the car and quickly closed the window to seal off the outside heat.

"Just Nieman-Marcus?" Blaney asked as he drove off.

"What does that mean, 'just Nieman-Marcus'?"

"Nothing. It's just that last week, well, I thought I saw you with that tennis bum from your club."

"Don't call him a tennis bum. He has a wonderful ground stroke. And what business is it of yours, anyway?"

"None, I guess."

"None, I know," Sherry said. "Look, Blaney, you can be Gus's chief cook and bottle washer if you want. You can be his snoop if you want. You can lick his boots in the morning if you want. But what's between Gus and me is between Gus and me and you've got nothing to do with it. So piss off."

They sat in silence until he let her out at the front entrance of the large department store. Without even glancing behind her, Sherry walked quickly into the store. Once inside, she stopped, fingering leather purses on a counter, and watched until she saw Blaney's golden Thunderbird pull away from the curb. She stepped back outside quickly, in time to see the car turn right at the next corner.

She walked to the curb and hailed a taxi to the Holiday Inn. Inside, she walked to the house phone with the directness of a person who had used it before.

"Please ring Mr. Frank Everts's room."

"One moment, please," the operator said.

Sherry heard the telephone buzz, then a voice answering cautiously, "Yes?"

"Me, honey," she said.

"Come on up. Room 1127."

It was the standard room of a standard commercial hotel. Paintings picked by a committee, rug and upholstery fabrics chosen carefully not to offend and generally failing. The man who opened the door for Sherry was in his early thirties. A generation earlier, his thinning blond hair would have been combed into a pasted-down plastic pompadour, but now it was curled into tight ringlets. He wore light-blue polyester slacks, a white synthetic shirt, and an anxious look. Sherry tossed her purse onto the nearer twin bed and hurled herself into his arms, holding him tightly and rocking back and forth.

"It's so good to see you again, Frank," she said. "God, I miss you. I just wish you'd come out and see me at the ranch."

"C'mon, honey, we've been through this before," the man said. "You know Gus would run me off with a shotgun if I went out there. Anyway, I've got a living to make back in L.A."

"I know, but I miss you so much sometimes I could just spit. I didn't bargain on spending my whole life on that ranch and never seeing you. Why the hell did you have to tick Gus off by trying to hustle that poker game?"

"I didn't plan on him catching me," the man complained. "Christ, he like to break my arms."

"Oh, Frank," Sherry said mournfully. She cupped his face in her hands, stared at him longingly, then kissed him again. He held her tightly for a long moment, then reached down and swatted her bottom.

"C'mon, you're getting me all steamed up," he said. "Still Scotch?"

"Anything but bourbon."

Sherry looked around the room as Frank Everts mixed two highballs from a setup tray atop a dresser. The only luggage visible in the room was a cheap attaché case on the dresser. The open closets were empty.

Everts handed her one of the drinks, and they clicked glasses before sipping.

"Like I told you on the telephone, Adam finally came up with a price," she said. Quickly, she outlined Adam's proposal.

When she was done, Everts said, "Not bad, kiddo."

"Not good enough, though." She took a long pull on her drink. "I'm just confused, Frank."

"Why?"

"Well, I know I should have told Gus the first time Adam talked to me about the stock. But I thought it was a chance to get closer to Adam and his family. Now I don't know. It's gone on so long and if I tell Gus... well, I don't know what he'll do."

Everts shrugged. "What can he do?"

"You forget, Frank. When Gus and I got married, I signed that damned agreement. If he drops me, I don't have a nickel. I have 'renounced totally and forever all claims against said Augustus Griffin and his property and his estate.' Hell." She sipped savagely at her drink. "I wouldn't be so spooky if it was just me. But there's Tina to think about. She loves it there on the ranch, riding her horse all the time. And clothes. And private school. College when she's ready. Gus treats her like his own daughter. Maybe I could start over again, but I don't want her to have nothing. I've been there. Nothing sucks."

"A hundred thousand isn't exactly nothing," Everts said.

"It's nothing compared with losing Gus."

"You're the one who keeps telling me he's seventy-five years old, Sherry. Suppose someday he wakes up senile and doesn't remember who you are and Adam talks him into divorcing you. What then?"

"You tell me," Sherry said.

18

Everts put his glass down on the dresser and sat on one of the twin beds next to Sherry. He put one arm around her shoulders and with his other hand patted her knee. "When you called me and told me what was happening, I talked to my lawyer. And that's why I called you to meet me here. My lawyer says you have to protect yourself. He says in a fight between Adam and Gus, you're just going to wind up hurt if you stay in the middle."

"But I *am* in the middle."

"Frank Everts to the rescue," the man said with a smile. "That's what I told my lawyer, and that's the good news I've got for you."

"Oh?"

"Yeah. My lawyer said he'd take an option on your stock himself, just as a speculation, just to see what happens to Griffin Oil."

"And what do I get out of it?"

"Better than Adam's offer. A hundred thousand. For one year. At the end of the year, if he wants to renew the option, he'll pay another hundred thousand. If the company does go public, he'll buy your stock for a million dollars or the offering price, whatever's better."

"Jesus, Frank, that's not bad." She drained her drink, then a puzzled look came over her face. "Wait a minute. What does your lawyer get out of it?"

Everts laughed. "Some goddam kind of tax-shelter thing. You know how lawyers are. They figure out ways that somebody can make money by losing money. He's got investors who'll put up the dough. But that's his problem. What it does, honey, is it gets you out of the middle. Gus and Adam can't pull you back and forth between them. Just tell them to see your lawyer."

"Frank, that's terrific. That can solve everything."

"I thought so."

"What do I have to do?"

Frank Everts walked over and opened the attaché case. "I just happened to have brought my music," he said. He turned, holding a sheaf of blue-jacketed legal-size papers. "I've done it all," he said. "All you've got to do is sign."

"And my money?"

"It's still at the lawyer's office in L.A. Sign this, and he'll transfer it over to your account."

19

Sherry glanced through the papers quickly, nodding all the while. "I want this, Frank. I really do. Do you know, I think my husband has that goddam snoop of his keeping tabs on me?"

"Well, as long as you're not doing anything wrong..."

Sherry smiled at him. "I never do anything wrong." She stood up from the bed and put her arms around him, hugging him tightly. "I knew I could count on you. I knew I could."

He kissed her lightly on the forehead, then more forcefully on the neck as he moved her back toward the bed where they both sat.

"You and me together, Sherry, always and forever. What's a brother for, anyway?"

"A foster brother," she corrected. "You trying to make us sound dirty?" She giggled as she started to unbutton his shirt.

Downstairs in the hotel lobby, Doyle Blaney called the Griffin Oil offices. This was the delicate part, he told himself.

"Hello, Gus, it's Doyle. She spent an hour in Adam's office this morning. She left a little before noon."

"What's she been up to since then?" Gus demanded.

"Seeing store clerks. Wandering around, shopping," Blaney said. "Relax. She hasn't bought anything yet."

"That won't last," Griffin grunted. "Come back whenever you want to."

"I'll probably get a drink first," Blaney said.

"Enjoy it."

Griffin hung up. Blaney said into the dead telephone, "I intend to, Gus. I intend to."

Then he went up to the eleventh floor, found a comfortable chair near the main bank of elevators, and sat down to wait.

CHAPTER THREE

Sherry was halfway down the hotel corridor before she noticed Doyle Blaney in the chair. Her step faltered for a moment, then she strode up to him defiantly.

"What are you doing here?" she demanded.

He smiled at her lazily, stood up, and sauntered back down the corridor to Room 1127, followed by Sherry. He tapped lightly on the door.

When it opened, he nodded to the startled Frank Everts. The smaller man just stared back. Blaney reached for the knob and pulled the door shut again, then turned and strolled back toward the elevators, ignoring both Sherry and her flustered foster brother, who had opened the door again and stepped tentatively into the corridor.

"I'll handle this, Frank," Sherry told him. She hurried after Blaney, reaching him as he pressed the down button. She grabbed his other arm and tried to swing him around.

"What the hell are you up to, Blaney?"

He smiled at her again, a not-nice smile that reminded her of a cartoon cat about to pounce.

"I figured it was him," Blaney said.

"So? You bastard."

"Now, don't make a scene and embarrass yourself, Sherry," Blaney said quietly. "I'm going to stop at the bar downstairs before I head back to the office. Join me?"

"I'd rather go strolling with Jack the Ripper," she snarled.

Blaney shrugged. "Suit yourself," he said agreeably. The elevator arrived, and he walked in without a backward look. Sherry angrily followed him. A uniformed porter was in the car, along with a middle-aged executive in a vested suit and a much younger woman with tousled hair who stood carefully apart from each other, looking belligerently innocent. Sherry bit her lip and remained silent until they arrived at the main floor and walked into the lobby. She grabbed Blaney's arm again.

"Goddammit, stand still and look at me and tell me what's going on," she hissed.

He stopped and looked down at her. "There's probably not too many people in the bar at this hour," he said quietly. "We should be able to get a nice quiet booth. I'm not going to stay too long, though. I hate that rush-hour traffic."

"Too goddam bad what you hate," Sherry said, but she followed him into the bar. Blaney chose a booth in the rear and asked the waiter for Scotch sours for both of them. They sat silently until their drinks were brought, the tension mounting steadily in her.

"All right," she snapped as the waiter moved away. "What are you doing here? Were you following me?"

"Of course."

"Why?"

"Just doing my job."

"You mean Gus told you to follow me around?"

"Let's say he suggested that I keep an eye on you. For your own protection, of course."

"That son of a bitch."

"Your husband and the man you love," Blaney said mockingly.

"You and him. You deserve each other," she said.

"Temper, temper."

"You go ahead and tell Gus," she said. "Don't bother. I'll tell him myself. And I'll tell him a few other things too."

"I said that Gus told me to keep an eye on you. I didn't say that I was going to tell him you were seeing your brother, Frank, the noted card player."

"You bastard, I wouldn't trust a thing you said, and neither would Gus if he had any sense. I wouldn't believe you if you said it was Wednesday."

"Some days it is Wednesday," he said, then leaned forward. "It's true, Sherry. I didn't even tell Gus about the tennis pro and your private lessons."

"What private lessons?" she asked blandly. "What tennis pro?"

"And I didn't say anything about the two hours your car was parked at that airport motel last Thursday."

"I was visiting a sick friend. A sick *girl* friend."

"I wouldn't be a bit surprised," he said.

"You really enjoy playing Mr. Super Sleuth again, don't you?"

"Just like old times," he said. "Only I'm a lot better paid now. And, of course, there are fringe benefits."

"I'm not one of them, in case you're getting any ideas."

"That's too bad, Sherry. I was hoping we might get to be friends. Even close friends."

"Forget it. You make me sick to my stomach. You're worse than those sleazy cigar-chewing producers I used to fight off."

For a moment, Blaney reddened. He had big white teeth, and he showed them all. Sherry didn't like his teeth. "You didn't fight them all off," he said. "And of course there's Adam. Messing around with Gus's son."

Sherry gaped at him in amazement, then laughed. "You jackass. Adam? That twerp? I'd have a better chance of making it with the Pope. Adam's got less use for me than I have for him." She laughed again.

"Easy to say. So explain the lunches and all the office visits." He asked it casually as he sipped at his drink. Sherry slowly smiled.

"So that's what this is all about," she said. "I might have known. Oh, you rotten bastards." She stood and picked up her purse. "You know, Blaney, your timing was all wrong. Six weeks ago or six days ago, even six hours ago, you might have been able to squeeze me with what you think you know. But now you're too late."

The thought of the papers she had just signed emboldened her, and she squeezed her way out of the booth. "Now I'm going back to the office to tell my loving husband where to get off. I hope you choke on your drink, you goddam sneak."

"We haven't finished our talk," Blaney said. "You still have your drink."

"You know what you can do with it. And please leave the stirrer in." She marched out of the cocktail lounge.

Blaney waited until Sherry had left the darkened lounge before he allowed himself the luxury of a smile. He waved to the waiter for another drink, got to his feet, and

23

headed for a telephone booth, whistling lightly under his breath.

"Velma, it's Blaney. Let me talk to the boss."

A moment later, Gus Griffin's voice rasped: "What is it?"

"Your beloved brother-in-law is in town."

"That thieving shitpoke? How do you know?"

"I followed Sherry. She stopped in his hotel room."

"Dammit. She said she was going to stay away from him."

"Yeah, I know. Anyway, while I was in the hallway trying to figure out what room she was in, she popped out and saw me. I tried to calm her down by buying her a drink, but—"

"What are you telling me all this for?" interrupted Griffin. "You know I hate talking on the phone. Give me the details later."

"I just wanted you to be ready for her. I think she's on her way up to your office with blood in her eye. She yelled about me spying on her and then she said if I didn't tell you about it, we might be 'very close friends' in the future."

"She said that, did she?"

"Afraid so, Gus. And she got pissed when I asked her about her and Adam. I don't know what the hell she's going to tell you."

"Okay. I'll talk to you later."

Gus Griffin hung up. Blaney dropped another dime into the coin slot.

"Adam? Doyle. It's done."

"Yahooo."

"Everything went the way we expected. I think she's on her way back there to see your father, so you may want to sneak our friend out the back way."

"All right," Adam Griffin said. "I'll take care of everything. Good job, Doyle."

"I just want you to know, Adam, I never would have done this if you hadn't made it clear to me that I'm actually looking out for Mr. Griffin's best interests."

"It's true, Doyle, you are."

"I believe it. I think you have the vision to make Griffin Oil a great company."

"Thanks, Doyle. *We'll* make it a great company. I want

24

you with me every step of the way." His voice seemed filled with emotion.

"You know you can trust me, Adam. I just want to help. Talk to you later."

Blaney hung up and strolled back to his booth in the cocktail lounge, still whistling tunelessly under his breath. *Yes, Adam, sure, I just want to help you. And I most certainly am going to help myself.*

Sherry brushed past Velma, her husband's secretary, without even a nod and walked into Gus Griffin's office. He looked up at her as she perched on the arm of the chair facing his desk. The black patch over his right eye contrasted sharply with his ruddy skin, and Sherry found herself wondering again if there wasn't a different kind of patch he could wear—some other color, perhaps—that wouldn't make him look so piratical and so ferocious. She put the thought out of her mind. He deserved to look ferocious, the bastard.

"Guess who I ran into this afternoon," she said brightly.

"Who?"

"Doyle Blaney."

"Oh, yeah? Where?"

"In the hallway of the Holiday Inn, spying on me, like you told him to do," she flared.

"Yeah? And what were you doing in the Holiday Inn?" Griffin's voice had started to rise in volume.

"Visiting my brother that I haven't seen in eight months," she said defiantly. "Any objections?"

Griffin stared at her coldly. "What other thieves you been seeing lately?"

"Why don't you ask Mr. FBI in Peace and War Blaney for my goddam itinerary?" she yelled.

" 'Cause I'm asking you."

"None of your damned business who I see."

"The hell it ain't," he yelled back. "You're my wife. You were a two-bit actress when I met you and almost ready to turn tricks. I married you and I gave you every goddam thing you've got, so don't tell me what you do ain't none of my business. I ain't too old to take you over my knee if I feel like it."

"You lay a hand on me and I'll—"

25

"You'll do shit," he said flatly, "'cause there's nothing you can do and no place you can go. Anything you've got in this world belongs to me."

"You think so," she hissed, leaning forward, her eyes blazing. "Well, that's just what the hell you think. Maybe once but not now."

Griffin grasped the arms of his ornate swivel chair, then relaxed with an effort and leaned back, studying her.

"You know what I've got against that brother of yours?" he asked, suddenly mild.

"Yeah. He's forty years younger than you are."

Griffin shook his head. "He's a thief, and the worst kind. He'll steal from kin. He tried to steal from me. That's why he's on my list. And that's where you're going to be too if you don't watch your step."

He stared levelly at her for a long moment, then abruptly terminated the conversation by spinning around and resuming work at his desk.

Sherry stood and walked slowly toward the door, biting her underlip. She paused, then turned to face her husband's back.

"You go to hell, Gus Griffin," she said. "And take your list with you."

She slammed the door behind her and again brushed by her husband's secretary without a word. The tall, lissome, dark-haired girl ran after her into the hall.

"Mrs. Griffin," she called.

Sherry turned back, angry with her husband, with Blaney, with the world, even with dark-haired young women with flawless complexions for whom wrinkles were always tomorrow. Especially with them.

"What do you want?" Sherry said.

"Mr. Adam called. He wanted to see you before you left the building."

"Tell him ... no, wait. How did he know I was here?"

Velma shrugged. "I don't know, Mrs. Griffin. He just called and left that message."

"Another goddam spy network," Sherry muttered. "All right, I'll go see *Mr.* Adam. I might as well tell one more Griffin exactly what I think of him."

She walked down the long flight of steps to Adam's office floor. Adam's secretary, Mrs. Penrose, seemed to be expecting her, because she smiled and said, "You can go right in, Mrs. Griffin."

"How nice that everybody in Houston knows where I'll be every minute of every day," Sherry said. When she walked into Adam's office, he was standing behind his desk, looking out the window. Behind him, she could see the city spread out, sprawling and busy, dusted over with the smog that others hated, but that Sherry always thought was a small price to pay for proof of life, proof that people were doing things here.

"What do you want?" she said to Adam's back. "And by the way, I've decided you can shove your offer."

Without turning, Adam said softly, "There are going to be some changes around here. Griffin Oil is going to be a lot more businesslike in the future. One thing we'll do to see to that is to keep out of the building a lot of people who don't have any real business here. That includes you."

Sherry blinked her eyes in surprise. Just what the hell did that mean? Still without turning, he said, "You lower the class of the place, and I don't want you around here anymore."

"What are you talking about?" Sherry said, and then, as Adam turned, her stomach rolled over and she felt her heart skip once. In his hands he held a sheaf of blue papers, the same kind of paper she had signed less than an hour ago in her stepbrother's hotel room. *They weren't the same. They couldn't be.* Adam waved them toward her with a smile.

"You made a mistake in not dealing with me," he said, "instead of that shabby little conman brother of yours. I have my doubts that you're ever going to see a penny of the money for this option you were dumb enough to sign. But bleached blondes are generally stupid, aren't they?"

"Adam..."

"Remember, I don't want you around here anymore," he said coldly. "You have no real business in this building."

Sherry bit her lip to prevent tears from flooding her eyes. "All right," she hissed. "You win this one. But the day will come when I'll be back to throw you the hell out of here."

"You won't have to," Adam said. "If the time ever comes when you have a reason to be back here...well, before I'd

27

deal with you, I'd sleep in the street." He looked up from the blue sheaf of papers and smiled. "You could give me some tips."

Confused, she repeated, "Some tips?"

"About sleeping in the street. You've spent a lot of time on the street, haven't you?"

Sherry backed away to the door.

"You bastard. I'll get you," she said as she fled from the office.

She rode the elevator down to the main floor in a panic, not seeing anyone, hardly knowing where she was. She ran out into the street to stop a cab and ordered him to speed to the Holiday Inn. Handing the driver the first bill she felt in her purse, she ran into the hotel and picked up the house phone.

"Mr. Frank Everts. Room 1127."

"Thank you. Just a moment," the operator said. After a few seconds, the operator was back on the line. "I'm sorry. Mr. Everts has checked out."

"Ooooooh."

Sherry held the telephone in her hand for a moment. Her stomach was tumbling wildly. She rode the elevator up to the eleventh floor.

The door to 1127 was open. Inside, a maid was busy stripping the bed. When she saw Sherry in the doorway, she flashed a polite smile and asked: "Can I help you, ma'am?"

Sherry numbly shook her head.

"Nobody can help me," she said. "Nobody." She walked back to the main floor, down all ten flights of steps, knowing that she had really done something wrong this time. Seriously wrong.

CHAPTER FOUR

Adam Griffin paused outside his father's office door. He glanced over toward Gus's secretary. She was looking at him with a faint smile on her face. He noticed that as usual she was not wearing a brassiere. Adam looked away, took a deep breath, then rapped once on the massive dark mahogany door, opened it, and walked inside.

His father looked up with a scowl from the papers on the desk.

"Do you always have to look like an insurance salesman?" Gus demanded sourly. "Why don't you buy some decent clothes? Some boots? Look like a Texan."

"I'd rather look like a businessman. I talk like a Texan."

"You talk like some dipshit from the Harvard Business School."

"Have it your own way, Dad."

"To what do I owe this honor?" Gus asked.

"I'd like to talk business."

"If you've come to talk about us expanding and buying more companies and doing all those other stupid things that they teach you in school, forget it."

Adam cleared his throat.

"You're not m-m-making this any easier," he said.

"Stop that goddam stammering."

"All right. I guess this is as good a way as any other. You don't control Griffin Oil anymore. I do."

Gus Griffin leaned back in his chair. "Is that so?" he said mildly. "When did this miracle happen?"

"Just now. Sherry signed over her stock. I've got voting rights."

"Well, wasn't that kind and obliging of her. How much did it cost you?"

"I'm sure she'll tell you about it. I tried to be fair, though."

29

"Oh, you tried to be fair? Isn't that just fucking sweet? I knew something was up, the way she's been tiptoeing around. You bet she'll tell me about it."

"Dad, we ought to talk about the company."

"Don't Dad me. This is my company. I started it. I own it. It's my company and it's always going to be my company." He leaned forward in his chair and pounded his fist on the desk. "You hear me, goddammit?"

Adam paced back and forth in front of his father's desk. Finally, he wheeled and slammed his own fist on the desk.

"If you can't be civilized, then act like an animal and I'll treat you like an animal. Yeah, you started this company. But it's not yours anymore. It's mine. You got that? Mine. I control the stock and I control the company, and from now on I'm running things my way, not bumbling and stumbling along the way you'd have us doing for the next twenty years. We're going to expand and diversify. I'd like you to help. But if you won't, I'm going to do it anyway."

"Like hell," Gus roared and jumped to his feet, surprised that Adam did not flinch and pull back. "I've heard that goddam speech of yours so often it makes me sick. I don't give a shit what those Harvard professors told you, you don't have to keep growing to be successful. You want to shoot craps, you go to Las Vegas, not to Griffin Oil."

Gus was leaning across the desk, the tendons in his ruddy neck swollen and distended. Adam shook his head, his face only a foot from his father's.

"Wrong, Dad. It's what we have to do. We're selling stock. We're going public. Whether you like it or not."

There was a long pause. The silence hung heavy in the room. Gus sat back in his chair.

"You can do anything you want, I guess, to ruin this company, but you better know, you're not getting any of my forty-five percent to sell off. You can bet on that."

"Suit yourself, Dad. I won't need it." Adam sat down in the chair across from the desk. "I'll make you rich anyway." He tried a smile, but got no response from his father, except a vicious one-eyed glare.

"I wanted your advice on something," Adam said.

"A little late for that, isn't it?"

30

"What do you think about my making Doyle Blaney the treasurer?"

"Blaney? Is he involved in this stupidity too?"

"No," Adam assured him. "But he's been with us now for nine years and knows everything about the company. And he's an accountant and an ex-FBI man. I thought he'd be a good man that we can trust."

"Who ever knows who you can trust?" the old man said bitterly. "I thought I could trust you. And Sherry. Go ahead. Take Blaney. What do I care?"

"Dad, he can keep working for you just like he always has. I just want him to oversee the financial end of things. As this company moves ahead."

Gus Griffin walked to the bar and poured a water glass full of tequila. Without turning, he said: "Please get out of here."

Adam hesitated, opened his mouth to speak, then thought better of it. He finally shrugged and quietly left the office.

He walked down the flight of stairs to his own office floor, hoping he would meet someone, wondering if they would notice any change in Adam Griffin. But there was no one in the stairwell. As he walked down the hall to his office, his stride quickly lengthened until he was almost marching. His rubber heels made dull little thuds against the marble floor. Maybe he would buy some boots, he thought.

Inside his office, he buzzed for his secretary.

"Mrs. Penrose, call Eustace McBride at McBride and McBride, please. And tell Mrs. Winslow that I want to see her. Right away."

"Yes, Mr. Griffin."

A moment later, his telephone buzzed twice.

"Adam Griffin," he announced.

"Hey, old buddy, this is Mac. What's happening?"

"Mac, do you remember that hypothetical discussion about taking Griffin Oil public?"

"Sure do."

"Get started. We're going public."

Eustace McBride whistled loudly over the line. "Gus changed his mind?"

31

"It's not really his decision anymore. Just get started, Mac. We want to do this with some speed."

"Congratulations, Adam. I'll put Benjamin Hirschfeld himself on it."

"You're not going to take care of it?" Adam asked.

"You want the best, I'll give you the best. Ole Hirsch knows more about stock offerings than anybody in Texas. That's his specialty. He does the work and then I walk it through Washington. I'm a politician, Adam. I hardly practice law at all anymore. Trust me. Hirsch is a genius."

"Well... whatever you say. Let's just get going."

"He'll be in touch with you soon to get started. Congratulations again, pal."

"Thanks, Mac," Adam said.

Shortly after Adam hung up his phone, it buzzed again, and a middle-aged woman entered his office.

"Hello, Adam," she said, calling him by his first name as she had for fifteen years.

"Take a seat, Mrs. Winslow," he instructed brusquely. "There are going to be a number of personnel changes made in the very near future. I want you to get the paperwork started. Here is a list of people who are being retired or let go."

He handed her a slip of paper. She looked at the names, and then back up at him with confusion on her face.

"So that you don't have to ask, Mrs. Winslow, I'll make it clear. I am taking over full operating control of the company. A stockholders' meeting next week will approve that. You will not have to worry about what my father might think of these changes. He has nothing to do with them. You just do them. You understand?"

"Y-y-yes, Mr. Griffin."

"That'll be all," Adam said. As the personnel director reached the door, he stopped her with a word. "One other thing," he said. "I've noticed that some of the younger women have taken to... well, they don't seem to find it necessary to wear undergarments. Above the waist, that is. I know that my father has allowed this in the past, but I would like you to inform the young ladies that hereafter they are to report to work fully clothed. Fully."

The woman seemed confused.

"Do you have a question?" Adam asked.

"Well, sir. It was...Velma Waldor...your father's secretary. Even her?"

Adam thought for a moment of the patronizing smile on Velma's face as he had hesitated outside his father's office door.

"Yes, Mrs. Winslow. *Especially* her," he said.

CHAPTER FIVE

If a professional basketball player could have been crossbred with a basset hound, the result might have looked something like Eustace Calhoun McBride. He was six and a half feet tall, lean and active at thirty-seven, but his face was that of a man of seventy-three. Jowls swung loosely under his jaw, and the bags under his eyes looked as if they could be used to store acorns. He seemed a role model of athletic dissipation.

But his blue eyes twinkled brightly, and he was rarely seen unsmiling. McBride was one of the best-known and best-liked men in Houston—liked even by men who were uneasily aware that their wives, too, found him engaging and appealing.

McBride was working on his third marriage, and this time he was mildly optimistic that it would last. Dolores was bright, well educated, reasonably attractive, good in bed, and, thus far, satisfied with their marital arrangement. Which meant that she did not question him when he called to say he would be working late, perhaps all night, and he, in turn, agreed cheerfully to her occasional shopping trips to Dallas and Las Vegas and San Francisco, even though she rarely bought anything.

Actually, McBride often did work late, occasionally all night. Despite his breezy, casual manner, he was a top-drawer lawyer with a keen, well-trained mind, a deep respect for the law, and a prodigious appetite for work. The other McBride in McBride and McBride had been Eustace's father, Erasmus McBride, the founder of the firm, who had died three years earlier. The senior McBride had thought very little of his son's marital and extramarital adventures, but Eustace, who had deeply loved the father who had raised him alone after the death of his mother, was proud of the fact that he had never given his father cause to criticize his legal work. An oil painting of the old man hung on the wall in Eustace's office, and, as he always did when the firm got a new case or a new client, he now knocked on the heavy wooden frame with his knuckles for luck.

Then he left his office and loped down the hallway to talk with Benjamin Hirschfeld. He stopped abruptly to stare down the blouse of Hirschfeld's secretary as she leaned forward over her typewriter to correct a mistake.

"Oh, wow," he said.

"Oh, you."

"I'm going to have to do some research. There's just got to be a law against a blouse like that."

"There isn't. I checked it out."

"If you say so. But one of these days, or nights, I might want to check into that myself. Meet me in the law library at one a.m. Bring pajamas."

She giggled as McBride plunged past her and into Hirschfeld's office. Inside, he tossed himself casually into a chair, one leg dangling over the arm. Hirschfeld, a short roundish man with thin graying hair and thick horn-rimmed glasses, smiled at him and began packing a pipe with tobacco.

"How ya doing, professor? How's the smartest Jewish lawyer in Houston?"

"Well, today I was not shot at. My house was not bombed. I received no hate mail and no obscene phone calls. All in all, a rousing success."

"I'm sorry Houston doesn't offer the cultural attractions you Northerners are used to. If it'd make you feel more at home, I could arrange for somebody to start a fire on your lawn."

"No, thank you," Hirschfeld said. "I wouldn't want to keep you away from your other duties with the firm." He slowly lit his pipe and blew an elaborate plume of smoke. McBride wrinkled his nose as the first scent of the burning tobacco reached his nostrils. The man had the ability to find the only pipe tobaccos in the world that smelled worse than cigars.

"So is this business or a pleasure visit?" Hirschfeld asked.

"Strictly business. I found another sucker for us to fleece," McBride said.

35

"I give up. I wonder if I did the world a favor when I trained you in the law."

"There are two women out there collecting alimony checks who say nightly prayers to you in Yiddish."

"You're sure you're not here to get my advice on another divorce?" Hirschfeld asked.

"Not yet. So far, what's-her-name and I are deeply in love. One of the great romances of the ages. Actually, I came in here to try to get you to make some money for the firm."

"How will I accomplish this miracle?"

"I've heard from Adam Griffin. He's taking the company over from his father and he wants to go public. We're doing the legal work. I figured it's right up your alley. Can you handle it?"

"Of course. This Adam Griffin. Does he know what's involved in the process of going public?"

"Adam Griffin doesn't know how to find his way to the men's room unless someone leaves him a toilet-paper trail to follow. He's the only son of the crabbiest, surliest go-to-hell man I ever met. Poor Adam was crushed before he ever crawled out of the playpen."

"And yet you say he is taking Griffin Oil over from his father?"

McBride shook his head. "Yeah. And I can't figure out how he managed to do that. He's been talking about expanding the company ever since he staggered out of Harvard, but Gus, that's the old man, just laughed at him. Gus made his pile and he just wants to sit on it and not take any chances."

"Who owns the company?"

"Gus, I think. He's got fifty-five percent of the stock as I remember. Adam inherited forty-five percent from his mother. Gus's father-in-law, Jeb Morrison, the old hardware man, gave Gus the stake that got him going, but he made sure his daughter and all her children would be protected. Just in case the wildcatting worked out and the marriage didn't. The mother died and Adam was the only child, so he got all her stock. He's had the title of president, but no duties and no authority."

"Obviously, that has changed," Hirschfeld said, considering the smoke from the bowl of his pipe.

36

"Yeah, but I don't know how. The company's solid. I mean, it's not Exxon, but it's solid. It could have done a lot more than it has, even out of its own assets, if Gus wanted. But he's always played his cards so close to his vest that he has to take his shirt off to see what he's holding."

"Maybe his son is dreaming that he has taken over the company. Is he delusional?"

"I would have thought so, except that just a couple of minutes after I got off the phone with Adam, I got a call from John Billings. He runs the Houston Trust and Guaranty. That's Gus's bank, and he's one of the old man's drinking buddies. He told me he heard that we were going to do the work on taking Griffin Oil public. Well, he kind of hinted that no one's feelings would be hurt if we did as little background digging as possible on the application to the Securities and Exchange Commission."

"That's interesting," Hirschfeld said. "And you? Before I start this, what is your position on the matter?"

"I want you to find out everything those bastards have ever done. If they farted in the tub twenty years ago, let's dig it up. Let's find out everything."

"I am happy with that," Hirschfeld said, "but why the excess zeal on your part?"

McBride said, "It's something personal, but let's turn over all the rocks in the Griffin empire."

Hirschfeld waited, but McBride offered no more explanation.

"Eustace, I will probably need assistance on this project, particularly if Adam Griffin is in a hurry to get his stock on the market. What if I asked Christopher Caldwell to assist me?"

"Chris? Good idea. Maybe he can use the money. He still in Puerto Rico? You got his number?"

Hirschfeld nodded and flipped a Rolodex file on his desk.

McBride stepped around behind the older man, read the number, then dialed it himself.

A man's voice answered.

"Hello."

"Chris, you old rummie, this is Mac. What are you doing?"

"Getting laid."

37

"She any good?"

"I don't know. I was just getting ready to find out when I was interrupted by some baggy-eyed shyster."

"Well, listen. I don't want to bother you. I just wanted to ask your advice on some piece of arcane constitutional law. It shouldn't take but an hour of your time. She'll wait."

"You mean right now?"

"Of course I mean right now," McBride said.

"Fuck you. Strong letter follows," Caldwell said. The telephone went dead in McBride's hand. Laughing, he replaced it on the receiver.

"He was otherwise occupied, professor, but you call and offer him the job. Better wait an hour, though. And if he won't take it, we'll get somebody else."

McBride waved cheerfully and headed for the doorway, but slowed to a halt halfway across the room. Then he turned, tugging absentmindedly at the loose flesh on his neck.

"You know, I just thought of something," he said, staring blankly at the far corner of the ceiling. "Gus Griffin doesn't own fifty-five percent of his company. He only owns forty-five percent. He gave ten percent to his present wife when they got married. Maybe Sherry threw in her stock with Adam's. That would give Adam control."

Hirschfeld waited patiently, an encouraging smile on his face.

"No, it couldn't be," McBride decided. "She wouldn't dare. Gus would kill her if she pulled a stunt like that, and no jury in Texas would convict him."

"No?"

"It's one of the three unwritten laws in Texas on when a man can kill his wife and get off. One is if he catches her in bed with somebody who's not rich. Another is if he catches her rooting for Arkansas or Oklahoma against any Texas football team. The third is if she costs him an oil well by doing something stupid. Now, if Sherry cost Gus a whole oil company, he could kick her to death on the steps of the capitol and the governor would lead the cheering."

"I love the high culture of Texas and of Houston,"

Hirschfeld said dryly. "I wonder if my ancestors, when they were building the Temple of Solomon, ever realized that one day all this would be mine."

"There you go being smart again," McBride said as he pushed out through the door. As the door closed, Hirschfeld could hear his secretary squeal. He really hadn't expected his former law-school student to be able to pass that secretary twice without savaging her low-necked blouse. The choice was the girl's: She would either tone down her wardrobe or eventually find her way onto the couch in McBride's office. Neither alternative bothered Benjamin Hirschfeld; he had lived too long and seen too much to worry about men's and women's lust to sleep with each other. Particularly in Houston, where it seemed one of the few activities one could engage in and not meet more than one other Texan at a time.

Hirschfeld waited a few minutes for his secretary to regain her composure, then asked her to place a call to Adam Griffin. They agreed to meet the next morning in Griffin's office. The lawyer did not know exactly what he had been expecting, but Adam Griffin's voice on the telephone was firm and fully in control. Hirschfeld thought to himself that people might be making a mistake if they underestimated Adam Griffin.

The gray-haired lawyer ordered a sandwich for lunch and sat at his desk, chewing morosely, annoyed that the delicatessen had managed to ruin good roast beef by putting catsup on it. Texans, he had long since decided, had a way with food that was lunatic. How many lives had been lost, how many sacrifices made, so that Texas could produce the most tender beef in the world? And yet to a Texan, cooking a steak meant throwing it into a fire until it was burned into charcoal-crisped leather.

Still, Texas had been all right to him. After the death of his daughter and grandchild, he had lost the urge to teach anymore. Every young woman who sat in his law classes had begun to remind him of Zhava, and he found himself stopping in the middle of lectures, staring, totally out of control. It had not been an easy time in his life. Then Eustace McBride had offered him a senior partner's position with McBride and McBride, and Hirschfeld had surprised himself by accepting. He was glad that he had. The work was interesting; it was good to be back in court once in a while; and there was very little chance that any of the women he met in Houston were likely to remind him of his daughter, who had been a woman of exotic and rare beauty, who had been young and brilliant and eager and full of life. Just thinking of her in his office, he realized how deep his loss had been. And then there was Christopher Caldwell. How great had been his loss?

Hirschfeld looked up Caldwell's number and dialed Puerto Rico.

"Dive shop," a deep voice informed him with bland disinterest.

"Good morning, Christopher," Hirschfeld said. He was not surprised that his eyes were suddenly threatening to fill up. "Or is it afternoon there now? I can never remember time zones."

"Dad, how are you?" Caldwell's voice was suddenly alive and vibrant. "It's late afternoon here now. Hey, is anything the matter?"

"No," Hirschfeld said quickly. "Everything is fine. I just wanted to talk to you."

"I'm not that far behind on my letters, am I?" Caldwell said. "Not that I ever have anything to write anyway."

"You say what you have to say, Christopher. Your letters show health. I have the feeling that you are healing from your wound."

"Maybe," Caldwell said, his voice flattening. "I'm okay."

Even as he spoke, Hirschfeld knew it was a lie and that the younger man knew it was a lie too.

"Yes, you are," Hirschfeld said. "And you will continue becoming more okay every day. You have life ahead of you."

"Yes, Ben," Caldwell agreed politely.

"I didn't call to lecture you. I called to offer you a job."

Caldwell chuckled. "Still trying to get me out of my little grass shack and back to the States? No thanks, Ben. I think it should be the life goal of every man to stay out of Texas."

Hirschfeld ignored the *pro forma* refusal. Quickly, he

40

outlined the Griffin Oil Company situation.

"I could use your help," he said.

"When are you and that shyster employer of yours going to stop trying to dream up jobs for me?" Caldwell asked. "You don't need any help with a simple stock offering. And even if you did, any first-year clerk with an ounce of sense could do the legwork you need. No thanks, I pass."

"Christopher, it is possible that I might need your special skills on this project."

"My special skill is swimming underwater," Caldwell said.

"There's water in Houston. We have the Houston Ship Canal. People go boating and, God help them, fishing in the reservoir and Lake Conroe."

"And I've got the Caribbean and I prefer Puerto Ricans to Texans. McBride is the only Texan I ever met who didn't set my teeth on edge."

"I am a Texan too," Hirschfeld said.

"Shucks, podner, I forgot. All right, two Texans I can stand. But that's all. No, Ben, I think I'll stay here, enlightening tourists to the glories of the world below the waves."

Hirschfeld sighed. "What a waste. A fine legal mind. Blowing bubbles at fish. Playing tag with mermaids. All right, Christopher, I'll leave you in peace."

"Ben, anytime you really need me, I'll come running. Look, another six weeks or so, things slack up around here. Maybe we'll get together then, okay?"

"I'll look forward to it."

"Okay. Say hello to Mac for me. We didn't get much of a chance to talk when he called before."

"I will. Goodbye, son." Hirschfeld paused. "Christopher."

"Yes."

"Don't dive too deep."

"It's a big ocean, Ben. There are a lot of depths I haven't reached yet."

"The deepest plunge is into oneself."

"I know," Caldwell said. "I've been down there."

"Goodbye." Hirschfeld put the telephone down slowly. He looked at the photograph on his desk of the tall strong man, and the smiling dark-eyed woman and the dark-haired little girl. He felt his eyes filling up again. Some wounds never healed.

Christopher Caldwell was frowning as he hung up the phone. He didn't want his father-in-law worrying about him and inventing work to bring him back to the States. He was content with his placid existence. Just so long as he didn't have to think or remember.

"You ready now, Mac?" asked a paunchy man in a bright-yellow sports shirt, tapping a diver's face mask gently against the edge of the counter.

Caldwell froze, rigidly containing a sudden, irrational urge of pure rage. He eyed the man coldly.

"Do you want to buy that mask or are you just practicing your Morse code?"

The man flushed and stopped tapping the mask. "I just want the best you got for my little girl here," he said. He handed the mask to his teenage daughter, who looked up at Caldwell through her long lashes with practiced coquetry.

"The best mask is the one that fits best," Caldwell said. He took the mask and pressed it against the girl's face. "Take a deep breath in through your nose," he said.

She inhaled and he released the mask, which fell from her face. He shook his head. "Too big for her face," he said. "She needs something smaller."

Caldwell walked behind the counter, put the mask back on a rack on the wall, and selected another. That one clung tightly to the girl's face when she inhaled, its thin rubber edges sealing perfectly around the smooth bones and skin of her head.

"This is a good mask," Caldwell said. "Tempered glass, purge valve, and it's shaped so she can squeeze her nose if she goes deep."

"What's that for?" the girl asked.

"It's easier to clear your ears if you can hold your nose and pretend that you're trying to blow it. The deeper the water, the more the pressure on your ears. It gets unbearable if you can't clear them."

"Okay," the girl agreed. She looked up at him through her lashes again. "Whatever you say." She smiled at him.

Caldwell smiled back. He took a credit card from the girl's father and wrote up the bill.

"I'll see you tomorrow morning," the girl said. "I'm in the hotel diving class."

"Okay. Practice using the mask this afternoon in the hotel pool."

The girl skipped out, followed by her lumbering father. Caldwell sighed, shook his head, and glanced at his watch. A pretty, slim Puerto Rican girl wearing a Hotel Excalibur T-shirt and light-blue shorts came into the store from the back room.

"I've got a class, Lisa," Caldwell told her. "Mind the store."

A half hour later, Caldwell was powering a small motorboat out to a nearby reef for an hour's diving. His passengers were two young couples and a girl in her early twenties.

They had all received training in using underwater breathing equipment, so he contented himself with a brief review of the fundamentals and a warning against straying away from the group, or feeling around in dark crevices where moray eels could be lurking.

His mind kept returning to his father-in-law's telephone call, though. What had Hirsch meant, that he might have use for Chris's special skills? He had a nagging feeling that he hadn't been listening closely enough.

He put the thought out of his mind as the boat neared the reef, and he dropped a heavy sea anchor. He helped the others don their tanks, made sure their equipment was properly fitted, then went first into the water after a quick, careful look around. As always, his cares seemed to wash away when he entered the ocean. Part of his mind focused on the immediate situation, checking his own equipment and keeping a sharp eye on the other divers.

But another part of him seemed to float away from the here and now, drifting off into the sea itself, becoming absorbed in the shapes of the different kinds of corals and the bright colors of the abundant fish life. Large parrot fish moved warily away to peck at the hard coral with their sullen pouting mouths. Brightly striped sergeant majors danced curiously around the group, sometimes goggling directly into a face mask, apparently unafraid of

43

these large alien invaders. Tetras streamed in a long neon ribbon through a passage between two stands of coral, surging with the gusts of water currents, in an eerie precision, turning all in the same moment to face the divers.

One of the women pointed excitedly at a small squid scuttling across the top of a brain coral. When she approached, it froze and seemed to disappear before their eyes, its colors changing magically to mimic its surroundings. When her partner extended his flipper cautiously toward the top of the coral, the squid squirted a small cloud of ink into the water and jetted to safety down the side of the living rock and vanished out of sight.

The two couples were paired off, and Chris watched them long enough to be sure they understood the buddy system of diving and knew how to use their equipment. The single girl was still by the boat, having trouble with her weight belt.

Caldwell swam over to her and took the belt off her narrow waist. She held onto his arm, to keep from rising, while he made the belt a little smaller, then buckled it again around her waist.

He knew from the way she pressed against him that with any encouragement, she would welcome a brief, meaningless affair. She was attractive enough, a blond girl from the Midwest in a yellow bikini. He tried to smile at the blond girl, but all he could see was the bright wheatfield color of her narrow bikini.

The color reminded him of Zhava, and the words of a song came into his head. The song was on a record Zhava had bought of a young folk singer from Maine, and when she played it for him, she stopped it after a line and repeated it for him.

"You will play in yellow fields in the morning sun," she had said. Chris had held her and told her that she made all fields yellow for him.

And then she was dead—she and Shoshana, their daughter—and the yellow fields of life had all gone dry and brown, burned in the explosion of some terrorist's bomb. A bomb that Caldwell knew had been meant for him.

Zhava and Shoshana had brought beauty and cleanness

44

to his life, but they had all been powerless against the ultimate obscenity of death.

He had an urge to rip the bikini off the blond girl. What did she mean, wearing the color of Zhava's life?

The back of his throat was suddenly dry, and he knew that when they got back he would welcome a drink. And another. And another.

He wanted to tell the blond girl that it wasn't her, that she was really attractive, but that for Christopher Caldwell, the relief came in a bottle, not in a bed.

He glanced at his watch and saw they had been down for almost forty minutes. With the blond girl in tow, he began rounding up the other divers, waving them back toward the boat. As usual, he found himself wishing that he were alone on the reef, with no clients to distract him or claim his attention and concern.

For the hundredth time, he promised himself that when he finally decided to commit suicide, he would do it in the ocean. It could be done so easily and so pleasantly. Just one last, leisurely look around the underwater world he loved so much, then begin diving down, down, down... until the overload of nitrogen forced into his system by the mounting pressure of the water brought on that strange drunkenness known as rapture of the deep, a rapture so glorious that it carried with it a total disregard for life, a willingness, even an eagerness, to rip out one's mouthpiece and tear off one's mask and laugh one's body full of choking drowning water.

More than one diver had vanished on such deep dives, and others had had to be forcefully restrained from sacrificing themselves, dragged protesting back to the surface by companion divers who had not felt the rapture.

For some reason, he thought again fleetingly of Benjamin Hirschfeld, but he put his father-in-law out of his mind and concentrated on getting his small group of divers headed back in the right direction.

He could worry about Hirsch later.

And if he drank enough, he would not worry about Hirsch or Zhava or Shoshana.

Or himself.

45

CHAPTER SIX

Gus Griffin parked his six-year-old Chrysler Imperial at an angle across two spots in the four-car garage at his ranch just off Route 59, twenty-five miles south of Houston.

He stalked into the sprawling house and asked the maid quietly: "Where's Mrs. Griffin?"

"By the pool with the children, Señor Gus," the young woman answered.

"Gracias," he grunted.

Sherry was sitting in the shade of an umbrella, watching her daughter, Tina, and several other young girls screaming gleefully as they jumped off the low board into the cool waters of the kidney-shaped pool.

"Sherry," he called out. "Step inside. We've got a few things to discuss."

He smiled grimly as his wife jumped. She looked at him anxiously, and he turned away and strode around the side of the house to his den without looking back.

Gus was leaning against his desk, arms folded, when Sherry entered, clutching a terry-cloth robe over her white bikini bathing suit.

"Close the door," he growled.

She hesitated. "I'm afraid to."

"Close the goddam door."

She slowly closed the door, eyeing him warily across the length of the room.

"Why'd you do it, Sherry?"

"Do what?" she asked, her blue eyes big with innocence.

"You know damn well what. Why did you help Adam take my company away from me?"

She shrugged childishly, as if the world were filled with events over which she had no control. "I didn't want to, Gus. I didn't know it was going to happen."

"No? You signed your goddam stock over to Adam and you didn't think anything was going to happen? You

46

thought it was just going to be business as usual?"

Griffin's face started to redden, and he scratched with his right index finger under the black eyepatch. Sherry could tell he had been drinking, but he was still on the sane side of drunk.

"I didn't sign it to Adam. He wanted me to sell it to him but I wouldn't. I signed it to somebody else who was supposed to keep me out of your battle, but he gave it to Adam."

"Who?"

She looked down at the carpet. "My brother."

"You dumb bitch. After all that's happened, you trusted that scumbag. What did he pay you?"

"A hundred thousand for a year's option with voting rights. But I don't think I'm going to see the money. I think Frank's going to take off with it."

Gus Griffin laughed aloud, a mirthless laugh without humor or warmth. "Good. I hope your brother takes that money and spends it on some Mexican whore and gets a case of syph that rots his frigging brain. You're so stupid you deserve him."

Sherry rubbed the sole of her high-heeled shoe across the deep-blue carpet.

"What gets me is you have the nerve to come back here like nothing happened," he said.

"I thought about packing up and grabbing Tina and heading for Los Angeles, but I knew I'd have to face you sooner or later. So what was the sense of running? You could always find me if you wanted to."

"I'm gonna kill you, Sherry," he said.

She whitened but shook her head. "No, you won't," she said, her voice quavering slightly.

"Oh, no? Why not?"

"Because you're not that crazy and because it's not worth it to you. Because it's already over and done with, so killing me wouldn't do you any good." She tried a small smile. "Because you love me."

"Sure," he said sarcastically. "I trusted you too, Sherry, and you handed me up. To my own son. You think I'm just going to forgive and forget?"

"Oh, I know you, Gus. There's no way you're going to

47

let me get away with it. But you're not going to kill me."

"Then what do you think I'm going to do?" he asked, softly, ominously.

"I think you're going to brood about this and brood about it and start drinking heavy and then one night, you're going to drag me out of bed and just plain whip the shit out of me. And I'm not looking forward to it at all, only I got to admit I got it coming."

Her voice sounded lost and forlorn, like a little girl's, and Gus looked at her sharply, trying to determine if she was really sorry or if she was just using her actress tricks on him. But her expression of sad concern told him little, and he looked away with a heavy sigh.

Finally, he said, "We're through, Sherry."

"Is it so bad, what Adam wants to do? You know, make the company bigger?"

"You don't know what kind of can of worms you opened," Griffin said.

"Gus, I'm sorry. I didn't want this to happen. I was just trying to get out of the middle of you and Adam, and I thought Frank could help me do it. Now I've got nothing. I don't have you and I don't have the money and I don't know what to do."

Tears filled her eyes. She blinked them back, carefully watching her husband.

Without turning to her, he growled, "Can I have the envelope, please? Best performance by a treacherous wife. Sherry Griffin." He wheeled toward her. "Shove those tears. I've seen it all before."

"You want me to leave?" she asked.

"No. You just stay here until I tell you to go. And I mean stay here at the ranch. Don't go getting any ideas about running into Houston to see Adam. Or anyone else. Just stay here so if I get ready to kill you, I don't have far to look."

"All right, Gus. Whatever you say," she answered submissively. She left the room. Outside, on the patio, she wiped her eyes with the belt of her robe, then walked back toward the pool. She was smiling. The worst was over, at least for now.

Griffin had waited until the door closed behind her, then kicked his desk savagely. He walked around his wood-paneled office, stopping to straighten one of the four oil paintings on the wall. Finally, he sat down behind the desk and dialed a telephone number in Houston.

"Blaney," the voice answered.

"Congratulations," Griffin growled.

"About what, Gus?"

"You didn't hear?"

"Hear what?"

"Adam got Sherry's stock. He's running the company now. He's going to make you treasurer."

"Me? What the hell for?"

"Who knows? Who knows what that clown is thinking?"

"I don't," Blaney said. "Gus, I don't have to tell you where my loyalties are. What do you want me to do?"

"For some reason, Adam trusts you. I want you to get close to him. Be treasurer. Stay close to him. Let him think you're handing me up if you have to, but keep me posted on what he's doing."

"All right."

"One other thing," Griffin said.

"What's that?"

"Sherry's brother. He beat her out of a hundred thousand. I don't think he should keep it."

"How'd he do that?"

Quickly, Griffin explained what Sherry had told him. "It's bad enough that Sherry sold me out. But the idea of that thief with that money galls me."

"If he did it for Adam, I'll try to find out what it's all about," Blaney said. "You want Sherry to get the money?"

"Better her than her brother," Griffin said.

"I'll see what I can do."

"Stay in touch," Griffin said as he hung up the telephone.

He looked around the office again, his good left eye fixing on the four paintings hung above the smooth leather sofa.

"Bastards," he hissed under his breath. "Bastards."

It was after five, and the office staff of the Griffin Oil Company had left for the day. Blaney walked down the flight of stairs to the fourteenth floor, tapped once on Adam's door, and walked in.

49

Adam Griffin looked up from behind his desk and smiled.

"Like a charm," he said.

"I know. I just heard from Gus. He told me to keep an eye on you for him."

"Good. You do that. I've already got McBride started on the stock offering. We don't want Dad to gum it up."

"That brings up one thing," Blaney said.

"What's that?"

"Sherry's money. Gus is bent out of shape that the brother might have skipped with Sherry's option money. If we let that happen, he's going to brood about it for a while and then, maybe, think that he can overturn the whole thing for fraud. I think Sherry's got to get that money."

"That makes sense," Adam said. "Get hold of that lawyer in Los Angeles that I deposited the money with. Tell him the money has to come back here. Have him send the check to you. Frank Everts gets the ten thousand we agreed on. Nothing more."

"All right. I'll take care of it," Blaney said. "Anything else?"

"Just keep an eye on Dad. Let him think you're spying on me for him."

"Sure," Blaney said casually. "Just so you know that I'm on your side."

Adam Griffin got up and came around the desk. Formally, he presented his right hand to Blaney, who stood up from his seat and shook the younger man's hand.

"I know that, Doyle," Adam said. "I know I never could have pulled this off without you. Heck. I couldn't even have thought of it. You'll find out that I won't forget."

Blaney nodded. "Better go home, Adam. Things are going to be hectic around here for a while. You need your rest."

"Yes. Tonight's a night for celebrating anyway. Tomorrow we start work."

As he left the office, Blaney realized that Adam had not asked about Sherry, about what might have happened to her when Gus learned of her treachery. Blaney nodded to himself; Adam was learning.

50

Upstairs, Blaney walked past his own door to the office of Gus Griffin. With a key from a large ring, he opened the door, stepped inside, then locked the door behind him.

He walked to Gus Griffin's desk and dropped to his knees. From under the desk, he removed a small tape recorder holding an oversized cassette of recording tape. He removed the tape and inserted a fresh reel from his inside jacket pocket, then carefully slid the recording machine back onto the brackets under the desk. His fingers expertly turned on the voice-activation switch. He stood up, put the recorded tape into his jacket pocket, and let himself out.

Later, he would return to Adam Griffin's office and get the tape from the identical machine he had installed there, and later tonight, he would listen to both tapes, checking out all the telephone calls, all the private visitors, that Adam and Gus had during the day.

It was knowledge, and knowledge was power.

CHAPTER SEVEN

Christopher Caldwell was at the pool of the Hotel Excalibur teaching a beginner's class in scuba diving on the Saturday morning, ten days later, when the call came from Houston. He called back an hour later from the dive shop. The telephone was picked up personally by Eustace McBride.

"No, I won't go to work for your law firm as a senior partner. Not even as a junior partner," Caldwell said when he heard McBride's voice.

"Chris, it's bad," McBride said quietly.

"What is it, Mac?"

"Hirsch. He's dead."

Caldwell closed his eyes in pain and took a deep, shuddering breath. Another of the lifelines holding him to the past, perhaps the strongest, last line of all, had snapped.

"When, Mac?" he asked numbly. "Why? His heart?"

"I don't know. I came to the office to get some work done, and the police called here. Hirsch must have gone out fishing this morning in Lake Conroe and fallen overboard and drowned. Maybe it was his heart. We won't know until the medical examiner looks."

"Hirsch was doing what?"

"He was out on the lake. Fishing, I guess. He rented poles and stuff."

Caldwell stared blankly out the window at a party of happy tourists strolling in casual attire in the bright Puerto Rican sunlight. The palm trees on the other side of the pool seemed unreal to him. He had been content here, away from the real world of sorrow and death and killing, happy in an artificial paradise of sun and rum. But now he had realized that one could never run away far enough or dive deep enough to escape the harsh light of reality.

"Chris...I know how this must hit you." Eustace McBride's voice brought him back to reality. "I feel god-awful too. Hirsch was a lot more to me than just somebody in my firm. I can't...well...I'm stunned, that's all. I don't know what to tell you."

"Wait a minute, Mac," Caldwell ordered.

He put down the phone and walked slowly across the room, staring blindly at the display of diving masks. His face was blank at first, as he tried to force himself to accept the reality of Hirsch's death. Then, abruptly, his lips thinned and his fists clenched. He walked quickly back to the phone.

"Mac, I'll be on the first flight I can get to Houston."

"There's a flight on American. Four o'clock your time. I looked it up while I was waiting for you to call back."

"That sounds good. It'll give me time to pack some clothes and make arrangements with the hotel to have my assistant run the dive shop while I'm gone."

"I'll pick you up at the airport," McBride said. "You can stay with Dolores and me."

"Maybe. But I'll probably stay in Hirsch's apartment."

"Whatever you say, Chris. And...I'm sorry."

"I know you are, Mac. I'll see you in a few hours."

Behind the counter of the dive shop, Lisa, his lovely Puerto Rican assistant, pursed her lips in concern. She hated the thought of Caldwell's leaving the island, because she knew he would not return on her account. He was unfailingly pleasant and polite to her, and on several rare evenings he had made love to her, but he was not really part of this world and she knew it.

She wondered what his world was like. But she knew too that he would never take her to it. He might return from this trip, but she knew that sooner or later he would go away and never come back.

"I'm sorry, Chris," she said.

"Thanks, Lisa," he said, idly picking up an underwater spear gun and running his thumb across the sharp barbed point. He spoke as if addressing himself to the weapon rather than to the young woman. "You know, once death is your life, you can't ever go back to the world of the living. All the dead and their memories won't let you. They never let go of you."

The American Airlines DC-10 was half empty, and Caldwell had a window seat. He stared down at the ocean, flat and featureless so far below him, and thought of the teeming life and the brutal death its bland gray surface so totally concealed.

With Hirsch dead, Chris had no links left to the world in which he had been raised. He was an only child, and his parents had died while he was young. An aunt, herself long dead, had reared him until he went away on a scholarship to college. His ROTC training had brought him to Vietnam as a second lieutenant, and he had volunteered for the Green Berets.

A yearning for order and precision, born out of the chaos of a jungle combat where friend and foe were indistinguishable, had sent him to law school, where he had met Benjamin Hirschfeld, and later the professor's only daughter, Zhava. The elderly teacher had become far more a father to him than the relatives he could barely remember, even before he had met the sloe-eyed, incredibly beautiful Zhava.

Hirschfeld had seemed to take a special liking to Caldwell and had invited him to dinner one night at his small apartment, off the campus of the University of Virginia Law School.

It had been raining, Caldwell's ratty old car had broken down, and he was late. When he arrived, Hirsch had taken his coat and moved him right to the dining-room table. Caldwell sat down and noticed three places were set.

Hirsch had hoisted his glass in an informal toast, then called out to the kitchen, "We are ready, woman."

Caldwell had looked up toward the kitchen door. He had heard somewhere that the professor had a daughter, but he was not ready for the vision that walked from the kitchen, carrying a large wooden bowl of salad greens.

His jaw must have hung open. Zhava smiled at him. Hirsch said, "This is my daughter, Zhava. Zhava, Christopher Caldwell."

"Mr. Caldwell," she said. Her voice was as musical as he would have expected it to be.

Chris tried to answer her. Only with effort was he able to close his mouth. Finally, he said, "It won't work, professor. Sorry, Zhava. First of all, I'm old fashioned. I believe in long engagements. I won't ask her to marry me

54

at least until next Wednesday."

She laughed. "That's good," she said. "I'm booked up through Tuesday anyway."

Hirsch said, "What? Busy? Here, an impending offer from this fine young Wasp and you're busy? Think of that when he's a bigshot lawyer on Wall Street making nine hundred million dollars a minute and you're running a steam press in a dry-cleaning shop."

"Poor but honest," she said. "You always told me it was ennobling."

"Yes," said Hirsch, "but I was rationalizing our poverty. Rich and honest is just as ennobling and much more fun."

"Mr. Caldwell," Zhava said, "as long as your mouth is open anyway, why don't you put some salad into it?"

On schedule, the following Wednesday, he asked her to marry him. She chided him for taking so long, for lacking confidence, for not caring enough about her, but she accepted, as long as they waited until he was out of law school.

Halfway through his senior year, Caldwell realized what it was that had been gnawing at him, making him edgy and nervous. He did not want to practice law.

He told this to Zhava, who shrugged. "Don't practice law," she said. "What do you want to be when you grow up?"

"Do you think we can get a job acting in pornographic movies? All I want to do is make love to you."

She kissed him and said, "Practice makes perfect."

A month later, the Central Intelligence Agency recruited Caldwell. He was interested in the offer, and when he asked Zhava's advice, she said, "You don't need my advice. Take the job. A person should be ready to give something for his country."

They were married the week after he was graduated from law school. His duty stations were in the Middle East, mostly on courier duty from Israel to Egypt and to Iran.

In the meantime, Zhava was building her own career. She had used her degree in fine arts to establish herself as a dealer for U.S. galleries, specializing in Middle Eastern art and antiquities. So she managed to be with Caldwell more than half of each year, and she insisted upon

55

being in Israel for the birth of their daughter, Shoshana.

"I want her to have two countries," Zhava had told him. "The United States and Israel."

Shoshana, who at four was already the mirror image of her mother, traveled with them to Iran, where Caldwell had a courier mission. While he went to deliver some secret papers, he left Zhava and Shoshana scouring the markets of Tehran for Persian miniatures. He had promised to meet them exactly at noon. He was five minutes late, and when he reached the appointed corner, he saw a surging crowd milling through the street. Panic blinding him, he fought his way through the mob to find that their red rented Fiat had been blown to pieces. Zhava and Shoshana were dead. A Palestinian organization claimed responsibility for the bombing, calling it a blow against the Zionist-Fascist United States imperialists and promising to carry out even more glorious attacks on spies. No one was arrested in the bombing, even though the CIA told Caldwell that the shah's secret police had tried to find the terrorists. It was not that they cared all that much about the death of an American woman and her child. They just did not like bombs going off in Tehran, Caldwell knew.

Chris tried to stay on after that, but his work seemed meaningless and empty. The CIA insisted upon putting him behind a desk and burdening him with administrative duties, hoping perhaps that he would lose himself in the drudgery of paperwork, while his psychic scars healed.

He could not, so he left.

The CIA did not try to stop him. He knew they were disappointed in his continued apathy. Although politely sympathetic, they distrusted him toward the end, judging him weak and broken and compromisable, perhaps even a threat to the organization.

Of course they were right, he realized later. What place was there in that organization—in any normal American organization—for someone who no longer cared? Who didn't care about Communists or Russia or China or advancement or security or power or the fate of the world? Who didn't even care about revenge upon the faceless shadows who had placed that bomb and then walked away, not even watching to see who it killed or crippled? It was as impersonal as if his wife and daughter had been killed

56

in an earthquake. Could he shake his fist at the insufficiently solid earth, howling curses at the planet itself? Particularly since he knew where the real blame lay.

Hirsch had come to his side then, imploring him to join him at Eustace McBride's law firm. Caldwell had refused.

"I'm sorry, Ben," he had told the old man. "But law deals with logic, and so it's a lie. There is no room for logic in a world that would kill the only things we ever loved."

"And now you run away from this world?"

"Why not? That bomb was meant for me and it killed me, just as sure as if I was behind the wheel of that car. The only thing not fixed yet is the day of my funeral."

"You will always be a Christian," Hirsch had said. "You will never run out of cheeks to turn. I prefer the Old Testament. I prefer an eye for an eye."

"And when you run out of eyes?" Caldwell asked. "Can you weep without eyes?"

"I always know how to weep. I weep for you, as I weep for Zhava and for our Shoshana."

Caldwell looked down at the sea and wondered why he was bothering to return to Houston. What good would it do to be there when they buried Hirsch? Why bother to pack the old man's few belongings when there was nobody in the world now, except for Caldwell himself, to give them to? What good would they be to Caldwell, a disillusioned man with almost no possessions of his own, because he had no hopes and dreams of his own to try to wrap possessions around? Why bother?

Then he remembered why, and his fists clenched again, and a tiny red spark glowed deep in his dark-brown eyes.

Somewhere, sometime, the killing had to stop. Someone had to stop it.

The plane was late. A message sent Caldwell to the airport cocktail lounge, where he found McBride slumped like an ungainly hound on a bar stool, morosely studying a nearly empty Tom Collins.

"I'll buy you another," Caldwell suggested, sitting beside him.

McBride shook his head. "This is my sixth today. I'd better pass. How about you?"

"Yeah. A big one. And then a bigger one."

McBride looked at him in surprise. "Hirsch was worried that you were drinking too much. I couldn't believe it. Hell, even when we tied one on in college, you always stayed cool while I was knocking things over and making a jackass out of myself."

Caldwell ordered a double vodka on the rocks from the bartender. "Yeah, well, people change," he told McBride. "I'm not that bright young guy you roomed with a hundred years ago back in Charlottesville. I'm a tired old man, and there isn't much in life that doesn't look better if you look at it through the bottom of a glass. So here you are. Your old buddy's a lush, Mac."

"Not you, Chris," McBride said. He threw some cash on the bar and said, "Let's go."

"It's a shame to waste vodka," Caldwell said. "Think of the starving alcoholics in India." When the bartender brought his drink, he drained it in one motion.

"Now I'm ready," he said. They reclaimed Caldwell's two small suitcases and went to McBride's car, which was parked in a no-parking zone in front of the terminal building. As they were driving into Houston, Caldwell finally asked: "Hear anything more from the police?"

"No, not yet. They were supposed to do the autopsy today. I made the arrangements with a Jewish funeral home. There'll be prayers tomorrow afternoon, and the funeral home took care of the cemetery arrangements."

Caldwell nodded. "That's nice. It doesn't mean anything except to us, but it's nice. Thanks, Mac."

"If I could think of anything else to do for Hirsch, I'd do it," McBride said.

"Well, there is one thing we might do," Caldwell said.

"What's that?"

"We could find out who killed him."

"What?"

McBride turned his head to stare at Caldwell.

"Watch the road," Chris snapped.

"What do you mean, find out who killed him? What are you talking about?"

"Hirsch was killed, Mac. I don't know what any autopsy is going to say, but somehow he was killed."

"How much did you drink on that plane?"

Caldwell shook his head. "It's not the booze. It's because

58

I knew Benjamin Hirschfeld. I sat in his house and listened to stories of what his life was like in Germany before the war. I listened to what happened to him in the camp at Dachau."

McBride had mastered his surprise. "Keep talking," he said in a cool, trial-lawyer voice.

"Did you ever see Hirsch eat fish?"

"Mmmm...I don't remember. Now that you mention it, maybe not. I don't think so. But that doesn't mean he didn't."

"Take my word for it, he didn't," Caldwell said. "Hirsch hated fish. He hated fishing. He hated the water. Zhava told me about it. Hirsch was just a kid in that death camp. He was always hungry, because he was slipping most of the little food he got to his mother and his sister. Then one day, he was out of the camp on a work detail, alongside a little stream. He was digging a sanitary trench. There was a little sunfish flopping on the bank, maybe it was dying already, and he grabbed it and he was so hungry, he ate the damn fish raw, Mac. While it was still alive. He just bit into it and gagged it down. Scales and all. That's how hungry he was. That's how desperate he was. He fought not to vomit it up, 'cause he knew he needed it if he was going to live.

"Zhava told me about this. Hirsch never mentioned it. Anyway, a couple of days later his mother died. And Hirsch couldn't help thinking that if he had smuggled that fish back into the camp and given it to her, maybe she wouldn't have died. He was wrong. Of course, they would have killed his mother in the gas chamber, just like they did his sister when she got too weak to work. He carried that all his life. Mac, don't tell me he was out anywhere fishing today with rented poles and boats. That's all a lot of bullshit, Mac. That wasn't any accident."

There was a long silence, and finally McBride shook his head. "Hirsch never told me that story," he said quietly. "I'm glad he didn't and I'm sorry you did."

Caldwell turned to look at his old friend. He smiled slightly and nodded. "It's a hard world, Mac. You know that."

"But it doesn't prove murder," McBride said.

"No. Not yet. But that's why I came here. To find out."

They drove in silence for a few more minutes before McBride asked: "What do we do, Chris? Tell the police?"

"Think they'd believe us?"

"Maybe."

"More likely not," Caldwell said. "Just maybe they have more pressing problems on their hands than worrying about the obviously accidental death of one lonely, insignificant old man with a paranoid son-in-law."

"A private detective?" McBride suggested.

Caldwell sighed deeply. "Just give me the name of a good men's clothing store."

"Why?"

"Because when I come to work for you, I have to look the part. Was Hirsch working on anything important besides that Griffin Oil Company business?"

"No. Just some trivial stuff. Why?"

"Because I'm taking you up on your offer, Mac. I'm going to work on that Griffin application. I'm rusty as hell, but I've got to satisfy myself that this project wasn't the reason Hirsch died."

McBride drove another block before answering. "I still think, maybe a private detective."

"You forget. I know something about this work myself," Caldwell said.

"Okay. You can move into Hirsch's office. As long as you're not going into court or signing anything for the firm, there won't be any problem about your not being admitted to the bar anywhere. Any help you need, you'll get. I don't know whether you're right or not, Chris. It seems unbelievable that anyone would want to kill poor Hirsch. But if that's what happened, I'm with you a hundred percent. If it's true, then—"

He broke off and pounded his horn savagely at a car in front of them.

"Watch the traffic, Mac," Caldwell said quietly.

Caldwell closed the door of Hirschfeld's apartment, which was in a cluster of small buildings on West Dallas Avenue. He stood for a moment inside the living room, looking about. He had been there before on brief visits, but for the first time, the furniture had an impact on him. It was the same furniture that had been in Hirsch's apartment on the night that Caldwell had first met Zhava, so long ago.

As he turned on the light, Chris felt a sudden pang of sadness at the sight of the familiar overstuffed armchair beneath the floor lamp, where Hirsch was accustomed to reading late into the night. "Old men don't need much sleep," his father-in-law had told him. "I'll have all the rest I need soon enough."

It was typical of Hirsch that there was no television set in the room. But one entire wall had shelves from floor to ceiling, all filled with well-worn books.

Caldwell sighed, memories again crowding into his mind. Then he shook his head. Time for reminiscence later. He had things to do.

He went back to the door to get his two small suitcases. Something on the rug with its old-fashioned design of large maroon flowers caught his attention. It was a little gray smudge, and he knelt to inspect it more closely. It looked like the ashes from a cigarette. But Hirsch smoked a pipe.

If they were ashes, they had been stepped on, Caldwell decided. He wished for a moment he had been in the FBI rather than the CIA. He could plant a bomb or defuse one, but he doubted if he could tell cigarette ashes from ordinary household dust. He touched the little gray smudge and rubbed it together between his fingers. Cigarette ashes. For sure.

He carried his two suitcases into the bedroom and put them on the bed. He draped his jacket over the back of a chair and rolled up his sleeves. He stood in the middle of the floor for a few moments, slowly turning, looking intently at everything in sight, seeking any hint of the unusual, anything that did not square with his memories of Hirsch's possessions and his knowledge of how the old man had lived his life.

The bed was unmade, and that was unusual. Hirsch was uncommonly neat, and if he had scheduled himself to go somewhere, he would have gotten up early enough to make his bed. The only mess ever to be found in his apartment might be a pile of books next to his reading chair. Caldwell remembered that he did not even own a vacuum cleaner but paid the superintendent's wife to come in once a week to give the apartment a quick cleaning.

He was rusty. He couldn't think anymore. He opened one of his suitcases and took out a pint bottle of vodka. Going into the kitchen, he turned on the light. There wasn't a glass on the sink, as there would have been in Caldwell's small house. Instead, all the glasses were clean and dry in the cabinet over the sink.

He poured himself a drink, straight, and as he sipped it, noticed that there was an ashtray on the sink. That was a little unusual. If Hirsch had washed an ashtray, he would have dried it and put it back on the table where it belonged.

He had a thought, and, carrying his vodka, he went into the bathroom. He flicked on the light and bent over to investigate the toilet seat. Sure. There were tiny flecks of gray on the edge of the seat. He touched them with his index finger. They left a light, almost white dusty smear along the wooden seat.

Cigarette ashes.

Somebody had smoked a cigarette in this apartment, then had dumped the ashes in the toilet and washed out the ashtray before leaving. He looked closely at the chrome-plated toilet handle. In the bright fluorescent light, he could see it sparkle evenly and cleanly. It had been wiped clean to make sure no fingerprints were left.

Caldwell finished his vodka and went back to the kitchen to pour another glassful. Then he began the tedious task of carefully searching every drawer in the room, every garment, every box in the closet.

Three hours later, Caldwell wearily closed the lid of the secretary in the corner of the living room. He felt as exhausted as if he had spent the time swimming through ten-foot waves. He had looked through everything in the apartment, saving the desk for last. That had taken the most time. He had been touched to find all his letters of the past two years from Puerto Rico kept together in one cubbyhole. But there was nothing that could give him a reason for Hirsch's having been killed.

Had someone else looked through the desk? There was no way to tell. Fingerprints, he knew, meant very little, unless there was a full set and a suspect to match them.

There was nothing.

Only an unmade bed, and a possibility of cigarette ashes

on the rug and in the toilet, and the fact that a glass ashtray had been washed out and put on the kitchen sink to dry.

But an ashtray on the table beside Hirsch's reading chair still held a small pile of half-smoked pipe tobacco.

Someone who smoked cigarettes could have gone through Hirsch's desk, then washed out the ashtray later to leave no evidence of his visit. Might have. Could have. Suddenly Caldwell was very tired.

A sudden thought sent him to the apartment door. He opened it and examined the area around the lock carefully for scratches or any sign of forced entry.

Again, nothing. It was a cheap snap lock that had come with the garden apartment as standard equipment. On an earlier visit, Caldwell had urged Hirsch to install a better lock, but the old man had laughed and said, "Who breaks in to steal books?"

A credit card would have been enough to open the snap lock.

Caldwell washed his face and hands, then paused uncertainly for a moment. On previous visits, he had slept on the couch. He shrugged, turned off the lights, and got into the bed. It felt strange to be sleeping in his father-in-law's bed. In a way, it seemed disrespectful. But Hirsch would have laughed at him for feeling that way. And even while he mulled that thought, the exhaustion and stress of the long day and night overcame him.

The sound of the radio woke him up the next morning. He listened with half an ear to the news broadcast and weather report and was dozing off again when a shrill beeping began coming from the radio. He fumbled sleepily for the control that would cut off the doze alarm.

Then he was wide awake, staring at the radio in the dark of the room. The luminous hands read seven o'clock. The radio was a cheap common type. Unless it was turned off, it would play continuously.

According to McBride, the police had said that Hirsch had rented a boat early yesterday morning. Before seven o'clock. And then died without returning home.

If he had turned off the radio before leaving his apartment yesterday, it wouldn't have rung this morning. The only way it could have rung today would have been for someone to find it ringing the previous day—after seven o'clock—and press the off button on the top of the radio.

And Hirsch couldn't have—because by then he was probably already dead.

Eustace McBride liked to sleep late on Sunday, so he was groggily surly when the telephone rang at 7:15 A.M. It was Caldwell.

"Mac, did you come to Hirsch's apartment yesterday?"

"Wait a minute. Let me clear my head," McBride said. "Uhhh, yeah. With the police. They wanted to see if there was a suicide note."

"Think carefully, Mac. When you came in, was the clock ringing or the radio playing? Think carefully. Did you or the cops turn off the radio?"

"No, Chris. Why?"

"Because I think it means I can prove Hirsch was killed."

CHAPTER EIGHT

Caldwell was on the telephone in Hirschfeld's living room, talking to a car-rental agency, when he felt someone behind him.

He turned slowly. Two men were inside the door. Each had a gun in his hand.

"Hang up the telephone nice and gentle," one of them said. He was a tall husky man with a ginger-colored mustache and sloping muscular shoulders that his expensive sports jacket could not disguise. He wore a broad, flat-brimmed hat that looked like the Old West version of the porkpie. The other man was black and shorter, with tightly trimmed short hair. The two men moved apart from each other so that in case Caldwell was armed, he would not be able to take them both out at once.

"What the hell is this?" Caldwell asked. He felt his muscles tense as he looked at their guns. His stomach knotted, more in anger than in fear.

"We'll ask the questions," the white man said. "Houston Police. Hang up that phone."

Caldwell could hear someone squawking at him over the telephone. He said, "I'll call back," and hung up the receiver. His muscles relaxed. For a moment, he had thought that perhaps whoever had taken Hirsch on that final fishing trip had returned.

"I'm Christopher Caldwell, Mr. Hirschfeld's son-in-law. Mr. McBride, the attorney, can verify that. He's home now if you want to call."

When the black detective made a phone call to McBride, Caldwell noted that he took the number from a small telephone book he carried in his pocket. He put his pistol down, near Caldwell, on the end table while dialing, and Chris unconsciously commented to himself that the technique was sloppy and dangerous, even though he was still covered by the white detective.

The black officer spoke a few sentences into the tele-

65

phone, then handed the phone to Chris.

"Hello, Mac."

"Okay. I ought to let them arrest your ass. It might be the only way I get any sleep. Put the fuzz back on."

Caldwell handed the phone back to the detective, who listened to McBride for a moment, said thanks, and replaced the receiver.

He nodded to his partner, and both men put their guns away. The white detective said, with a touch of disappointment, "I thought we had a good grab."

"What brought you here?" Caldwell asked.

"We handled the old man's death yesterday. Then a little while ago the super of this building called. They heard someone moving around in the apartment. When the call came in, we took it. We used the super's key to get in."

"You scared the shit out of me."

"We like scaring the shit out of people," the big detective said, a happy cherubic smile under his moustache. But the smile stopped before it reached his eyes. They were not happy.

"You investigated Hirsch's death?" Caldwell asked. "My father-in-law?"

The black man nodded.

"What did you think?"

"What's to think?" the detective said. "He called to rent a boat and fishing equipment. He got there real early, paid for the boat, and went out. Somebody found the boat drifting around later. His body was hooked on the anchor rope. He must have fallen over and drowned and just luckily got hooked onto the rope."

Caldwell thought for a moment of telling the detectives his suspicions, but he thought better of it. To them, it was cut and dried. He would sound like a hysterical relative.

Instead, he said, "No doubt it was an accident?"

"Unless you got something better," the black officer said.

"Guess not," Caldwell said casually. "Were you the two who came here yesterday to search the place with McBride?"

"Yeah," the white detective said. "Thought it might be suicide. Maybe he left a note."

66

"Did you notice, was the radio playing when you came in?"

The white officer shrugged. "No," said the black man.

"Neither of you touched the radio?"

"Not me," said the black detective. "You?" he asked his partner. The white man shook his head.

"Why?" he asked.

"No reason," Caldwell said. "The autopsy said Mr. Hirschfeld drowned?"

"Yes. Water in the lungs."

"No bruises?"

"Nothing he wouldn't get falling overboard. You a detective?" the black officer asked.

"Not in a long time," Caldwell said. He asked the two detectives for their names. The white man was Detective Albert Potter, the other man Sergeant William Walders. He wrote both names down, and the police took his name and address.

As they were leaving, Caldwell asked casually, "I ran out. Either of you have a cigarette?"

"Sorry," the white man said. "We've both kicked the habit."

After they left, Caldwell locked the front door and took a long shower. He dressed himself in his only suit and went downstairs.

He found the superintendent's apartment in the basement of the building. The woman who answered his ring was squat, and pear-shaped, with massive upper arms and blond hair so stringy and unhealthy-looking it appeared to have been bleached with sulfuric acid.

"I'm Chris Caldwell," he said. "Mr. Hirschfeld's son-in-law. I'm going to be staying in his apartment for a while."

The woman nodded.

"The police were just there," Caldwell said. "Everything's all right."

"Okay. I hope they didn't cause you no trouble, but I heard sounds in there and I didn't know what else to do."

"No, you did the right thing," Caldwell said. "I just wanted you to know everything's all right."

He turned to go. The woman stepped out from behind the barrier of the half-open door. "I always cleaned his apartment on Sunday. You want me to do it for you?"

"Yeah. I'll be out most of the day, so any time is good," he said. "You weren't in the apartment yesterday?"

"No, not me. I wasn't in there," in a tone of voice that saw accusation where none was intended.

Caldwell patted his jacket pocket. "I forgot my cigarettes," he said. "Could I trouble you for one? Just to get me to a store?"

"Sorry, Mr. . . ."

"Caldwell."

"Yeah. No. I don't smoke. Eddy and me, we both quit last year, 'cause the prices was getting so high and all and between the Arabs and their gas and inflation and everything, you can't even make . . ."

"Yes. It's tough, isn't it?" Chris said. He walked down the hall to go outside and find a taxi to take him to the car-rental agency. He hoped the liquor stores were open on Sunday.

Caldwell found McBride and his wife, Dolores, waiting for him at the funeral home. They were sitting alone in a small room with a closed plain pine casket, both looking extremely uncomfortable. They greeted him with relief, Dolores McBride putting her arms around Chris and hugging him tightly.

"This is the damnedest thing I've done in years," McBride said in a hushed whisper. "Are we going to be the only ones here for the ceremony?"

"If we are, there won't be a ceremony," Caldwell said. "You have to have ten men for a minyan to have a ceremony. Jewish men. The rabbi or the funeral home will take care of that."

As if on cue, a mournful man in a somber suit ushered in a dozen elderly men wearing yarmulkas. Some of the headpieces were black, some white, a few were elaborately beaded. The man in the suit gave Caldwell and McBride yarmulkas to wear. A few minutes later, the rabbi, a stout smiling man, bustled in and came over to them.

"I am Rabbi Levin," he said. "You are friends of the deceased?" He looked down at a small card in his hand. "Mr. Hirschfeld?"

"Yes," Caldwell said. "I am his son-in-law. This is Mr.

68

and Mrs. McBride, his friends. Mr. Hirschfeld had no surviving relatives that I know of."

The rabbi nodded. "Would you happen to know if Mr. Hirschfeld was Orthodox or not?"

"I don't think so," Caldwell said. "Maybe Reformed. He kept the holidays, but he wasn't devout. He didn't eat ham or shellfish."

Or any kind of fish, he reminded himself silently, stubbornly.

"We will have an Orthodox ceremony if you have no objections," the rabbi said.

The rabbi and the silent group of elderly men donned prayer shawls and began a litany of prayers and responses in Hebrew that lasted for almost half an hour. Caldwell winced as he listened; he had heard the prayers before when his wife and daughter were being put into the ground.

At the end of the prayers, Caldwell saw Dolores unobtrusively cross herself. He smiled warmly at her. She looked embarrassed.

At the cemetery, there were more prayers. The rabbi looked at them and asked, "Do you have any words you would like to say?"

"Only that he was a good man," McBride said somberly. "He was my teacher and my friend."

"He was my father," Caldwell said.

Caldwell followed the McBrides to their large split-level home in the swank River Oaks section of the city. The two men sat on the patio, beside the pool, while Dolores checked with the cook about dinner. McBride sipped at a Tom Collins while Caldwell gulped straight vodka from a water glass.

It was their first chance to talk privately.

"I didn't tell Dolores anything about your suspicions," McBride said.

"Good."

"What'd you mean when you called this morning?" McBride asked.

Caldwell explained to him about the radio's going off and awakening him. "Somebody had to reset it," he said.

"Somebody who was in the apartment after Hirsch died."

"I guess," McBride said with a sigh. He shook his head. "But I...I don't know, Chris. It's still all kind of unbelievable."

"It is to me too. But there's an answer and I'll find it."

"You're really serious about that, aren't you?"

"Dead serious," Caldwell said.

"Why would anyone want to kill Hirsch?"

"I don't know, but I'm going to find out."

"Soup's on," Dolores called.

They drank during and after dinner, and when Caldwell finally left, after dark, he took a bottle of McBride's vodka with him.

"I'll see you tomorrow at your office," Caldwell said.

"Your office now too," McBride said.

Caldwell was tired, but before he could force himself to sleep, he had drunk half of the quart of vodka.

CHAPTER NINE

Christopher Caldwell entered the well-furnished offices of McBride and McBride, occupying half a floor of a downtown office building, later than he had planned. It was already ten o'clock.

On the few occasions in the past when he had visited Houston, Caldwell had stayed at Hirsch's apartment, venturing into midtown only after dark, to find a meal or a drink or a woman. So, unconsciously, he still had an idea of Houston as a flat spread-out Texas town where one could drive for miles without meeting another soul, and he was not ready for the torrent of traffic that flooded the city's heart every day. It had taken him almost half an hour to find a parking garage four blocks from McBride's office that was not already filled up.

A young receptionist with bright-red hair and an attractive toothy smile sat behind the desk, just inside the glass entrance doors to the office complex.

"Chris Caldwell to see Mr. McBride," he told her.

"One moment, please." She picked up her phone, spoke briefly, then looked at Caldwell with increased interest. "He's waiting for you in his office. All the way down that hall, last door on the right."

"Thank you," Caldwell said politely, turning away. The girl's eyes followed him as he walked away, and she cocked an eyebrow and smiled at an inner thought.

Another secretary, a woman in her thirties wearing a tailored suit that seemed somehow to match exactly her intelligent, attractive all-business face, sat outside McBride's office, but the tall lawyer bounded out to usher Caldwell inside. "This is my new boss," he informed the startled woman. "He's taking over the joint. He made me an offer I couldn't refuse. Chris, this is Sylvie Arnoff, my right-hand woman. She can't type worth a damn, but she's got a great pair of lungs. Come on in."

Caldwell grinned and shrugged helplessly at the woman

as McBride threw an arm over his shoulders and almost dragged him into the office.

"I told Sam Fischer, our office manager, that you'll be in some time today to fill out forms, insurance, taxes, all that bullshit," McBride said.

"Okay. I'll fill out your forms."

"So go to work already. My clock's running and at a hundred and fifty an hour, you're costing me a fortune wasting my time here."

"What do I do?"

"Go to Hirsch's office and get started. You know you're not here to do an SEC application. You're looking for something else. Do as little or as much as you like. Use the work here for a cover, if you need it. Only you know what you have to do, Chris."

"I don't know enough about the SEC work to use it as a cover."

"Well, you poor bastard, you've got an assistant. Check that. Make it an *associate*. She'll tell you what to do. And she'll tell you and tell you and tell you."

"Who is she and why do I hate her already?" Caldwell asked.

"*She* is named Susan Millard and she is a goddam legacy handed down to us from Washington on high by Mr. Justice Oliver Wendell Brooks of the Supremest Court there is."

McBride pulled down the corners of his mouth in a dour expression that made him look like a hound dog offered asparagus for dinner.

"Try again, Mac, you lost me. Who the hell is Susan Millard?"

"Who she is is some kind of niece or cousin or something to the late Mrs. Justice Learned Hand Brooks. She got her law degree a couple of years ago—from Harvard, no less— and she's been working as a special assistant to Mr. Justice Earl Warren Brooks. Until two weeks ago, goddammit."

"Mac, rev down. I don't know what the hell you're talking about. Brooks, I guess, is Supreme Court Justice Otto Brooks?"

"That's right. The last bastion of hope for liberal America, I think *Newsweek* called him. And it's all your fault."

"What is?"

72

"Two weeks ago, when you wouldn't take the job with Hirsch, Brooks called me. He said he wanted to find a spot for this girl who had been on his staff. He suggested she could work on that SEC application with Hirsch, get some federal-type work under her belt before she comes back to Washington as Attorney General or President or something. Because I didn't have you, I didn't have any way to say no. So she's been here ever since."

"And you don't like her, obviously. What have you got against her?"

"What I have against her is that I don't like Mr. Justice Brooks and I don't like his shoving his people into my office. And, having met her, I'm not all that crazy about Miss Susie Baby Millard, either. Anyone who could spend three years working with good old Uncle Otto has got to be either a complete opportunist or a dyed-in-the-wool knee-jerk jerk. I think she's both." He gave a theatrical shudder of disgust that seemed to send ripples up and down his lanky frame.

Caldwell laughed. "If you don't like the girl, why sic her on me?"

"Three reasons, good buddy. For one thing, Hirsch needed somebody to help with the scut work involved in this kind of project, and I was afraid to expose her to any of our important clients. The first time we sat down to talk here, she wanted to know how many hours a week our firm volunteered to defend the poor without charge. I told her we donated all our time to the prosecution to get muggers off the street. She almost went into cardiac arrest. All she's interested in is social progress and the plight of the suffering masses. But I think she might be a good lawyer, so maybe she can be some help to you. How many reasons is that?"

"I don't know," Caldwell said. "One, two, three, eight, I don't know."

"Stop counting. Another reason goes back to what I said before. I'm prejudiced against this girl. I didn't like her even before I laid eyes on her, and she hasn't done anything to improve my opinion since then."

"Then why'd you hire her?" asked Caldwell. "Why didn't you just tell Brooks that you didn't have any work for a new associate?"

"Because I did and he knew it. He wanted her to work on the Griffin Oil thing. And besides, whatever Uncle Otto wants, Uncle Otto gets," McBride said. "He started this company with my father. It used to be Brooks and McBride. My dad did all the goddam work, but Otto was the front man and it was Otto who got picked to be a Senator and then a Supreme Court Justice. He carries a lot of weight in this town. A lot of people didn't think I was old enough or good enough to head this firm when my father died. Otto could do me a lot of damage with a couple of words here and there if he felt like it. So I've got to smile and be polite to the old bastard, including when he calls up and chuckles and tells me that as a special favor to the son of his old friend, he's unloading a Radcliffe radical on me."

McBride threw both arms high in the air, then slumped in his chair, a picture of hopeless despair. Caldwell laughed again at his friend's histrionics.

"Why did she want to come to Texas?" he asked.

"I don't know. Otto said something about pushing her out of the nest. Washington. A nest for birdbrains. And she said something about wanting to get involved in the actual practice of law instead of the academic atmosphere of the Supreme Court, whatever the hell that means. Not that I take anything either of them says at face value, of course. Maybe good old Uncle Otto was putting it to her and she started getting ideas of being Mrs. Supreme Court Justice, so he shoved her off on me. With the Chief Justice just dying, some people are talking about Otto becoming Chief Justice. All he needs is some bippy wife one-third his age and he can forget that. Or maybe she got involved in some sticky situation and Otto's getting rid of her before it rubs off on him. Who knows? Anyway, she's here now and she's all yours."

"You still didn't explain why."

"As I said, I don't like the girl, but maybe she really is a good lawyer. You've got good judgment, Chris, and you don't have my emotional involvement. I want you to look her over good and tell me if I should keep her or find some excuse to tie a can to her tail."

Caldwell frowned. "I'm not real crazy about that idea, Mac."

74

"Yeah, but I'm the boss, see, and those are things that employees have to do around here. Anyway, it's not that bad. She'll knock your eye out when you see her. You didn't think I'd stick my old roomie with some frumpy-looking hag, did you?"

"Yeah. You did it twice on double dates back in college. But I don't give a damn what she looks like. She can wear a sack over her head for all I care."

"Listen," McBride said. "Hirsch's secretary is named Celeste Thompson. I don't think you ought to expect too much of her for a few days. She thought the world of Hirsch, and she just may resent you sitting in that office. Take it easy with her until she gets over it, okay?"

"Sure, Mac. I understand."

"Anything else you need from me?" McBride asked.

"Well, I need to know about Griffin Oil."

"There's a file on your desk, and Sam Fischer can fill you in pretty good. And Susie Baby should know what the hell is going on. And if you need background stuff that isn't in the file, I can fill you in on that."

"Okay. One last thing. What do I say about...well, my background?"

McBride grinned slowly, looking pleased with himself. "I thought about that in the car coming over here this morning, and I figured honesty is the best policy. So I called in Rob White and Kenny Brown and a few of the other top guys and told them you'd be coming on and who you are—that is, Hirsch's son-in-law. I said you were my roomie at law school and had better marks than me and that you had worked for the feds for a number of years. Then I dropped my voice mysteriously and said, 'It was the CIA, but we don't like to talk about that.' And I told them not to ask you about it and that you had been in private business for the past few years and that I've been after you a long time to come here. I didn't tell them you never passed the bar exam. So they were all very impressed and I guess some of them might assume you're still with the Outfit, working here as some kind of cover. You'll be romantic to them, Chris. They'll be asking for your autograph. The secretaries will love you."

"You think telling them all that was wise, Mac?"

"I had to say something, and it seemed easiest to tell

the truth. So they won't be asking you a lot of questions. Let's just see how it goes." His face turned sober for a moment. "One last thing, and I guess I better lay it right out. I know what you think about Hirsch and all, and I don't know if you're right or wrong...."

"I'm right, Mac."

"Maybe, so you ought to know this. When I gave Hirsch the Griffin Oil job, he asked me how hard he should dig. You know how those SEC applications are. Twenty questions about this. Twenty more about that. They want a look at every barnacle in your corporate butt, but a good lawyer sometimes can hide maybe one barnacle from them. So Hirsch asked me what to do and I told him I wanted him to dig up everything. He seemed kind of glad about that. Anyway, I don't care much for Adam Griffin, and I don't like old Gus."

"Why?"

"It was Gus's money that sent Brooks to the Senate in '42. Mr. Justice was going belly-up in his first campaign, and Gus pumped a hundred big ones into his campaign in the last minute. Got him elected by a couple of votes, and that was that." He shook his head forlornly. "It should have been my father's seat. But Brooks made some kind of deal with Gus Griffin, so it was Brooks. I'll never forget that and I'll never forgive it. Anyway, I told Hirsch to dig deep. I just want you to know that. I don't know if his digging had anything to do with him being...with his death, or what, but you ought to know."

"You know, Mac, that I'm digging all the way too. If Griffin Oil had anything to do with his death, I'll find out."

"I know that."

"You'll back me up?"

"Right to the wall," McBride said.

"All right. Knowing that, I can even face up to dealing with your Susie Baby Millard."

"Christ, don't call her Susie. It's Susan."

Caldwell left the office, nodded at Mrs. Arnoff, and walked slowly down the hallway toward Hirschfeld's old office. He felt suddenly reluctant to enter that room.

An attractive young woman with reddened eyes was

76

sitting at the desk outside the office door, and Caldwell offered his hand to her.

"Miss Thompson, I'm Chris Caldwell, Mr. Hirschfeld's son-in-law. I'm going to be using his office for a while. I just want you to know he was the finest man I ever knew. He was like my own father, and I can understand how you felt about him."

The girl collapsed in giant racking sobs. Caldwell put his hand around her shoulders, and when she finally regained her composure, he ordered her to take the rest of the day off. She was reluctant at first, but agreed at last when he explained that he would not be in the office much for the rest of the day.

He left the girl dabbing her eyes, hesitated a moment, and entered Hirsch's private office.

Again, as he had when he entered Hirsch's apartment two nights before, he had the feeling of wrongness, of almost sickening incompleteness. Hirsch should be sitting behind that desk, looking up with his quick bright smile of pleasure, leaning back to gaze down his long nose in a fondly measuring way, reaching for the plain well-worn pipe, puffing an occasional neat plume of smoke as he considered an answer to a question.

But Hirsch wasn't there. Hirsch would never again sit behind that desk, and Chris was alone now—alone with his determination to find out who had killed the man he knew as his father.

To find out... or to punish?

Closing the door behind him so he wouldn't be disturbed, Chris sat in Hirsch's chair, and ignoring the sudden, irrational twinge of guilt, asked the operator to connect him with Sam Fischer. Chris introduced himself and asked Fischer to send over all the forms he needed to fill out. He promised to have them returned the next day. He also told Fischer that he had told Celeste Thompson to take the rest of the day off because she was visibly upset by Hirschfeld's death and would be useless in the office anyway.

"We'll all miss Hirsch," Fischer said. "I'll get somebody else to watch your phones."

Caldwell eyed the thick manila envelope in the center

77

of the desk and decided he would take it home with him and begin reading it tonight.

Home. He thought it strange to be thinking of Hirsch's apartment as home, but perhaps it was more home to him than anywhere else.

He looked through the desk. The wide center drawer held a jumble of pencils, paper clips, a half-used pouch of tobacco, another pipe, and his own latest letter of several weeks before.

He opened it and read it. It seemed foolish to him—a childishly sarcastic description of the behavior of a group of drunken tourists and a sophomoric attempt to relate his disgust with them to the peace and calm he felt while diving.

The telephone rang, startling him. It was Sylvie Arnoff, McBride's secretary. "He wants you to come down here right away. He's holding a call until you get here."

Caldwell trotted down the hallway and into McBride's office. The lanky lawyer was sitting relaxedly, his feet on his desk, arms behind his head, slouched down so far in his chair that he was almost horizontal. "It's Adam Griffin," he explained. "I thought you might as well listen in."

He sat up and pushed a button on a small box next to the telephone receiver.

"Hello, Adam? Sorry, pal, I was long distance to Washington, and you know how those tax-suckers are when we're paying for the calls." He winked at Caldwell, putting a warning finger to his lips.

"That's all right. I know you're busy," said a fretful voice from the telephone's loudspeaker. "But I heard about that lawyer of yours drowning and I wondered if that's going to set things back or cause any serious delay. I mean, it's not going to make problems for me, is it?"

Caldwell's lips tightened, and McBride, glancing at him, shook his head sadly.

"I put a new man on the project this morning, Adam. He's going through the files now. It depends on how much poor old Hirsch had of his notes typed up, I guess. If his notes were rough, we might have to backtrack a little."

"And answer all those questions again?" asked the younger Griffin.

"Let's hope it's not necessary, Adam," McBride said.

"This is really very annoying."

"Adam," said McBride, "Benjamin Hirschfeld is dead. I don't think your troubles matter a shit compared to his."

"No, no. Of course. But you'll move this as fast as possible?"

"Yes, Adam," McBride said in his humblest voice. "Everything will be all right."

Caldwell frowned, then grabbed a pencil from the desk and looked for a piece of notepaper. Not seeing any, he took his last letter to Hirschfeld from his pocket and scribbled on its back: "How'd he know about H?"

"Okay, I trust you, Mac. I know you'll move this along," Adam Griffin was saying.

"I will," McBride said. "By the way, Adam, how'd you hear about Hirschfeld's death?"

"Doyle Blaney told me about it a little while ago. I guess he saw it in yesterday's paper."

"Okay, Adam. Talk to you later." He hung up the telephone. Caldwell filed the name of Doyle Blaney away in his mind and told himself to check the Houston papers to see if any of them had carried a news story on Hirsch's death.

CHAPTER TEN

When Caldwell returned to his office there was a new girl replacing Celeste Thompson at the outer desk.

She handed him a note with a smile.

"Miss Millard. Please call her back."

Inside the office, he asked the switchboard operator for Susan Millard. She picked up her phone on the first ring and crisply announced her name.

"Susan Millard."

"Chris Caldwell."

"Oh. Mr. McBride told me we'll be working together on that Griffin Oil application. Can we get together on it?"

"Sure," Caldwell said. "We'd better if we're working together."

"How about right now?"

"Sorry, I'm going out of the office," Caldwell said.

"Lunch?"

"I'll be gone."

"Later this afternoon?" she said.

"I don't know if I'll get back to the office," Caldwell said.

Her voice chilled over. "This *is* the Christopher Caldwell who works for Eustace McBride of McBride and McBride, isn't it?"

Caldwell felt a quick flash of anger.

"Yes. And this *is* the Susan Millard of Radcliffe, Harvard, and the United States Supreme Court, isn't it?"

For a few long seconds, there was only silence over the phone.

"All right. Maybe I deserved that," the woman's voice said. "When can we get together? And it's Wellesley, not Radcliffe."

"What time do you quit?" Caldwell asked.

"Five o'clock."

"If I get back before then, I'll call. I'll buy you a drink or dinner or take you to the roller derby or whatever you want. What do they do in Houston? Want to go bust a bronco?"

"God, no. But drinks sound good. I've got a dinner date. I'll be in the office all day. I hope you call."

The telephone clicked dead in Caldwell's ear, and he replaced the receiver with a small smile. He wondered what Susan Millard looked like. He discounted McBride's description and eloquent eye-rolling, because he remembered only too well Mac's alluring descriptions of girls he had induced Chris to date back in law school.

He put her out of his mind; he had other things to do first.

It was almost noon when he arrived at Lake Conroe, where Hirsch had taken his fatal fishing trip. He found the boat dock McBride had described, a long thin wooden finger pier with a number of canoes and rowboats, some with small trolling motors.

A short fat Mexican-American sat behind the counter inside the concession building. His eyes widened when Chris began to ask questions about the drowning.

"Why d'you wanna know?" he demanded. "Who're you?"

For a moment, Caldwell thought about telling the man the truth. But what was the truth? That he was almost a relative who almost had evidence that Benjamin Hirschfeld had been murdered and hadn't just drowned by accident? That if Caldwell had listened to the man more closely two weeks ago, he might have come right to Houston and maybe Hirsch wouldn't be dead?

Could he tell the man all that? Any of it?

Chris reached into his wallet and from a deep back inside compartment, took out a hard plastic card, its corners clipped sharply to make it roughly octagonal in shape. It identified Christopher Caldwell as an agent of the United States Central Intelligence Agency.

"I'm your friendly neighborhood CIA man," Caldwell said. He was not smiling. He handed the card forward just long enough for the man to glance at the picture and to see the words "Central Intelligence Agency" printed in a fine gray screen over the yellow background of the card, then replaced the card in his wallet.

"What is this, a big spy thing?" the attendant said.

Caldwell ignored the question. "Mr. Hirschfeld was not

81

known to fish. That's all you need to know. Were you working on Saturday morning?"

"Yeah. Regular man's sick a lot, because he drinks too much. So I came to fill in for him. I get here at six o'clock to open up and this man, he comes a couple of minutes later. He rents a rowboat with a motor and he wants a rod and reel and some bait and he goes out. It's still almost dark and I'm busy so I don' see him much."

"What happened next?"

"Later it gets busy, then it slows down. 'Bout ten o'clock, somebody says they see a boat floating around with nobody in it. I take a boat out there to look. I find him twisted up to the anchor chain. He drowneded."

"It was the same man who rented the boat?" Caldwell asked.

The Mexican shrugged. "Sure. I mean, it was early and he was wearing that yellow poncho up over his head and sunglasses. I don' see his face all that good but it was him. I seen that poncho. That cop, he ask me about that too." The idea stirred a memory in the attendant. He seemed about to say something and Chris waited. He had learned the virtue of silence when questioning someone. Silence could be almost painfully awkward; some people, to fill that silence, would babble on about anything.

"That cop, he remind me about the poncho. I guess I didn't really see the old man's face. And like he said, people don't look the same after they been in the water a couple of hours. This Hirschfeld, he's an important man, I guess."

"Yes. He was very important. Why?"

"He's not just any old lawyer. Too many people asking about him."

"Yeah? Who?"

"Well, the policemen Saturday. Today, that insurance man."

"What was his name?"

"I don' know. He didn' tell me."

"What did he want?"

"Like you. Talk about the accident."

"Did he ask you anything I didn't ask?"

"No. Except he want to know if Mr. Hirschfeld, he was alone."

"Was he?"

82

"Yeah. I din't see nobody with him. Just him. He had that big bag."

"What bag?"

"Like a big bag, like soldiers carry. A...a..." His English failed him.

"A duffel bag?"

"Yeah. Like that. Maybe bigger. I see him with it. Like it was heavy and he lugging it." He stopped. "Hey, that's funny."

"What's funny?"

"That bag wasn't in the boat when I brung it in." He shrugged hugely, the gesture of those to whom all life is a puzzle and puzzles are just not worth working out. "Probably it fell overboard. Maybe it's got something heavy in it and it sank. Someday it'll come up."

"Did you tell that to the policeman?"

"No. I didn't think of it except just now."

"You tell it to the insurance man?"

"Maybe he asked about it and maybe I said I didn't see it anymore. I don't remember. He didn' ask no questions like you. But we talked a long time."

Caldwell nodded. He had met insurance investigators, and this was no insurance investigator. He had done what Caldwell would have done if his skills hadn't all been lost someplace, at some bar, in some bottle, drowned in some pool of personal sorrow. The insurance investigator had let this man talk and had picked his brains and memory clean.

"This insurance man. What did he look like?" Caldwell asked.

"A big man. Bigger than you. Tan suit. Curly hair."

The question reminded Caldwell of something. "Mr. Hirschfeld," he said. "He was a big man too." It was half statement, half question.

The attendant shrugged. "Like you, maybe. Bigger than me." The fat man grinned. "Everybody bigger than me."

Caldwell thanked the attendant and gave him twenty dollars. The man refused.

"You don' have to do that. Just glad to help you any way I can."

"Thank you," Caldwell said. For a moment, he felt a touch of warmth toward the man. It was nice to find some-

83

one, anyone, who wanted to help nowadays. "Take it, please," he said. "It's on my expense account. You'll pay it back in taxes."

"Taxes. You bet. I pay my share," the attendant said. He took the bill and stuffed it into the pocket of his oily paint-flecked jeans.

"If I think of anything else, I'll call you."

"Anytime. My name is Rafael. You just ask for Rafael. Or Ray. Some people call me Ray."

"Okay, Ray."

In his car in the parking lot, Caldwell took a small spiral-bound notebook from the glove compartment. In it he had written the names of the two Houston detectives who had come to the apartment the previous day. Detective Albert Potter. Sergeant William Walders. Potter was the white man. Caldwell circled his name. He jotted down notes on what Rafael had told him. What had he said? The white cop had "reminded" him about the poncho. Did that mean anything? Was the cop trying to give Rafael a reason to believe that Hirsch himself had rented the boat? Or was Rafael's command of English too tentative for Caldwell to draw conclusions on the basis of a single spoken word?

Chris did not remember Hirsch's having a poncho. The old lawyer was a man who took taxicabs. Ponchos were for people who were outdoors in bad weather, but Hirsch had once told Caldwell, "If God had wanted people to be rained on, he wouldn't have invented houses. Rain is for artichokes to enjoy, Arabs to envy, and human beings to avoid."

Rafael had said the man who rented the boat was as tall as Caldwell. But Chris was a full six inches taller than his father-in-law. It didn't mean much; people were notoriously bad at estimating the heights of others. But it was just another link in the chain.

Back in the heart of downtown Houston, Gus Griffin glowered at the man who stood in front of his desk.

"All right," Gus said, "you've been waiting out there all morning to see me. You won't tell my secretary who you are or what you want. I never saw you before in my life. I'll give my curiosity about sixty seconds and then I'm going to throw you out of here on your ass."

84

"If I have all of a minute, I might as well sit down," the man said. He stepped back and sank into the soft glove-leather high-backed chair. "Nice," he said, then folded his arms and was silent, as if mentally clicking off his allotted sixty seconds.

Griffin slammed a heavy fist down on his desk blotter. The thump knocked a pen out of its desk-set holder.

"Just who the hell do you think you are?"

"I have papers that identify me as one Frederick Kirchner. I believe I am supposed to sell motorized bicycles for a living. Do you want to buy a motorized bicycle?"

"Get out of here."

"Not just yet. I have another thirty seconds." The man leaned back confidently in his chair. Griffin got to his feet. His left eye was squinting, his face turning red, and he lowered his head like a range steer preparing to charge.

The man in the chair shook his head. "You really do not remember me, do you, Griffin?"

"Why should I?"

"We have met before. Many years ago."

"Just get to it. Who the hell are you and what do you want?"

"The name Kirchner will do for the time being. My real name is of no concern to you. You would not recognize it, although some others might." He shrugged. "If you wish, you may call me by some other name. Sam Houston, perhaps?"

Griffin sank back slowly into his swivel chair. His seamed leathery face was rigidly expressionless, but his bristling gray eyebrows writhed like a pair of wounded caterpillars.

"I don't think much of your sense of humor, mister," he said. The other man bowed slightly in apology, but a trace of a smile lingered in his expression. Griffin had seen that look before. It was the expression of a poker player with two aces showing and a third one in the hole.

"What do you want here?" Gus said.

"I want to give you a lot of money, Mr. Griffin. Many millions of dollars."

"Good," Griffin said. "I never turn down many millions of dollars. Just stick it in an envelope and leave it with my secretary. She'll know how to handle it."

85

The other man ignored the sarcasm. "Imagine, Mr. Griffin. You will be one of the richest men in Houston. The Griffin Oil Company will grow beyond your wildest dreams."

"And how do we work this wonder?"

"By giving your company access to unlimited supplies of oil. Iranian oil, Mr. Griffin. Oceans of it. All the oil that you can sell—and at a price far below the world market price."

Griffin's face remained carefully guarded against emotion, but his eyes glittered. "And just why would you want to do that when you can sell all you pump to Japan and anywhere else at top dollar?"

"American dollars still have their value. They can buy many things."

"In case you hadn't heard, locked away at the funny farm, this country doesn't get along very well with Iran. No one will buy Iranian oil."

"A detail. There are ways around it. This oil could come in as Venezuelan oil, for instance. You have holdings in Venezuela."

"They don't produce anymore."

"They could recover their former vigor."

"It would take a miracle," Griffin said.

"Sometimes miracles happen," his visitor said, his smile growing broader and more confident.

"It'd take a second miracle to pull off something like that without being caught. I stopped taking chances a lot of years ago, after I made my pile. Now I keep it tidy and safe. Thank you kindly for the offer, but no thanks."

"It was not an offer, Mr. Griffin," the other man said softly. "It was an announcement."

Griffin studied the other man intently. The stranger, "Frederick Kirchner," was a tall, thin man probably in his late fifties or early sixties. He was dressed in a white suit. His hair was a light blond, thickening in texture where it was silvering, and his skin was darkly sunburned. He sat composed and quiet, and he spoke firmly and with confidence. His English was excellent, but hinted at a slight accent, which gave him a touch of arrogance, the look and sound of a man who felt in total command of a situation. He made Gus feel uneasy, as if this Kirchner knew more than Gus did.

"Not an offer but an announcement," Griffin repeated mildly. "Mind explaining that?"

"My country—the government I am representing—is anxious to do business with you. It is in your best interests."

"Why me? If you've got oil, you can sell it to anybody. Why would you even think about little old Griffin Oil?"

"Because you are unique. You are a privately owned company, only just going public. It is more efficient to deal with you. And safer. No one will ever associate Griffin Oil with Iranian oil."

"No one'll ever have any reason to." Griffin glanced at his watch. "I have another appointment, Kirchner, and you're still beating around the bush."

His visitor smiled coldly. "You really do not remember me, but we met many years ago. In Venezuela. You ask what we want? It is simple. You will no longer attempt to block your son's efforts to make Griffin Oil public. Our lawyers will arrange for much of your stock to be transferred to us at a fair market price. The people I represent will provide your company with large quantities of Iranian oil at low prices. We will arrange to ship it to you so it appears to come through Venezuela. This will make your company much larger, much more profitable."

"And what do you get out of it?"

"From time to time we might make suggestions on things the company should do."

"And of course you can't tell me what these proposals are right now?"

"That is correct."

"Get out of here. This is Abscam, right? You're all taped up and you've got a goddam TV camera in the end of your nose and you're trying to hang me by my balls. Get out of here."

Frederick Kirchner stood. "I am not from your authorities. And you have no choice in this matter. You will do as I say."

"Yeah? Why?"

"Because I know about the Red Moon." Without even

87

a nod, Kirchner turned and walked to the door to the outer office. At the doorway, he stopped.

"I know *all* about the Red Moon, Mr. Griffin. And I have too much time and trouble invested in this project for me to allow it to fail. Particularly because of one stubborn old man. I will contact you with further instructions in the near future. Good day, Mr. Griffin."

Gus Griffin stared at the door as it closed behind the man, then sank back heavily in his chair and wheeled around to look out the window at Houston. It was his town, he was an important and respected part of it—could his unwelcome visitor really pull him down into the gutter? The Red Moon. He hadn't heard those words spoken in more than a quarter century, but now he had heard them twice in one week.

He spun back to his desk and jabbed the intercom button.

"Get me Doyle Blaney. Right away."

Five seconds later, Blaney's laconic male voice drawled into the phone. "Yes, Gus."

"Listen, there's a guy just left my office. Six feet tall, gray hair, wearing some ugly white suit that makes him look like a preacher or something."

"Yeah?"

"Follow him. Find out where he goes and who he sees. I want to know who he is."

"Okay."

The intercom crackled off, and Griffin pressed the button again. "No calls but Blaney," he instructed his secretary curtly, then he turned to look out the window again.

Down in the lobby, Frederick Kirchner walked toward the revolving front doors. He paused before them to light a cigarette, then turned to face the lobby as he inhaled deeply.

Doyle Blaney stepped off the elevator. His eyes met those of Kirchner. The white-haired man nodded slightly. Blaney smiled, then stepped back into the elevator.

Frederick Kirchner dropped his match on the floor and walked out into the hot Houston sun.

Blaney finished the cup of coffee in his office before he went to Gus Griffin's office. He walked in with only a pro forma tap on the door. The old man looked at him expectantly.

"Sorry, Gus, he skipped."

"Shit."

"Left the building before I could get the guards. He wasn't out on the street. Want me to have the cabs checked to see if anybody picked him up?"

"If you want," Griffin said morosely.

"Okay. Who is he, anyway?"

"Aaah, just somebody."

CHAPTER ELEVEN

Christopher Caldwell was halfway back to his office before he sensed that he was being followed. He glanced into his rearview mirror but saw only a random caravan of cars and trucks following him in the usual rush of midday Houston traffic.

Still, he knew he was being followed. He did not know by which car or truck, but he knew. He realized that unconsciously he must have been checking the mirror and seen one vehicle too many times. When he was with the CIA, he had developed the habit of continuously varying his road speeds so that no one had a reason to get on his tail and stay there for too long a time.

He looked in the mirror again. There was a long string of vehicles behind him. A red pickup truck was closest. Behind that, there was a gray Cadillac, two black Fords, and a Volkswagen. Far behind the line he saw a bright-yellow car. None of them registered in his mind.

On impulse, he pulled off the highway at the next exit ramp. He drove slowly around a block, then parked at the curb. He drew a blank. For the next five minutes, no car pulled into the small side street. He found his hands were sweating and his armpits were wet. Across the street, he saw a red neon sign for Tinny's Tavern, and he locked the car and walked across the street into the dark bar. Taking a seat at the window, he ordered vodka on the rocks.

He drank three while watching the car, but only a handful of cars drove down the street, and none of the drivers seemed to pay any attention to Caldwell's gray Chevrolet.

The sweating had stopped. He must have been dreaming, he told himself. But as he paid the bartender, he shook his head. He had been followed. He knew it.

He drove slowly back to the highway and made sure that no car followed him up the entry ramp. On the highway, he melted in with the traffic, then stomped on the gas pedal and sped back to his office.

He stopped in a lobby telephone booth to call upstairs.

He was surprised that he had remembered the number. He had never called the law firm's main number, but he remembered seeing it on the telephone on his desk, and out of habit he had placed it into his memory. Some good habits died hard; others couldn't wait to expire. Back on the highway, when he had realized he was being tailed, he should never have driven off the roadway. Not, at least, until he was sure who was following him; not until he had gotten the license number of the car and a look at the driver. He had done everything wrong that he could possibly do. He smiled as he thought of identifying himself to Rafael as Chris Caldwell, CIA man. Chris Caldwell, junior G-man, charter member of the Nick Carter Secret Circle fan club, would have been more like it.

When McBride's receptionist answered, he asked for Susan Millard. As her cool voice answered the phone, he said, "Chris Caldwell. I'm down in the lobby. I'm ready for that drink now."

"It's only three o'clock."

"I'll put a word in for you with the boss. I know where the bodies are buried."

She hesitated. "All right. I'll meet you at the elevators in five minutes. How will I recognize you?"

"I've got a Groucho Marx mustache. I'll be wearing a putty nose, pink-tinted horn rims, and stick-on eyebrows. My suit is gold and my carnation is blue. I'll be the only guy loitering near the elevator. How do I know you?"

"I'll be the only blond that you can't enter in the Dolly Parton look-alike contest."

"Fair enough." But Caldwell didn't need the description, because for once McBride had been right. Susan Millard was tall and slim, wearing a fashionably designed and obviously expensive pin-striped suit, with a lacy blouse open only to the first button. She had dark honey-blond hair worn in a casual style. Her cheekbones were high and her eyes were set wide apart, giving her a faint look of surprise. He judged her to be in her late twenties.

She smiled as he stepped toward her.

"Chris Caldwell?"

"Here to kidnap you for the Dallas Cowboys cheerleaders," he said.

"Exploitation," she said. "Besides, I hate those stupid

91

white plastic boots that they wear."

"Me too," Chris said. "Generally I like to keep women barefoot."

"And pregnant?" Susan asked with a small smile.

"Only occasionally. You pick the saloon."

"Cochran's around the corner," she said. "It's a rare find. No disco, no country and western, and no mechanical bulls to attract the local degenerates."

"Lead on," Chris said. He reached out tentatively to take her arm as they started through the lobby, but almost without seeming to notice him, she stepped on ahead of him. When he caught up with her, he jabbed his hands into his pockets.

On the sidewalk outside, she said suddenly, "I just want you to know how terrible I feel about Mr. Hirschfeld's death. I know you two were close. He was very kind to me...and, well, he was a nice man."

"He was a *mensch*," Caldwell said.

"What's a *mensch*?"

"It's a man who is a real man, a man of character, a man without posturing as a man. It's a Yiddish compliment."

"I see. Do you speak Yiddish?"

"Only seven words. Six of them dirty," Caldwell said.

"You've got to teach them all to me. It'll wow them back in Westport," she said.

At just a few minutes after three, Cochran's Corned Beef Emporium was almost empty, and they picked a small corner table far away from the jukebox, which was blessedly quiet.

The waiter came and glanced at Caldwell for the order. Susan ordered for herself. A Rusty Nail, not too sweet. Chris ordered vodka on the rocks, with a glass of club soda on the side.

"I understand that you haven't practiced law for some time," she said.

"Word gets around fast. Actually, I've never practiced law."

"Working for the government, I hear."

"That's right."

"Mr. McBride seems to have a high regard for your abilities, though," she said. He thought he heard a slight

92

edge to her voice, and he studied the salt and pepper shakers for a moment before looking up and meeting her eyes. They were a brilliant jade green, flecked with tiny dots of amber that made them look as if they were continuously being hit by a bank of colored spotlights.

"Are you trying to tell me something, Miss Millard?"

She flushed. "I...never mind. And please call me Susan."

"Mac has a higher opinion of my abilities than I do. We've been friends for a long time, and that affects people's judgments. But I was a good student. I probably would have been a good lawyer if I had bothered to take the bar, and if I didn't think I could handle this Griffin Oil stuff, I wouldn't have signed on."

He wondered how many others in McBride's law firm might hold the same opinion this girl seemed to have. For the first time, it occurred to him that Mac might even be running some risk to his own legal reputation by giving Caldwell the chance to use the law firm as a cover for his investigation of Hirsch's death. He made a small mental resolution to try to avoid embarrassing McBride.

Susan Millard picked her words with care. "I'm sorry. I had no right to jump to any conclusions about you without knowing you. Mr. Hirschfeld lectured me about that."

"You've just gone up ten notches in my book," Caldwell said.

"Why? Because he told me I was wrong?"

"No. Because he bothered to talk to you at all. Dad...Hirsch always said that only a fool bothers to try to teach a fool. That he thought you were worth lecturing says he thought you were made of real goods."

"I'll accept that compliment. That's the nicest thing anyone has said to me since I got to Houston. Are you planning to start practicing law? Take your bar?"

He delayed answering until their waiter had set their drinks on clean paper napkins in front of him. He glanced around the room. The bar had two sets of steer horns mounted high on the wall, but that no longer surprised Caldwell. His first visit to see Hirsch had convinced him that every wall in Houston had steer horns on it.

Susan hoisted her drink. Caldwell looked at his glass of vodka and glass of soda, remembered his foolish dem-

93

onstration of incompetence back on the highway, then disregarded it and raised the vodka. They clicked glasses and drank.

"I don't know," he answered her question. "I'm here to see if I like the law. Maybe I'm not cut out for lawyering. Maybe I'm too old. I'll find out. What are you doing here? Isn't Houston a comedown after the Supreme Court?"

"Houston's a comedown after civilization," she said. "But Justice Brooks says I should get some practical experience. He said that this Griffin Oil matter might be a chance to see the government legal bureaucracy from the other side. I wasn't sure, but Otto's like a father to me, so I came down here. It doesn't hurt to do what he suggests."

Chris remained silent but raised his eyebrows slightly. Susan burst out, "Not you too. Somebody else made a snide crack the other day. For your information, Otto's like a father or an uncle. His wife and my mother were half sisters."

"Whoa, tiger, let me off. I didn't say anything."

"Don't even think it. Some people have minds like garbage cans. It really pisses me off."

Caldwell blinked but said nothing.

"That's right," she said, nodding her head up and down for emphasis. "Pisses me off. That's another thing I don't like about Texas. I have to watch my language so they'll think I'm a lady. What's so important about being 'a lady'? Screw 'em all."

"Save six for pallbearers," Chris suggested solemnly.

She looked at him, her eyes flickering with anger, ready to find abuse in his glance. He covered his eyes with his hands, and she began to laugh.

"All right," she said. "You ought to see me when I'm intense."

"I couldn't take it," Chris said. "My blood pressure's already got a contact high."

"You called Mr. Hirschfeld 'Dad.' It slipped out. Were you related?"

"I was married to his daughter, but she died."

"Oh. I'm sorry."

"It was a long time ago," Chris said. "It's all right."

"Were you with the government then?"

Caldwell looked around the bar. The steer horns outnumbered the customers. There were two men sitting at the bar, and at a table near the door was a husky man with a ruddy face, wavy brownish hair, and a well-tailored summer-weight beige suit. The man's eyes met Caldwell's for a moment before casually moving on.

"Yeah," Chris said. "I was with the government then."

"Mr. McBride told some of the people you were in the CIA."

"Yes."

"Did you like it?"

Chris shrugged. "What's to like? I was pretty much a clerk type."

"Too bad," Susan said.

"Why too bad?"

"Oh, I thought you were going to be a dashing agent, writing a spy book, and I'd get to know all your dirty little secrets first."

"The only dashing I did was to catch a bus across town. And the only secret I know is how to make the worst coffee allowed by law. Enough already. What about you? How do you find oil country?"

Susan Millard laughed softly. "What's the old joke? 'How did you find your steak?' 'Easy, I just brushed aside the lettuce and there it was.'"

"That's an awful joke," he said.

"And I get worse. Anyway, that's the way I feel about this place. Every time I push aside my lettuce, there's Houston staring at me. And I hate it. I guess I'm doomed to be a member of the effete Eastern establishment. Besides, how many times do you think I can stand being called 'girlie' before I crack?"

"Give me that complaint when you're fifty and wrinkled," Chris said.

"Not a chance," she said. "The women in my family are immune to wrinkles. Must be good genes or something. If we're still sitting here fifty years from now, people are going to look and say, 'What's that fresh unwrinkled beauty doing sitting with that old relic of a man?'"

"If you don't tell me about Griffin Oil, we may *be* sitting here fifty years from now," Chris said. "How was that SEC application going? How did you and Hirsch work?"

"It was a real experience," Susan said. "Mr. Hirschfeld

was brilliant. And patient. He let me do most of the work. If somebody else had done that, I might have felt put-upon. But not with him. I knew he wanted me to do it so I'd know forever how to do it. He was a teacher as well as a lawyer."

"Yes, he was," Chris agreed. "Tell me, did he ever say there was anything unusual about the application? Something unique, maybe?"

Susan looked puzzled, then shook her head. "No. Not that I remember. Why? Unique what way?"

"Nothing, really. I was just wondering what kind of work was involved."

"I think it's pretty much routine," she said. She hesitated a moment, then said, "Chris."

"Yes."

"I want you to know I was prepared to resent you today. I didn't know why they would bring you in to work on Griffin Oil when I was capable of handling it. And your not being a lawyer didn't make me feel any better either. I thought it was some typical male power crap, but... well, I feel better now, having met you."

Caldwell smiled. "Just count me as part of Eustace McBride's make-work program for unemployed would-be lawyers. He probably figures I could learn something from you. And maybe he figures if you've got a man hanging around with you, it'll make your job a little easier." He twirled the end of an imaginary mustache. "Keep all those cowboys away, girlie," he said with a leer.

Susan smiled and nodded her head in agreement. "All right," she said. "I can live with that." She glanced at her watch. "I guess we ought to go back to work."

"I guess. We can talk about Griffin Oil tomorrow."

Susan insisted upon paying for the drinks as his welcome to Houston. He reached into his pocket for a dollar for a tip, expecting Susan—as women usually did—to carefully compute ten percent of the total bill, then divide that amount in half, and then round it off to the next lowest quarter, and leave that as a tip. But instead she took her change, dropped a dollar on the table for the waiter, and jammed the rest of her change into her purse without counting it. Chris was impressed.

He rode up with her quietly on the elevator and walked

her to her office, which was smaller than his.

"First thing in the morning," she said, "we'll go over the Griffin Oil material."

He nodded, and she turned away, leaving him standing in the hall. He was smiling as he entered his office. McBride, for a change, had not been exaggerating: Susan Millard *was* beautiful. But in his scornful description of the young woman's mental processes, Mac had just been off the wall. There was nothing in McBride's description that even faintly resembled the bright young woman he had just shared a drink with.

He felt vaguely pleased with himself until he saw the fat manila folder marked Griffin Oil on his desk. Caldwell opened it quickly and groaned at the pile of papers it contained. He decided he would read it tomorrow, after talking to Susan Millard.

Under the desk, he saw Hirsch's battered old attaché case. He opened it. It was empty, and the Griffin Oil file fit comfortably. He put it back under the desk.

Gus Griffin walked into his son's office without knocking. Adam was on the telephone, but when he saw his father, he quickly excused himself and hung up.

"Hi, Dad," he said, venturing a smile at the older man.

Gus wasted no time. "I've decided not to fight you about taking the company public."

"Oh, Dad, that's terrific. I knew that—"

"You know shit," Gus Griffin said, turning on his heel and walking out of the office.

Chris Caldwell went downstairs and started walking toward the garage, but then decided it was time to buy his lawyering suit. He turned around to walk back toward a long block near McBride's building that housed a string of boutiques and men's and women's clothing stores.

The street was packed with people going home. One of them stood out. Chris got only a glimpse of the man who stepped into the front door of an office building, but the man was tall, with brown curly hair and a beige suit. Was it the man who had sat at the table across from him and Susan at Cochran's? Was he being followed again? Caldwell felt a little tingle at the base of his spine. He had learned years ago that it was often necessary to trust one's instincts.

Veering off from his planned route, Caldwell walked quickly to the office building he had seen the man entering. He pushed along with the crowd in through the air-tight revolving doors into the cold air-conditioned lobby. The lobby was packed with people milling about. He looked along the walls, toward the areas that would command a view of the street outside, but he didn't see the man in the beige suit. Caldwell posted himself near a bank of public telephones with a view of both the front and side entrances and the main bank of elevators. He waited ten minutes, but did not see the man again.

Casually, he looked at the building directory, but none of the names meant anything to him. Who would follow him? Why? He knew one thing: It wasn't some dissatisfied scuba-diving student. It had to have something to do with Benjamin Hirschfeld's death.

Presumably, his tail knew who Caldwell was and what he had been. If so, he might well have expected Caldwell to have spotted him by now. Caldwell decided to act like a man who knew he was being followed and see where that took him.

He left the office building and walked along the block. Twice he went into men's clothing stores and then quickly came back out. One time he stopped to buy a handkerchief. But he saw no sign of the man in the beige suit. Was it a government man? Did he quit his goddam spying job at five o'clock? Was there a union now negotiating wages and hours for secret agents?

At the end of the block, he stopped into a clothing store that, thank God, had something besides cowboy suits in its windows and spent a leisurely half hour having a neat conservative dark-blue lightweight wool suit measured and fitted. As he checked suits, he kept glancing toward the front display windows but did not see his tail.

The tailor promised that the suit would be ready the next afternoon.

The street had lost some of its pedestrian traffic when Caldwell went back outside. He walked straight to the garage where his car was parked.

When he left the garage, he drove half a block, pulled

to the curb, and waited, but no car followed him out of the garage. A few cars passed him, but he could have been a fire hydrant for all the attention the drivers gave him. He hoped he had not shaken his tail, yet he was feeling excited and curiously exhilarated. Somebody following him meant that he might have stumbled onto the right track. His suspicions about Hirsch's death weren't just some kind of lunatic by-product of an overworked guilt feeling. They were real. And sooner or later, Caldwell would confront the people responsible.

Sherry Griffin was at the ranch, where she had been banished by her husband, when Doyle Blaney arrived. He walked out to the swimming pool and found her lying on a chaise alongside the pool, wearing a skimpy white bathing suit. As he stood alongside her chair, staring down at her body, she carefully draped herself with a towel.

"Don't stare like that," she said. "I hate to see grown men drool."

"I always do when I'm hungry," he said.

"Try starving. It's good for the soul."

"You'd be better off being nice to me," he said.

"Blaney, what do you want?" she said in a tone of bored disgust.

He reached inside his jacket pocket and pulled out a check. He removed the towel from her body and laid the check gently on her belly, letting his fingers dwell on her smooth flesh for a moment before lifting his hand.

"Here," he said. "Don't tell me everybody always gave you a hundred thousand."

"No. Some people didn't give me anything. But they were human, so I went easy with them."

His face frosted over. "That's the money you earned double-crossing your husband. I hope you enjoy it."

She picked up the check and looked at it.

"Thank you, Doyle," she said. She smiled at him, a large white smile. She put the check under the top of her bikini, alongside her left breast. "I'll take good care of it."

Before he left the office, Gus Griffin had drunk almost half a bottle of tequila, feeding his thirst as well as his anger.

99

Who was Frederick Kirchner? And what about the Red Moon? Griffin had not uttered those words in over a quarter of a century, and now it was all coming back. How did Kirchner know? How could he know?

His anger fed on itself. Anger at Adam, who now controlled the company.

And anger at Sherry, who had made Adam's power grab possible. Especially anger at Sherry, who should have been more loyal.

"Bitch," he grumbled under his breath. The Griffin offices were dark when he left. Two cleaning women saw him and smiled greetings at him, but uncharacteristically he did not respond.

His Chrysler was parked downstairs at the curb where the building maintenance men were instructed to put it every day at five o'clock. He got into it and drove across the business district to the southwestern corner of Houston. Inside a large converted one-family home was the Spread, a private club for rich men, and Griffin sat at the ornate bar, drinking, spurning all attempts by acquaintances to draw him into conversation.

When he arrived at the ranch, just before midnight, he was drunk and he knew it. Mumbling "Bitch" under his breath, he let himself into his office through the private side entrance and poured himself another drink. He sat behind his desk, sipping it, looking at the oil paintings on the wall.

Periodically the glass moved up to his lips, then down again. His other hand began flexing, forming a fist, then relaxing, clenching and quieting.

The glass rose again, but stopped just short of his thin bitter lips. He held it there for a moment, then slapped it down on the desk. Standing, he walked carefully, but steadily, out of the room. At the top of the stairs, he turned to his wife's bedroom, opened the door without knocking, and went in.

Sherry, who was seated in front of her vanity, removing polish from her nails, looked up in surprise as he came in. In the mirror, he could see her face pale.

"What is it, Gus? Anything wrong?"

Gus closed the door behind him. He approached her

100

slowly and stood towering over her. Their gazes met in the glass of the mirror.

Unconsciously, Sherry clutched her negligee closed at the neck. "You've been drinking," she said in a flat dry voice.

"Yup. I've been drinking and I've been thinking. Know what I've been thinking about, Sherry?"

She flinched and her face tightened. "How about if I make us both drinks?" she said with forced brightness.

He ignored the remark. "I've been thinking about us, Sherry. I've been thinking about what a goddam whore you are."

"Gus, don't say that. You don't believe that."

His hand swept forward in a roundhouse slap that knocked Sherry backward off her vanity stool and onto the thick white rug. She crumpled into a ball at his feet, giving a shuddering moan.

"Get up," he snarled, reaching down and grasping her arm. He dragged her roughly to her feet.

"I could kill you right here and now," he said in a slow grating tone. "I could break your goddam neck. You know that."

Her face still looking toward the floor, Sherry nodded silently.

"Look at me," he snarled, reaching down with his free hand to wrench her head upward. "Look at me and tell me you deserve to live."

He twisted her face toward him. Her eyes were shut and the tears continued to flow down her cheeks.

"Look at me," he yelled again, and she forced herself to open her eyes. His face, up close to hers, was red-blotched and livid. His black eyepatch made him look like a movie madman.

She took a deep breath.

"You don't want to kill me, Gus," she gasped. She reached out a hand to touch his cheek, and when he did not recoil, she moved her body closer so it pressed against his. "No," she said again softly, near his ear, "you don't want to kill me."

Gus glowered down at her pale face, still streaming tears, her golden hair splashing over her lips, which trembled uncontrollably. Then he dragged her over to the bed, tossed her onto it roughly, and began to open his trousers.

Their coupling was brief. Her hips worked feverishly and she moaned in a parody of erotic ecstasy, holding him tightly to her to prevent his changing his mind and hitting her again.

Griffin gave a loud grunt of triumph as he spasmed into her. He slumped bonelessly against her for a moment as she crooned wordlessly and caressed him.

Abruptly, he pulled himself free, pulled up his trousers, and glowered down at her.

"You're not done yet, Sherry," he said. "You got a lot more punishment coming your way."

"I know, Gus," she whispered, not moving. He looked at her again, then stalked from the room, zipping up his trousers as he left.

Sherry lay quietly on the bed, watching the door close behind him. Her face was afire where Gus had slapped her, but she felt relief. She had gone through Gus's first raging anger, and she was still alive. She could handle anything else he was liable to throw at her.

Christopher Caldwell ate dinner in a Mexican restaurant, then drove back to Hirsch's apartment. He parked in the small lot next to the apartment building and let himself in through the locked side door. After checking the empty mailbox, he walked up the stairs, slid his key gently into the lock, and eased the apartment door open quietly.

The living room was empty.

He shrugged, closed the door behind him, and stepped into the living room. From the corner of his eye, he saw the hall closet door swinging open.

He spun around, feeling sickeningly defenseless, as the tall man in the beige suit stepped out of the closet. He held a pistol, pointed unwaveringly at Caldwell's stomach.

"Mr. Caldwell, I presume," the man said in a deep, harsh voice with a British accent.

"You know it goddam well," Caldwell said. "You've been following me all day. What's this all about?"

"I think I'm going to have to kill you," the man said. There was a soft sadness in his eyes as he spoke.

102

1943

A large man, wearing a light-blue chambray shirt and washed-out blue jeans, entered the cabin of the tanker warily. He frowned at the sight of the small wooden box and the large crate, touched a cautious finger to his mustache, then nodded to the white-haired young man in the rumpled suit.

"Señor," he said.

"I speak better English than Spanish," the younger man said, in a tone that indicated he found both languages beneath him. "You are Herr Sam Houston?"

The husky man ignored the question. "What is this shit in the big box?"

"Payment. Somewhat different in form from what you're used to."

Herr Sam Houston eyed him coldly.

"Our deal's the same as it always is. Cash or gold. Nothing else. No gold, no oil. Case closed."

His voice was as flat as the smooth sea the ship rested on.

"You have no real choice in this matter," the younger man said. "The small box is gold. It was somewhat difficult to assemble this time. We had to resort to . . . well, unusual methods to put this shipment together."

"That's your problem, not mine," the older man with the mustache said.

"Our problem," the younger man said. "Most of the payment is in gold. The rest is in works of art. There are four extremely valuable paintings in that carton. They will be worth more than gold when the war is over. Any one of them would make you wealthy."

The older man studied him intently. "Things aren't going so good for you guys, are they? Getting a little tight over there, huh?"

"Temporary setbacks. But soon there will be a major counterstrike and we will again cleanse Europe."

103

"Yeah, sure. If you say so." The older man shrugged. "Let's see the gold."

The small box was pried open. It contained several ingots, each somewhat smaller than a brick. The man hefted each suspiciously in his hand.

"They seem different from what I've been getting," he said.

"They were melted down in haste from...jewelry. Do you wish to inspect the paintings?"

"No. A waste of time. I couldn't tell one from the other. I don't like this. I've got a half a mind to tell you to take all this crap back to wherever it came from."

The blond young man smiled. "That would do no one any good. We have come all this way; I don't think the captain of this craft would choose to go back empty."

"Is that a threat?"

"No, Herr Houston. It is a reality. My nation has very little patience with those who fail. The captain might go to extreme measures to make sure he does not return with an empty ship."

"And what kind of measures would *you* take?"

The young man shrugged again. "I do not like failure either," he said.

The big man with the mustache looked into the bland unlined face of the young German, then nodded. "All right. I'll take your word for it that you're not pulling a swindle. Let's get this stuff on my boat and tell your men to hook up. And let's be quick about it. Get it and go."

"I understand."

"Good. *Adiós.*" He nodded and left the cabin. He watched quietly as seamen from the Panamanian tanker lowered the small carton and the large crate into the back of the unpainted, battered powerboat tied up to the side of the tanker's boarding steps. The men followed him to shore in another small boat, tying up at a rickety dock that jutted out into the ocean like a twisted arthritic finger of wood. On shore, they loaded the two cartons into the back of a waiting pickup truck.

From the cab of the truck, the man with the mustache could see a work crew already moving flexible piping off large coils on the tanker's deck. The flexible pipe would be strung from the ship, a hundred yards toward shore,

104

where it would be coupled with an underwater pipe twelve inches in diameter.

The man waited until the two Spanish-speaking crew-members headed back toward the tanker, then he drove the pickup off the beach. As soon as he was out of sight of the ship, he peeled the false mustache off his upper lip and threw it out the open window of the truck.

He followed a narrow dirt road into the jungle. No more, he thought. The Nazis, those stupid bastards, were losing the war. He had guessed wrong and it was time to get out of the game.

Several hundred yards deep into the jungle, he stopped the truck at a large pipe, elevated by stone supports two feet above the jungle floor. The pipe stretched off to the right and left as far as one could see, until it was swallowed up by jungle. The man hopped from the truck and turned a large spin valve, opening the pipe. With a key, he turned on and started a gasoline-powered pump the size of a large washing machine.

He backed the truck up and drove off down another narrow dirt road cut through the jungle. He drove casually and expertly, paralleling the beach for almost two miles until he came to a low wooden house just at the water's edge. He locked the truck carefully in a garage next to the house and walked inside.

A baby was crying.

"I'm home," he called. "How's the baby?"

"Just teething. He's fine."

He walked into the kitchen and kissed the neck of a plump, pretty woman who stood over the sink washing dishes.

"Hold dinner," he said. "I'm going back out. Some trouble with the pumps."

"The men can't handle it?"

"Those bozos couldn't find their ass with both hands. I'll be back in a while."

"Be careful."

"I always am. And when I come back, I've got some good news."

The woman turned with a questioning smile.

"Later," he said.

He worked in the detached garage for three hours. It

105

was dark when he finally left, carefully carrying a wooden box. He drove back through the dark jungle, stopping two hundred yards from the rickety pier. He lugged the box down to a rowboat lying on the sandy shore, put it aboard, and rowed implacably and strongly out into the night, carefully skirting the tanker, finally anchoring the boat fifty yards away from the tanker on the seaward side.

He worked slowly and carefully. It would take almost all night for the ship to pump its tanks full of the thin Venezuelan crude oil. It would leave with the morning sun and morning tide.

The water was colder than he had expected. It was also oily and dirty, but he did not hesitate. Four times he swam between his rowboat and the tanker, each time carrying a flat cylindrical object in a bag strapped to his naked back.

He was shivering with cold and exhaustion as he rowed the boat back to the beach and drove home. Supper had long since been forgotten. He took a brief shower before climbing into bed next to his wife.

"We're going home," he said.

"Oh, thank God. You sure?"

"Yeah. I'm sure. We've been here long enough."

"When?"

"As soon as we can. Tomorrow. The next day."

The sun had already risen, but the bedroom was darkened by heavy drapes. He woke with a start and glanced at his watch with the luminous face.

It was 7:30 A.M.

"Auf Wiedersehn, amigo," he said softly. He was smiling in the dark.

His wife grunted and said, "Did you say something, dear?"

"No. Nothing important."

BOOK TWO

CHAPTER ONE

Susan Millard fussed with the spaghetti straps of her peacock-blue dress, looked at herself in the full-length mirror on her bathroom door, and whirled experimentally. The dress flared out, then draped smoothly.

Her first date since she had arrived in Houston, and she wondered if Doyle Blaney was going to behave or if she would have to fight him off at the end of the evening. Although she did not mind losing a wrestling match every so often, it was annoying to have it happen almost every time she went out with a man.

She hadn't been surprised when Blaney had called her in the morning and asked her to dinner. They had met a week ago, and he had looked her over carefully, then invited her to dinner that night. She had said no and he had said he would try again.

She was surprised at herself, though, for accepting the date on such short notice. Normal tactics would have been to put it off for several days. But that was the kind of manipulative role-playing her older sisters excelled in and she had always looked down on. This was just a dinner date, she told herself. And she was going stir-crazy, sitting alone in her apartment every night.

Besides, Doyle Blaney promised to be interesting. He reminded her of a New Jersey Congressman she had met when she first went to Washington. He had the same burly good looks and the same cool assurance. It was challenging, in a way, to be with a man who was obviously interested in you but was even more obviously interested in his own plans and pleasures.

Blaney was that. He was direct. That damned Christopher Caldwell today had been so remote she had felt as if she were talking to him from another room. It hadn't been that he acted aloof and superior, just distant and uninterested. He was strange. She had imagined CIA agents would be furtive, but Caldwell seemed honest and straightforward in his distant way.

Since he was the son-in-law of Benjamin Hirschfeld, she wondered if he would turn out to be tied up with Hirschfeld in this whole mess. At any rate, she had done her best to strike up a friendship with him, and she would just have to wait and see where it led. She wondered what it might take to bring him to life—and what she would feel if he began looking at her with the interest and speculation she was used to arousing in men.

There was something boyish and vulnerable about Caldwell, a sort of sad expression to his eyes, and she admitted to herself that she found it appealing.

The telephone rang and the lobby clerk informed her that Doyle Blaney had arrived. She told him she would be right down, but as she went out the door, she hesitated. She was supposed to make a phone call. She pursed her lips, then closed the door quickly behind her. The telephone call would wait, and she was hungry.

Two hours later, sipping a brandy, she looked around with approval. The steak had been fine, and the large dining room of the Wildcatter Restaurant was almost filled with well-dressed couples. A three-piece combo was playing quiet dance music.

It wasn't Washington, but it wasn't bad, she conceded. Even Doyle Blaney had been okay. She had expected him to be hard, loud, single-minded, but he hadn't been. They had chatted about her career, about Justice Brooks, about college and Texas. Blaney sometimes gave the impression that he was pumping her for information, but that was probably his background and her imagination, she decided.

"So how do you like this new man you'll be working with? What's his name, Caldwell?"

"Chris Caldwell. We met today."

"And?"

"He seems nice enough. Very quiet. Maybe he's shy or

108

something. I guess with his father-in-law dying..." She left the sentence unfinished.

"I just hope this Caldwell is as competent as his father-in-law was," Blaney said.

"I don't know. He went to school with Mr. McBride, but he never practiced law. He went into the CIA instead."

Blaney had been lighting a cigarette. He clicked the lighter closed and put the still-unlit cigarette into the ashtray.

"The CIA? He's a CIA man?"

"Not now. He left a couple of years ago, I understand."

"Since then?"

"I don't know. I didn't ask. McBride said something about private business." Susan found herself resenting Blaney's sudden loss of interest in her. "Why are you so interested in Christopher Caldwell?" she said. "You have something against the CIA?"

"Should I?" he asked, surprised. He lit his cigarette.

"I've been in Washington. You used to be FBI. Everybody knows that the FBI and the CIA don't get along all that well."

He laughed. "I've heard that too, but it never bothered me. I was too busy chasing bank robbers and car thieves and other riff-raff to worry about the CIA."

"Why did you join the FBI?" She shuddered delicately, as if astonished that anyone could voluntarily enlist in a law-enforcement agency.

"To make money."

"But FBI agents aren't paid that much," she said.

"The salary's decent. Particularly when you're a kid accountant facing the prospect of going to work in a bank."

"Why'd you leave?"

"To make more money. Gus Griffin offered me a job. Twice my salary. And I was tired of worrying about whether J. Edgar Hoover would like the color of my suit or how long my hair had gotten, so I quit."

"Any regrets?"

"No, how could I have any? I've got a good job with a company that's moving. And I'm having a good dinner with the prettiest woman in Houston."

Pleased with herself that she had gotten the conversation off Chris Caldwell and back to herself, Susan asked

109

Blaney if he liked to dance. But as he led her to the dance floor, she cautioned herself to be careful or she would have one hell of a struggle when he took her home tonight. Chris Caldwell might just walk away from her apartment door, but not Doyle Blaney.

"...think I'm going to have to kill you."

"Mind if I ask why?"

"No, Mr. Caldwell. Just so long as you do not mind that I don't answer."

The man's English was precise and the British accent seemed to come and go, occasionally giving way to speech inflections that seemed earthier, more guttural.

He stood against the wall next to the closet. He seemed casual, but his evil-looking gun was held at his waist, close to his hip, instead of extended away from his body where a lucky kick might jar it loose. And the barrel of the blue-metal pistol was pointed at Caldwell's belly, the most central target in the body, where there was the most margin for error.

The man was a professional, so Caldwell stood motionless, wishing that he had drunk less during the day, annoyed because his mind came up with so few options. A roll onto the floor, a vault over the couch, a sudden charge, throwing the end-table ashtray which was close at hand. But each alternative seemed puny and futile when he looked at the muzzle of the gun.

"Please move away from that table," the man said. Caldwell took two steps into the center of the room. Still covering him carefully, the man went to a tufted cushioned chair, lifted the cushion, and satisfied himself that nothing was hidden under it. He replaced the cushion and with the tip of the gun motioned Caldwell to the chair.

"Sit down, please," he said.

Yes, he was very good. There were two occasional chairs in the room. The man had picked the one that was against the wall, so that Caldwell could not push the chair over backward and perhaps get to a hidden weapon. The other chair, Hirsch's reading chair, in the middle of the floor, was dangerous. On such little edges did agents live to retire.

Caldwell sat down and folded his hands in his lap, in

full view. If the man were going to kill him that easily, he would have been dead by now. The man, whoever he was, wanted to talk first. Chris was going to give him no foolish reason to begin shooting.

"Are you the one who killed Hirsch?" Caldwell asked.

"Oh? Was he killed? I heard that it was a fishing accident."

"That might be what other people believe, but you and I know better than that, don't we?"

"*I* know better than that. What exactly do you know, Mr. Caldwell?"

"I know that Hirsch never died in any fishing accident. I know that I'm going to find out who killed him. I know that if you killed him, you'd better pull that trigger now, because if you mess it up, I'm going to leave your body in the gutter."

"You know a great many things," the man said. He remained standing against the closet wall. "And how well do you know Ernest Wessel?"

"Who?"

"Aaaah, I have found something that you do not choose to share with me. Perhaps you will tell me where I can find Ernest Wessel."

Suddenly, Caldwell was tired. It was all coming back, the circular games, the questioning that seemed to go around and around, on and on, never making a point but slowly zeroing in on what it was the questioner sought. Chris knew it well. He had been on the other side of that gun many times, asking just the same kind of questions. And he was tired of it. He put his hands on the arms of the chair.

"Easy, Mr. Caldwell," the man said.

"I don't know any Ernest Wessel. I don't know where he is, whoever he is, and I don't give a good goddam. That answer it for you?" He kept his hands on the arms of the chair.

"Who told you to come to Houston?" the man said.

"No one *told* me to come. Hirsch was my friend. He died and I came."

"No one suggested to you that there might be a profitable opportunity for you to go to work at the offices of Mr. McBride? Perhaps some of your Iranian friends?"

111

"If I wanted a job with Mac, I could have had one any-time in the past three years. I don't lawyer. And I don't have any friends in Iran. Just memories. Now you pull that goddam trigger or you tell me what you want."

The telephone rang. Caldwell looked toward it, then at the man. But the man in the beige suit was already walking toward the telephone.

"Just behave yourself," he said. He picked up the telephone but said nothing.

He listened a few moments, then said simply, "Yes. Go ahead."

After sixty long seconds, he said, "Thank you," and replaced the receiver.

He looked at Caldwell, smiled, and put his pistol back into a shoulder holster.

"You may get up, Mr. Caldwell. I suggest you make us coffee. We are going to be here for a while."

"Sugar and cream?" Chris said.

112

CHAPTER TWO

As he heated water for instant coffee, Chris thought for a moment of jumping the man and trying to take away his gun. But what purpose would it serve? The man seemed ready to talk to him, and Chris wanted to talk. He wanted to hear himself frame questions; he wanted to hear answers. He wanted someone else's opinions and facts.

He poured the water, over instant coffee, into cups and placed them on the small round table in the kitchen. Seeing the man seated there brought back more memories.

"Who are you?" Caldwell asked.

"My name is Yoel Tsurnick. I am with an organization that is involved with the security of Israel."

"You have a business card, of course."

"No. I am afraid that my supply just ran out. I should have more in three or four years. Will you wait?"

"I don't have much choice, do I? I have to take your word that you're a snoop for the Mossad."

The man took a small folded piece of paper from the breast pocket of his light jacket.

"You entered Israel by El Al Airlines from Dulles Airport on June 27, 1978. You gave your occupation as an insurance agent with the Prudential Insurance Company of America. You carried Passport Number B2851623 made out in your name. Three days later, you were joined by your wife, Zhava, and your daughter, Shoshana. You were on courier duty. You picked up a small package from one George Brinkley in the King David Hotel on the day after the arrival of your wife in Jerusalem. Two days later, you flew to Tehran with your family, where you delivered the package to one Faud Shamikar. You and your wife expected to spend a few days in Tehran, where she wished to shop for local art. She and your child were killed that same day by a bomb that exploded in the trunk of your rented car. The bomb was seven sticks of dynamite, ignited probably by a wristwatch activator. The power came from

113

a nine-volt battery of West German manufacture. The Palestinian Association for National Unity said it set the bomb. No arrests were ever made. You returned to the United States immediately after the burial of your family in Mount Moriah Cemetery. You were placed on administrative duties at Langley, but you left your agency in December of 1978."

He looked at Chris, who had closed his eyes during the calm dispassionate recital of the facts that had torn apart his life.

"I'm sorry, Mr. Caldwell," Yoel Tsurnick said. "But you asked for my business card. Will you accept that only my organization, and, of course, the one that you once represented, would have all that information available to it? And would you also accept my sympathy on your loss? Your losses?"

"Have your coffee," Caldwell said. It never changed. Whenever two snoops got together, they drank coffee in a kitchen, almost as if they were embarrassed to bring themselves and the work they did into the other rooms of the house. What would dealers of death do in a "living" room?

As he sat down, across the narrow table from Tsurnick, Caldwell had his first chance to look at the man without the distraction of a pistol pointing at him. Tsurnick was in his late thirties. His shoulders were broad and bulky. He was well tanned, and like Caldwell's, it was a year-round tan, the result of living in the Sunbelt. His jaw was square, and his lips were narrow and did not move much when he spoke. His blue eyes were large and crinkled at the corners, but the wrinkles were not laugh lines; they looked sad. As the Israeli put his hand around the coffee mug, Caldwell noticed the man's knuckles. The main fist knuckles of the right index and right middle finger were gone. In their place was a single solid mound of callus. Caldwell had seen it before. It was a self-inflicted deformity chosen by some experts in the art of hand-to-hand combat. Karate practitioners called it a superknuckle. The purists scorned it, but in close-quarters fighting, it was as good as carrying a club in your hand.

"Is your left hand like that too?" Caldwell said.

Tsurnick nodded. "Yes. A childhood enthusiasm. Not

attractive, but utilitarian. You make awful coffee."

"Not tasty, but utilitarian," Caldwell said.

"Score one for the Yanks, but it's hardly either." Tsurnick stood up and went to the stove, where he put another teaspoonful of coffee crystals into his cup.

"Educated in England?" Caldwell asked.

"Yes. My first instructor in this business told me that it was important to look like an Englishman and think like a Jew. Unfortunately, he died the first time he left the classroom. One of your colleagues told me that the problem was that he looked like a Jew and thought like an Englishman. Why tempt the fates? I keep my accent."

Caldwell smiled. The memories came back to him in a flood, the long nights spent in kitchens like this, spy with spy, swapping stories of the other side's or their own cupidity and stupidity. He knew that since he had left the Company, he had a reputation for being taciturn and silent. But why not? He had no urge to talk about death and torture and double-dealing. The fact was that Caldwell had very little to say to polite company.

Something of the same thought might have been stirring in Tsurnick's mind, because he was staring into his coffee cup as if it contained the collective memories of his race and his profession.

"Who's going to ask the first question?" Caldwell said.

"You have many." It was a statement and not a query.

"Sure," Caldwell said. "What are you doing in Houston? What are you doing in Hirsch's apartment? Why were you following me? Why do you think I killed him? Who was that telephone call from just now? Even if you were sure I killed him, why should you involve yourself in the murder of an American citizen? Just for openers."

Tsurnick nodded, sharp little chops of his head as if he were trying to promote the meaning of nod from "yes" to "yes, yes, yes, yes."

"Good questions. All in good time. Mr. Caldwell—"

"Try Chris."

"And Yoel. All right, Chris. Suppose you tell me what you know and what you think. Everything. Then I will tell you what I know."

"Okay."

Caldwell knew it was correct procedure. Yoel Tsurnick

obviously knew more than he did, and the man with the most information was always better off listening to the other's story first. By the precedence of time, he might be nearer to a solution and the newer man might have gathered just that one small fact that could fill in a critical void. On the other hand, if the man with more information spoke first, it generally clouded the new man's memory, making it difficult for him to differentiate between what he actually knew and what he had just been told.

"I don't have much for you," Caldwell said. "Hirsch was my father-in-law. You knew that. He called me a couple of weeks ago—"

"What was the day?" Tsurnick interrupted.

"Let's see. This is Monday. He called me twelve days ago. On a Wednesday. He offered me a job working with McBride's law firm, where he worked. He told me that he was working on an application to the SEC to let the Griffin Oil Company go public. It wasn't unusual for him to offer me a job. He and Mac were always trying to get me back from Puerto Rico. That's where I've been living since I left the Company. You know that?"

"Yes. You live on Isla Verde and you are drunk most nights."

Caldwell winced. "About the job. This time, Hirsch sounded a little more insistent than he usually was. As if he really could use me for something and it wasn't just makework to try to rescue the soul of his only son-in-law. He talked about my special talents, but I wasn't listening. I didn't think too much of it at the time, and I turned down the job. I didn't hear from him again." Caldwell paused, thinking. "It's funny. His last words to me were something like 'Don't swim too deep.'" Caldwell shook his head. "It was advice to me, but maybe it was advice he needed himself. Anyway, on Saturday, McBride called me. He said that Hirsch was dead. He said killed in a fishing accident. I caught a plane and got up here Saturday night. We buried Hirsch yesterday. I moved in here and I looked around the place, but I didn't find any clue to who killed him."

"When did you know he had been killed?"

"As soon as Mac called. Forget a fishing accident." Briefly, Caldwell recounted Hirschfeld's history, his lifelong aversion to fish. "There was no way he was going to

116

rent a boat to go fishing. When I was here yesterday morning, the radio alarm went off at seven A.M. That's the time Dad woke up. But he was seen at the fishing pier the day before at six o'clock." Chris looked at Tsurnick to make sure he was following this thread. The Israeli's eyes were bright and intense, staring at Caldwell.

They discussed the radio alarm, and Chris mentioned the cigarette ashes he had found.

"Today, I figured I'd start at the office. I went there, but I found nothing that meant anything to me. I also went through this apartment as well as I could. I didn't see anything that would give me a clue about who killed Hirsch. Anyway, from work this morning, I went out to Lake Conroe to the fishing dock. I met the attendant who was working Saturday. He remembered Hirsch coming in around six A.M., but he never saw his face. He said Hirsch was wearing a yellow poncho and it covered his face. He had on sunglasses too, even though the sun wasn't up yet. He was as tall as I am. He rented the boat and then went out. The attendant saw him later carrying what looked like a heavy duffel bag down to the boat. Then somebody found the boat drifting later, and when the attendant went out, he found Hirsch twisted around the anchor rope. Drowned. But Hirsch didn't own a yellow slicker. And I think the attendant made the identification just on the slicker. Who would wear sunglasses at six A.M., before sunrise, except someone trying to hide his face? Wait a minute."

Caldwell went into the living room and came back with his small spiral-bound notebook.

"Detective Albert Potter," he read. "He investigated the death, and he was here yesterday to question me. I can't be sure, but it almost sounded like he convinced the attendant that Hirsch rented the boat because he was wearing a poncho and so was the man who rented the boat. And where was that heavy duffel bag? It wasn't in the boat, and nobody found it floating. What was in there? The boathouse guy remembered Hirsch's accent, though."

"Many people have German accents, Chris," Tsurnick said stolidly.

"Anyway, I want to get my hands on that poncho. Maybe it will tell us something. Why am I telling you all

117

this? You were at the boathouse. The insurance man, right?"

Tsurnick said, "Yes. I was the insurance man. I found out about the poncho too. I took the liberty of borrowing it from Houston Police headquarters. It was brand-new. You know how rubberized material like that cracks with wear. This was fresh. Brand-new."

Chris shrugged. "Maybe he had just bought it?"

"If he had, would he not buy his own size? A small or at best a medium. Not a large."

"All right. Then I came back, but you know that, of course, because you followed me back."

Tsurnick looked up sharply.

"When?"

"Today from the boathouse."

The Israeli shook his head. "I did not follow you from the boathouse. I picked you up for the first time this afternoon when you left your office to go to the bar down the street. With the blond woman. Who is she?"

Caldwell's mind churned. If Tsurnick had not been following him back from the boathouse, then who had? Was it just a guess gone wrong? Or had the years of liquor finally worked their poison even on his instincts until he was given to bad dreams and worse judgments?

No. He had been followed. He was sure of it.

"The girl is named Susan Millard. When I didn't take the job with Hirsch, she took it. McBride hired her as a favor to Supreme Court Justice Otto Brooks. She used to work for him, but she wanted to leave. I spotted you when I left the office and I bought some clothes, had dinner, and came home. That was you following me?"

"Yes."

"Where did you go? I followed you into the lobby of that building. I didn't think anyone could move away so fast."

"I was outside," Tsurnick said. "I knew you had made me and I guessed you would follow me. I went through the revolving door and took off my jacket and folded it over my arm. I put on my sunglasses. Then as you came in the revolving door, I stooped a little and walked out. We were only a foot and a plate of glass apart. I stood outside watching you. Then I followed you on your shopping trip."

118

"Christ, I've gotten old," Caldwell said.

"No, just somewhat rusty. When you stopped for dinner, I came here to search the apartment. Are you sure you were followed back from the lake?"

"Yes. I've been thinking about it, and I'm sure."

"Good. Or not so good, depending upon what you decide."

"Isn't it about time, Yoel, that you told me what's going on here?"

"Of course. Do you have any more of your abysmal coffee?"

"Make your own. Coffee's in the jar, water's in the faucet. Make it yourself and I don't have to listen to your complaints."

"Fine. You too?"

"Yes."

Tsurnick was a big man, a full two inches taller than Caldwell's six feet even, and broader and thicker through the shoulders and chest. But Caldwell noticed he moved quietly, light on his feet, as he poured water, set it on the stove, and began rinsing out the coffee cups. Good spies were always good bachelors. They cleaned up after themselves. They washed dishes. They didn't leave food out. They lived in a world in which there was precious little order, and they compensated by imposing order on everything they could. Even at his most drunken, Caldwell was meticulous, hanging up his clothing when he took it off, clearing away dishes, doing his laundry.

With his back still turned, Tsurnick said, "First, what do you think of Israel, Chris?"

"I think you people are altogether nasty and vicious. On the other hand, counting the numbers against you, I'd say polite and gentle would close on Saturday night and your country would be out of business."

"And the Mossad, our secret service? You think what we do is necessary?"

"You're talking to a man who's loved three people in his life. His Israeli-born wife. Her father. My daughter, who was born in Israel. I'm the last of the Zionists, Yoel."

"Not the last. There are a few of us left. But one of us died Saturday," Tsurnick said.

119

"Hirsch?" said Caldwell. "Yes, I know. When we were together, we often talked about it. He loved Israel, just as he loved America. Just as he loved the Germany that once was before Hitler."

"Then you will believe me when I tell you that the professor was one of us."

"Us?"

Without turning, Tsurnick said, "Mossad. He worked for us. Oh, not as I do. But we could call on him when we needed him. As we did this time."

The world closed in again around Chris, and he shook his head. Was his life always to be ruined by spy work? Would it go on, this dirty little game of cat and rat until it destroyed everyone he had ever loved? But they were all dead now. Would the game still go on? Who was left to destroy? But even as his mind framed the question, his heart spoke the answer. It would go on a little longer. Until the person who killed Hirsch was dead. Or until Chris himself was dead.

Laconically, he said, "Yeah."

Tsurnick was silent as he spooned instant coffee into the two cups. Two spoonfuls for Chris, three for himself. He added water, stirred, and screwed the cap tightly back on the jar of coffee. He brought both cups to the table and sat down again.

"I'm going to tell you this because—"

"—because you need me," Chris said.

Tsurnick smiled with his sad blue eyes. "Yes. And I believe I can trust you. And that we are on the same side."

"Not quite," Chris said. "We ought to get that straight. Whatever it is, you're after the enemies of Israel. I'm after the killer of my friend."

"And if they are the same?"

"Then we're on the same side. Only then," Caldwell said.

"I can live with that," Tsurnick said. "I will talk and you will listen and then you decide. And remember that Professor Hirschfeld was my friend too."

"Fair enough."

"After the revolution in Iran, it was necessary for us to expand our intelligence activities there," Tsurnick said.

120

"We always maintained a presence, but we added more men under the simple assumption that once Iran no longer had ties to the United States, it became a serious threat to our existence. At any rate, about six weeks ago, one of our agents was made. The details are not important, but this agent got word to us that there would be an attempt by the Iranians to take over an American oil company. Unfortunately, he died before we could learn any more. Good coffee."

"If you like mud."

"It is what we have spent our lives in, Chris," Tsurnick said. "I was assigned to look into this rumor. I solicited the help of many of our friends in this area. Including the professor. He contacted me two weeks ago and told me about the Griffin Oil Company's planning to become a public company. We met and I told him our sketchy information. Of course, he agreed to work with me closely."

"'Of course'? He hated spy work."

"He loved Israel," Tsurnick said. "He did not shrink from his obligation. Early Saturday morning, he tried to reach me. I was out of town and he left a message on my tape recorder. Someone was going to talk to him."

"Who?" Chris asked.

"He did not know, or at least did not say. He said he thought it might be the information we were looking for. It will be no solace to you, Chris, but if I had been at the telephone I would not have let him go to any such meeting. Not alone, anyway."

"Someone should have been on your phone," Chris said bitterly.

"Yes. Except that the Israeli presence in Houston is not exactly battalion-size. Basically there is me. I learned later in the day that he had died."

"And you don't know who he was talking to?"

"No."

"Or what they were supposed to talk about?" Chris asked.

"Maybe I know that. I think they were talking about the Red Moon."

"The Red Moon? What's that?"

"I don't know. It was something we received from our

121

agent in Iran. Just sketchy details about the Iranian infiltration of an oil company. The Red Moon. He did not live long enough to explain it."

"It could be anything," Caldwell said. "Maybe just a code name."

"Or it could be more. It isn't likely that anyone would call the professor and offer him information about the Red Moon if it were nothing but a code name. There is a meaning there, but I do not know what it is."

"And you don't know what, if anything, Hirsch learned?"

"No."

"Why were you after me?" Caldwell asked.

"Perhaps anger at myself. The professor had mentioned you to me before. Then he died, and I thought of you some more. And I remembered that you had served in Iran. And you had spoken to your father-in-law only a few weeks before. You had left the service under a cloud. I thought to myself, what if this loving son-in-law left because he was somehow connected with the Iranians? And what if he slipped into Houston on a plane and killed his father-in-law, and then flew back? And what if he now shows up to do the father-in-law's work, just to make sure that nothing goes wrong with his Iranian employers' plans?"

"That's all pretty thin to think about killing me for," Chris said.

"If it had been true, it would have been more than enough," Tsurnick said.

"And that telephone call tonight?"

"That was from a friend of a friend in Langley, Virginia."

Chris nodded at the reference to CIA headquarters.

"It was confirmation that you were nothing more than you seemed to be. Your Company has been watching you since you left the service. You have made no contacts with foreign nationals. You have had no connection with Iran. And you were with a woman on Friday night. Until very late."

"Those bastards," Chris spat. He had resigned because he was dying of grief, and the heartless bastards had kept checking up on him as if he were a possible double agent.

"You would have done the same thing," Tsurnick said. "At any rate, in my mind that cleared you of any involvement in the professor's death. And so now, here we are, and I am asking you to take over his work. Work with me and find out what this is all about."

"A couple of things I don't understand. When you got this tip out of Iran, why didn't you just give it to the CIA?"

"Things have changed at Langley, Chris. If your agency should find out something that affects the security of Israel, what guarantee does my nation have that anything would be done about it? The CIA has changed, and not for the better. It is now a democratic institution." He laughed bitterly.

"Fair comment, I guess," Chris said. "Why would Iran want to take over an American oil company?"

Tsurnick's quick sad smile flashed across his face. "Ah, Chris, it's a good thing we were both field agents. Exactly the question I asked. But people in my government who are very smart and are paid to think about these things explained it for the benefit of my leaden brain. The opportunities for mischief would be vast. First, there is the amount of money that can be made. Iran could get its oil out into the market in a world which doesn't want to deal with it. If it doesn't, Iran can drink its oil. But with a pliable company, the oil could be disguised as coming from another source. The next time there's another oil squeeze, the prices that could be charged might stagger the mind. Those profits could be used to influence United States foreign policy by reaching United States officials. Some might be reluctant to take money directly from Iran, but could always find a reason to be bribed by an American oil company. You know yourself that much of what your Congress does could be changed by the swing of only a dozen votes or so. Iran could buy that dozen and dozens more."

"For a dollar and a half," Chris said bitterly.

"And think about other things," Tsurnick continued. "Suppose massive oil spills tarred the shores of Mexico and created an international crisis between your country and its neighbor? Suppose somehow an oil ship exploded in the Panama Canal? These are just some of the possibilities. The fertile minds in my government have dozens more."

"All right. I'm convinced. We're looking for the Red Moon, whatever it is."

Tsurnick smiled again at the use of the word "we."

"Yes," he said. "We are."

"What do we do?"

"You do," Tsurnick said. "You go through Hirschfeld's files. You look for any promising lead. You follow it up but you take no chances. You keep in touch with me. You say someone is already following you, so you might be on the right road already."

He had said to take no chances, but Christopher Caldwell knew what Tsurnick was proposing. He was telling Chris that it was up to him, but the best thing to do was to get out and stir up the waters and call attention to himself and try to get whoever killed Hirsch to come after Caldwell too.

"I understand," Chris said. For a brief moment, his eyes locked with Tsurnick's.

"Do you have a weapon?" the Israeli asked. "In case someone decides to take *you* fishing?"

"No. I haven't carried a gun in years. I don't even own one. I thought I had left all that behind me."

"We never leave it behind us," Tsurnick said. He reached into his outside jacket pocket and removed a small .32 caliber pistol. "Hold on to this," he said. "Efficient and not bulky. And I recommend that you do something to make this apartment a little less easy to enter without a key."

"Yes." Chris put the revolver on the table.

Tsurnick drained his coffee and pushed his chair back from the table.

"Anything else?" he asked.

"Don't give me that crap," Chris said. "You know there is." He hefted the .32 in his hand, surprised as he usually was at the weight of a handgun.

"Oh?" Tsurnick said.

"Who's Ernest Wessel?"

Tsurnick pulled his chair back into the table.

"Now that you are no longer a suspect, I am sure he is the man who killed Benjamin Hirschfeld."

Doyle Blaney insisted on taking Susan Millard up to her apartment door.

"Houston's filled with muggers," he said with a small smile. "House burglars. Thieves. Perverts and rapists."

"It's those rapists I worry about," Susan said in the elevator.

When she unlocked the door of her fourth-floor apartment, Blaney insisted upon coming in to look around. "No point in being careless," he said.

He satisfied himself that the apartment was empty, then said, "How about a nightcap?"

"I hope you don't mind, Doyle, but not tonight. I've got a big day tomorrow."

"That's all right," he said. "I've been rejected before."

"You're not being rejected now," she said. "I really am tired." She was surprised at how mildly he was taking it.

He started for the door, and she began walking with him. Just inside the door, he wheeled and took Susan in his arms. He pressed his lips hard against hers, pulling her body close to his.

When he released her mouth, he pressed his lips to her ear, but while he spoke softly, there was a harshness in his voice that frightened her.

"I don't mind being rejected," he said. "Once. But not the next time we go out."

Before she could respond, before she could tell him that there would never be a next time, he had let himself out through the front door.

CHAPTER THREE

"**D**o you want a drink?" Chris asked.

"No. And neither do you."

"I don't?"

"No, you don't," Tsurnick said. "There may be people out there who want to kill you. I don't think you should give them any edge by drinking yourself into soddenness as you have been doing for the last three years."

"Christ, my reputation has preceded me," Chris said.

"The professor told me about your drinking. It bothered him."

Chris shrugged. "I don't even know if he had anything to drink around here."

"Just some ceremonial wine, in the cabinet over the sink," Tsurnick said.

"All right, I'll pass. Who is Ernest Wessel?"

"In Haifa, there is the Documentation Center on Nazi War Crimes. Inside, there are ten gray filing cabinets filled with names and references to records. The records themselves are kept elsewhere, and microfilm of them is kept in yet two more locations. The names in these filing cabinets are what is left of the Nazis who escaped justice at the end of the war. I was in Haifa the day the file on Adolf Eichmann was pulled and marked closed."

"Most of them are dead by now," Caldwell said.

"Probably. Many of them would be of advanced years. Many probably have died. In Israel, however, we do not deal in ifs and probables. When elephants forget, we remind them. Until we are sure of a death, the file stays open. Only in the hands of God is a Nazi safe from our hands."

Tsurnick got up and put on more water for coffee. The man's capacity for caffeine was bottomless, Caldwell thought.

"By far the biggest files now belong to Joseph Mengele and Martin Bormann, both probably dead. It is strange to think—here are cabinets containing just pieces of paper, and paper is lifeless and cold. To open one of those cabinets is eerie. Your mind says, pieces of paper. But one can almost hear the anguished cries of six million souls. It is as if their spirits were locked inside those cabinets and when you open them, the screams pour forth. It is an awful responsibility to open one of those cabinets. You do not wish to go back to them until you are ready to pull a file and mark it closed. One of the files that sits in those cabinets, one of the largest files, belongs to Ernest Wessel. It is still open."

The water boiled and Tsurnick built himself another liquid monument to bad nerves and indestructible stomach. He glanced at Chris, a question in his eyes, but Chris waved a hand in an I'll-pass gesture.

"Wessel's is a very large file," Tsurnick said as he sat back down. He sipped his coffee and went on, almost as if reciting a lesson learned and memorized.

"Ernest Wessel was the only son of Max and Helga Wessel, a wealthy family of Frankfurt. The elder Wessel was an art dealer. Mrs. Wessel was a promising pianist who still taught students part-time, and she assisted her husband in his business. Their son, Ernest, went to the university at Frankfurt. He was a very good student, majoring in mathematics. It is amazing, is it not, how often mathematicians are drawn into a search for final solutions? Ernest Wessel also had a natural talent for languages and early could speak English and French as well as German. Later he learned Spanish and Parsi, we know

"He received a commission in the German army when he was just twenty years old, in 1939. Even then he was a striking man. Tall, broad-shouldered, blue-eyed, with a full head of almost white blond hair.

"Wessel went to work in the Nazi procurement office, later the Office of War Supplies. We do not know too much of what he did in the early days of the war, but we suspect, based on his background, that it was at his suggestion that the Nazis began to systematically loot the art works of all the captured countries and send them back to the Third Reich, where they could one day be used as currency if necessary. If it wasn't his idea, Wessel helped perfect it. With the help of his mother—his father had died—he

127

made lists of the great artworks to be found in both private and public collections all through Europe, and commanders in the field carried these lists with them when they moved into another country.

"A little later in the war, 1942 perhaps, Wessel had an idea that was to win him a place of honor in those files in Haifa. The Nazis by now had their concentration camps in good order. The Jews who were marched into the gas chambers were stripped of their belongings, their jewelry, rings, eyeglasses, even their clothes, all used to fuel the Nazi war machine.

"It was Wessel's idea to loot not only the living but the dead. We found the memorandum in Eichmann's files and confirmed it after we captured him and placed him on trial. They called it Operation Reclamation. Eichmann confirmed that the idea to chisel the gold from the teeth of dead men, to cut the hair from their heads to stuff mattresses, even more grisly acts of vampirism, this idea had come from Ernest Wessel. It was so clear and so obvious that no one had thought of it before. The Nazis knew a good idea and a good man when they saw one. They adopted the idea and promoted Wessel.

"Late in the war, he disappeared, although it did not concern us then. Israel did not yet exist. Wessel was a man of low profiles, then as now. It was only after the war that we began to run across his name and his legacy.

"I said that his father was by that time dead. That was before the Mossad. Our intelligence service in those early days was called Shai. When our men went to Frankfurt to question Mrs. Wessel about her son, she could not believe what our men told her about her son's activities. They showed her proof. She swore she knew nothing of her son's whereabouts. She insisted he was a good son. After our men left, she took poison. It is astonishing how those who helped the Nazis were always grief-stricken afterward. Never did so many have their eyes closed so tightly for so long."

"You're hard on the woman," Chris said. "Maybe she was just naive."

"Her son, with her help, was hard on my people. They never had a chance to grow up naive," Tsurnick said. "Six million of them, all killed by fun-loving Bavarians, not a
128

Nazi in the crowd. No thank you, I reject that." He paused as if waiting for an argument, but when none came, he went on.

"There was no trace of Ernest Wessel at the end of the war. But in the late 1940s and early '50s, there were reports that he was living in South America. Always we checked them out. Always they turned out empty. The reports were of a striking similarity. Ernest Wessel had dyed his hair black. He was now an art dealer or a collector and he was in Buenos Aires or Rio de Janeiro or here or there. They came regularly, these reports, never more frequently than two years apart, never less frequently than thirty months. Finally, that regularity impressed someone at the Haifa Center. Our agents went back and checked out the tips themselves. Where had they come from? How did they get to us? The information was being planted by Ernest Wessel himself. Every two years or so, he would send someone to one of these cities and they would talk about their great rich friend with the dyed-black hair who used to be a Nazi and was now an art collector and whose name was Wessel and there was a big reward on him from the Israelis. He was using agents to manipulate people to give us false reports."

"Where the hell was he?" Chris asked. "Did you ever find him?"

"Yes. He was in the Middle East all the time. Under our noses. The safest place to hide is in the middle of the crowd that is chasing you, because their eyes always look in only one direction. We were looking toward South America, and Wessel was in Egypt and Libya and Lebanon. He helped train certain PLO operatives.

"We learned this much later. In 1976, we finally found him, but it was too late. He was a member of the shah's government in Iran, a high officer in the Savak. He was in charge of interrogation. This presented us with great problems. He was wanted by us. But the shah's Iran was an American client, just as was Israel. While we had no delusions about where the shah would stand in an all-out war against us, we simply could not sneak in and kidnap one of his officials. Not without ramifications that we did not want to deal with. So we waited.

"When the shah fell, we thought that here, now, was

129

our chance to get Wessel. But the new government was even worse than the shah. Without provocation, they were calling for a *jihad,* a holy war, against us, against you. Trying to get Wessel out of that country was too dangerous. It would surely touch off a shooting war, and in those early days, Iran's armed forces were still potent. So we decided to wait and see what happened. After all, Wessel should be a piece of meat, a victim of the revolution himself. A high officer in the shah's torture brigade? Presumably the ayatollahs would do our work for us. But they did not. Somehow Wessel survived. We decided that it was time to go in and get him. After all, Iran and the United States were at each other's throats. The United States would not be upset. To prevent Iran from looking foolish and stupid in the eyes of the world, it was agreed that we would say we captured Wessel in Argentina.

"Our men got into Iran but Wessel was gone. Our men inside Iran report that Wessel had not been seen for two months. Then we received the report about the Iranians wanting to take over an American oil company, and at the same time, there was a report that Ernest Wessel had entered New York. Someone matching his description flew soon after to Dallas."

"What do you think?" Caldwell asked.

"I think Wessel is here in Houston. I think he killed Benjamin Hirschfeld. I think he is behind the Red Moon, whatever it is. I think he will try to kill you. And if you are drunk, he will probably succeed."

CHAPTER FOUR

After Yoel Tsurnick had left, Chris went into the kitchen to straighten up. He carried the cups to the sink and without hesitation reached into the overhead cabinet and took out the lone bottle of wine there.

It was a cheap grape wine. The bottle was two-thirds full. It was better than nothing, and he reached for a glass on the next shelf.

He had the plastic stopper out of the bottle and was ready to pour it when he stopped. Had the liquor taken hold of him so thoroughly that he *had* to drink, disregarding Tsurnick's warning, disregarding his own common sense? He thought for a moment, then replaced the glass and put the stopper back in the bottle.

After washing the dishes, he went to bed. He fell asleep quickly, but he dreamed.

He was back again on that street in Tehran. The red Fiat was parked in front of the bazaar market. He could see Zhava in the driver's seat. Shoshana was looking out the rear window. She saw him and she waved. He could see her mouth the word "Daddy." There was someone in the front passenger's seat. It was Hirsch. He was wearing a yellow rain poncho.

Caldwell was far away, but he could clearly see Zhava inserting the ignition key.

He shouted, "Don't," and began running toward the car, but even as he ran, he saw her turn the key and saw the car explode—the red metal vanishing in a flash of fire and light and noise.

There were people milling around the fire scene as he tried to get through. But one man was walking away. He was a tall husky man with white-blond hair, and when he turned, his eyes met Christopher Caldwell's, and he smiled. The horrible nightmare faded.

Chris awoke to feel sweat covering his body. In the room

he could almost smell the scent of the fire and the burning gasoline and rubber.

He sat up. He smoked a cigarette, hoping that somehow his unconscious would bury that dream before he fell asleep again. This time when he slept, he did not dream.

Chris arrived at the office before nine o'clock the next morning and immediately began reading through the thick file on the Griffin Oil Company he had left under his desk. He and Tsurnick had agreed that there might be something in Hirsch's notes, some tip, some clue, but instead the file consisted of letters back and forth between the oil firm and their attorneys over the years, along with a variety of documents, yearly reports to state and federal agencies, and other technical papers. Caldwell at first tried to read carefully, but after a while he found himself scanning rapidly through the thick file.

He finished as the wall clock reached eleven. He now had a general grasp of the company's history and activities, along with a mind-boggling welter of technicalities and trivialities carefully preserved in triplicate for the edification of governmental nit-pickers.

But there was nothing in any of the papers relating to a Red Moon; nothing relating to Iran; nothing relating to anything that might have been a cause for Hirsch's death.

Celeste Thompson was at her desk, and Caldwell asked her if she knew where Mr. Hirschfeld's personal notes were.

"I'm sorry, Mr. Caldwell, but I don't know." The girl had recovered from yesterday's attack of grief. She also obviously had heard about Chris and his background, because she looked at him with frank and obvious interest. She came into his office with him and pointed to the five-drawer file cabinet in the corner.

"If he kept any personal notes on the Griffin matter, they *might* be in there," she said.

"He didn't give you anything to type for him?" Chris asked.

"No, sir. I'm sorry."

"So am I."

He was about to call Susan Millard to ask her to come

to his office when McBride buzzed him on the intercom.

"Early lunch, old buddy?" McBride said.

Chris realized that he had had no breakfast. He was hungry and his body felt dried out, the way it so often did when he'd drunk too much the night before.

"You have early lunch," he said. "I'll have late breakfast. If I look at another Griffin income-tax return, complete with exclusions, deals and amendments and carryovers and stashaways and roll-forwards and obvious lies and fudgings, my eyeballs will fall out and roll around on top of the desk."

"What do you mean, 'obvious lies and fudgings'? When oil lawyers and accountants lie and fudge, we do it as delicately and deviously as anyone in the business. Some of those returns are works of art, Chris, masterpieces of corporate law."

"If you say so. The hell with it. Let's eat."

At lunch, McBride ordered an extra-dry martini. Chris thought twice before opting for Perrier water, with lime.

"Heard you had drinks with Susie Baby yesterday," McBride said. He leaned forward. "How was she?"

"Shame on you, Mac. Miss Millard is a lovely young lady. She's bright and well educated and full to the brim with noble ideals."

"Screw that. You get lucky yet?" McBride asked.

"No," Chris said. "But I'll tell you the truth. Under different circumstances, if I were here for a different reason, I wouldn't mind taking a serious run at Susan Millard. She's bright and she's funny and she's beautiful," he said. "And unfortunately, she's not on my agenda for things I have to do."

"More's the pity," McBride said.

"Try her yourself," Caldwell suggested.

"I never fool around with professional staff," McBride said. "Only secretaries and receptionists."

"Oh, of course. Forgive me for suggesting you might trample on office etiquette."

"Forgiven. Anyway, I have to watch my step with her, because it wouldn't surprise me a bit if she was sending regular reports back to dear old Uncle Otto, that sneaky old fraud."

133

McBride had finished his drink and put the glass down sharply. The waiter approached with a questioning look, but McBride shook his head.

"Mind if I ask you a question?" Chris said.

"Go ahead."

"How did your father feel about Brooks going to the Supreme Court, instead of him?"

"He didn't give a damn. But he would have made a hell of a lot better justice than babbling Brooks. He sure wouldn't have been a fall guy for every crackpot. My father, Chris, didn't just do the legal work in the firm; he did the political work too. He was the one who got the hundred grand from Gus Griffin that elected Brooks. But he just didn't care. Once I bitched about it and he said he wouldn't have traded Houston for Washington. He said he preferred crude oil to refined bullshit."

"He was probably right," Chris said.

"Maybe. But I still think Otto is full of shit."

"Susan Millard doesn't," Chris said. "Her eyes glow when she mentions him."

"I know. And that's why I'm not going to pinch her ass, as much as I'd like to. You could, though. Christ, you even made a hit with Dolores the other day."

Caldwell thought of Dolores, McBride's tall svelte wife.

"What the hell are you talking about, Mac?"

"Don't get upset. Dolores told me she hadn't realized you were so handsome. So don't be surprised if you find her one night sniffing around your apartment door."

"Not for me, pal," Chris said.

"Don't get unctuous," McBride said. "Dear Dolores likes to sleep around. If she's got to, I've got no problem with her sleeping with a friend. New rules these days, buddy. You've been out of touch."

"I like the old rules better," Caldwell said. The direction of the conversation was disturbing him. "Did Hirsch ever say anything to you about a red moon? Or the Red Moon? Something like that?"

"No. I don't think so. What are you talking about?"

Caldwell had been thinking about telling McBride some of what was going on. But it might lead to too many questions, and he decided against it.

"Nothing," he said. "I just found a note in Hirsch's

134

apartment. Said something about a red moon, and I thought maybe it had something to do with Griffin. You know how bad his handwriting was—you couldn't tell anything about what he was writing."

"No. You got me," McBride said.

When the two men returned to their office, Chris found Susan Millard talking with Celeste Thompson. Susan nodded to Chris and walked into his office before him. As he looked at her swaying walk, the lunch conversation came back to him. He wondered about her life in Washington. Was sex a casual thing with her, like a pick-up tennis game? What would it be like to have an affair with her? he wondered. Would she prove experienced and aggressive in bed, or timid and shy?

"Why are you staring at me?" she said, intruding on his thoughts.

"I was just wondering about your sex life," he said.

"Remind me to tell you all about it sometime when you've got three or four weeks to spare," she said. "Or an evening."

Was it an invitation? Chris wondered. And if the invitation came more strongly, what would he do? He was relieved to see Sam Fischer, the office manager, bustle into the room.

"You didn't fill out your forms," he chided Chris. Fischer was a small man, in his early thirties, but fat with the fat that had been deposited on him in childhood and that had never been attacked or even questioned.

"This afternoon for sure, Sam," Chris said.

"I'll hold you to it. Otherwise, you don't get paid."

The three spent the next hour going over the procedures that Griffin Oil had to follow to make its public stock offering. Fischer was detailed and precise. He said that the law firm had just about everything in hand that it needed to file the preliminary application to the SEC.

"A few more tax returns, some corporate records, but mostly paperwork. No big problems," he said. Susan nodded.

"Then we don't have to lose a lot of time because of Hirsch's death?" Caldwell asked.

"Not really," Fischer said.

"Don't take this wrong, Sam," said Caldwell. "But if

135

you and Susan have everything in order by yourselves, just what was Hirsch doing? Why have a partner in the firm involved in this at all?"

"Two reasons," Fischer said. "One is psychological. The client likes to see a lawyer—forgive me, Susan—a lawyer with some clout with the firm working on his application."

"No, you're right," she said.

"The other reason," Fischer said, "is it takes an expert on this to see if there's anything tricky. Anything that could cause a big problem. Legal work on this level is as much prevention as cure."

"And did Hirsch find any big problems?" Caldwell asked.

"Not that I know of," Fischer said. He looked at Susan Millard. "You?"

"No." She was staring at Chris.

"He never mentioned that he thought Griffin might have trouble with its application? Or why it might?" Chris asked.

"Not to either of us," Fischer said.

"Have either of you run across his notes?" Chris said. He quickly added, "I just thought if he had run into some problems, he'd have them in his notes. It might save us from getting egg on our faces."

"No," Fischer said. "Hirsch always kept his notes on sheets of legal paper, but I didn't see any of them."

"And he never mentioned anything to me," Susan told Chris.

"I still want to talk to the principals of the Griffin company," Caldwell said. "Just to satisfy myself and get a feel for this whole thing."

After the conference was over, Susan stayed behind while Chris telephoned Adam Griffin.

He introduced himself and said, "Miss Millard and I would like to talk to you about the stock offering."

"Are we going to have to go over all that same ground again?" Griffin asked.

"Not all of it. We've just got a few questions."

"Well, I'm busy today. Tomorrow? Ten o'clock?"

"Fine. We'll be there," Caldwell said.

"What happened to Mr. Hirschfeld's notes?" asked Susan when Chris hung up.

136

"I don't know." He pointed at the file cabinet. "They could be there somewhere, neatly filed away under P for Prospectus or O for Oil. Hirsch had a great mind, but he wasn't much on administrative details. Plus, of course, his notes might not mean anything anyway. You couldn't read them. I even had trouble making out his signature at the end of a letter." He paused for a moment, then decided to gamble. "Like the Red Moon."

"That again?" she said.

"What?" asked Caldwell.

"You mentioned the Red Moon."

"You've heard it before?"

"Sure. Mr. Hirschfeld asked me about it. Asked me if I'd ever heard of it."

"What'd you tell him?"

"That I'd never heard of it. He asked Adam Griffin about it too."

"What did Griffin say?"

"He had never heard of it either."

CHAPTER FIVE

Adam Griffin dropped the telephone back on the stand and complained, "Why can't things ever go smoothly? It looks like they lost old Hirschfeld's notes. I spend most of an afternoon answering stupid questions and now I've got to do it all over again."

"Damned inconvenient," Doyle Blaney agreed.

"I guess the old man couldn't help it if he had a heart attack or fell overboard or whatever the hell happened to him, but I wish he could have picked some other time. I never knew a simple stock offering could take so much time and trouble. That damn McBride is probably just making it involved so he can run up his bill."

"You know government regs," Blaney said. "You can bet, with a stock offering this big, the SEC is going to be into every detail with a fine-tooth comb. Mind if I sit in on that session tomorrow? I might learn a few things I should know."

"Yeah. Might as well, Doyle."

"Okay, if that's what you want, I'll be here."

Actually, there was no need to sit in at the meeting tomorrow, Blaney reflected, as he walked up the single flight of stairs to his office. He would have the entire session on tape anyway. There was nothing that happened in Adam Griffin's office these days that escaped his electronic surveillance—or in Gus Griffin's office either. But it was always preferable to hear things firsthand when you could see the expressions on people's faces as they were talking.

And tomorrow's meeting would give him a chance to size up this former CIA man, Christopher Caldwell, and an opportunity to talk again to the fast-assed Susan Millard. She had put him off last night, but that wouldn't last. He was confident that Susan was his when he was ready for her.

138

As he walked by Gus Griffin's office, he saw that Velma Waldor was wearing a brassiere. He liked it better the old way. Gus Griffin's office door was shut. It usually was these days.

Blaney was dictating a memo to the payroll department an hour later when his telephone buzzed. "It's Mr. Griffin," his secretary told him. That meant it was Gus. When Adam called, the secretary would say, "It's Adam Griffin."

"Doyle, I was just telling Adam that Justice Brooks was on the phone a few minutes ago. He's coming down tonight for a couple of days, so I told him to come out to the ranch tomorrow night. We'll have a little party. Help Sherry with the arrangements, will you? Give her a call and see what she needs. Got a pencil? Invite these people." Griffin rattled off a list of two dozen, ranging from state senators and commissioners to oilmen and ranchers. "Invite Mc-Bride too. Tell everybody they can bring their wives or their girlfriends, but not both."

"Sure, Gus. Say, is it okay if I invite Susan Millard, who just joined McBride's firm? She's the one who was working with the judge."

"Sure. Why not?"

"And maybe McBride would appreciate it if we invited this Caldwell guy he just hired and put in charge of the stock-offering project."

"Who?"

"Christopher Caldwell."

"Who's he?" asked Griffin.

"He's an old friend of Mac's who's taking over for Hirschfeld. The old guy was his father-in-law."

"He's a Jew?"

"No. But he was married to the old man's daughter. He's a former CIA man, they tell me. Anyway, he's working with Susan Millard on the stock prospectus. They'll be here tomorrow to talk with Adam, and I guess they'll be getting around to you in a day or so."

"More goddam questions, huh? Well, all right, if you think so. Maybe Caldwell can bring the Millard girl out to the ranch?"

"I was planning to do that myself."

"Oh, like that? Well, I don't want to spoil your fun, but

139

you really ought to be at the ranch tomorrow. You know Sherry always forgets to do half the things she's supposed to for a party." The old man chuckled. "Don't feel bad. It's not who brings her but who takes her home. Give Sherry a call and see what she needs. And find out what you can about these two lawyers."

The old man hung up without bothering to say goodbye. Blaney glared at the phone, then slapped it down angrily. "See what Sherry needs." He knew what Sherry needed, all right. He wondered what the old man would think if Blaney stuck it to his big-titted blond wife.

Now now, he told himself. Plenty of time later. Somehow, now that he was treasurer of Griffin Oil, serving as Gus Griffin's Man Friday too was becoming increasingly irksome to him.

But he was not about to make an issue of it. Not yet, at least. Gus did not make too many demands on his time, and Blaney wasn't ready to try to put more space between their relationship. Not until he was sure that Adam's plans would actually work out. Because Adam's plans were the first major step toward his.

He hurriedly completed his memo to the payroll department, looked at the notes he had scribbled while Gus was talking, sighed, then began looking up numbers and making Gus's telephone calls.

Gus Griffin tugged at an earlobe and thought about what Blaney had told him, trying to restrain his anger. He knew the Millard girl. He had met her once in Washington, and he supposed she was smart enough, but why the hell wasn't she doing what she was supposed to be doing?

He did not like being surprised, and this Christopher Caldwell was a surprise. How did he suddenly appear on the scene, involving himself in Griffin Oil affairs just after his father-in-law had conveniently drowned? And what was the business about the CIA, for God's sake?

It was bad enough giving the SEC a chance to rummage around in his corporate affairs. But the CIA? How did they get to be involved? Or were they involved? Blaney had said a "former" CIA man. But how much did that mean?

Doyle Blaney's FBI experience and contacts were useful

to Gus—but only because he had quickly made sure that Blaney's love of money and power far outranked any notions the FBI might have put in his head about honesty and corporate integrity.

He had smelled the hustler in Blaney when he first met him and had been amused at the man's subtle but clear attempts to attract Gus's notice and get himself placed with Griffin Oil.

Gus had hired him, and then had tested him by giving him opportunities to augment his healthy salary. He was pleased when Blaney prudently avoided any minor temptations, such as chiseling on expenses or reaching for penny-ante kickbacks from suppliers. But he was relieved when Blaney promptly took advantage of a chance for a sizable payoff, riding along secretly on a real estate deal of questionable integrity that Gus had arranged for Blaney to "overhear" him making.

With that assurance, Gus had involved Blaney more and more in his activities, such as having him arrange payoffs to some labor men, and beatings of other labor men who were not quite so willing to do business. He knew he need have no fear of his personal assistant's law-enforcement past when Blaney personally beat a union troublemaker so badly that the man was hospitalized for several weeks.

Yes, Blaney could be trusted—trusted to be ruthless, greedy, ambitious, and clever, a sharp-edged tool that had to be used carefully lest it cut the user.

But a former CIA man?

He reached for his telephone. "Velma, get me Eustace McBride," he barked.

When McBride came on the line, Gus was equally abrupt. "What's this I hear that you've got that girl from Brooks's office working on our stock offering?"

"That's right," McBride admitted cheerfully. "Equal opportunity strikes again. The judge asked me to give her a job a couple of weeks ago, and she was working with Hirschfeld before he died. Don't worry. She's a good lawyer."

"I worry about everything," Griffin said. "That's what got me where I am today. She's just a baby, that girl, and I'd rather deal with a man."

"You will. She's working with another new member of
141

the firm, an old friend of mine named Chris Caldwell."

"Caldwell, huh? What's his background?"

McBride launched into a brief but glowing biography of Caldwell but was promptly interrupted.

"What the hell does a CIA man know about stock offerings?" Gus demanded.

"He left the CIA years ago, Gus. He's been doing private work since then." McBride crossed his fingers, hoping Griffin wouldn't press him on what kind of private work. How could he explain that he had assigned a skin diver to deal with Griffin Oil?

"Well, all right," Griffin said. "By the way, Doyle Blaney call you yet?"

"Not today."

"He will," Griffin said and hung up.

The housekeeper in his Georgetown home had packed his bags, so Supreme Court Justice Otto Brooks had time for another cup of coffee before the limousine arrived to take him to the airport.

He sat in his wood-paneled study and could not resist again opening *The New York Times* to its editorial page.

The lead editorial was headed: "An Obvious Selection." He had almost memorized it by now.

"If, as he claims, the President of the United States is serious about selecting the best available candidates for vacancies in the federal court system, he need not look far to fill the post of Chief Justice of the United States.

"The obvious selection is Justice Otto Brooks of Texas. In his fourteen years of service on the high court, Mr. Justice Brooks has raised a standard to which the wise and the honest and the compassionate can repair enthusiastically.

"He has been..."

The telephone rang. It was his private line. Brooks thought for a moment about not answering it. But who knew? Perhaps the President of the United States had just gotten around to reading *The New York Times*. Brooks put the newspaper on an end table and reached into the pocket of his blue pin-striped suit to check his watch. Still ten minutes before the car would arrive to take him to the airport.

He picked up the telephone, clearing his throat first.

"Hello."

"What the hell is going on with you?" Gus Griffin's voice barked through the earpiece of the telephone.

"Hello, Gus. What's the problem?"

"The problem is that dipshit girl that you sent down here."

"What's Susan been doing?"

"Obviously nothing," Gus snarled. "I have to find out for myself that McBride has hired some fucking CIA agent to go snooping around my oil company. And who do I hear it from? From Blaney. And how does Blaney hear it? From your Girl Friday. But does she tell you? No. Does anybody tell anybody anything the way they're supposed to? No. What the fuck is going on?"

"What's his name?" Brooks asked. He should not have answered the telephone. The editorial had just been getting to the good part.

"Christopher Caldwell, and I want you to check him out. Pronto."

"I don't know, Gus. What reason would a Supreme Court Justice have to ask about a CIA employee?"

"Maybe he's a former employee. How the hell do I know? Think something up. For Christ's sakes, Otto, you have the CIA director at your house for dinner. Give him a call. Tell him somebody wants to offer this Caldwell a job. Do something."

"You sound like he worries you, Gus."

"What worries me is people who don't do what they're supposed to do."

"But how could this man possibly be of any concern—"

"You know goddam well how he can be of concern, and I don't want the CIA or anybody else rooting around in my affairs. And neither do you, Otto. Neither do you."

There was silence from Brooks for a moment.

"It can't wait until Susan tells me what he's up to?"

"No, it can't. Who knows what she's doing?"

"All right, Gus. I'll see what I can do."

"Do that. We'll have lunch tomorrow," Griffin said. "Call me here at the office in the morning." He hung up abruptly.

Brooks replaced his telephone slowly, shaking his head.

He was extremely unhappy, and he looked it. He checked his watch again. Five minutes. And he had two telephone calls to make.

Gus Griffin sat in his office for a long while, idly fingering the stiff leather patch over his right eye. He looked at the mounted head of the wild boar on his wall and said aloud, "You ought to be working for me. At least you're better than what I got now."

He punched the button for his private line and dialed a number in Arcola, a few miles outside Houston.

When a man answered, Griffin said, "Kirchner, this is Griffin. We should talk. I think we've got trouble."

CHAPTER SIX

Chris Caldwell spent the rest of the afternoon methodically ransacking Hirsch's office. The file cabinet proved to be less of a chore than he had expected. It did not take too long to make sure that none of the folders the drawers held had anything to do with the Griffin Oil Company.

The large wooden desk was more of a problem. One double drawer was a built-in cabinet filled to bursting with legal papers, documents, correspondence, and other items stuffed carelessly into manila file folders, most of them with a hastily scrawled and generally illegible identification on the side. Each had to be opened and scanned.

As he finished, he put each file into a cardboard box provided by Celeste Thompson. She could integrate them with the files in the metal cabinets or distribute them to the lawyers who were taking over Hirsch's previous assignments.

The other drawers in the desk held random papers and a few file folders. One folder contained copies of several letters from Hirsch to Adam Griffin and other officers of the Griffin Oil Company, confirming dates for interviews.

There was no sign of the notes Hirsch had taken at those interviews, though. Caldwell became increasingly certain that any notes Hirsch had must have been in the apartment and had been taken after Hirsch was killed. Assuming there had been notes. Maybe there weren't. Maybe he was spinning his wheels, looking for something that didn't exist or, if it did exist, would be of no value to him.

He was interrupted when Susan Millard strolled in. Her closely fitted skirt showed off her fashion-model figure flatteringly, and he noticed that she had opened another button on her blouse since their early-afternoon meeting with Sam Fischer. He realized, with something close to surprise, that he was pleased to see her.

145

"Need any help?" she asked as she perched on the arm of a chair.

"Not unless you've got a special on extra eyeballs," he said.

"Still looking for Mr. Hirschfeld's notes?"

"Yeah. No sign of them."

"Am I bothering you? Should I go away?" she asked.

"No. You're the best thing that's happened to me this afternoon. Anyway, I need a breather." He pulled out a pack of cigarettes and offered them to her.

She wrinkled her nose. "I hate menthol cigarettes," she said, but took one. She stood and leaned over the desk to allow him to light it for her. Chris found his gaze dropping to focus on the open throat of her blouse. He could see the faint swell of her breasts, then the top of her bra, before his view was obscured. He wished she had opened another button.

Annoyed with himself, he looked up to find her gazing at him, a faintly mocking smile on her face. He lit his own cigarette, looking directly at her. He saw a healthy, alert young woman, well made up with artful casualness.

He wondered what she saw.

Did she see a fellow worker? An office companion? An eligible bachelor? A possible friend to have fun with, to laugh with? Or did she see him as he increasingly saw himself—aging and weary, tired of life, a man without hopes or dreams or expectations?

"Don't you ever laugh?" she asked. "Or even smile? Not something polite with your lips, but really happy?"

He shrugged. "I'm just not the cheery type, I guess. McBride's the smiler. I trudge around with the world on my shoulders."

"Big shouders, though," she said. "Weight-lifter, right?"

"Swimmer. Don't tease an old man. It's not nice."

"Who cares about nice?" she said. "My mother says I'm brazen."

"Brazen's in this year," he said.

"Good," she said. "I'm glad you appreciate my style. How's *your* love life?"

"I don't have one."

"No girlfriend that you're keeping secret? No frenzied orgies in nameless places in the dark of night? No close encounters of the worst kind with shadowy ladies of the evening?"

He thought of Lisa, his dark-haired clerk back in Puerto Rico, and of the rare nights they had spent together. He thought of some of the others, tourists mostly, one-night stands, and he could not remember any of their names.

"My life in Houston is one of unimpeachable rectitude and astonishing emptiness," he admitted.

"Isn't everybody's?" she asked. "Anyway, here comes the real brazen part. I'm taking you to dinner tonight."

"Why?"

"Because I'm bored and lonely and tired of sitting around in my apartment and you can't walk anywhere in this town at night, you have to drive, and I don't even know where to drive, and why are you making me beg to take you to dinner?"

"If you're going to appeal to my sense of guilt, I'll go," he said. "But I'm warning you, I'm too old and too morose for you."

"I like old men," she said. "Dodder over about seven-thirty." She whirled and walked briskly out of the office without a backward look.

Chris kept looking at the doorway, as he sat down again behind the desk. There was the Red Moon, and Hirsch had mentioned it to Susan Millard. And just maybe, in a leisurely mood, over drinks or dinner, maybe she might remember something worthwhile. Something he needed to know.

Chris tried to tell himself that, but he knew it was just rationalization. The fact was that he would have accepted Susan's dinner invitation under any circumstances.

When he resumed digging through Hirsch's desk, he found himself whistling softly under his breath.

Doyle Blaney waited until the secretarial staff had been gone for more than half an hour before he entered Gus Griffin's office carrying a file folder. He locked the door behind him, dropped the file folder onto Gus's desk, then knelt down, fumbled briefly, and removed the tape recorder from its brackets. He placed a fresh tape cassette in the device, put it back in its holder, and quickly returned to his own office.

147

He glanced at his watch. He had enough time to listen to the tape. He dropped the cassette into a player and put an earphone in his ear so that the tape could not be heard by anyone but himself.

His eyebrows rose as he flipped through the tape and heard Gus Griffin chewing out Supreme Court Justice Otto Brooks. And they rose even higher as he listened to the judge's meek compliance with Griffin's demands.

Blaney knew from remarks made by Griffin over the years that he and Brooks had known each other most of their lives and that Griffin was contemptuous of the man who had gained national stature as "the Lone Star Liberal" since his appointment to the high court. So he was not surprised to discover that his employer held some secret authority over Brooks, but the naked, brutal expression of it shocked him.

And there was Susan Millard. So the girl was Otto Brooks's plant in McBride's office? And she was reporting to Brooks, who reported to Gus. Good to know, he thought.

He sat up straighter as the next pair of voices came on the tape. Gus Griffin and Frederick Kirchner.

He heard Gus ask, "Do you know about this Caldwell?"

"I have heard of him," Kirchner said blandly.

"I don't like this," Gus complained. "First the old Jew lawyer dies and now the CIA. Goddam that dumb son of mine."

Kirchner grunted indifferently.

"I'll be seeing Brooks for lunch. Maybe he'll know something then," Griffin said.

"And I will see you tomorrow night," Kirchner said.

"Can't. I'm having a party at my ranch."

"I *will* see you tomorrow night," Kirchner said flatly, not raising his voice.

"Can't, I told you."

Kirchner spoke as if he had not heard Griffin or as if what he said were not worth responding to. "I will be by that small building behind your pool at eleven-thirty. You will meet me there."

Griffin was silent.

"You understand?" Kirchner said.

"Yes."

"Eleven-thirty tomorrow night," Kirchner repeated, and the connection was abruptly broken.

"Goddam son of a bitch," yelled Griffin, and Blaney flinched at the sudden crash of the telephone receiver.

There were only a few more sounds on the tape as Griffin left for the day. Blaney slowly pulled the earplug from his ear, frowning. Kirchner had more hold than he had realized over Gus Griffin.

It was time for Blaney to have a good long heart-to-heart talk with Mr. Frederick Kirchner. He had gone as far as he would go on faith. It was time for some answers.

Christopher Caldwell stood up wearily and rubbed his eyes with the backs of his hands. His fingers were grimy from handling so many papers, including a number of old-fashioned carbon copies.

Hirsch's notes were definitely not in this office, and the chilling thought came at him again: You're wasting your time. There are no notes.

No. He knew Hirsch too well. The man was methodical and detailed and careful. Somewhere there were notes. Somewhere.

He thought about telling Tsurnick that he had drawn a blank, then dismissed the idea. Time enough for that later. No news, in this case, was definitely not good news.

Looking out the window, he saw the clouds piled up, black, over the city. It would be raining in just a few minutes.

He walked quickly to the men's room and washed his face and hands. When he returned to the office, the skies had burst. Heavy sheets of rain dropped vertically onto the city.

"Damn," he mumbled. No raincoat.

He opened the long clothes closet in the office to see if there was an umbrella secreted in there. In the far corner of the closet there was a raincoat. A ratty-looking old tan raincoat. Hirsch's raincoat.

He felt the pockets. There was a long cylindrical bulge in one of the pockets. He pulled it out. It was a packet of papers, folded and folded again. He smiled as he remembered Hirsch's habit of jamming papers into his pockets,

149

all types of papers, cocktail napkins, matchbooks on which he had written telephone numbers, pieces of restaurant menus from which he had torn a corner to make a note.

Carefully he checked all the other pockets of the raincoat. They were all empty.

He went back to the desk, pushed aside the papers that littered it, and sat down. He looked at the folded sheaf of papers on the desk without opening them for a moment. He felt as if it might contain some last message to him from his dear old friend. Taking a deep breath, he opened the papers and smoothed them out.

Inside were several typewritten sheets with biographies of Augustus Griffin and Adam Griffin, prepared by a public-relations firm for the Griffin Oil Company. They were scribbled over with various words and phrases in Hirsch's hen-track scrawl.

There were four yellow legal-sized sheets of lined yellow paper, also containing notes.

He had found what he was looking for, but what would it tell him? He started to read carefully, laboring over the almost-incomprehensible writing.

As he fought through the mystery, line by line, page by page, his spirits started to sink.

Benjamin Hirschfeld's marginal notes were mostly prosaic office jottings.

"Remember to get tax returns for partners."

"Lists of holdings."

"Early profit statements."

The notes were what a lawyer preparing an SEC application would be keeping to remind himself what he needed for the application to be thorough enough to meet federal requirements.

But Caldwell's heart skipped a little faster as he got to the last yellow sheet of paper. In the upper right hand corner, Hirsch had written: "Red Moon."

And under it he had written: "100K."

He had drawn a small box around the two entries.

Chris looked at it.

Red Moon.

100K.

What did it mean?

In the lower left corner of the same page was another

150

box. Inside it was written: "Brooks." And on the next line: "4B."

A box was drawn around the two lines.

What did it mean? He hunched himself over the desk, going back through the rest of the notes, unable to find anything in them that could connect with the Red Moon. With 100K. With Brooks. With 4B.

What did it mean?

Red Moon. 100K. Brooks. 4B.

What?

Justice Brooks?

Chris wondered and then, just as quickly, remembered Susan Millard. He glanced at his watch. It was seven o'clock.

He wanted to talk to her tonight.

He closed his eyes a moment, forcing up Yoel Tsurnick's telephone number from his memory. He dialed it on the outside night line and heard a mechanical approximation of the Israeli's English-accented voice.

It did not identify itself. The message said simply, "This is a recording. Please leave your message at the signal."

When he heard the beep, Caldwell said:

"Y., this is C.C. I'll call later. I may have found something."

Then he hung up and tried to put Yoel Tsurnick out of his mind for a while. He would try to relax and enjoy the evening and, just maybe, find out from Susan Millard some kind of clue on what Red Moon, 100K, Brooks, and 4B had to do with one another.

CHAPTER SEVEN

Chris was almost a quarter of an hour late when he was announced by the front desk. Susan punished him by making him wait another ten minutes in the lobby before she emerged from the elevator, splendid-looking in a moss-green silk jersey dress that clung tightly to her body.

He smiled apologetically, then pulled a small old-fashioned nosegay of flowers from behind his back.

"You're forgiven," she said. "How can anybody be mad at a man who brings flowers?"

"You know how tough it was to steal them from the front yard without the desk clerk noticing?" he said.

"See? Your training was good for something after all," she said.

Susan picked the restaurant, Juarez's near the main business district, and they drove over in Chris's rented Chevrolet. Inside they waited briefly and then were shown to a balcony table overlooking the main dining room.

"Too bad," Chris said as he held her chair. "You should be downstairs where everybody can gawk at you."

They ordered drinks—a Margarita for Susan and Perrier for Chris. Susan explained to Chris that only in Houston in the entire world did they know how to make Margaritas properly.

"What's proper?" he asked.

"A slice of limon, not lime. Triple Sec, not Cointreau. Cheap tequila. Just a little salt on the glass, not a big enough goddam lick for a steer. Shake. No blender."

"You're making it sound too good," Chris said.

"Try one."

"No. I've retired."

"Since when?"

"Last night. I saw the error of my ways. Funny, though, when I was drinking, I didn't care what the drink tasted like. I didn't care about the brand. All I wanted was alcohol. If you didn't have good vodka, cheap vodka would do. Or Scotch. Or rye. Alcohol dishwater. Maybe you're in trouble when you stop tasting the drinks and just start downing them."

"Christ, now I'm feeling guilty," she said.

"It'll pass. Order up."

She glanced at the menu and decided quickly to have lobster tail. She looked at Chris as he was studying the menu. He really was a handsome man, she decided. He hadn't seemed so at first, but that was probably because he was so quiet and withdrawn and his face showed so little animation. Perhaps that was part of his CIA training. She didn't know any other spies, but she doubted if they were flamboyant in appearance and personality. Probably not if they wanted to live, she decided.

The thought gave her a small chill. Sitting across from this gentle, mild man and thinking about killing. Had he killed? If he had, had he done it with a smile? With a laugh? Was it possible that he laughed and smiled only when he was murdering someone?

Why not? Appearances could be deceiving. Chris Caldwell looked like the original nice guy. But she knew better. Justice Brooks had told her about him. It was a shame that he was what he was.

"Where are you?" She heard Caldwell's voice and realized he was speaking to her.

"Hmmmm?"

"I was just wondering where you were. You weren't here with me," he said.

"Just daydreaming. Did you ever kill anybody?"

"Yes. The last woman who asked me that question," he said. He quickly changed the subject to food.

She interrupted him and reached across the table to touch his hand. "I'm sorry. I don't know why I asked that."

"It's all right," he said. "With McBride going around spreading stories about me being the best thing since James Bond, it seems like a natural question, I guess. Actually, I was more of a messenger. I delivered things."

She decided immediately that she didn't believe him. The waiter came with their drinks, and Chris ordered dinner for them. Her lobster tail and a steak, very rare, for him. The waiter looked at him questioningly.

153

"Very rare," Chris repeated. "Juicy, blood running out, soaking everything in its path." When the waiter left, he told Susan, "I'm a dangerous man. To prime beef. All right, time for you to 'fess up and tell me the pitiful story of your life. All I know about you is that you're forty-three years old, you've had reconstructive surgery to make your figure a joy to behold, and you're independently wealthy."

"Close. Wealthy. Twenty-eight years old and skinny, and surgery won't help. I checked. And I'm glad I went to Wellesley and Hahvahd because now I can pahk a cah." She stuck her tongue out at him.

"Very pretty tongue," he said.

"Should I show you the rest of it?"

"This conversation is getting entirely too deep and serious," Chris said. "Let's stick to trivialities. How many times have you been married?"

"Nobody would ever have me."

"No one's ever had you?" he said. "Poor child. Tell me about Justice Brooks."

"I'm not sure I like that arrangement of comments," she said, her expression frosting over. "Are you implying again?"

"Nope. Innocent. I was just wondering how you got to work for him and how you got here. I've been out of the country for the last couple of years and I was just wondering about him. Is he going to be the next Chief Justice?"

"I hope so. And I think being from Texas will help him. The President could really use a Westerner, and how could he find a better one than Otto? I mean, a man who understands that the law is a tool to be used for the betterment of people's lives."

"Sold on him, aren't you?"

"Yes. I've been with him for three years now. I told you, he was a shirttail relative, and you're supposed to like relatives, not respect them. You know, seeing warts and things. But he doesn't have any warts."

"A paragon, eh?" Chris said lightly. "What did you quit for? Why did he send you down here to work on an SEC application?"

"He didn't. Well, not to work on the Griffin thing. He and I decided I need some real courtroom and law-office work. He asked Mr. McBride to hire me. He did, and when

154

I came down, the first thing he gave me to do was the SEC work on Griffin Oil."

Chris nodded, but he was puzzled. He was sure that McBride had told him that Justice Brooks had asked him to make sure the girl worked on the Griffin Oil application.

"Life's funny, isn't it? Your first job is with Gus Griffin. He and the judge are close, aren't they?"

"For years. Otto says that without Gus, he wouldn't have been anything but a country lawyer."

"Oh, that's right. That first Senate election," Chris said.

"Right. Griffin came in at the last minute with a lot of money. A hundred thousand, I think, and it probably swung the election. He gives the credit to Griffin."

"Can't blame him. Nothing's deader than yesterday's losing candidate," Chris said. "You still talk to the judge?"

"Once in a while by phone. He's coming down here tomorrow. Mr. McBride told me there's a party at the Griffin ranch. I'm invited."

"Me too."

"I know. Mr. McBride told me you'd probably take me there."

"I accept," Chris said. "How's the Margarita?"

"No better than the ones they make in Washington. You know, I get this idea that I'm being interrogated."

"I'm sorry. I was in a business that involved talking with people and finding out things. I was good at it, and I guess some habits are hard to break. Fact is, though, that I'm interested in you."

"At last you say something nice."

They were interrupted by their meal, and they ate mostly in silence. Chris was wondering about the girl. It was a lot of coincidences that she had been sent by Brooks to work in McBride's office and just happened to be assigned to Griffin's application. And that she talked to the judge on the telephone still. Was it possible that she had been sent to Houston to keep an eye on things and to keep the judge informed? But informed about what?

About the Red Moon? Whatever it was.

Susan had Sambucca after dinner. Chris tried another Perrier. She said, "Now it's my turn. You really liked Mr. Hirschfeld, didn't you?"

"He was my father-in-law. I loved the man."

"When did you meet him?"

"Law school. He was my professor in business law. He was Zhava's father."

"What was she like?" Susan asked.

Chris looked at her, startled by the question. How could he tell her about Zhava? How could he tell this charming, pleasant, liberated American woman about the beauty that he found and lost? How tell her about the large piece of him that had gone up in smoke with Zhava's life?

"She made all fields yellow in the morning sun," he said.

"I'm sorry," she said. "I know that means something to you. Something special."

"Yes."

"You must have been shocked by Mr. Hirschfeld's death."

"He was all I had left in the world. And then when I heard he was...he died..." Careful, Chris, he told himself. Too close.

"But what made you come here and take over that SEC job? You're not even a lawyer."

"I don't know. Just something to do with unfinished business," he said.

"You're still working for the CIA, aren't you?"

He was being pumped. Susan Millard, the sweet little thing, was pumping him. He decided to string the game along.

"My lips are sealed," he said with a smile.

"Now why would the CIA be interested in an oil company stock offering?" she asked.

"You'll have to wait to read all about it in my book."

"Do I get a chapter?"

"If you earn it."

"Right after the chapter about the Red Moon?" she said lightly.

"I guess so. If I can ever figure out what it's all about. You say Hirsch mentioned it to you?"

She nodded and sipped her Sambucca, carefully keeping her lips almost closed so that the coffee beans floating on the syrupy liqueur did not slip into her mouth.

"How? How'd he bring it up?"

"I don't remember," she said. "We were in his office, I

156

think. And he was telling me all the things we had to look for, and I think he said, 'And the Red Moon too.' And I said to him, 'What was that?' And he said something like it was just something he had heard about. But he didn't know what it was. What the hell is it, anyway?"

"I don't know. I just found it in a note that Hirsch wrote. Just the name. The Red Moon. Nothing else. I thought you'd know, working so closely with him."

"No," she said. Chris could tell she was being honest.

"Did you ever mention it to anybody?"

He could see her body tense slightly. She waited a beat too long before answering. "To whom? Mention what? It doesn't mean anything to me."

"Me neither." Suddenly he had an urge to get out of the restaurant. He signaled the waiter for the check. Susan made a production of reaching for her purse, and Chris feigned shock, and they traded quips before she allowed herself to be forced to accept the status of dinner guest.

They were silent during the short ride back to her apartment. At the front door of the building he paused as if to say goodnight, but she looked at him scornfully. "Haven't you got any manners? Aren't you going to see me to my door?"

"If you want," he said. But what he wanted was to call Yoel Tsurnick and talk to him.

Still, Tsurnick could wait a few minutes.

Susan nodded to the desk clerk, who waved to her and looked at Chris enviously. Susan held Caldwell's arm tightly in the elevator. She felt a steady glow building inside her body. I really want this man, she thought. And it's got nothing to do with Otto. I want him.

At the apartment door on the fourth floor, Chris paused again, ready to leave.

"Oh, come on in," she said, opening the door. "It's been such a nice night and I want to kiss you goodnight."

"Here will do," he said.

"And ruin my reputation in the building? Come on in. I'm not going to rape you."

He followed her in, and she turned on a small lamp on a hall table. In the living room, she put her purse and flowers on the coffee table in front of the couch.

"How do you like my apartment?" she asked, crossing

157

the room to turn on the radio to a program of quiet music.

"It's becoming to you," he said. He trailed her reluctantly into the living room.

"Sit down there," she said, pointing to the couch. "Would you like a drink?"

"I'd love one, but I won't have one." He sat down. Susan turned the lamp beside him to its lowest setting, then went back into the foyer to turn off the light there.

Back in the living room, she kicked off her shoes, knelt on the couch beside Chris, put one hand on his shoulder, and slowly lowered herself onto his lap. She looked down at his face with an amused smile, then lowered her lips onto his.

Chris put both his arms around her, pulled her gently toward him, and returned the kiss. Susan shivered at the feel of his hands on her back. The glow within her grew more insistent. She pressed her lips harder against his, then pulled away.

"Thank you for a wonderful evening," she said, close to his left ear. "You're a nice man, Chris, and now I'm going to try to make it a wonderful evening for you, too."

She lowered her mouth to his again, and this time her warm tongue slipped out to caress his lips. After a moment, his mouth opened. His hands tightened on her back; she felt a pressure rising against her bottom. She squirmed against him.

She lifted her head again and reached over to turn off the lamp. She removed Chris's hands from her back and placed them on her breasts. She gasped with pleasure as his fingers tightened convulsively, squeezing her hard nipples.

"I lied to you, Chris," she said in a husky whisper. "I am going to rape you."

CHAPTER EIGHT

Chris woke with a start, disoriented and confused. Where was he? Whose naked back was pressed against his?

Quick memories of the evening returned to him in a flood. He relaxed and found himself smiling as he listened to Susan Millard's faint ladylike snore, a delicate buzz.

Then he remembered Yoel Tsurnick. Chris lifted his head slightly to look at his wristwatch, propped on the bed table beside him. Its luminous hands told him it was five o'clock in the morning.

Quietly, moving softly, naked, he got up and went into the living room. He closed the bedroom door tightly behind him.

He dialed Tsurnick's number.

It rang four times. There was no immediate click of a tape-recorded message coming in.

Then Tsurnick's voice answered, his accent almost overwhelmed by his sleepiness.

"Yes? Who is it?"

"Chris Caldwell," he said softly.

"Are you all right?"

"Yes, I'm okay," Chris said softly.

"I got your message, but when you didn't call..."

"I know. I'm sorry. When can we get together?"

"Well, the rest of this night is ruined, chappy. How about now?"

"Okay. Better give me a half hour or so. I'll be waiting in my car in front of my apartment."

"Right." Tsurnick clicked off the telephone.

Chris turned around. Susan Millard, nude, smiling, stood in the doorway to the bedroom.

"Another woman? Already? Haven't you got any shame? Or limit, for that matter?"

159

"Sorry," Chris said lamely. "I remembered a call I had to make."

"Business, of course," she said with a smile.

"Of course," he agreed. How much had she heard? Had he said anything compromising? He racked his memory; he didn't think so. She was talking.

"What kind of business do you have at five A.M.?"

For a moment, Chris realized how ridiculous they might seem to anyone else. Two naked people, facing each other across ten feet of high-pile carpeting, the woman politely prying, the man dodging questions. To get his clothes in the bedroom behind her, he would have to answer her questions. Or move her some other way.

"What'd you say?" he said as he walked toward her, oddly unembarrassed although naked in front of this woman he hardly knew.

"I said, 'What kind of business?'" She was smiling still, but her tone was serious.

"Monkey business," Chris said. And he put his arms around her and squashed her mouth under his. He kissed her strongly, with passion, then grunted in her ear, "Enough talk. I've got something else in mind."

She purred with pleasure as Chris marched her back into the bedroom and the waiting bed.

Twelve minutes later, Chris left her lying contentedly in bed and dressed quickly. He bent over to kiss her and murmured in her ear, "See you."

"Yes, CIA man," she whispered.

Chris pecked a kiss on the tip of her nose, faked a punch at her chin, and left the bedroom.

Chris pulled up in front of Hirsch's garden apartment building and unlocked the passenger door. He glanced at his watch. He was five minutes late. He waited, lights out, motor running, for thirty seconds, and the door opened. Yoel Tsurnick, unshaven and still sleepy-eyed, slid into the passenger seat.

"Morning. What have you got?"

"I found Hirsch's notes," Chris said. He reached into his inside jacket pocket, pulled out the thin stack of papers, and handed them to the Israeli agent.

160

"Drive a little bit," Tsurnick said. Chris turned on the lights and began to drive aimlessly around the streets of his neighborhood.

"What's in them?" Tsurnick asked.

"Not much," Chris said. "A couple of words and phrases are marked. Red Moon. One hundred K. Four B. Brooks."

"Brooks?" asked Tsurnick.

"The only one I know that has anything to do with this is Supreme Court Justice Otto Brooks," Chris said. "He's a close friend of the Griffins'."

Tsurnick opened the glove compartment. Leaning forward, he looked at the papers in the glow of the map light. Chris glanced down and saw him staring at the paper on which Hirsch had doodled the four lines.

"That's all there is," Tsurnick said. He was unable to keep the disappointment out of his voice.

"I know. I thought maybe some of your people could go over them, find something there that I missed. Hirsch's handwriting was so bad I couldn't..."

"I know. Red Moon. A hundred thousand. Br—"

"What'd you say?" Chris asked.

"A hundred thousand. Isn't that what a hundred K means?" Tsurnick said.

"No. A hundred M is a hundred thousand."

"You've been on the beach too long. Nowadays it's a hundred K," Tsurnick said.

"That's interesting," Chris said.

"What is?"

"Twice now, Susan and McBride both have told me that when Brooks first ran for the Senate, Gus Griffin put up one hundred thousand dollars. It helped get him elected. Oh, and that's another thing."

"Yes?"

"I don't trust Susan Millard. I think she was sent here by Brooks to keep an eye on Hirsch and what he was doing with that application. She might be reporting back to him for all I know. I think she is. And Hirsch mentioned the Red Moon to her."

"He did?" Tsurnick could not conceal his interest in that.

"Yes. He was just rattling off a list of things to do, and
161

he dropped it into the list. I don't know why, but Hirsch didn't do things without a reason. Maybe it was to test her somehow."

"You think she might have told Brooks about it?" Tsurnick asked.

"I don't know. Yes. I think so," Chris said.

"I'll have to have our people look into this Susan Millard."

"And Otto Brooks," Chris reminded him.

"This is getting, as you people say, heavy," Tsurnick said. "A Supreme Court Justice." He stopped talking as a pair of headlights turned the corner behind them at high speed and pulled up on the tail of Caldwell's car. As Chris looked into the rearview mirror, a flashing police light began spinning on the dashboard of the trailing car.

"We've been made," Chris said as he pulled over to the curb.

"My name is David Benjamin," Tsurnick said. "I'm your house guest. We're coming home from a tavern and took a wrong turn looking for a diner."

"Right."

The car pulled into the curb behind them. In the side-view mirror, Chris could see a man get out of the car. He was wearing a civilian suit, but as he approached Caldwell's car, he pulled open his jacket and hooked it behind the holster on his right side.

Chris rolled down his window. As the man stepped closer, Caldwell recognized him. It was one of the detectives who had come to Hirsch's apartment on Sunday morning. Chris tried to remember his name.

"License, please," the red-mustached detective said.

"Badge, please," Chris said.

The policeman was wearing his broad, flat-brimmed hat, but even in the shadow that shrouded his face, Chris could see the man's eyes flash, as if in anger.

The policeman reached into his inside jacket pocket, pulled out a billfold, and flipped it open. He flicked on a flashlight he held in his hand and pointed it at the gold badge inside the wallet. Chris looked at the picture on the ID card next to the badge.

"Detective Albert Potter," Chris said aloud. "We've met before."

"License, please," the detective said stolidly, taking the billfold back and returning it to his pocket.

Chris took his license from his wallet and handed it to Potter, who stared at it long enough to memorize it.

"This says you live in Puerto Rico. What are you doing here?"

"You know I'm visiting in Houston," Chris said. "What did we do wrong?"

"Driving around this neighborhood at night. Just driving around like you're going noplace. Where are you going?"

"We were on our way home and we decided to stop for coffee. I must have taken a wrong turn."

Potter handed the license back to Chris and flashed his light in Tsurnick's face.

"Who are you?"

"My name's Benjamin," Tsurnick said, turning his voice into its most British. "I say, really, what is this all about?"

"Do you have identification?"

"My passport."

"Let me have it, please."

"Christopher, do we have to put up with this?"

Before Caldwell could speak, Detective Potter said, "We've gotten complaints about this car of yours wandering about the neighborhood. If you want to go to headquarters, maybe you can straighten it out down there. Or give me your identification and we can clear this up by ourselves."

With the light still in his face, Tsurnick shrugged and reached carefully into his inside jacket pocket. He handed his passport past Caldwell to the detective, who looked at it, at the picture, and again at Tsurnick.

"David Benjamin," he said.

"That's right," Tsurnick said.

The detective handed the passport back.

"I remember you, Mr. Caldwell," he said. "I thought you'd know your way around better by now."

"So did I until I took the wrong turn."

"If you're going to the Hirschfeld apartment, it's back two blocks and then left three."

"Thank you," Chris said. "Can we go?"

"Yeah, go ahead. Drive carefully."

163

Potter walked back to his car. Chris turned left into a driveway, backed out into the street, and drove back past the detective's car. The officer had the dome light on and was writing on a pad. He looked up as Chris passed. The car he sat in was a yellow Plymouth. Chris knew he had seen it before. When?

He remembered. Coming back from the boat shop, it had been one of the cars he had seen behind him.

He waited until they were half a block away before he said, "That's the car that followed me back from the lake."

"Are you sure?"

"Almost swearing sure."

"Did you notice how our detective was dressed?" Tsurnick asked.

"No."

"His shirt was buttoned incorrectly. Our Detective Potter dressed in rather a hurry. You were with Susan Millard tonight?"

"Yes."

"Talk to anyone else?"

"No."

"Did she know you were meeting me?"

"She knew I was meeting somebody. She heard me on the phone."

"Your Miss Millard has some strange friends."

They were back at Chris's apartment.

"You want to come up?"

"No," Tsurnick said. He handed back the pile of Hirsch's notes. "You make a copy of these yet?"

"No."

"Copy them today, then give me the originals. I'll meet you in that bar, Cochran's, at five o'clock."

"Okay."

Tsurnick stepped out of the car. Chris looked in both directions but saw no headlights anywhere. Tsurnick leaned back in through the open window.

"Christopher, be careful. I think we're getting close."

"You too," Caldwell said. Despite himself, he smiled. No one had called him Christopher since . . . since Hirsch.

"You're not carrying that gift I gave you, are you?" Tsurnick asked.

164

"No."

"Carry it." It was an order. "Five o'clock today. Do try to be on time."

Caldwell got to the office at nine o'clock. Celeste Thompson showed him where the Xerox machine was, and he made copies of the four pages of Hirschfeld's notes.

Back in his office, he put the copies in his pocket and the originals in a long white envelope, which he sealed. He stuffed the envelope in the back of his center desk drawer.

He got a fresh legal-size notepad from his secretary and put it into Hirsch's attaché case, then hurried down the hall to Susan Millard's office.

She was wearing a fresh white dress as he came in, and she looked up and smiled. He smiled back, but the question lingered: Had she handed him up only a few hours before?

Adam Griffin kept them waiting for ten minutes before having them shown into his office. Then he killed another five minutes with idle talk, waiting for Doyle Blaney to arrive.

"Sorry I'm late, Adam. Your father was on the phone with some more instructions about that party tonight." Blaney turned to Susan. "How are you, Susie? Looking nice today."

"Thank you," she said. Chris noticed she looked flustered and decided Blaney's calling her Susie was somehow offensive.

The woman introduced Blaney and Caldwell, and as Chris stood to shake the bigger man's hand, he felt an instant and strong dislike for Blaney. He wondered if it was a touch of jealousy, hearing Blaney greet Susan so familiarly, and decided that was stupid. Hell, he had slept with the woman the night before. What did he care what somebody else called her? But he did care. He cared about her feelings, and he didn't like the idea of Blaney stomping all over them.

Still, he would have disliked Blaney under any conditions. The bigger man's hand closed more tightly than necessary around his during the handshake, and Chris

165

thought he could see a trace of amusement on Blaney's face.

"Nice to meet you, Blaney," Chris said mildly.

"I hope this isn't going to take too long," Adam Griffin fretted.

"It shouldn't," Chris said. "It's mostly formalities." He quickly double-checked the information that had been on the brief press release prepared three years earlier when Adam had been appointed by his father, as the new president of Griffin Oil. Griffin made a change in the list of schools he had attended and added a new bank directorship to his list of affiliations.

Chris pulled the copy of Hirsch's notes from his attaché case and looked it over.

"These are some of Mr. Hirschfeld's notes. I just ran across them, but they're almost unreadable, so it's necessary to go through some of this again. For instance, he mentions three things: tax returns of the partners, lists of holdings, and early profit statements. Have you provided any of those things yet, Mr. Griffin?"

Griffin shrugged, and Blaney spoke up. "Mr. Hirschfeld asked me for those last week," he said. "I was preparing them when he died."

"Do you have them for us now?" Chris asked.

"I should have them by tonight," Blaney said.

"Good," said Caldwell. "There's one notation here that puzzles me. Something about a Red Moon. Do you know what that means?"

Adam Griffin looked blank, but from the corner of his eye, Chris saw Doyle Blaney lean forward intently.

"I don't know what you're talking about," Griffin told him in an annoyed tone of voice. "I told Hirschfeld that too. I never heard of any Red Moon."

Chris believed him. He had a feeling that Adam Griffin wouldn't know a red moon if it fell on him.

He stood up and put his notes away. "That's all we need, then, at this time. But we'll still have to talk to some of your other officers."

"You might as well start with Doyle here," Griffin said. "He's our new treasurer, and he can put you together with the rest of the staff."

"We can all go down to my office," Blaney said.

As they left Griffin's office, Adam called, "See you to-night, Doyle. Tell Dad that Annie and I will be a little late."

"Will do."

Walking down the short flight of steps to his office, Blaney took Susan's arm in a possessive manner and bent down to talk quietly in her ear. He paused outside his office door to allow Caldwell to enter first. As Susan followed behind him, Caldwell heard her give a startled squeak.

He turned and saw her face flushed and annoyed as she sat down. Blaney had a bland, innocent expression on his face, and Chris had an urge to punch the other man in the mouth.

Blaney fished in his top desk drawer and found a press release, only three days old, announcing his appointment as treasurer. "All that biography is up to date," he said as he handed it to Chris. He also gave Caldwell a list of the corporation's top staff members and offered to help set up any appointments he needed.

"Thank you," Chris said. "We'll be in touch if we need more. Do you know anything about this Red Moon business?"

Blaney met his eyes directly as he shook his head. "It's news to me. Are you sure that's what Mr. Hirschfeld was asking about? Maybe you just can't read his writing."

Caldwell pretended to consult the notes and shook his head. "No, it's Red Moon," he said.

"Let me see," Blaney suggested. "Maybe if I look it will ring a bell." He held out his hand.

"I'm afraid I couldn't do that," Chris said. "There might be something in there that's privileged. There's another notation that's puzzling, though. 'Four B.'"

"'Four B'? That's it?" asked Blaney.

"Yeah."

"Another blank. Sorry," said Blaney.

Susan and Caldwell waited for a few minutes while Blaney arranged appointments for them that afternoon with the company's executive vice-president and four operational vice-presidents.

"I'll look forward to seeing you tonight, Susie," Blaney called after them as they left. "Sorry I can't bring you to

167

the ranch, but maybe I can take you back home after-wards."

"That's all right, Doyle," she answered brightly. "I'll manage."

"And, Caldwell. If you find out what that Red Moon business is about, how about letting me know?"

"Sure thing," Chris said. He looked back at Blaney, who was smiling at him.

Chris stopped in the doorway. "By the way, Mr. Blaney, how'd you find out about Mr. Hirschfeld's death? Adam Griffin said you knew about it on Sunday."

"Yeah? I guess I read it in the paper."

"It wasn't in the paper," Caldwell said.

Blaney shrugged. "Oh, yeah, I remember. I heard it on the radio. The news."

"Oh. Okay. Thank you," Chris said. He was glad to see that Doyle Blaney was no longer smiling.

Doyle Blaney looked at the door as it closed behind Caldwell and Susan Millard, then walked to the small chest in the room and poured himself a drink.

That goddam Caldwell was just a little too smart for his own good, but let him dig. He could check forever and not be able to prove that the story of Hirschfeld's death wasn't on some radio program some time over the week-end.

But there was the damned Red Moon again. Blaney had heard it on the tape of Hirschfeld's interview with Adam Griffin. Then Hirschfeld had mentioned it when he talked to Gus Griffin in Gus's office. And Gus had mentioned it on the telephone to Kirchner.

And then Hirschfeld was dead.

What in the hell was the Red Moon?

Blaney tossed down the small glass of straight tequila and poured another. Things were getting a little too com-plicated, a little too sticky.

And then last night. There had been the call from Gus Griffin telling him to get his friend Detective Potter to keep an eye on Caldwell. Potter had followed Caldwell to Susan's and then to meet David Benjamin, a Brit with a current passport.

Potter had relayed the information to Blaney, who gave

it to Gus on the telephone. Gus had taken it down without a word of explanation.

Kirchner again? Was he behind it?

Probably.

And tonight, after Kirchner met with Gus, he was going to meet with Doyle Blaney. It was time for some answers. The danger in playing both sides against the middle was that sometimes one could get squeezed. Blaney wanted no squeeze plays used on him.

He threw down the second drink and decided it was time to get to the ranch to see how Sherry Griffin was messing up the party.

The owner of the small coffee shop recognized Gus Griffin immediately. With his black eyepatch, his suits festooned with white piping, and his hand-tooled boots, the old man was well known in Houston. But it took an extra few seconds for the owner to realize who the shorter, portly, white-haired man was who walked in behind Gus.

It was Otto Brooks of the United States Supreme Court, and maybe the next Chief Justice, if you could believe what the Houston papers said.

The owner spent so much time fawning over them, trying to get them more coffee, making sure the cream was fresh, seeing that they had enough sugar, that everything was all right, that the air-conditioning wasn't on too high, that finally Gus Griffin growled, "Get the hell out of here and leave us alone."

The owner looked hurt. He looked at Justice Brooks, who gave him a helpless we-both-know-he's-crazy-but-what-can-I-do-about-it look.

Finally, they were left alone in their corner booth, far from the door, sipping their coffee.

"Anything check out last night?" Brooks asked.

"Yeah. I checked it out. I don't know if it means anything yet," Griffin said noncommittally. "I got somebody looking into it. Tell me again about that Caldwell. Exactly what he said."

"There isn't much, Gus," the judge answered in a low voice. "I talked to the CIA director. He told me Caldwell resigned from the service three years ago. Personal reasons. Probably never got over the shock of having his wife and daughter killed in a bomb explosion. He had a good record. He could have stayed on if he wanted."

"Is he still working for them?"

"No. I couldn't come right out and ask. I had to keep it light and casual, but for what it's worth, he says Caldwell's on his own."

Griffin gnawed on a scarred knuckle of his right hand. "I don't like it."

Brooks shrugged. "Not much you can do about it. One funny thing, though. Caldwell never passed the bar exam anywhere as far as they know. He's not really a lawyer."

Griffin looked up quickly, his left eye wide with surprise. The eyebrow lifted above the patch over his right eye. Brooks looked away. He had always found the eyepatch a little grotesque; if it had been his accident, he would have gotten an artificial eye.

"You didn't mention that on the phone," Griffin said.

"I just remembered it."

"That opens up new avenues."

"Like?" asked Brooks.

"Like you can tell Eustace McBride that I don't like CIA people poking around in my affairs, and nobody else in this town would like it either if I told them about it. And I especially don't like guys who aren't qualified working on my company's projects. Tell him to get rid of this guy or at least get him away from Griffin Oil. That's not too much to ask."

Brooks looked around casually to make sure no one was within earshot, then leaned forward.

"Gus, think about that. You start making noises because some former CIA man is asking a few questions and you're going to start a lot of people looking closely at you. Do you want that?"

"The guy's unqualified. He's not a lawyer. Tell me, is that kosher? Should McBride have a non-lawyer working on this job?"

"Well, actually, he shouldn't," Brooks conceded. He sipped his coffee and leaned back, hooking his thumbs into the vest of his dark-brown suit, looking calm and confident and distinguished.

"Then you got every reason in the world to complain to McBride."

170

"How am I supposed to have found out about it?" Brooks asked.

"Your girl, what's her name, Susan. She could have told you."

Brooks nodded reluctantly. "She could have," he said. "The whole thing's funny, you know," he mused. "First, Hirschfeld is working on your application and then he dies. And now an ex-CIA man who was related to him." He paused. "You know, maybe that's got something to do with it. Maybe he's here because of the old man's death and not really working on your application. It's odd."

Griffin looked down at his coffee. "Talk to McBride. I'm paying him and I don't expect to be shot at from inside my own stockade. If this Caldwell is nosing around into something else, let him nose hungry, not on money McBride pays him that I pay McBride."

"All right. I'll talk to Eustace tonight."

"And I want you to talk to this Caldwell tonight too," Griffin said.

"About what?"

"About the Red Moon," Griffin said.

Susan waited until she and Chris had left the Griffin Oil building and were headed for a restaurant down the block. Halfway there, she squeezed his arm and demanded, "Isn't it about time you leveled with me?"

"Making demands already and we're not even engaged," Chris said.

"Don't get cute. What is all this about a Red Moon?"

"In the restaurant. I don't like to talk on the street," Chris said.

Susan sat by his side in the booth in the crowded luncheonette. This was his last chance, she thought, as he ordered for both of them. He was a good man and he hadn't done anything wrong yet, and if he would just tell her the truth, she could help him straighten it all out. But it started with his telling the truth.

The waitress left and she demanded, "All right. Red Moon. What is it?"

"I don't know," Caldwell said. "It was in Hirsch's notes."

"Chris, I'm sorry, but you're a liar. You asked me about the Red Moon *before* you found Hirsch's notes."

171

"He mentioned it to me on the telephone before he died," Chris said.

"I suppose he could have," Susan said. It was too bad, she thought, too bad that he couldn't be honest with her. Otto was right. He had said that Caldwell was blackmailing the Griffins just as the old lawyer had been. It didn't look as if anything was going to change that.

"Last night," Caldwell said, "when I left your apartment, I was stopped by the police. They were waiting for me. It's almost as if they knew I was coming."

"So?"

"I wonder how they knew I was coming."

"I wouldn't know. Maybe they keep an eye on all suspicious characters in Houston." She laughed.

"Yeah, maybe," Caldwell said. It wouldn't work, Chris realized. She belonged to the other side. Somehow she was mixed up in this with the Griffins and Brooks and Detective Potter and Doyle Blaney, and too deeply mixed up in it to try to recruit as an ally. He told himself to forget it.

"What was that shrill scream of agony when we went into Blaney's office?" he asked.

Without looking up, Susan said, "Blaney's a pincher. He bought me dinner one night and now he thinks he owns me."

"Does he?"

"Not him and not you. Not anybody."

Chris said nothing, but in his heart he hoped that that statement were true.

As they left the restaurant, Susan said, "Chris, I really like you. I wish you could level with me. Really."

He glanced at his watch. "We'd better hustle if we don't want to be late for our appointments."

The afternoon appointments with the Griffin Oil staff passed quickly. None of them had ever heard about the Red Moon, and Caldwell believed them.

But when he thought back to the morning's conversation with Doyle Blaney, he felt again the faint tingle in the back of his brain, a kind of teasing itch that told him his instincts were sending alarm signals. Blaney might not know much of anything about the Red Moon, but his interest in the subject was too strong and immediate to suit Caldwell. And he knew too much too soon about Hirsch's death.

Susan Millard might just be a pawn being moved about by someone, but Doyle Blaney was involved. Knowingly and willingly. Chris was sure.

He relayed his suspicions to Yoel Tsurnick late that afternoon, sitting at a rear table in Cochran's with the Israeli, where he gave him the originals of Hirsch's notes.

"That's all I got out of today," he said. "Other than Blaney, it was a washout. Blaney and Susan, that is. Of course, I haven't talked to Gus Griffin yet. That's tomorrow."

"Maybe that will be productive," Tsurnick said. "In the meantime, you know what you've done."

"Yes," Caldwell said.

"Yes, you do. By asking the question about the Red Moon, you've made yourself every bit as much of a target as Professor Hirschfeld."

"I want it that way."

"Be careful. We don't want to lose you too."

Caldwell smiled slowly. "I won't be as easy as Hirsch," he said quietly.

CHAPTER NINE

Ernest Wessel stripped off his robe and stepped into the bathtub. He sat down, then sank in the tub until the hot water reached almost to his ears. He rummaged around in the bottom of the tub for the bar of soap.

He hoped it would all soon be over and he could leave this cursed country, but he had his doubts that anything would be neat and quick. There were too many people involved.

There was Doyle Blaney. Driven by simple greed. Since the first day Wessel had met him and explained what he knew about the former FBI agent, Blaney had belonged to Wessel. He had transmitted Wessel's plan to Adam Griffin and had carried it out, bringing Griffin Oil to the public market. That had worked. And Blaney's tape recordings of the conversations in the Griffins' offices had been valuable.

But Americans could not wait. Greed translated into a desire for the quick score. Not the big score but the quick score. Something measurable right away. Blaney would have to be brought in deeper, harder, to ensure his continued loyalty in the service of his greed. It might soon be time to put a gun in Doyle Blaney's hand.

Gus Griffin was another matter. The old man was driven by fear. Fear of exposure. Fear of loss of face. He had almost panicked when the old lawyer had mentioned the Red Moon. It was the tape recording that had let Wessel know of it. Griffin already had brought Justice Brooks into the picture. It was a good idea, but in time, if Hirschfeld had kept digging around, Griffin would have panicked. He had been saved by Hirschfeld's death.

Wessel had not known how Hirschfeld had learned of the Red Moon, and the lawyer would not tell him. Even faced with his own death, he would not talk. The man was stubborn.

Wessel lathered his body, and as he soaped his genitals,

174

he thought of Susan Millard, but quickly put her out of mind. The girl was a dupe, used by Griffin and Brooks without her knowledge. One did not cry over a broken hammer. One bought a new hammer.

The detective. Potter. In the beginning, he had merely delivered tapes to Wessel from Blaney. But he was diligent and had the eyes of a killer. And he liked money. Wessel thought he would reach Detective Potter soon and talk to him directly.

It was annoying that the Israelis were involved, but he knew he should have expected it. They would always be after him, just as they had been after him for more than thirty-five years.

It was another reason to hurry, to get Griffin Oil safely in the hands of Iran so he could get out of this damned country and back to Iran, where there was safety. The Iranians were fools too, but they were fools who knew how to hate. And whom to hate.

So far, he had managed to keep everyone apart, no one knowing what any other was doing. He could not do that much longer, and soon he might have to bring them all together and explain what he had done and therefore what they were party to.

It would be an interesting meeting.

But that was for later.

For now, there was the Israeli, Yoel Tsurnick, to deal with.

And Christopher Caldwell.

CHAPTER TEN

Doyle Blaney carried the last case of beer into the pantry, started to enter the kitchen, then stepped hastily aside as Gloria, the young Mexican maid, bustled past carrying a large empty tureen. He wandered through the kitchen and into the dining room, where Sherry Griffin stood frowning at a list in her hand.

"How's it going?" he asked.

Sherry looked up distractedly. "You got the booze and wine and beer?"

"Yeah."

She sighed and brushed a lock of blond hair out of her eyes with the back of her hand.

"Stop worrying," Blaney said. "Everything'll be fine as long as we don't run out of booze. And we won't."

"I have to worry. Gus is mad enough at me these days as it is."

Blaney grinned crookedly. "You blame him?"

"Leave me alone," Sherry snapped angrily, turning her back on him. She walked into the long living room. Blaney, still grinning, followed her. As she passed the door to Gus's study, he reached out and caught her by the arm.

"Step in here for a minute," he said. "I want to talk to you, and I don't want anyone listening in."

Sherry wrenched her arm away. "We don't have anything to say to each other," she said.

Blaney sighed loudly with exaggerated patience. "You're not listening, Sherry. I didn't say we're going to talk to each other. I said I'm going to talk to you and you're going to listen. It's important."

"Go to hell, sneak."

"Do you want Gus to go to jail?" he asked.

Sherry's eyes widened. "What are you talking about?"

"If you'll listen instead of running your mouth off, I'll tell you," he said curtly and walked into the den.

176

She followed him slowly, pausing by the door.

"Close the door," he ordered.

She eyed him suspiciously but obeyed.

"That's better."

"All right, what are you talking about?" she asked.

"Do you know what Gus is up to these days?"

"He doesn't talk business with me. Even if he did, I wouldn't tell you."

"We're in the same boat. I don't know what's going on either. I don't want Gus doing anything that'll hurt all of us."

"You sound like you're trying to dance me around with your pipe dreams," Sherry said.

"Just listen. One of our guests tonight used to be a CIA man. For all I know he still is. And he's been asking some funny questions around the office."

"What kind of funny questions?"

"About Gus. I don't know if Gus is in trouble or not, but I don't like the CIA messing around. If Griffin Oil goes belly-up, we're all in trouble."

"Aaaah, you're talking nonsense. CIA. Gus in trouble. I don't believe it."

"If the company dies, your option's not worth anything. If Gus is mad enough to change his will and *he* dies, you're not worth anything. You willing to risk it?"

"Get to it," she said. "You've got something on your mind."

"This CIA man, his name is Chris Caldwell. He's with McBride's firm. I want you to be extra-friendly to him tonight."

"Yeah, swell. Gus'll love that. Me making a pass at a guest."

"You don't have to be obvious. Just be nice to the guy. Get him talking and pump him."

"I don't know. What does Gus think?"

"We can't tell him what we've been talking about, about him maybe being in trouble. But when he gets here, I'll suggest to him that he have you lean into Caldwell. You can take the suggestion from him if he goes along. All right?"

"Okay," she admitted grudgingly. "That's the only way I'll do it."

177

Blaney smiled confidently. "You think I'm trying to trick you, Sherry, get you in trouble with Gus. But you're wrong. I just want what's best for all of us."

"You're doing what's best for you, and I don't trust you a nickel's worth," she said sullenly.

"Sherry, someday you're going to know I'm your best friend."

"Someday horses'll fly."

"And when you do, you're going to pay me back."

"Fat chance," she said.

"You'll see." He stepped forward abruptly, wrapped his heavy arms around her, pulled her tight against himself, and lowered his mouth onto hers. She froze for a moment, then began struggling wildly, trying to twist her face away from the mouth that was crushed against hers. She tried to knee him, but he was too close, so she began kicking at his shins.

Blaney released her and stepped back, satisfied.

"Someday, Sherry, I'm going to have you. Not now, but when the time is right. And when that time comes, you're going to ask me for it."

"You bastard. I'm telling Gus."

"Go ahead. Think he'll believe his lying sell-out wife? Or his trusted assistant?"

She glared at him with a look of pure hatred, then turned and fled the room. Blaney strolled slowly after her, pleased with himself. He knew she wouldn't tell Gus. Even if Gus believed her, he would think that she had brought on the attack herself. Anyway, in her present position with Griffin she was too afraid to risk any further strains between them.

And the day would come. She was a physical woman, and while she might be on her best behavior now, the day would come when she would yield. And Blaney would make her beg for it.

Blaney glanced at his watch. Gus would be getting back to the ranch soon. He had things to do before then.

Blaney went quickly to his car, opened the trunk, and took out a small paper bag. He walked around the house, stood on the patio in back looking at the pool for a moment, then sauntered past the pool and through the fence to the

178

small shed that housed the pool's filtering system and supplies.

The overhanging corrugated-metal roof of the shed slanted down from front to back. Standing on his toes, he reached up and attached a tiny microphone to the roof with electrician's tape.

He slipped the microphone wire through a crack in the top of the shed's metal wall. Inside the shed, he hooked it up to a small tape recorder that he hid in the back of the shed, behind a large drum of filtering powder. The recorder had a fresh cassette in it. Blaney set it to be triggered by nearby sounds. Two men talking would activate the recorder, and Blaney could come back and retrieve the tape later.

He closed the door of the shed and walked back toward the house. He would convince Gus that Sherry should pay extra attention to Caldwell. And while she was attracting that damn spook's interest, Blaney would be making sure that the lovely Susan Millard was not feeling lonely and neglected. He heard Gus Griffin's car pull up. This promised to be an interesting evening.

Blaney found Griffin in the kitchen, testing the chili, complaining to Gloria that it wasn't hot enough.

"Boss, I've got to talk to you," Blaney said.

"What is it?"

Blaney nodded toward Gloria, and Griffin followed him into the living room.

"This Caldwell," Blaney said. "Do you suppose he's still working for the CIA?"

Griffin looked at him sharply. "Why would you think that?"

"He was asking some funny questions today."

"Like what?" Griffin asked.

"He asked Adam and me about a red moon. Does that mean anything to you?"

Blaney put the question innocently, but Griffin knew his assistant was watching him closely. He frowned. "A what?"

"A red moon."

Griffin shook his head. "Doesn't make any sense. Was he drunk?"

179

"No. He's a sharp guy, very smooth and professional. Knows his way around."

"He sounds crazy to me. Red Moon. What the hell is that?"

"I had an idea, but I don't know how you'll take it," Blaney said.

"Try me."

"I thought it wouldn't hurt if you told Sherry to pay a lot of attention to this Caldwell tonight. Maybe she can get some drinks in him and get him talking."

"You want her to go to bed with this guy?" Griffin said, eyeing him suspiciously.

"No. Come on, Gus, I wasn't suggesting that. Just play up to him a little bit."

Sherry passed through the living room on her way to the kitchen. "Hello, Gus," she said.

"Come here," Gus grunted. "We were just talking about you."

"Nothing bad, I hope."

"You can always hope," Gus said sourly. "One of our guests tonight, a guy named Chris Caldwell."

"Yeah?"

"We want to know what he's about. I want you to play up to him and see if you can learn anything."

"Whatever you want, Gus," Sherry said.

180

CHAPTER ELEVEN

A pair of Rolls-Royces, three Mercedes-Benzes, a half-dozen Cadillacs, and a pickup truck were parked along the twisting drive leading to Gus Griffin's sprawling ranch house when Chris and Susan arrived in her metallic-blue Porsche 914.

"I like the looks of this party already," Susan said, as she slid her car into a tiny space between two mammoth gas-guzzlers and hopped nimbly out from behind the wheel with a flash of long legs. Her apricot silk evening dress was slit well up both sides.

Beautiful, thought Chris as he watched her get out of the car. Beautiful but maybe treacherous.

They had driven out to the ranch making friendly small talk, as if they both realized that each had something in their life that was being kept from the other.

As they walked toward the front door, Chris cautioned: "Don't eat the chili. Mac says it'll curl your toenails."

"Nothing frightens a Wellesley girl," Susan said.

Her long imperious ring on the doorbell was answered by Gus Griffin himself, holding a tall drink in his hand. Caldwell was not prepared for this big bulky man with the patch over his right eye. What had he thought Gus Griffin looked like? He realized he had had no idea and had drawn no mental picture.

Griffin greeted him casually, then turned to Susan. "When Mac told me he had taken on a woman lawyer, I figured she was short and dumpy with a face like a wart hog. You're sure you're a lawyer?"

"Shore am," she drawled. Caldwell winked at her when Griffin turned to lead them inside.

"We don't do introductions here," Gus said. "We figure everybody knows everybody else. Even if you don't, make believe you do and they'll be so drunk they won't notice."

Doyle Blaney came up to Susan as soon as they reached the living room.

"You're the belle of this ball," he said, and pointed them toward the bar. Susan picked up a Tequila Sunrise from the black-jacketed houseboy while Chris had plain Perrier water. When they turned around, they were being rushed by Sherry Griffin, wearing a low-cut champagne-colored satin cocktail dress. She greeted Susan warmly but kept her eyes on Caldwell.

"Come on, I'll show you the house," Sherry said. "You can meet all these drunks later."

She linked her arms between Chris and Susan, guiding them from the high-ceilinged living room out toward the pool area in back. Chris could feel the swell of her large breast against the side of his arm.

There was a broad span of about forty feet of flagstone patio between the house and the pool.

"No pool lights," Chris said casually.

Sherry said, "You want them on?"

"No. I just guess that means this isn't going to be one of those parties where people push each other into the pool."

"Not with their clothes on anyway," Sherry said, turning toward Chris, pressing her bosom harder against his biceps.

An hour later, the party had filled out and Susan introduced Chris to Justice Otto Brooks. He certainly looked like a Supreme Court Justice, Chris thought. With his wavy white hair and sensitive face, he might have been sent over from Central Casting.

"Happy to meet you, Caldwell," Brooks said, as he took Chris's arm and steered him to an unoccupied corner of the living room. "I've been hearing about you. Mac's lucky to have someone with your experience working for him."

"Glad to meet you, sir," Chris said. Silently he damned Eustace McBride for apparently telling everyone in Houston about his pet spook. Chris might as well have tried sneaking into town at high noon wearing a black cloak and carrying a dagger in each hand. And one in his teeth, for luck.

"This law work must be quite a bit different from the work you're used to," the judge said.

"Quite a bit," Caldwell agreed, thinking wistfully of the

warm waters of the Caribbean and the beauty of the coral reefs. Susan excused herself to refill her glass. As soon as she had left, Brooks leaned closer and said, "Listen, son. If you need any assistance on what you're doing here in Houston, just call on me. We've got our faults, but not being patriotic isn't one of them."

"That's kind of you, judge. But all I'm doing in Houston is trying to help set up that Griffin stock offering."

The judge nodded as if he had been told an obvious lie but was too polite to disagree with it. "Certainly. Well, be sure to do a good job. Gus Griffin is a cantankerous old coot, but he's dear to my heart. He was our first client, myself and old Erasmus, Eustace's father. A little piddling one-man oil company. And look at this ranch. Times change."

"You've known Mr. Griffin a long time, then?" Chris said.

"Yup. My closest friend, I guess."

"Then maybe you can remember something I ran across that's been puzzling me. What has the Red Moon got to do with Griffin Oil?"

Brooks frowned and looked off into the distance, then a well-used smile spread across his face.

"The Red Moon," he repeated. "I haven't heard that name for thirty or forty years. Sure. That was Gus's first good well, down in Venezuela. Hit it just before the war. I remember his telling me it came in finally, one night just around midnight, and the oil was splashing up into the sky, and from where Gus was standing, the whole derrick and gusher were silhouetted against the moon. The moon was red that night. So he tagged it the Red Moon."

"Odd Adam Griffin didn't know."

"Adam wouldn't remember. By the time he was old enough, the well had just petered out. You need to know history, Chris, you've got to ask us people who are long in the tooth."

"Yes, sir," Chris agreed. Very convincing, he thought. The name of Griffin's first well. It was the way so many searches ended, not with a bang but with a boop. It might even be true, but he would have put a lot more faith in it if Brooks had not been so smooth. The man said he hadn't

183

heard the name for thirty or forty years. Chris couldn't buy that. He had no doubt that the judge had heard the name several times in the past couple of weeks from Susan Millard. And after the Justice had heard it, Benjamin Hirschfeld had been murdered.

Susan returned and handed Chris a glass of Perrier. She told Brooks there was someone he simply had to meet, and the gray-haired man smiled at Chris, the smile of a man forced reluctantly to do something against his will, and dutifully followed her off.

As the party began to thin out, Chris was standing alone near the sliding glass doors to the patio and Sherry caught up his arm again.

"Take a walk outside with me," she said. "All this smoke and old men's talk is giving me a headache."

"It is a little stuffy," he agreed politely, letting her lead him outside. All night long, he had been uncomfortably aware of her eyes upon him; it would be interesting to see what she had in mind for him.

Gus Griffin stood a short distance away, talking with another man. The man was younger than Gus but dressed like the oil man's clone, gabardine suit with piping, flowered shirt, and boots.

"Chris and I are going to walk around the grounds," Sherry called out.

Gus nodded disinterestedly. "Bring her back before midnight, boy. After that, I'll have to send a posse."

Before they could move away, Eustace McBride and Dolores came up. "Sherry, we're leaving," McBride said. "Dolores isn't feeling too well and wants to go to bed."

"Don't we all?" Sherry said with a giggle. Dolores McBride squeezed Chris's arm and smiled at him.

After the McBrides left, Sherry guided Chris to the end of the patio and onto a flagstone walk that led around the far side of the house. They stopped in the shadow of the house, looking at a cluster of various kinds of cactus, including a towering example of saguaro, standing almost eighteen feet high.

"Nice if you like cactus," Chris said.

"I like a lot of things better than cactus," Sherry said.

She took Chris's glass and set it down on a tree stump which had been smoothed and polished for use as a table.

"For instance," she said as she moved up against him. Chris put his arms around her. There was hardly anything else to do with them, other than holding them up in the air as if he were under arrest.

She released him and backed off. "Thank you," she said. "I needed that."

She took his hand again and continued walking with him down the flagstone walk.

"Beautiful home," he said, at a loss for anything else to say.

"Thank you. It's the kind of home I always used to see in Hollywood and always wanted."

"Were you an actress? You're certainly pretty enough."

"An actress but never a star, I'm afraid." She laughed, the kind of tinkly professional laugh that Chris expected an actress to have. "Just too much competition." She stopped again along the walk and turned to him, taking his left hand in both of hers. "What about you? I've heard you've lived the life of an adventurer. You must have stories to tell."

"Afraid not. I was with the government, but not much adventure. Really I was just a kind of glorified messenger. That's one reason I quit. It was too boring. I'm not allowed to talk about it, but even if I could, you wouldn't find it interesting, believe me."

I could tell you stories that would make you throw up in horror, he thought. Some of them make me want to throw up when I remember them. That's why I try not to remember them.

She squeezed his hand intimately. "I don't believe you, you know. I've always had an eye for those quiet, mysterious, dangerous men, and I can see you're one of them." She squeezed his hand again, and Chris uneasily returned the pressure, embarrassed to simply let his hand lie like a lump between hers.

"How do you like Texas?"

"I've been living in Puerto Rico," he said. "I like the islands better."

"I do too. This is nice, but it's lonely out here."

185

"There's always Gus," Chris said.

"Yes, there's Gus. But not always."

Otto Brooks caught up with McBride as the tall ambling lawyer was leaving the house with his wife.

"I want to talk to you a moment, Eustace," Brooks said.

"Sure. Dolores, get the car, will you?"

When the woman was out of earshot, Brooks said, "I've just heard something disquieting."

"Oh? What's that?"

"I've just been talking to your friend Caldwell. He's not an attorney."

"No, that's true."

"Do you think you should have him working on Gus's SEC matter, then? I mean, not even an attorney. How will that look for your firm?"

"If Chris does his usual good job, it'll look fine," McBride said casually. "Besides, Susan's a good lawyer. She'll keep an eye on him."

"You should think about replacing him," Brooks said, putting an arm around McBride's shoulders. "I'm just thinking of you and your father and the reputation of a firm that meant so much to me."

"I'm sure you are," McBride said.

Gus Griffin strolled nonchalantly around to the far side of the pool. He stood in the dark, looking toward the water, the patio, and the house beyond for a moment, with his hands stuffed into his pockets. When he was sure no one was watching him, he slipped through the gate in the split post fence and headed for the utility shed, twenty yards back, under a thick-based aspen.

Frederick Kirchner was there wearing dark clothing, standing in the shadows. It was the first time Griffin had seen him wearing anything but a white suit.

"It's crazy, you coming here," Griffin hissed.

"The path of true greed never runs smooth," Kirchner said in a hard, implacable voice. "We have a few problems."

"I've had nothing but problems since I met you."

"As ye sow, so shall ye reap," Kirchner said. "You created your own problems forty years ago."

"Yeah. You keep reminding me. What is it now?"

"The Israelis."

"What?"

"That man your friend Caldwell met last night is an Israeli agent."

"Now what in the hell are the Israelis doing in this? This is fucking Texas, not Tel Aviv."

"Everywhere they have a way of sticking their noses in where they are not wanted," Kirchner said. "But I had not thought the old man was connected with the Mossad."

"Old man? Mossad? What are you talking about?"

"The Mossad is the Israeli secret service. You know the old man."

Gus realized that Kirchner was talking about Hirschfeld.

"I thought we lucked up when that old bastard fell off the boat."

He realized Kirchner was staring at him.

"What's the matter?" Griffin said.

"You are not such a fool as to really believe that, are you?"

"What?"

"Mr. Hirschfeld did not fall off that boat. I threw him off and held him under until he drowned."

"Oh, no," Griffin said. "No. Don't tell me that. Murder?"

"Precisely. Do you think things are ever accomplished without having to remove some obstacles?"

"Obstacles? Dammit, man, we're talking about a human being."

Kirchner answered coldly, "You have not always been so squeamish about death."

Griffin looked hard at the man. In the bright moonlight, he could see that Kirchner was smiling at him, a smile without humor and without warmth.

"Brooks thinks that maybe Caldwell's looking into the old man's death," Griffin said.

"Let him look. Let the Israelis look. Let everybody look. If you keep your head, there will be nothing to see."

"All right. What do you want me to do?"

"Just stick to the story we have decided about the Red Moon. I will let you know what else needs to be done. Now go back to your party," he said curtly.

Without waiting for a reply, Kirchner turned and

187

walked straight away from the small toolshed, ducked lithely under a fence rail, and headed across a pasture. He must have parked his car on the dirt road on the far side of the pasture, Griffin realized.

When he stepped back through the gate into the pool area, Gus remembered to fumble with his fly as if just zipping himself up.

Murder. He had not counted on murder.

There was no one in the dining room except the maid, Gloria, busy, humming, transferring something from a pot to a large bowl on the table.

Susan took Judge Brooks to the far side of the room, where they stood in a corner, talking in whispers.

"What do you think?" she asked.

"He appears an affable young man," Brooks said. "But we both know what he is."

"I find it hard to believe, Otto," Susan said. "He really is a decent kind of man." She shrugged. "The idea that Mr. Hirschfeld was trying to squeeze money from Griffin Oil, and that now Chris is... it's hard to believe."

"I'm sorry, dear, but those are facts. Do you think I would have let you get involved, let myself get involved, if it weren't serious and it didn't concern my friends?"

"But why? How? You've never told me what they would have to blackmail the Griffins about."

"And it doesn't help you to know," Brooks said. He put his hand on the young woman's shoulder. "Susan," he said, "I hate this. I hate your being involved. But I didn't have any choice. I needed you to help me, but I don't want you any more involved than you have to be." He smiled at her and squeezed her shoulder in a fatherly manner. "You understand, don't you?"

"Yes, Otto. It's just... well, I was getting to like Chris," she said.

"Like him all you want. But just keep letting me know what he's up to. Together, we can stop this chicanery."

He recognized the sad look on Susan's face. "Who knows?" he said. "Maybe your young man is just an unwitting tool. If he is, I promise I'll make sure nothing happens to him. There doesn't have to be prosecution. But you mustn't let on that we're on to him."

"I think he already suspects me," Susan said.

Brooks smiled. "I'm sure you can convince him otherwise."

Sherry took Chris's hand and pulled him toward the house.

"Come on in here," she said.

She opened a door and led Chris inside. Carefully, Sherry closed the door behind her, then turned around, put a hand behind Caldwell's head, and pulled his face down to meet her lips. When Gus and Blaney had told her to be nice to this CIA man, she hadn't imagined that he would look like this. She had expected some surly, tight-lipped man with the look of a Republican Congressman. Instead, she had found this handsome, vulnerable young man, to whom she had spoken for the last forty-five minutes and found out exactly that he was a widower, lived in Puerto Rico, and occasionally taught skin diving.

She released his head and said, "I've wanted to do that all night. You didn't mind, did you?"

"Once I don't mind," Chris said. "More, it might get to be a habit."

"We won't let it," Sherry said. She reached behind her and flicked the light switch. Chris realized they were in Gus Griffin's private office.

The room was rectangular, bigger than most living rooms. The walls were paneled in deep-toned rosewood, and hunting trophies covered most of one wall. Gus's desk was at the far end of the room. Chris glanced quickly around, looking for file cabinets, but saw none. There were bookshelves and a bar, a couch, a few lamps, a coffee table, a large reclining chair and paintings on one wall.

There were four paintings, three small ones grouped together alongside a large landscape. The large painting showed a still pond, trailing away to a stand of trees. Slashing in across the painting from an angle came the first early rays of the rising sun. The scene was done in clumps of color that seemed almost to shimmer before Chris's eyes.

Sherry looked at Chris as he walked toward the painting. Gus had told her to play up to the young man, but nevertheless she was becoming nervous. She had spent an hour with Chris now and found out little more than his name. And it was not beyond Gus to jump all over her, as if talking to Caldwell had been her own idea. What she didn't need was Gus angry at her again. She wanted to get back to the party.

"Seen enough?" she asked.

"Just a moment," Chris said. He stood in front of the painting, then leaned forward to look closely. There. In the left-hand corner were the initials J.R.

"You like *that?*" Sherry asked. She had never liked the fuzzy painting, which always reminded her of an out-of-focus photograph.

"It's called *Morning at Giverny,*" Chris said. He reached out to touch the painting. The paint was real. And yet the original painting was supposed to have been lost to the world. Memories flooded his mind. He remembered Zhava, his Zhava, once showing him a photo of the same painting in an art book. The Nazis, she said, would have deserved condemnation if all they had done was to loot the world's art treasures and let some of them, like this one, vanish. Her soft, gentle voice had quivered with anger. The painting had been lost in the war, and yet here it was, in Houston. In Gus Griffin's house.

"You sound like it's something good," Sherry said, stepping up alongside Chris.

"It's a famous painting. Is it Gus's?"

"Yes. Let's go." She didn't want to talk about some dopey painting with a lot of paint splashes. She wanted to get back before Gus started to wonder why she was taking so long.

"Where'd he get it?" Chris asked.

"After the war, I think. Somebody got it for him in Europe, I think he said. Is it worth something?"

"Yes."

Leaving could wait a few moments, Sherry decided. "A lot?" she asked.

"Maybe a million dollars," Chris said. "Probably a lot more."

"Come on," Sherry said. She looked at the painting again. Who would pay anything for *that?* Maybe this Christopher Caldwell was a little loose.

Chris looked at the small paintings next to *Morning at*

190

Giverny. They were obviously original oils, but he did not recognize any of them. Zhava had tried to teach him to appreciate art, but his eye was lazy and his taste defective. Still, *Morning at Giverny* had meant something special to her, and so he had remembered it.

"Really?" Sherry said. "A million dollars?"

"At least," Chris said.

"Wow."

Chris was still looking at the landscape. Why would someone have this painting and then hide it in an office on a ranch outside Houston? Was it possible Griffin didn't know what he had? He couldn't. But the work belonged in a museum where millions could look at it and marvel at Jean Renelle's genius—not hang here where it served as a backdrop for chili bowls and Tequila Sunrises and cheating wives.

Chris had forgotten that Sherry was next to him for a moment, but then he felt her tug on his wrist.

"C'mon, Chris. We ought to get back. We'll be missed."

"I guess so," Chris said.

At the door, Sherry flipped off the light switch, but before opening the door, she reached up again and pulled Chris's head down toward hers and kissed him hard on the lips. Then she opened the door and led him outside.

Doyle Blaney was sitting in the front passenger's seat of Kirchner's car, waiting for the man to come back across the pasture. His mind was framing the questions he wanted answered. What the hell was the Rod Moon that everybody was so damned interested in? Why did he have to set Detective Potter on Caldwell? The order to do it had come from Gus, but he knew that it must have originated with Kirchner. It wasn't Gus's style to use intermediaries. If Gus had wanted to know whom Caldwell was meeting this morning, he would have gone after Caldwell himself, run Caldwell's car into a ditch, and shouted, "Who the hell's in there?"

Where was Kirchner? His meeting with Gus should have been over by now.

The passenger door was yanked open. Before Blaney could turn his head, he felt the cold point of a gun barrel pressed against his throat.

191

"It's me. Blaney," he said.

A hand roughly grabbed his hair and twisted his head around. Blaney found himself looking into Kirchner's cold gray eyes. The white-haired man shook his head, released his grip on Blaney, and took the gun away from his throat.

"Not very smart," he said. He slammed the door shut, walked around the back of the car, and got in on the driver's side.

"I didn't see you coming. I was looking for you," Blaney said.

"I have spent much of my life avoiding people. Well-trained people. What do you want?"

"I think we should talk."

"Then talk."

"I want to know what the Red Moon is. I want to know what the hell Caldwell is up to. I want to know what we're doing here. I want to know why I had to check out who was in Caldwell's car this morning. Yeah, I know it was your idea. I want to know why Gus can boss around a Supreme Court Justice."

"And knowing these things will enrich your life?" Kirchner said.

"Probably."

"They will not. What will enrich your life will be minding your own business. It will also lengthen it."

"This is my business," Blaney said.

"Not yet it isn't," Kirchner said. "Not until I tell you it is. I have told you I will make you president of Griffin Oil. I will. You have done good work for me, Blaney, and I have paid you good money. It would be a mistake to ruin this excellent relationship now. You do not need to know anything. Tacticians do not have to understand strategy."

"I'm not going on like this," Blaney said stubbornly. Suddenly the barrel of the gun was again stuck under his chin.

"You will listen to me," Kirchner hissed. Blaney could feel the man's warm breath against the side of his face. "I killed that old lawyer, and I will have no trouble with my conscience if I kill you too. You will do what you're told. Or your former superiors in the Federal Bureau of Investigation might find an interesting package of documents on their desk someday. Do you understand?"

Blaney gulped and said yes. Hirschfeld was murdered? He hadn't known.

Slowly the pistol barrel pulled away from his throat again. Blaney rubbed his neck and turned to Kirchner. The older man was smiling.

"Blaney, trust me. Everything will work out as we have planned."

"Do you mind my asking? Does Gus know I'm working for you?"

"No. Should he?"

"No," Blaney said.

"I don't think so either," said Kirchner. "Just keep sending me the tapes of what he and that fool son of his discuss."

"Okay. Can you tell me anything about Caldwell?" Blaney asked.

"Caldwell is dangerous."

"He's still with the CIA?"

"No. That is why he is dangerous," Kirchner said. "He is a free lance, but a trained free lance. However, I will take care of Mr. Caldwell."

The words "take care of" sounded ominous in Blaney's ears.

"Okay," he said quickly. "I better get back." He started to get out of the car but was restrained by Kirchner's hand on his arm.

"What car did Caldwell come in tonight?"

"He came with Susan Millard in her car. A blue Porsche. Why?"

"You will never get out of the habit of asking questions, will you?" Kirchner said.

He released Blaney's arm and pulled the door shut as the former FBI man got out. Blaney stood there, the car started, and Kirchner drove off.

CHAPTER TWELVE

Chris was standing by the pool when Susan found him. She was carrying her lightweight stole and her purse. Her mouth was tight.

"Are you ready to leave?" she asked.

"Let's go." He saw her look at his collar, and he felt his face flush. He had scrubbed Sherry's lipstick off his face in the bathroom, but there was nothing he could do about the red smudge on his collar.

As they left the house, without saying goodnight to anyone, Chris tried to take Susan's arm, but she jerked it away from him. He shrugged and followed her quietly to the car.

"I'll drive," he said.

"Why? I haven't had much to drink."

"And I've had nothing," he said. "Besides, if you drive in that mood, you're liable to push me out alongside the road." He tried a smile, but there was no response.

He held out his hand for the keys.

"Go to hell," she hissed. Her lower lip trembled, and he saw she was on the verge of tears. Now what in the hell was all that about?

"Anything the matter?" asked a voice from behind Chris. He turned and saw Doyle Blaney sauntering toward them. For the first time since he'd seen Blaney, the big man's hair was mussed.

"No problem, Doyle," Chris said easily. "Susan and I are just discussing who'll drive back."

"Lady's car. She wants to drive, let her drive," Blaney said. There was a faint, ugly edge to his voice, a hint of anticipation, and Chris realized that Blaney would like to show him up in front of Susan Millard.

Blaney smiled at Susan. "Or let Caldwell drive. I'll take you home."

"She'll go with me. And I'll drive," Chris said mildly, but he felt a tingle beginning to glow inside him.

"Susan?" Blaney said.

"You go to hell too," Susan answered. Blaney turned back to Chris.

"It looks like you've upset Susie," Blaney said. He stepped closer, squaring his shoulders slightly, and jabbed Chris in the chest with a thick finger. "You do what she tells you and stop arguing with her."

Caldwell slapped the hand away with the back of his own hand. "Don't, Blaney. Just don't."

He was going to be fighting Blaney in a moment, Chris realized, and a hot glow of pleasure swept over him. He didn't know if the man was drunk or just trying to show off in front of the woman, but he represented a convenient outlet for the anger that had been building up in him since receiving McBride's shocking phone call back in Puerto Rico. He *wanted* to hit somebody. Who it was didn't much matter.

Blaney stepped forward, put both hands on Chris's chest, and shoved him contemptuously against the Porsche. Chris bounced back with an overhand right that smashed against Blaney's unprotected nose, sending him staggering with a grunt of pain.

Susan stifled a shriek. "Stop it," she said shrilly.

Blancy put a hand to his nose, looked down in surprise and anger at the blood gushing out, then fixed his eyes on Caldwell.

"Okay, you son of a bitch."

Behind him, Caldwell could see people stepping out on the porch of the ranch house.

Blaney raised his fists and moved smoothly toward Chris, hunching over slightly and rocking his shoulders in small feints. Chris stood straight up, his fists at his shoulders, his forearms vertical. He took a short step toward the bigger man.

Blaney grinned confidently and whistled a left hand at Chris's face. The blow went over Chris's shoulder as Chris ducked low and stabbed with the stiffened fingers of his left hand deep into Blaney's solar plexus.

Blaney gasped, choked, and involuntarily clapped both hands to his stomach. Chris straightened, measured him coldly, then slashed down on the side of Blaney's neck with the hardened edge of his right hand.

195

The bigger man's eyes crossed, his knees buckled, and he slumped to the ground, still clutching his abdomen.

Chris bent over him. Blaney was still conscious, he saw, and was glaring at him helplessly as he fought to get air into his paralyzed lungs. He was making gagging sounds as he tried desperately to inhale.

"Stay there, Blaney," Chris said coldly. "Get up and I'll kill you."

He turned to look at Susan, who was standing wide-eyed, her hand pressed to her mouth. He held out his hand again.

"Give me the goddam keys and get in the car."

Behind him, people were walking from the house toward the driveway.

Susan stared at Blaney, then back at Chris. Her eyes narrowed. She slapped the keys in his palm so hard that it stung.

"Here. Take them, you…"

She stalked around to the passenger side of the car, wrenched the door open angrily, and flounced into the passenger seat. She slammed the door shut again and crossed her arms over her breasts and glared straight ahead.

Chris got into the car quietly. The evening had not been half bad. He had finally gotten someone to talk about the Red Moon, even if what he had been saying was probably a lie—or at least not the whole truth—and it had been fun knocking that big goon on his ass.

By the time they pulled off the small feeder road onto Route 59, heading back toward Houston, Chris had the feel of the peppy little racing car. On the highway, he settled down to driving instinctively, and glanced over at Susan. She was still glowering at the road ahead, chin high, arms still folded over her chest.

"I'm glad you had a nice time too," he said.

Her lips turned down scornfully, but she remained silent.

So much for humor. "Look," Chris said. "I'm sorry about what happened back there. But he picked the fight, not me. And I wasn't going to get pushed around."

She sniffed again and tightened her lips.

196

"Especially in front of you," he offered.

She turned and glared at him. "You've got your goddam nerve," she said. "You sit there with sweet old Sherry's lipstick all over your shirt and tell me you were fighting with Doyle because of me."

She snapped her head away from him. He said nothing, and her head snapped back.

"Just what did you two do?" she demanded.

"You'll have to be more specific than that," Chris said lightly. "What two?"

"You and Sherry, the *grande dame* of the barbecue pit," she snapped.

"The usual—she tried to rape me," he said.

"Did you let her?"

"I used my military training, wrestled her to the ground, and fought her off."

"You're very funny," Susan said. "Tell me, would you have mentioned this charming little interlude if I hadn't noticed you with her lipstick marks all over your shirt?"

"Probably not," Chris said. "I don't generally go around talking about other people. Another thing—the whole thing was so strange that I could hardly believe it myself."

There was another reason, he thought. It was none of Susan Millard's business what he did with Sherry Griffin.

They were silent again for a while. A truck roared past them on a downslope, rocking the small car with displaced air.

Susan glanced over at the speedometer. "Can't you drive a little faster? This is Texas."

Chris looked down. He was going a little over sixty miles an hour. Perversely, he slowed down to fifty-five miles. "I was speeding," he said.

Another truck gusted past them with a blast of sound.

"No one else seems to mind speeding," she said.

"But they're all in a hurry to get somewhere. Here I am, having a wonderfully pleasant time with a woman who's crazy about me, and I could just spend the rest of my life pooching along this highway at walking speed."

"Very funny," she said.

"What's going on between you and Blaney?" he asked.

She looked at him again, startled. "Why do you ask?"

197

"Come on, child. He didn't try to punch me out for no reason at all. He was showing off for you, and being pretty possessive about it too."

She made a face. "He came on pretty strong tonight," she said. "He kept trying to get me upstairs so he could show me the bedrooms. He seems to have some ideas about me that I don't have about him."

A large black sedan came up from behind and pulled almost past the Porsche, but the driver apparently changed his mind, and the car dropped back and slowed, quickly falling well behind. The lights of Houston glowed ahead.

"Listen, Chris," Susan said. "I'm sorry I'm bitchy. It's just that that damned Blaney was all over me and I kept looking around for you and you were off somewhere with Goldilocks. Forget last night. We don't have any locks on each other."

Chris did not answer. His eyes were on the rearview mirror, where the headlights of the black sedan were visible, leaping forward toward the tiny sports car at an ever-increasing velocity.

He flicked a look ahead. The sloping dirt shoulder on their right dropped into a drainage ditch. There was a car coming toward them from the opposite direction, but it was still far away. Chris pressed down on the accelerator and looked back to the mirror to see if the driver behind intended to pull out and pass them.

The car was coming straight at their rear end, and Chris realized suddenly that it was going to hit them.

"Well, say something," Susan said. "I don't know who's worse, Blaney with his pawing or you with your—"

She broke off her complaint as Caldwell abruptly swerved the Porsche sharply to the left, hitting the brakes and yanking back hard on the steering wheel as his left front tire bounced onto the far shoulder. For a moment, the two cars were side by side and Chris could see the shadowy outline of the other driver's face looking toward him.

It registered on Chris that the other driver was a big man, because he sat well up on the seat. In the reflected glow of headlights, his hair was light-colored. Blond. Or gray. Almost white.

Susan screamed as the sedan slowed and swerved to-

198

ward them. "Look out," Chris yelled, instinctively jamming the gas pedal.

The Porsche leaped forward like a frightened cat, but not quickly enough. The sedan's left front fender banged against the Porsche's right rear fender, and Chris suddenly found himself traveling sideways down the highway, the ditch on the right drawing threateningly closer.

He spun the wheel again, dimly hearing Susan's full-throated scream of terror. The Porsche clawed its way off the right shoulder, inches from the ditch, and spun to the left. Even as he wrestled the car back again, Chris could see from the corner of his eye that the sedan was still barreling straight at them. As he got control of the car again, straightening it out, the sedan thumped solidly against the rear of the Porsche, jolting it ahead. Susan screamed again.

Chris stomped on the accelerator and the Porsche began opening a gap between it and the sedan. Both cars were racing down the middle of the road toward the oncoming car, which slowed down and pulled onto the shoulder. Veering to the right, the two cars flashed past the third car, whose driver looked at them pop-eyed.

Caldwell hunched over the steering wheel and concentrated on opening up a sizable margin on the black sedan. A short distance ahead, he could see the major interstate leading into Houston. His speedometer showed over a hundred miles an hour.

"Slow down," Susan screamed. "You trying to kill us?"

"No. I'm trying to keep us alive."

He had enough of a lead now, and he tapped his brakes and slid onto the ramp leading off onto the main highway. Susan sat rigidly, her arm braced against the dashboard, as the tires of her car squealed their protest at the sharply curved downward ramp.

Chris downshifted and fed into the highway at a high but controllable speed. He slowed more and watched the ramp entrance behind him, but there was no sign of the black sedan. Apparently it had not chosen to follow them.

Susan sighed and took her hand away from the dashboard as Chris slowed down to legal speed.

"What the hell was that all about?" she said.

"Must have been a drunk driver," Chris said.

199

"Yeah. And the tooth fairy leaves money under your pillow," she snapped.

Chris shrugged.

"Oh, my poor car," she said. "And we could have been killed. Chris, I was afraid."

"So was I," he said, but he was lying. He had been too intent on surviving to be afraid, and then he had felt a surge of elation, almost joy, when he had realized the black sedan was trying to force them off the road.

What they had tried once, they would surely try again. Only next time, he would be ready. His fists tightened on the wheel as he thought of getting his hands on the man who had murdered Benjamin Hirschfeld.

Chris recalled his fleeting glimpse of the other car's driver—a big man with white hair—and was sure he knew who it was.

CHAPTER THIRTEEN

Susan Millard's fright was slowly changing to anger at the damage done to her expensive sports car. She insisted Chris take her to her door. He went inside and checked her apartment and found it empty.

"Do you want to stay?" she asked.

"No. Not tonight."

"Chris, I really want you to stay."

He shook his head. "You'll be all right here," he said, but he waited with her a few minutes until the young woman seemed again to be in control of herself. Then he kissed her lightly and left, walking back to his own car, which he had parked on the street near Susan's apartment.

Driving and looking for a phone, Chris was hit by a welter of feelings. Only a few hours before, he would have sworn that Susan Millard was part and parcel of the seemingly endless conspiracy that revolved around Hirsch's death.

But now he was not so sure. If Susan were part of it, would her cohorts have risked her life the way they had tonight? They must know that she and Chris were getting close to each other. Wouldn't tonight's murder attempt be enough to drive her into Chris's arms and he into her confidence?

But Susan had seemed totally confused and frightened by the night's events, and Chris began to think that maybe she knew no more about what was going on than he did.

He saw a brightly lighted telephone booth on a corner, pulled over to it, and dialed Tsurnick's number. The Israeli answered.

"We've got to talk," Chris said.

"What's up, laddie?"

"I think I met Ernest Wessel tonight."

Tsurnick whistled, then gave him the name of an all-night diner on Eleventh Street.

Tsurnick was sitting in a back booth looking toward

the door when Chris arrived. A cup of coffee was on the table in front of Chris's seat.

Quickly, Chris recited the events on the highway leading from Gus's ranch back to Houston. Tsurnick's big deformed hands clenched and unclenched on the table as he listened.

"It could have been Wessel," he said.

"If he's here in Houston as you suspect, who else?" Chris said.

Tsurnick nodded. "Who else would want to kill you? And it means you have been stepping on some toes."

"I guess," Chris said. "Judge Brooks told me tonight about the Red Moon."

"Yes?" Tsurnick said. His face came alive with interest.

"He said it was the name of Griffin's first well. In Venezuela back about the time of the start of the war. It came in at night and there was a red moon that night, and that's what Gus called it."

"Do you believe him?"

"I don't know," Chris said honestly. "It's a logical story. But he said he hadn't heard the words 'Red Moon' in thirty or forty years. I know that's a crock. I know Susan Millard has been feeding him information. Maybe it was the name of his well. But people don't get killed for finding out the names of oil wells. There's something more to it. Did you have any luck with Hirsch's notes?"

"We went through them very carefully," Tsurnick said. "There was nothing of importance there except what you saw. 'Red Moon, one hundred K, Brooks, four B.'"

"What the hell is so important about an old Venezuela well that it could get Hirsch murdered?" Chris snapped.

"If we knew that, we'd know everything," Tsurnick said.

"I hate this work," Chris said. "I had forgotten how much I hate it. How much I hate tracking things down and having nothing ever tie up. Every question you answer gives you two more questions, and the questions just go on and on until you get sick of them."

"You Americans," Tsurnick said. "You want it neat and tidy, total truth. And you want it right away." He shook his head. "But truth is never neat and tidy. It comes at you from all directions, when you least expect it, and its

202

shirttails are always hanging out. We are doing all right. We are answering a lot of questions as we go."

Chris looked disgusted. "Sure. Name two."

"We have some answers. Some stronger than others. But we know there is an Iranian plan to take over an American oil company. We know the Griffin Oil Company is involved. We know that Ernest Wessel is involved; he's been with the Iranians and now we're almost certain he is in Houston. The professor was working for us and looking into the Griffin matter. We had the name Red Moon. Hirsch started asking about it and then he was killed. You came to do the job in his place. You started asking questions about the Red Moon. Tonight, they tried to kill you. Probably Ernest Wessel himself. Last night, they had the police stop our car. That was to find out who I was."

"You think so?"

"When an American police officer stops a driver, does he usually ask the passengers for identification?" Tsurnick said. "Of course it was to find out who I was. Now the only person who knew that I was meeting you was Susan Millard. You said yourself that she has been pumping you. And she used to work for Otto Brooks. Brooks. The name on the professor's notes in the neat little boxes with Red Moon. Through it all, the question—the big question—is still: What is the Red Moon? That's the big question we haven't been able to answer up until now. Now, tonight, you got an answer. Maybe it's true and maybe it isn't. But we've got something, and now we just have to figure out how that piece goes in to complete the puzzle."

Chris swirled his spoon around in his coffee idly. "That cop who got your name last night. Detective Potter. You think that name went to Wessel?"

"Yes. And I think by now he knows who I really am and who I work for."

"I thought your people's security was better than that," Chris said.

"Money opens a lot of doors and a lot of mouths. There are as many Iranian spies in Israel as we have in Iran. Probably more. He knows who I am," Tsurnick said calmly. "Detective Potter, by the way, is a friend of Doyle Blaney's. They were in FBI training together, but Potter was washed out. When Blaney was assigned to the Houston FBI office, he got Potter named as the city police liaison with the FBI. Their association goes back."

"Blaney. That makes me feel better," Chris said.

"Why?"

"Because I punched him tonight." Quickly he recounted the scene outside Griffin's home. Tsurnick listened, nodding.

"Think for a moment, Chris. Do you think Blaney was trying to get Susan in his car?"

"I think he's just trying to get in Susan's pants is all," Chris said. "Wait. He did offer to drive her home, said I could go by myself."

"Give it some weight. On balance, what he said, does it strike you as a man who knew an attempt was going to be made to run that car off the road and he didn't want Susan in it?"

Chris thought for a few moments. "No. I don't think so. I'd like to think it so I'd have another reason for hating that bastard, but I don't think so. It was too casual and he dropped it too soon."

"All right," Tsurnick said. "Maybe he didn't know what Wessel had planned. If he did..."

"What?"

"It was possible Wessel was at the ranch tonight." He shook his head. "I should have thought of that possibility."

"Wessel? There? If I only had known," Chris said.

It was Tsurnick's turn to stare at his coffee.

"Somehow," he said without looking up, "all these people are tied up together. We just don't know how. We don't know which ones know what they're doing and which ones don't. But we'll find out. We know one thing. We have Wessel worried. He doesn't like to dirty his hands. He likes to use people and things, but tonight you flushed him into making a direct move on you himself. He's getting nervous." He looked up and smiled.

"There's something else," Chris said. "Tonight in Gus Griffin's study, I saw four paintings. Three of them I didn't know, but one of them I recognized. It's called *Morning at Giverny*. A famous French painting. My wife once told me it was taken by the Nazis, then lost in the war."

204

"So?"

"So what is it doing in Gus Griffin's study? How'd he get it?"

"I don't know," Tsurnick said. "I'll ask my people about it. Unfortunately, my specialty is Nazi history, not French art. But we have people who will know more than I."

"Find out what you can. I'm going to ask Griffin about it tomorrow."

"You're meeting him?"

"Yes, on the stock offering."

"Be careful, Chris." Tsurnick stood up. "I think we're getting very close. And if Wessel tried to get you tonight, he will more than likely try again. Are you carrying that weapon I gave you?"

"No, dammit."

"Wear it, as I told you to," Tsurnick said. "You have now been promoted to the rank of target. Where is your car parked?"

"Right in front."

"Wait a few minutes, pay the check, and leave. I'll follow you home, just to make sure that no one is following you. Be careful from here on."

The reassuring headlights of Tsurnick's car were in Caldwell's rearview mirror as he drove home. When he let himself into his apartment, he walked immediately into the living room and picked up the gun from under the chair cushion. He searched the apartment carefully, especially its closets. The apartment was empty.

Chris undressed and went right to bed. But he slept with the gun under the pillow next to his. He dreamed again. He dreamed of Zhava and Shoshana and the Nazi, Ernest Wessel. Somehow they were all jumbled up, the little red Fiat moving in and out, but the scenery was the scenic background of the painting, *Morning at Giverny*. And Hirsch's notes kept marching through his mind. Red Moon. 100K. Brooks. 4B.

The last guest left the Griffin ranch shortly before midnight. Gus had already gone to bed. Sherry stood with Blaney in the empty kitchen.

She smiled at his swollen nose.

205

"Looks like you stuck your nose where it didn't belong."

"Don't you worry about it. I'll take care of that bastard. Did you find out anything?"

"Sure. He used to work for the CIA and now he runs a diving school in Puerto Rico. He doesn't know anything about anything, except about art. He knows a lot about paintings. He's handsome, though. And I guess he's tougher than he looks."

"Bitch," Blaney growled. "I guess you liked your work tonight. Did you give him any?"

"Just a few nuzzles, Doyle. Just to keep him interested. If I had known he was going to punch the shit out of you, I would have done anything he asked."

Her laughter followed Blaney as he walked angrily from the house.

Before he went to his car, Blaney slipped around through the pasture to the equipment shed and carefully unhooked the microphone and retrieved the tape recorder. He rewound the tape and played it in the car while he was driving back to town.

The voices were indistinct, a little too far away from the microphone for perfect clarity, but he could recognize and understand them. Kirchner's soft chilling voice. Griffin's sharp-edged sound.

His stomach tumbled over as he heard Kirchner coldly refer to killing Hirschfeld. And now Israeli agents were involved. And the Red Moon again.

Blaney pressed his lips together tightly as the tape ran out. What the hell have you gotten yourself into? he asked himself. Just who *was* Frederick Kirchner? Why was Hirschfeld murdered? His mind went back to the earlier events of the evening, and he swore under his breath. What was Caldwell doing nosing around their operation? He had a lot of questions and very few answers, but he knew one thing perfectly well: If Kirchner wanted a volunteer to punch that Caldwell's ticket, he would not have to look very far.

When Chris arrived at the office in the morning, Susan was waiting for him near his secretary's desk. She followed him into his office.

"I've been thinking about it all night," she said, after

206

the door closed behind them. "I didn't have any right to be bitchy with you. Make it up to you?"

"Sure. Sometime. And you had a right to be bitchy. Somebody tried to kill us. I wasn't exactly a white knight myself."

He watched her face carefully for a reaction, but she simply shook her head. "Who would do that?" she asked. "I talked to Otto about it this morning and he said we probably had too much to drink. It must have been a drunk driver, he said."

"And you believe him?" Chris said.

"Well, I guess so."

"How much did you drink?" he asked.

"I don't know. A couple of highballs, I guess."

"And I didn't have any. I don't think we were drunk."

"Well, that other driver certainly was."

He saw that she was looking at him expectantly, as if for confirmation, and he shook his head. She wasn't part of any plot. She was just a patsy, and last night they had tried to kill him and did not even care if she was killed too. She was a dupe. And an expendable one. For a split second, he thought of telling her that, but he decided not to. Her capacity for fooling herself seemed limitless, when it came to Justice Brooks.

"Yeah, maybe he was," Chris said.

"Otto said he finally cleared up your Red Moon mystery for you," she said brightly.

"Now I've been told what it is," Chris said. "I just still don't know what it means."

"I don't understand, Chris. What do you mean?"

He looked at her and answered honestly. "I don't know," he said.

Chris and Susan were at Gus Griffin's office at 10:25. He kept them waiting less than two minutes before coming out himself to escort them inside.

Chris noticed the boar's head on the wall and walked over to look up at it.

"That's the bastard that got my eye," Gus said. "Sorry, Miss Millard. Got him in Tennessee."

"Not what I expected to see in your office," Chris said.

"No," Griffin said. "I guess every damned office in this

city has those stupid cattle horns on the wall. They're not for me."

"No," Chris said. "I meant artwork on the walls. Last night, Mrs. Griffin was showing us around the ranch. I saw those paintings in your office. Very beautiful. And valuable."

"That's what Sherry said. That you said the big one was really something good. I don't know. It might even be a fake for all I know. Some guy sold them to me in Europe in the '40s. Old oilman down on his luck. I kinda liked them. He was trying to tell me they was valuable too, but I figured that was just talk. Anyway, I paid him more than I thought they were worth. You know, nobody likes a handout, but he needed some help and it was the only way I could think to give it to him, without making it look like charity."

"That big painting might be worth a million dollars or more," Chris said. He noticed Susan looking at him, startled.

"Hey, you an art expert or something?" Griffin asked.

"I know a little bit about it," Chris said. "How'd you get them back into the country?"

"Listen, if they're worth something, that means I beat the customs people out of duties, right?"

"Probably."

"Then I better not tell you anything or you'll put it in your files and it'll mess up our application."

"I don't think the SEC will want to know about any artwork you own," Chris said.

"All right. If that's a promise. I left them over in Europe with somebody I knew. He shipped them back on a tanker a couple of months later, and I picked them up when they slipped into Houston. That answer your question?"

"Yes, sir. Sure does," Chris said. And why, he thought, if you thought the paintings weren't worth anything, did you bother to have them smuggled into America? But instead he just smiled and said, "We ought to get to work."

"Yeah, I guess so. I've got to meet some bankers pretty soon." He looked at Caldwell appraisingly, as if measuring him. "They must teach you CIA fellers a lot. Artwork. How to take care of yourself in a fight."

Chris colored and looked toward Susan. "I'm sorry about

208

that, Mr. Griffin. Just two men blowing off steam."

"Over a pretty lady," Gus said. "Can't say I blame either of you. Especially you. Blaney can get kind of pushy."

The interview went quickly and produced no startling revelations. Gus had started in the oil business in late 1939, in a corner of Venezuela far away from the major oilfields near Lake Maracaibo. He and his wife had moved to Venezuela to manage the well.

"Little pissant thing," he said. "Didn't do more than four barrels or so a day, and of course the government got all the oil, you know, the war, and so I didn't make any real money off it. But we saved a few bucks. Well went dry after the war and Venezuela started scooping up fifty percent of everything I made, so I came back here and lucked out. Dug a lot of holes and found a lot of oil."

"That first well, that was the Red Moon?" Chris said.

Gus's face brightened. "Yeah, that's right. That's what we called it. How'd you know that?"

"Mr. Hirschfeld's notes mentioned it. And last night, Judge Brooks told me about it."

"Yeah, that was our well. Our first." Gus looked off into space as if he were going to ramble on but then checked himself, looked at his watch, and said, "How we doing? I'm getting close to being backed up."

Chris looked at Susan. "We're done, I think. Unless Susan..."

"No, I don't think so," Susan said. They stood, and Griffin thanked them for coming to his party.

"Sorry we couldn't stay later," Susan said, "but I made the mistake of tasting your chili. I had to go home to pack my stomach in ice."

"It'll do that to you," Griffin said. He walked them to the door. "Take care of yourself," he said lightly to both of them, but he was looking at Chris when he said it.

It was one of those rare, balmy summer days in Houston when the heat is muted, and Chris and Susan walked the few blocks back to their office.

They did not speak much, each locked in private thoughts.

There had to be more to the Red Moon than that, Chris thought. More than a nickname for an old well. A man

209

had been killed over it and another murder attempted. Why? Because of the name of a well? More than that. And what about Gus Griffin's casual disregard of millions of dollars' worth of art on the walls of his study where no one was likely to see it? That didn't work either. Somewhere, somehow, Chris was missing something. Tsurnick had called it a jigsaw puzzle, but you didn't have to wait for the last piece of the puzzle to solve a jigsaw puzzle. You started with what you had. Chris had a lot of pieces on the table in front of him, but he seemed not to be able to find an edge or a corner to start assembling it.

For her part, Susan Millard was wondering just what kind of man Chris Caldwell was. She had been told by Otto Brooks that Caldwell was, as Hirschfeld had been, trying to dig out dirt on Gus Griffin, and then using the threat of it to force him to make payments in order for the SEC application to be approved. Maybe Eustace McBride was behind it. But why hadn't Griffin just dropped the McBride law firm? Wouldn't that have made more sense? And now Mr. Hirschfeld was dead, that nice old man who, she still felt, was no thief or chiseler. Chris claimed that the accident the night before hadn't been an accident at all, but an attempt to kill them. Why? Was Gus Griffin so worried that he would kill casually? Did Otto Brooks know about that? Every time she tried to talk to Brooks, he sloughed off her questions. Did he approve, she asked herself, an attempt to kill Caldwell that might have killed her too? It wasn't possible. She had known Otto Brooks too well for too long. But he had been very quick to dismiss last night's incident as a drunk driver and to suggest that she and Chris had had too much to drink. But that wasn't so; she had drunk little and Chris nothing, and that other driver wasn't drunk. He had intentionally tried to force them into an accident. Maybe even kill them.

Caldwell looked over to see her glancing at him.

"Do we both like it a million miles away?" he asked.

"Hmmmm?"

"'Cause that's where we both are. A million miles away."

"Sorry, Chris. I just can't get last night off my mind."

"Forget it. Stay away from me and nothing bad'll happen to you," he said.

"Who is it, Chris? And what is it? You can't even walk down the street anymore without your eyes going in all directions, looking to see who's near us."

"Force of habit, Susan," he said.

"Who is it, Chris? Who? And why?"

"It doesn't really concern you," he said.

After a pause, he said, "I'm looking for someone, Susan, and he's always a step ahead of me, almost as if somebody is tipping him off to what I'm doing."

He looked at her carefully and saw a hint of redness appear on her cheeks. And, of course, you're doing the tipping, he thought. And you probably don't even know it.

"But you can't tell me who you're looking for. Or why," she said.

"It's better for your health that I don't. Let's just drop it. Anyway, I suspect we've got just about everything we need for the Griffin SEC application. Our work together's almost done."

"And that's it? Our work's done and we're done?"

"No. But we won't be involved in the same things, and what I'm looking for won't be involving you anymore."

"You think Mr. Hirschfeld was killed, don't you?" Susan asked, realizing suddenly that she was beginning to suspect that very thing.

"I'll pretend you didn't ask that," Chris said.

Susan stopped in the middle of the sidewalk and grabbed his arm. People pushed by them on both sides.

"Tell me, Chris. Tell me. You think he was killed?"

"All right," Chris said, "I'll tell you. I don't think he was murdered. I *know* he was murdered. I know whoever did it has something to do with Griffin Oil. I'm looking for him and he's looking for me and last night he almost got me. I'm telling you more than I should, Susan, but I'm telling you for your own good. Whoever's involved, last night they would gladly have killed you just to get me. If you think these people are friends of yours, you're wrong. You're a piece of meat. Hirsch was a piece of meat. I'm a piece of meat. Satisfied?"

She looked up at him, her face reflecting indecision, as if uncertain whether to show anger or shock. Sadness came instead.

She put both hands on his arm, oblivious of the noon-

211

time crush of people buffeting them on the busy street.

"Chris, I'm sorry," she said. "Really sorry."

"Sorry about what?" he asked. "Sorry that that's what happened? Or sorry that I'm so delusional I think that's what happened?"

Her face colored again and he nodded curtly, took her hand in his, and began walking along the street. She had chosen her side, he thought, and it was *their* side. The side of Hirsch's killers. From now on, she was the enemy.

"You want lunch?" she said.

"I think not," Chris said.

"How about dinner tonight?" Susan asked. "I'll even cook."

"I think not," Chris said.

Later that afternoon, Eustace McBride put his head in the door of Chris's office.

"How's it going, champ?" he asked.

"Come on in."

McBride closed the door behind him as he entered the office, Chris noted. Usually Mac conducted business at the top of his voice and didn't care who heard it.

"What's with the Griffin application?" McBride asked.

"We've got all the data. Susan's going to write it all up."

"That's good. Give it that proper liberal flavor. A growing company concerned with the environment and the rights of little people. It'll make Gus Griffin puke, but it'll make it easier for me to walk it through Washington."

"She's not that bad," Chris said. "In fact, she's a good lawyer and she's got a good brain."

"Yeah, but how's her nookie?"

"You're disgusting, Mac. Did you come in here to swap tales of conquests?"

"No. I was wondering, did you talk to Brooks last night?"

"Yes. He was very pleasant. And I nodded and smiled a lot and agreed with everything, except when he started hinting about my still being a CIA man and offering to give me any help I'd need here in Houston."

McBride shook his head. "I don't get it. When he collared me later, he was trying to get me to get you off the

212

Griffin matter. Bad for the firm, your not being a lawyer and all. So what's that all about?"

"It proves that Brooks is up to something. It also proves that Susan is a pipeline to him, because except for you, I don't think anyone but her knew that I never took the bar exam."

"I'll keep it in mind," McBride said. "Mr. Chiefo Supremo Justice-o leaned on me pretty hard."

"Don't worry, Mac. I'm almost done here."

"You find out what you wanted?"

Chris thought for a moment about telling McBride what he had learned and what had happened last night, but he decided not to. There was no point in it. The less involved McBride was, the better off he would probably be. But he yearned to talk to a friend.

"No. But I'm going to be looking elsewhere, I think," Chris said.

"No clue? You still think Hirsch was killed?"

"I know he was killed. And I've got some leads and I think I know who did it, and telling you anything more than that isn't doing you a favor."

McBride waited for him to say more, but when Chris didn't, McBride sighed, unwound himself from the chair, and stood up. "Do what you have to do," he said. "But if I can be of any help, holler."

"I know," Chris said. "I know you're there if I need you, Mac."

CHAPTER FOURTEEN

When Chris entered his apartment, he saw a slip of pink paper inside the door. It was a post-office notice of attempt to deliver mail. It said he could pick the mail up at the branch post office after three o'clock the next day.

Who would be writing him? Caldwell wondered. And at Hirsch's address?

He tossed the notice onto the coffee table and went into the bathroom to shower. Later he would check in with Yoel Tsurnick.

Chris had just stepped out of the shower when the telephone rang. He slapped at himself with a towel and ran to get the phone in the living room.

Susan Millard's voice said, "Hi. What are you doing?"

"Standing here naked, dripping on my rug," he said.

"Sounds tempting," she said.

"Some women have been known to pass by without a sideward glance," he said.

"None that you've met in Houston," Susan said, then added quickly, "Listen, Chris. I'm just not satisfied with today. I don't want things between us to end just like that."

"I'm sorry, Susan."

"I was going to drag you over here and make you hold still for dinner while we talked," she said. "But I've just heard from Otto and something came up. I have to help him tonight."

"Do what?" Chris asked.

"We have to go out of town for a couple of days."

"Where are you going?"

"Puerto Rico. But I'm not supposed to tell anyone that. Because of reporters and all."

What the hell business did Justice Brooks have in Puerto Rico? Chris wondered. So he asked her that question.

"I don't know," she said. "He said it was important, though."

"Okay," Chris said. "Where are you staying?"

"The Caribe Hilton. Let's get together when I get back."

"Sure," Chris said.

As he dialed Tsurnick's number, Chris tried to sort out his feelings toward Susan. Under any other circumstances, he could have liked her without any reservations. But even though she might not know it, she was one of the enemy. Somehow, through some twisted set of connections, she was working for Ernest Wessel, and she had continued to work for him even though he had tried to kill her last night just because she happened to be with him. Chris would use her as he had to. He had told her at noon that he knew someone had killed Hirsch, just because he knew she would carry that message along and it would eventually reach Wessel. The Nazi now knew that Caldwell was dangerous to him and his plans. He would have to move soon.

There was only the tape recording of Tsurnick's voice on the phone. Chris decided he would call later and did not leave a message.

After dressing in jeans and a boatneck shirt, he went into the kitchen and found a can of soup. He heated it and brought it into the living room to eat.

Again wondering why anyone would be sending him mail at Hirsch's address, he picked up the pink postal notice and looked at it again casually. In the box marked for the identity of the letter carrier, there were two initials. Y.T.

Yoel Tsurnick.

Chris looked at the paper again for a long moment, turned it over, and held it to the light. What was Yoel trying to tell him?

Of course.

He went downstairs to the lobby and checked the mailbox for his apartment. There was an envelope inside. It was almost the first time he had looked into the mailbox since he had moved into Hirsch's apartment.

Chris got the mailbox key from the superintendent and took out the envelope. It bore no address or return address.

He carried it upstairs and locked the door behind him before opening it.

It was a handwritten note, covering one side of a piece of unlined paper, in a precise neat writing that seemed too tiny to belong to a man as large as Tsurnick.

But it was signed "Yoel." He sat down to read it.

Dear Christopher,

I tried to reach you but you were at G's office and I did not wish to call you there. Something has come up involving the R.M. that makes it necessary for me to go to Puerto Rico. I think we are closing fast. I expect to meet some of our more oily and white-haired friends there within the next 24 hours.

The piece of art we discussed has an interesting history. It was taken from Paris when it fell and moved to Goering's mansion at Karinhall. But after the war, it was gone. No one knew where. Goering said it had been taken from him. (By white-hair?) No trace of it has ever been found. My people say it was probably sold by Nazis to a collector to raise money for the war. Maybe I will have the opportunity to ask E.W. about this. I certainly hope so.

I will be at El Convento. I hope to finish my business in a short time and be back. Take care of yourself. The professor always worried about your diving too deep; soon, maybe, we will all be able to swim in shallow water, in sunlight, with the spirits of our dead at rest at last.

Meanwhile, don't forget the supplies I lent you. Use them wisely and on the slightest provocation.

Yoel

Chris stood, looking at the note in his hands. Yoel should know that Brooks was on his way to Puerto Rico too.

Caldwell got the long-distance operator and told her to get him the El Convento Hotel in San Juan.

When the hotel operator answered, Chris said, "Do you have a Mr....er, David Benjamin registered?"

There was a pause while the operator checked the room records.

216

"Yes sir. Should I ring?"

"Please."

After a few seconds, there was a metallic buzz as the room phone rang. It rang six times before the operator came back on the line.

"Benjamin does not answer."

"I'd like to leave him a message. I'm calling long distance."

"Yes sir. I'll take the message."

"Write this down, please. 'Brooks on way to P.R.' Sign it 'C.C.'"

"Okay."

"Would you read it back please?"

"Sure. 'Books on way to C.R. Sign C.'"

"No, no. It's not 'books.' It's 'Brooks.' With an R. B-R-O-O-K-S. On way to P.R. As in Puerto Rico."

"Oh, I got it."

"And sign it 'C.C.' Not just 'C.'"

"Okay, sir. I got it."

"Read it back, please."

"Okay. 'Brooks on way to P.R. Signed C.'"

Chris sighed. It was close enough. "All right," he said. "Thank you very much."

And then, because he didn't know what else to do but because he was sure he should do something, Chris decided he would go to San Juan himself.

He thought for a moment, then pulled his suitcase from the bedroom closet and filled it with an armful of clothes from his dresser drawer. Taking Yoel's gun from under the chair cushion, he unloaded it and slipped the gun into one sweat sock and the six bullets into another, then wrapped them in a sweatshirt and put them into the center of the pile of clothes in the suitcase. He had more room in the luggage than clean clothes, so he stuffed folded newspaper around the edges until the suitcase was bulging full and he was sure the gun wouldn't slip around.

He called the airport and found there would be another plane to Puerto Rico in an hour.

If he hurried, he could make it.

Yoel Tsurnick had gone to an early dinner at the Flamenco Restaurant, four downhill blocks along Calle Fortaleza from the El Convento Hotel. He loved Puerto Rico, and particularly old San Juan. It reminded him of a Latin Jerusalem. History was in every building, in every street cobblestone.

When his day came and he left his grisly business, he often told himself, he would spend his retirement days in the writing of history. It would be an excuse to travel, the kind of travel one could enjoy without always looking over his shoulder.

And in his next thought, he always asked himself whom he was kidding. No one left his business except feet-first. He could leave his business with a clear conscience only when the enemies of Israel were no more. That had not happened in four thousand years. He did not expect it truly to happen in his lifetime. It had not happened for poor Benjamin Hirschfeld, who had survived the death camp and made a new life in America only to be called again by Israel and to die.

Tsurnick hoped, though, that Chris Caldwell could escape. He had no stake in finding Nazis on the run. With luck, Tsurnick could see that justice was done to the killer of Hirschfeld and Caldwell could go back to his life and try to pick up the pieces again.

Perhaps.

The Flamenco was a small dining room with twelve tables, each with four chairs. In the right rear corner of the room was a small service bar, presided over by a fussy short man in his early fifties with a thin mustache. Only four other diners, two couples, were in the restaurant when Tsurnick arrived. A waitress in flamenco dance costume with a pearl-studded tiara met him inside the door and escorted him to a table. She motioned toward one chair, but Tsurnick nodded and moved to the other side of the table where his back was to the wall and he could watch the entrance door.

His home base had picked up the word in Iran. A meeting was scheduled for this restaurant tonight. He glanced at his watch. In four more hours, Ernest Wessel should be here, and so should a top intelligence official from Tehran. Tsurnick's assignment was to let them meet, find out what they discussed, and then capture Wessel.

He looked around the restaurant. It was unlikely they

218

would meet in the open at one of these tables. There were two doors in the rear of the room. One, a swinging door with glass windows, led to the kitchen. The other was a solid wooden door. It was open, and in the small dark room beyond, Tsurnick could see a rectangular table and six chairs. Beyond it was a window, and the dying sun through the dusty windows cast an orange glow over the room.

If he was holding a meeting here, he would do it in that room.

The waitress, a pretty sloe-eyed girl with her hair neatly spit-curled in front of each ear, stopped alongside his table.

"Cocktail, sir?" she asked in a thick Spanish accent.

"Por favor," he said. *"Una Margarita. No sal."*

"Oh," she said with a smile. *"Habla usted español?"*

"Un poco," Tsurnick said.

The girl nodded and went to the bar to get his drink.

Later when she asked him what he wanted for dinner, she started to rattle off the specials of the day in rapid-fire Spanish that he could not even begin to understand.

He raised a hand in supplication. "Slow. Slow," he said. *"Mi español es muy pobre."* In English, he said, "I'll look at the menu."

The waitress giggled as if he had just finished a rousing stand-up comedy act. She clapped her hand over her mouth and went over to the service bar. He could hear her whispering to the bartender. *"Es muy pobre..."* he heard her say. The bartender looked at Yoel and smiled. Tsurnick waved the man to come over.

"You speak English?" he asked the man.

"Yes, sir. Very well."

"Yes, you do. What did I say that was so funny? I thought I was doing all right."

"Actually, señor, you said your Spanish was *muy pobre.* 'Very poor.' But it doesn't translate that way here. Actually what you said was that your Spanish had no money. Lola thought that was very funny. I hope she hasn't..."

"No, of course not. I was just wondering. My name is David. Yours?"

"Philip, señor."

"You have a nice place here. Is that room for private parties?"

219

"Yes."

"Would it be available tonight?" Tsurnick asked.

The man looked pained. The ends of his mustache twitched. "I'm sorry, señor, but it has already been booked." He looked at his watch. "In another three hours or so. Perhaps tomorrow night?"

"Maybe my friend already booked it for us," Tsurnick said. "What was the name of the man who booked it?"

Philip walked back to the bar to consult a small notebook. He walked back to Tsurnick.

"The name is Wessel, señor. Is that your friend?"

"Sorry," Tsurnick said. "He's not my friend."

Later, as he ate the flaky fresh fish in tomato sauce, Tsurnick thought about Caldwell again. It was a shame that poor Christopher knew so little. He was a confused and tortured man, trying to escape a past that he had had no control over but for which he still blamed himself. Tsurnick vowed that when he got back to Houston, he would take it upon himself to straighten out Christopher Caldwell. The professor had been wrong; it should have been done before. Caldwell should be brought back to life; life was so precious.

Resolutely, he put Caldwell out of his mind. That was for later. Right now was now. Dinner was good and he felt good. This was the place and tonight was the night when a long manhunt would end.

Chris Caldwell rode in the back of the cab up cobblestoned Calle Sol toward the El Convento Hotel. His suitcase was on the seat next to him. The guidebooks described old San Juan as picturesque, a piece of sixteenth-century Spain in America, but most of it was a slum, some few streets of seventeenth-century charm, a bit of Times Square, and a twenty-four-hour traffic jam on streets that had been built only for an occasional horse.

He paid the cabdriver and carried his bag into the hotel and restaurant built into a restored seventeenth-century chapel. It was one of Chris's favorite places on the island, one of the few places he liked in old San Juan.

The desk clerk rang David Benjamin's room for him, but still there was no answer. He thanked the clerk, went to the phone booth against the other wall, and dialed the Caribe Hilton.

"Would you ring Miss Susan Millard's room, please?"

"*Uno momento,*" the operator said.

A few seconds later, she was back on the line. "I'm sorry, sir. Nobody by that name is registered."

"Are you sure? That's Millard." Chris spelled it.

"No, sir. No one by that name."

Chris thought briefly and asked, "Do you have an Otto Brooks registered? He came in today."

"I'll see," she said, but a moment later expressed more apologies. There was no Mr. Brooks registered.

Chris hung up the telephone, puzzled. Susan had told him the Caribe Hilton. Was it possible that she was staying under a different name? But why? Unless she was shacked up in Brooks's room and he was under a different name. He doubted it. Even if Brooks had taken her to Puerto Rico to boff her, he would hardly have been stupid enough to stash her in his room. Not with a Supreme Court promotion in the works.

Caldwell went back to the desk clerk.

"I'd like to leave a note for Mr. Benjamin," he said.

"Certainly." The clerk gave him a pen and notepad. Chris asked the time and the clerk said, "Eleven-fifty, señor."

Chris put the time on the note and wrote: "David. Call me immediately. I'm here in P.R., 555-0016. Chris." He handed the note to the clerk, who folded it and put it into the mail slot for Room 317. Chris saw another note in the same slot. That would probably be his earlier call.

Lugging his suitcase, Chris went back out front, knowing that there would be no cabs in sight, since there never were at El Convento. But a battered red Ford pulled up, discharging two passengers for the hotel, and Chris slipped into the back seat.

The cab did not have a formal cab sign on top, but many of the taxis in old San Juan were unlicensed—just private cars whose owners used them as cabs at night to make a few extra dollars.

Chris gave the driver the address on Isla Verde, the strip of San Juan leading out past the luxury hotels and into little residential enclaves before Route 187 drifted off into the small towns and tarpaper shacks of the eastern side of the island.

Yoel Tsurnick stepped out of the bar across the narrow roadway from the Flamenco. He allowed himself to smile at a rickety old red cab rolling down the street, heading out of old San Juan.

The street was quiet. A small group of tourists were looking at souvenir T-shirts in a late-night novelty shop four doors down the street.

Tsurnick crossed the roadway and stepped quickly into the alleyway between the restaurant and the pink stucco two-story building next to it. He picked his way through overflowing garbage pails until he was behind the old stone restaurant building.

Just over the level of his head, he saw the small window that looked into the private dining room. From his pocket, he fished a small suction cup, no bigger than a dime. Two shiny metal leads stuck out from the raised section of the cup. Tsurnick licked the belly of the cup with his tongue and pressed it to a corner of the window. From his inside pocket he took a small tape recorder with eight feet of thin wires leading from the microphone plug. Each wire ended in a small alligator clip. He clipped them to the leads on the back of the suction cup, which housed a delicate contact microphone. He took a roll of tape from his back pocket and peeled off three foot-long strips, tearing them with his teeth. He stuck the strips to the inside of his left wrist and put the tape roll back in his pocket. With the tape, he attached the tape recorder to the wall of the building, high enough off the ground so it would not be noticed by anybody who might wander into the back alley. He set the controls of the tape recorder to be activated by sound, so that anyone talking inside the room would trigger the recorder.

He stepped back to look at his handiwork.

It would do, he thought. It would do.

It was Yoel Tsurnick's last thought, because, close-up, a bullet was fired into the base of his skull and he dropped dead in the dirty alley behind the building.

His killer bent over him and stuck a folded piece of

222

paper into Tsurnick's inside jacket pocket. Then he ripped the tape recorder from the wall and the microphone from the window. He stuck them into his pocket and returned his gun to his shoulder holster.

A moment later, a husky man with a reddish mustache and wearing a wide-brimmed hat stepped out onto the street in front of the Flamenco. No one seemed to have heard the shot. He walked away to look for a cab to take him back to the airport.

Standing two blocks away, at a corner, was an overflowing mesh litter basket. The man reached in under the top layer of garbage and dropped in the tape recorder and microphone.

Then he took off his thin leather gloves and stuck them into his pocket.

CHAPTER FIFTEEN

He had been in Houston for too long, Caldwell realized when the taxicab turned off Route 187 onto La Playa Street and drove almost to the ocean before turning into the driveway of his home. He felt a surge of some comfortable joy looking at the small stucco building. His old red MG TC was in the driveway, clean and waxed, and he smiled. Lisa had been keeping an eye on it for him.

He paid the cabdriver. As he stepped out on the walk leading to his home, he looked off to the left to a similar house where Lisa lived with her aged aunt. He should stop in and say hello, to see if anything had happened at the dive shop while he had been gone, but he decided there would be plenty of time to do it tomorrow. He wanted to be home when Tsurnick called.

Inside, the small house was picture-neat, more of Lisa's work. When he had first bought the small house, he had carefully opened up its single floor so that kitchen, living room, bedroom, and dining area all were open to each other. If he wanted privacy, there was a folding screen that could be pulled out to seal off the bedroom. He tossed his suitcase on a couch and walked to the back of the house to the sleeping area. Through his large windows, he could see the sand sloping down to the light-blue waters of the Caribbean, warm, looking inviting even in the darkness of late night.

For the first time in two days, he really wanted a drink. He looked longingly at his well-stocked liquor cabinet. Perhaps, he thought, drinking was as much habit as anything else. He was in the habit of drinking when he was here, and the habit seemed to be grabbing at him, making the back of his throat dry. He went to the small bar and held a bottle of vodka in his hand. He could pour a drink, he knew, and then change his mind and dump it into the sink. Or he could just let it stand on the bar, untouched.

He opened the top of the bottle, then closed it again. It

was a trap. Once he poured the liquor, he knew its next stop would be his stomach. First pour it. You can always change your mind. Then smell it. You can always change your mind. Then put it to your lips. You can always change your mind. Then gulp it down before you have a chance to change your mind.

He walked to the telephone and tried Susan Millard at the Caribe Hilton again, but she still had not registered. Nor had anyone named Brooks.

He found a slim pile of mail on the little end table just inside his front door, and busied himself reading it. Bills and advertisements. The Franklin Mint wanted to know if he wanted to buy sterling silver "stamps" commemorating the world's greatest automobiles. American Express wanted to know if he wanted to buy durable and handsome vinyl luggage.

All he wanted was a drink.

He waited for an hour. Tsurnick did not call, and he called El Convento and asked them to ring Room 317. No answer. He left no message.

It was two in the morning when he slipped off his trousers and shirt and got under the light sheet he used as a bed cover. First he pulled the telephone, on a long cord, into the sleeping area and placed it on the floor next to the bed.

He was not aware of falling asleep. He had thought that he would just rest his eyes for a few minutes. But he slept, and when he awoke, there was someone in the room. He felt it. And his gun was in his suitcase.

Before he could move, a flashlight shone in his face and a cold voice said in neat English, "Do not move, Señor Caldwell. We are the police."

"Get that light out of my eyes," Caldwell responded in Spanish. "There's a light switch by the door."

The overhead light came on and Caldwell pulled on his slacks. There were two men in the room. One wore a lightweight blue suit, the other a policeman's uniform. Through the front windows, Chris could see the headlights of a car in front, parked next to his MG in the driveway.

"What the hell is this all about?" Chris asked. "What time is it, anyway?"

225

"It is four o'clock, señor. Do you know a man named David Benjamin?"

For a moment, Chris thought about lying. But perhaps Tsurnick was in some sort of trouble and needed him. The policeman at the door held his pistol in his hand. These two officers were obviously not investigating a traffic violation.

"Yes. Why?" Chris said.

"If you don't mind, Mr. Caldwell, I will ask the questions. When did you last see Mr. Benjamin?"

"In Houston, yesterday."

"Were you supposed to meet him here?"

"Yes. Will you tell me, goddammit, what's going on?"

"And tonight, where did you meet Mr. Benjamin?"

"I didn't meet him tonight. I couldn't reach him at his hotel." Chris's mind was clearing. The policeman who was questioning him was a tall man with metal-framed glasses which made him look studious. The uniformed officer was also tall. It had always amused Chris that on the mainland, most city police departments had done away with height requirements for recruits so they could attract more Puerto Ricans on the force, but throughout San Juan, the police department wanted only tall officers and made no bones about it.

The officer in the blue suit was looking around the room. His eyes seemed to settle on Chris's suitcase, open on the couch. Chris noticed a glint of light from under the bathroom door. He did not remember having turned it on.

"How long have you been here, Mr. Caldwell?" the policeman asked. "How long tonight, that is?"

Before Chris could answer, another voice answered.

"He has been here all night, with me."

He looked over as Lisa walked out of his bathroom. She was wearing a thin robe, which she pulled around her with her left hand. As she walked, her long bare legs pushed forward between the material. The top of the robe was open enough to show the woman was naked underneath. Her hair was tousled about her head.

The policeman looked at her with open admiration, then at Chris with new respect.

"This is true?" he said.

"Lisa, don't answer anything for this fool," Chris said

226

sharply in Spanish, "until he tells us what he is doing here and why he has broken into my house and how he will explain this to his superiors tomorrow when I have him censured for his conduct."

Lisa smiled at Chris. "I just want him to go, darling."

"Forgive me," the policeman said. For the first time, he seemed to lose his authoritarian poise. "I am Lieutenant Gomez. This is Officer Martín."

"Fine. Now what is this all about?"

"David Benjamin is dead, Señor Caldwell."

Chris winced and sat back on the bed. "Oh, no," he said. "When? How?"

"He was found shot dead an hour ago behind the Flamenco Restaurant in Viejo San Juan. In his pocket, we found this."

He handed a small card to Chris. It read "San Juan Dive Shop. Private instructions. Chris Caldwell" and gave his business number at the hotel.

"That's mine," he said. "I have a whole box of them on that table by the door."

"Mr. Benjamin's hotel key was in his pocket. When we went to his hotel, we found that you had been there. There was a message from you in his box and another message, perhaps from you. You left your telephone number and we traced it to this address. When were you at his hotel?"

"Just before midnight. He wasn't there, so I grabbed a cab and came home here. An old red wreck of a cab."

"He was here exactly at midnight," Lisa said, "and I haven't let him leave all night."

"And you are?" asked Lieutenant Gomez.

"I am Lisa Guzmán. I live across the street." She sat in one of the living-room chairs and crossed her legs. The policeman at the door stared at her. His gun was hanging limply by his side now. "Mr. Caldwell is my employer," she said.

"Yes. I see," Gomez said.

While Lisa distracted the policeman, Chris quickly put together his cover story, and when Gomez got around to it, Caldwell sketched it in for him. He had been in Houston on legal business. He had met David Benjamin there at a restaurant. He was an Englishman who did something in sales.

He had told Chris he was going to Puerto Rico for a few days, and Chris said if he could get free he would fly down and give him some diving instructions. At the last minute, Chris hopped a plane to the island. He went to the hotel to tell Benjamin he had arrived, but the man wasn't there. He left his number and came home and figured that Benjamin would call him eventually.

"You say he was a salesman?" Gomez asked.

"That's what he said."

"Then why did he carry a gun?"

"A gun? I know nothing about his carrying a gun," Chris said.

"Nevertheless, he carried a revolver in a shoulder holster," the policeman said triumphantly.

Chris shrugged.

"And who is this Mr. Brooks?"

"Mr. Brooks?"

"Yes."

"I don't know," Chris said cautiously.

"You left a note earlier. It said that Brooks was on his way to Puerto Rico. Who is that Brooks?"

"No. That damned operator. David asked me to buy him some books on diving. I got them and put them in the mail to him. I just wanted him to know they were on their way. That message said 'books,' not 'Brooks.'"

Lisa yawned. "Can't you finish this tomorrow, lieutenant?"

"You are prepared to swear to your whereabouts tonight?" Gomez asked Caldwell. "And you, too," he asked Lisa.

She nodded.

Gomez looked around, and again his eyes fixed on Chris's suitcase.

"You will not mind if I look into your suitcase, Mr. Caldwell," he said.

"Damned right I mind," Chris said. "Not without a warrant."

"Oh, Christopher," said Lisa. "Let him look. That may be the only way to get him out of here."

The lieutenant accepted her offer before Chris could speak and began poking around in the open suitcase. Chris

228

could not remember having opened it before.

There was a lump in Chris's throat as he watched Gomez feel around in the suitcase. Finally, the officer turned to Chris and said, "You are not a very neat packer. Do you always carry folded newspapers?"

He closed over the top of the suitcase.

"It fills out the bag," Chris said. "Saves it from damage at the airport. And I'm pretty neat for a bachelor."

"I would not know, señor. How long will you be in Puerto Rico?"

"I came down to see David. I'll probably go right back."

"You will not leave the island without talking to me first," Lieutenant Gomez said.

"Yes, of course."

"Then we bid you goodnight." His eyes danced behind his glasses from Chris to Lisa, then he spun on his heel. He barked at the uniformed officer, "Put that gun away and come, Martín."

A moment later, their auto headlights swept the room as they backed out of the driveway, turned, and drove off.

Chris went to the front door to make sure they had gone. When their taillights disappeared, he looked inside his suitcase for the gun.

"It's not there," Lisa said.

When he turned to look, Lisa was smiling. "It's in the bathroom in the bottom of the clothes hamper," she said.

"How did...?" he started as he walked past her to retrieve the gun.

"I was out tonight," she said. "When I came home, my aunt told me she had seen lights in here. I let myself in quietly and saw you asleep. I decided to unpack your suitcase for you, and I found the gun and bullets in your socks. I decided not to unpack the clothes, and I sat over there watching you, waiting for you to wake up. When the police car pulled up in front, I did not know what was right to do, but I grabbed the socks and took them into the bathroom and threw them into the clothes hamper. Then I thought and I thought the police might not ask so many questions if I looked as if I had been sleeping here, so I took my clothes off and put on this robe."

"Lisa, you're a charm," Chris said, as he removed the

229

gun and bullets from the socks and put them behind a pile of books on a high shelf over his bed.

"But, Christopher, that business card?"

"Yes?"

"Earlier today, my aunt said she saw someone here. I came over, but there was no one. I did not think much of it, because Rosa's eyes are no longer so good. But maybe someone came and took that business card to leave it, to make things bad for you."

"Probably."

"Who is David Benjamin?" she asked.

"He was my friend," Chris said. "He was a brave, good man and he was my friend. And like all my friends, he was killed."

Chris woke at nine o'clock, seven in Houston, and placed a long-distance call to Susan Millard's apartment. He could hear Lisa in the kitchen area making breakfast. She had slept beside him during the night but he had not made love to her.

Susan answered on the first ring.

"You're not in Puerto Rico," Chris said.

"Obviously, Chris, if I'm here to answer the phone," she said brightly. "Where are you?"

"How come you're not in Puerto Rico?" Chris asked.

"Oh, Otto's plans changed at the last minute. He's impossible these days. I tried to reach you but you weren't home. Are you home now?"

Again, Chris ignored the question. "Think, Susan," he said. "It's important. Why did you happen to call me yesterday afternoon to tell me you were going to Puerto Rico?"

"What's this all about?"

"Please, Susan. Just answer the question. Please."

"Oh, I don't know. I just thought since I was going out of town and you might try to reach me . . ."

"It was your idea to call?" he said.

"Well . . . mine and Otto's, I guess. He said I should call anyone I was planning to meet and cancel my appointments. I think he said something about calling my 'young man.' He thinks you're my young man. What's this all about, anyway? Where are you?"

230

"In Puerto Rico, looking for you."

"Come on," she said.

"I am," he said.

"Oh, I'm sorry, Chris."

"If that makes you sorry, try this," he snapped. "A friend of mine was murdered here last night. Somebody else who knew I was going to Puerto Rico tried to frame me for the killing. Now you can just tell *your* friends I'm coming back. And they'd better not miss again. Because I won't."

He heard her saying "Chris" as he hung up the telephone. He had been set up. Someone had lured Tsurnick to Puerto Rico, knowing he would tell Caldwell he was going. And then Brooks, through Susan, had told Chris they were going to Puerto Rico too. They knew that this would bring Caldwell to the island, where they killed Tsurnick and tried to frame Chris for the murder. Fortunately, Lisa had given him an alibi or he might right now be in a San Juan jail cell charged with murder.

Chris had now issued a direct challenge to the plotters, and he knew the next attempt on his life would be open and direct. He rubbed his hands together, looking out his rear window at the water. He looked forward to it. He looked forward to meeting face to face with Ernest Wessel.

In Houston, Susan Millard stared at the dead telephone in her hand, then dropped it onto its stand and sank back into a living-room chair. She bit her lip to try to prevent tears from flowing, but they came anyway to her eyes. The tears were tinged with fear. What was going on? Was Mr. Hirschfeld murdered? And someone else? Some other friend of Chris's? Was Otto Brooks somehow mixed up in something shady? Could he be? She wiped her eyes with the sleeve of her robe. There were just so many questions, she thought to herself. And it was time she started to get some answers.

Lieutenant Gomez was sitting behind his piled-high desk, looking tired and drawn, when Chris arrived in mid-morning.

"I want to go back to Houston, lieutenant," he said.

"Yes," Gomez said. He took off his glasses and rubbed his eyes. "We found the cabdriver who took you from El Convento to your home last night. It was immediately after you left the note for Mr. Benjamin. The desk clerk remembered the time. So you are free to go. But will you please tell my clerk outside where you may be reached, Mr. Caldwell."

"Of course."

Gomez stood up. "I have the feeling, señor, that this is not just a simple killing on the street."

"Why is that?"

"One gets a feeling," Gomez said. "He talks to an embassy and asks about a dead foreign national. And suddenly no one wishes to talk. Conferences. They will get back to me. One wonders about such things. It would seem as if a traveling salesman had never been killed before."

He reached into a pile of papers on his desk and pulled out a lump of dull-gray metal, with a cardboard tag attached to it.

"This is the bullet that killed your friend," he said. "A .38 caliber slug."

Chris looked at the bullet. A little lump of heavy metal worth maybe a fraction of a cent. And a good man was dead.

"You still have no clues?" Chris asked.

"You would not know a Mr. Wessel, would you?"

"Who's he?" Chris asked casually, but he felt his heart pound sharply.

"Last night, Mr. Benjamin ate in the Flamenco. He asked about renting the back room, but it had already been rented to a Mr. Wessel. Mr. Wessel never showed up to use the room."

"Maybe he's your man," Chris said.

"Perhaps. I wonder if that is the name of the man with the red mustache."

"What man is that?" Chris asked.

"Someone saw such a man walking away from the restaurant at about the time Mr. Benjamin met his death. We are looking for him."

"What did he look like?"

"He was big and had a red mustache. He wore a wide-brimmed hat. Do you know any man like that?"

"No, sir. I'm sorry."

"So am I."

Gus Griffin was just leaving his ranch house when the telephone rang.

"Otto, Gus."

"Yeah?"

"Maybe this doesn't mean anything and maybe it does."

"Well, suppose you tell me and let me decide," Griffin said.

"I just heard from Susan."

"What did she say?"

"Not much," Brooks said. "But she was trying to pump me. Questions about you, me, our relationship, your oil business."

"They weren't just business questions?" Griffin asked.

"I don't think so. There was kind of a hard edge to them," Brooks said.

"Do you think she knows what happened in Puerto Rico? Do you think she talked to Caldwell?"

"I don't know," Brooks said.

"Christ, you're a bundle of information," Griffin said. There was a pause and he said, "That sucker might just come back here. I think it's about time to straighten out Eustace McBride."

"Oh, I don't like that, Gus."

"I don't care what you like."

"You think it's wise?" Brooks asked.

"I think it's necessary," Griffin said.

1943

Pedro Lorca was amidships when the first explosion broke the back of the small tanker. The blast hurled him through the air and into the water. Stunned, he fought his way back to the surface, battling instinctively, even though only half-conscious, against the horror of drowning.

He broke the surface and saw the vessel already listing to the port side. He started to swim back toward the ship. There was a second explosion.

A babel of screams and shouts filled the air, accompanied by a deep groaning as the ship began to break in half.

Lorca saw their passenger, the young white-haired man in the white suit, cutting loose a life raft near the bow of the ship. The man pushed the raft over the low railing and jumped into the water after it. Amidships, two men worked frantically to free a lifeboat from its davit. Four more seamen were throwing life jackets into the water.

Then there was another explosion, followed by a hiss, a roar, and then a frightful red, ear-piercing blast as the cargo of oil exploded.

"Holy Mary, save us all," Pedro Lorca said. An oily wave slapped him in the face. He saw men in the water. He saw the passenger in the white suit using a single paddle to move the balsa life raft away from the sinking ship.

Lorca kicked off his shoes and began swimming awkwardly toward the life raft. As he swam, he saw five more seamen converging on the raft.

With a final screech of tortured metal, the ship turned over and sank. The entire disaster had taken less than fifteen minutes.

The men pulled themselves into the raft.

"What happened?" one gasped. "The boilers?"

"No. The explosion was too far forward," another said. "It must have been a torpedo."

"It was not a torpedo," the man in the white suit said flatly in his harsh guttural Spanish.

Pedro tried to say "Maybe a mine," but no words came from his mouth. He knew he had been hurt badly. He touched his right temple and saw blood on his fingers. His neck ached. His stomach churned from the oily salt water he had swallowed.

"We must go back to see if any of our shipmates are still in the water," one sailor said.

"We cannot take on any more men," the man in the white suit objected. "We are overloaded now." Several men grunted agreement.

"Look," the passenger said. He pointed to the sea, again silent and morose where the ship had been in fury only moments before. There were floating boxes and drums, bits of wood, pieces of furnishings from the boat, but no signs of swimmers.

The men slowly looked away, accepting that death had been triumphant.

"Does anyone know where we are?" the passenger said.

"Pedro. He knows." Pedro Lorca could see eyes on him. He wanted to talk, to tell them that they were about thirty-five miles offshore, but no words would come.

"He is hurt bad," said one of his crewmates. Pedro tried to nod. His head ached worse than ever. The sun already was beating down savagely and his clothes were growing stiff with salt. The men sprawled about in complete exhaustion, each sunk deep in his thoughts.

"Oh, God, look," exclaimed one of the men suddenly, pointing behind the raft.

Pedro turned and saw the dorsal fin slicing lazily through the water.

The next three days passed in a merciful delirium for Pedro. He was only dimly aware of the blazing tropical sun, the welcome relief of rain squalls, the cold nights, the gnawing hunger, the constant thirst.

Occasionally, he tried to mumble "Thank you" as one of the men on the raft wet his lips with a trickle of water. Then there were no more men wetting his lips with trickles of water.

Pedro lay motionless and unconcerned, barely conscious. One night, he heard sounds. They sounded like

235

more explosions. He screamed. There were five explosions very quickly. He struggled to open his eyes.

The moon, large and red, was shining down on the raft. There was no one left on the raft but himself and the passenger in the white suit. The passenger was aiming a pistol at Pedro. He squeezed the trigger. Click.

He squeezed again. Click. Pedro wanted to shout "Don't shoot! Don't shoot!" But no words came out.

The white-haired man cursed in some language Pedro did not know, then reached down and tossed Pedro Lorca into the sea. Pedro tried to swim. He drifted. He prayed to Mary that when the sharks came to tear him apart, they would be merciful and quick.

His body bumped against a piece of driftwood, and he held on to it. He was found twelve hours later by a fishing boat, more dead than alive.

Pedro Lorca tried to tell them what had happened, but he could not remember it. In the small fishing village, a doctor treated him as best he could and told the men who found him that Pedro would never be the same again, would never be right in the head.

He lived in the village for a year, until someone from Pedro's home port of Irapa happened to pass through and recognized him.

Pedro went home then. He did not remember his wife and his son, but they remembered him and they took care of him.

He grew stronger and sometimes was able to go to church, although he could never remember the responses of the mass. He could speak a little as time went on, but he did not remember what had happened on that day his ship went down.

He tried hard. People asked, but he could not remember. Sometimes, though, he dreamed and often woke up screaming from a nightmare, seeing again the pitiless blazing sun, the circling fins of the remorseless sharks, the pistol in the hand of the man in the white suit as he was silhouetted against the high overhead moon. And he would sometimes yell out numbers and scream aloud, "The moon! The moon!"

But no one knew what he meant.

BOOK THREE

CHAPTER ONE

The death of Yoel Tsurnick finally got to Christopher Caldwell as he sat aboard United Airlines Flight 202, heading back for Houston, and forced a decision on him. To celebrate his decision, he ordered a Finlandia vodka on the rocks, then corrected the order to a double vodka.

He was done. He would not have a part in any more people around him being killed. There had been Zhava and Shoshana and Hirsch. And now Tsurnick.

Done and done. No more. Let the already dead be dead and let them be lonely. Let some of the living live.

Caldwell was going to do one more thing. He would write a report on everything that had happened, everything he had learned, and make sure it got into the right hands at the CIA. Then it was their baby. And Caldwell would go back to Puerto Rico, back to his bottle, back to his diving equipment, back to those inviting waters far beyond the reef.

He celebrated his decision with another double Finlandia. He decided he would have no more than three. By the time the plane landed, he had had five. And he was very pleased with himself, because in his jacket pocket he had two little airline bottles of vodka that clinked together comfortingly as he walked.

He had been in his apartment only ten minutes when the telephone rang.

"Hi, Chris," a woman's voice said. "This is Dolores McBride."

It took Caldwell, who was a little fuzzy from the liquor, a moment to place Eustace McBride's elegant wife.

237

"Yes, Dolores. How are you?"

"Calling you all day," she said.

"I was away."

"Can I come over and see you?"

Caldwell hesitated. The woman said, "It's important, Chris."

"Sure. Come on over. Hey, do me a favor?"

"Sure. What?"

"Bring some vodka?"

He left his suitcase tossed onto the couch, unopened. When Dolores McBride arrived fifteen minutes later, he was sitting in a chair, drinking the last of the airline vodka.

She had a pint bottle of liquor in her purse. Only a pint. He supposed he would have to offer her a drink. How many drinks did she think you could get out of a pint, anyway?

"You want a drink?" he asked.

"Sure. Whatever you're having."

He made them both drinks, vodka over ice, gave her the small one, and sat on the chair facing her as she sat on the couch. Dolores looked nervous, Caldwell thought.

"What's the matter?"

"This is tough for me, Chris," she said.

"Plow right ahead," Caldwell said. "If it makes it any easier, I want your body too."

She laughed nervously and took a long gulp of her short drink. "Chris, I want you to quit."

"Okay," he said.

She looked shocked. "Just like that? Okay?"

"Yeah."

"Don't you want to know why?" she asked.

"If you want to tell me. But it's not really important to me," Caldwell said.

"Mac's been under a lot of pressure because of you," Dolores said. "Brooks has been after him to get you off the Griffin matter. The Griffins think you've been prying into their personal business. You know how important Brooks is to Mac. It's because of that relationship that Mac can get things done in Washington. You're going to hurt the practice, Chris. You already have. And Mac just doesn't have the heart to fire you or ask you to quit, because you're his friend. That's why *I'm* asking you to quit."

"Consider it done," Chris said. "I quit. Have another drink?"

"No, I don't think so. I don't understand."

"Dolores, everything I touch turns to shit. I'm quitting before it happens to Mac too like it happens to all my other friends. You don't mind if I have another, do you?"

"No. I think maybe I'd better go. Chris, there's one more thing."

"What is it?" Caldwell said. He wished she would go so he could go out in the kitchen and make his drink. Maybe he would bring the bottle in here.

"Mac doesn't know I came here. He'd go through the roof if..."

"Quitting's my idea. Don't worry about it. He'll never know you were here." He stood up to walk her to the door, before she changed her mind and said she would have another drink.

She stopped with her back to the apartment door.

"Are you going back to Puerto Rico?"

"Yeah, I think so. Houston doesn't seem to agree with me."

"You're a good man, Chris. I wish we had gotten to know each other better."

Caldwell shook his head. "You wouldn't like me. To know me is to die."

She looked confused.

"Never mind," he said. "It's too complicated."

Dolores McBride stretched upward to kiss him. He bent his head and offered his cheek, but Dolores put her left hand behind his head, pulled his face down, and kissed him hard on the lips.

"Maybe sometime, Chris."

"If you ever get to Puerto Rico," he said.

"If that's an invitation, I accept."

He pulled her hand free from the back of his neck and glanced at the glass in his hand. Good, he had not spilled a drop.

"Get out of here before I'm tempted not to wait," he said.

When she got downstairs, Mrs. McBride looked back into the lobby of the building. Caldwell had not followed her. She walked to the corner, then fifty yards down the side street, and got into a waiting Cadillac.

Eustace McBride was behind the wheel.

"Did he buy it?" he asked.

"Sales tax and all," she said.

"Good girl," McBride said.

Chris was halfway through his next drink when Susan Millard telephoned.

"I've been trying to reach you," she said. "Come on over."

"What for?"

"What do you mean, what for?" she said. "I want to see you."

"I don't travel too well today," Chris said.

"You've been drinking?"

"Yes. A lot."

"I'll come over there then and make you coffee."

"Just coffee. No temperance lectures," he said.

True to her word, when Susan arrived, she went right into the kitchen and made a pot of real percolated coffee. Women, Chris noted, always seemed to be able to find things like coffeepots and ground coffee in strange kitchens. All he could ever find was a saucepan and a jar of instant coffee. She brought him coffee in the living room, putting it down on the table in front of him, then took his glass of vodka and put it on the table near her seat. He leaned over and took the glass back and set it next to his coffee.

Susan sat on the edge of the couch, next to his still-unopened suitcase, facing him.

"Otto's asked me to marry him," she said.

"Tell the Lone Star Liberal he doesn't have to do that," Chris said.

"What does that mean?"

"That means I'm leaving so he doesn't have to worry about keeping you away from me."

"That's not very flattering," she said. "You think he might not want to marry me just for marriage's sake?"

"Sure. Maybe he wants to. I don't know. You're sexy and he's old. I saw him look at you at Griffin's party. There wasn't much uncle in those eyes."

Chris sipped the coffee. It was pretty good coffee. With

240

a little brandy in it, it might have been great coffee. The girl had untapped talents, but he doubted if she was carrying any brandy in her purse.

Susan looked hurt. "What happened to us, Chris?" she asked.

"Nothing. We were on different sides from the git-go."

"How can you say that?"

Chris wanted to tell her to forget it. It was all a million years ago and everybody involved had long since died, including him. But her light-blue eyes were fixed on him, earnestly, almost as if challenging him to convince her.

"Look," he said, "we've gone through it already, but if you need it one more time, here it is. You were sent here by Otto to keep an eye on Hirsch and the Griffin application. And then Hirsch was killed, and I think maybe it's because you reported a little bit too much to the judge—"

"Now, wait a minute."

"No. You wait a minute. And then I think he told you to stay close to me, and for all I know, that's what you're doing here now, staying close to me. And I think he told you to tell me you were going to Puerto Rico because they wanted me to go down there."

"We were going to Puerto—"

"You know what happened in Puerto Rico?" Chris snapped. "A friend of mine was murdered. Another man involved in this Griffin oil mess. And they tried to set me up as the killer. They knew I was coming and they tried to set me up."

"You're sure of that?" Susan asked.

"Yes."

"Chris, I talked to Otto after I talked to you this morning. He said he had been asked to go to Puerto Rico to meet somebody from the White House, perhaps about his being appointed Chief Justice. It was all supposed to be hush-hush, and then the White House canceled the meeting at the last minute."

"You believe him?" Chris asked.

Susan said nothing for a long moment. Then she said simply, "No. I don't."

For a fleeting moment, Chris recognized an opportunity. Susan was weakening; he could turn her, bring her

241

over to his side and have a pipeline into the enemy's camp. But then he remembered that he was done, finished with the Red Moon. He didn't need anyone in the enemy camp, so he said cheerily, "Congratulations. Welcome to the world of reality."

"But, Chris...I just can't believe...Mr. Hirschfeld murdered? Somebody else killed in Puerto Rico? I can't believe..."

"Believe," Chris said.

"You've got to tell me what this is about," Susan said. She looked up from the table, and her Wedgwood eyes fixed on his face. Her voice was soft and plaintive as she said, "Chris, who are you? What's going on here? What's the Red Moon? Help me, Chris."

"I am going to help you, Susan. The best way I know how. I'm going to leave here and I'm going to get out of your life. With me gone, nobody'll have a reason to kill you, as they almost did the other night."

"Who? Chris, who? For God's sake, tell me who."

"No. The less you know, the better off you are," he said as he picked up his glass of vodka and took a long swallow. "I think you ought to go now."

"What about us, Chris? Don't you have any feeling for us? For me?"

She reached out and touched his hand, but he withdrew it and picked his glass up again.

"Some other time, some other place, we might have been good," he said.

"But not here and not now?" she asked.

He shook his head. "Not here, not now."

"Okay," she said. She got up from the sofa, picked up her purse, and walked to the door.

"You going to marry Brooks?" he asked as she put her hand on the doorknob.

She answered without turning around. "No."

"Why not?"

"Because I don't love him. I think I love you," she said, then walked quickly from the apartment. Chris stared at the closed door of the apartment for a few moments, then took his still-full coffee cup into the kitchen and brought back the pint of vodka. Tomorrow he would tell McBride that he quit. All done. Goodbye, Houston.

Glass in hand, he walked around the apartment, looking at it really for the first time, knowing he would soon see it no more. He would have to pack some things. Maybe McBride could get somebody to empty out the apartment and throw everything away. He saw on the bookshelves the few things that Hirsch had held dear. A piece of crystal in the shape of an eagle. On a small easel was an ancient coin found in Israel, bearing the likeness of Alexander the Great. There was a piece of colored glass, a shard from a Roman dish. They had all come from Zhava.

It hurt suddenly to look at them. He turned away. There were more bookshelves on the other side of the room. Mostly law books. But on the top shelf, something else caught his eye. It was a brown fabric-covered book, and along the spine was printed in large black letters: PHOTOGRAPHS.

Knowing it was going to hurt him to look, but powerless not to, Chris stood on a hassock and pulled the book from the top shelf.

He took the album to the couch, turned on a floor lamp, and sat for a long minute with the book on his lap before opening the cover.

The first photograph was an eight-by-ten, brown-tinted and ripped at the edges. It was a head-and-shoulders of a middle-aged couple, the man balding, the woman with her hair carefully and immaculately marcelled. Beneath the photo, Hirsch had written "Mother and Father, 1935."

The photographs were in a rough chronological order. There was a snapshot of Hirsch in Israel, after the war, with his Sabra wife, a round little dark-eyed woman in whose face one could see the beginning of the beauty that would reach its culmination with Zhava. Hirsch was thin to the point of starvation, but his eyes were the bright happy eyes of a free man.

Those eyes were even happier in the next photographs, a group of three of Hirsch and his wife holding their infant daughter, Zhava. There were two more pages of pictures of Zhava, a baby, a little girl, growing up, a teenager, becoming painfully more beautiful with each snap of the camera shutter.

Chris turned another page. There was a picture of him and Zhava standing together on a beach in Virginia, and on the following page was their wedding picture.

Another page. Zhava with the baby, Shoshana. Chris holding Shoshana in his arms.

He felt his eyes grow moist, and there was a chill of sadness, sorrow, pain, in the front of his elbows, a shiver that ran up and down his arms.

He couldn't look anymore. This was what a man's life had come down to: a dozen pages of faded photographs in an album. He would take the album back to Puerto Rico with him, and on the day of that final dive, he would take it down with him. All the Hirschfeld family would be buried together, with him.

He flipped his thumb along the edges of the pages, unable to look, but not wanting to put the book down.

There was an envelope stuck into the book behind the last page of pictures.

He removed it and looked at the front.

It was addressed simply: "Christopher."

He held the envelope in his hand. It was a legal-size plain white envelope, probably with two pieces of paper inside.

Finally, he set the book on the table alongside him and opened the envelope.

Dear Christopher,

I am writing this on July 2, 1979. Zhava and the baby have been dead for exactly one year and you are still deep in your grief. We both are, but I grieve and go on living, and you grieve and go on killing yourself.

It is my hope that you never read this letter. If you do not, it will prove that I have been man enough to tell you something that I should have told you during this year since Zhava was first taken from us. I do not know if I will ever attain that manliness.

The truth is, although it is no excuse, that at first I did not know and I was filled with pain and wanted someone, everyone, to share my suffering. You were convenient. That I used you this way is a shame I will carry with me to my grave.

You have been sinking in your sorrow for the past

year because you blame yourself for the death of Zhava and Shoshana. You think they were killed by those savages because of your work, because someone was striking out at you. At first, I believed that too.

Christopher, believe me now, because in this letter, I have no reason to lie. If you ever find it, I will not be here and there will be no need for me to be anything less than honest.

Zhava was not killed because of you. She was killed because of who she was and what she was. My daughter, your wife, worked for the Mossad. The bomb that killed her was meant for *her,* Christopher. For her, not for you. She had done occasional work for them for at least two years before marrying you. I told her to tell you but she chose not to, and as you know, our Zhava made her own decisions. It was her feeling that, knowing, you might worry and might expose yourself to unnecessary dangers.

Believe me, Christopher, this is not a fantasy I am spinning for you. I too have worked on and off for, and will again work for, the Mossad. Why me, a college professor? Why Zhava, an art buyer? Because we are Jews, Christopher, and Israel is the fruit of our centuries of suffering. If it is allowed to be destroyed, the destruction will make meaningless all the pain and the hurt of our people.

There is one question left. Why did I not tell you this before? First, because I did not know it. I needed someone to share my suffering, and I thought you were right. I thought that that obscene bomb *had* been meant for you. I learned the truth only months later. By that time, you had retreated into yourself and I could not tell you simply because you would not have believed me. You would have thought it a kind gesture by a nice old man. And, too, perhaps I lacked the courage to tell you, because I feared I had caused you such hurt.

At any rate, I want you now to know the truth. I want you to live your life without its being haunted by the specters of sins you did not commit, of crimes

245

of which you are not guilty. You are as much my son as Zhava was my daughter. I love you as she did.

It was signed simply "Dad."

Christopher Caldwell wiped his eyes and read the letter again. The tears running down his face made it difficult.

Not guilty. All his mind could focus on was that he was not guilty for Zhava's death. For Shoshana's.

But he knew it was not that simple. If Zhava's life was to have meaning, if Shoshana's brief tragic life was to mean something... and Hirsch's... and Yoel Tsurnick's... then Christopher Caldwell could not just run.

He was not ready to go back to Puerto Rico.

Not just yet.

CHAPTER TWO

A woman with black hair, streaked with gray, sat behind a desk just inside the front door of the small white stone building around the corner from Houston's Greenway Plaza.

A uniformed police guard sat on a chair behind the door, almost out of view of people entering the building. The woman looked up expectantly as Caldwell walked to her desk.

"I would like to see your intelligence officer," he said.

The woman's smile was immediate and forced. "I'm sorry, sir, but this is only a consulate. We have no one here in that capacity." She glanced toward the policeman in the corner.

Chris handed forward his expired CIA identification card.

"Yes, of course," he said blandly. "I'll wait."

"I'll see if I can get someone to help you," the woman said as she looked at the card. Chris sat on a hard chair, across the narrow hallway from the policeman, who eyed him warily. The woman spoke softly into a telephone.

Two minutes later, a young slim man with tanned face and sun-streaked blond hair came out and stopped at the woman's desk. He was jacketless, wearing a striped shirt, its sleeves rolled halfway up his forearms. He looked at Caldwell's identification card, then walked over to Chris, looked at him, then at the card again.

"Mr. Caldwell," the man said.

Chris nodded.

"This card has expired."

"I know. I'm retired. It's just by way of identifying myself."

"What can I do for you?" the man said.

"Where can we talk?" Chris asked. "Privately."

The man shrugged. "What do we have to talk about?"

Chris stood up and spoke softly to the man. "About who killed Yoel Tsurnick."

"Come with me," the young man said. He led Chris

247

down a long corridor and into a small room with a table and four chairs placed around it.

After he closed the door, the young man said, "I'm Major Paul Ravitch. I'm the intelligence officer."

"I guessed."

"Oh?"

"The shirt. I've been in embassies. Only snoops walk around without jackets."

Ravitch smiled.

"You mentioned a Yoel Tsurnick?"

"Let's not fence, major. I'm hung over and I'm not up to it. Yoel Tsurnick was an agent with the Mossad. He was in Houston checking into an Iranian takeover attempt of an American oil company. Another man was helping him. Benjamin Hirschfeld. Hirsch was my father-in-law, and he was murdered. Two nights ago, Yoel was murdered in San Juan. He was carrying a passport made out to David Benjamin. I was in San Juan at the time. The killer tried to pin the murder on me. I was lucky and the frame didn't take."

"Stay here," Ravitch said.

He left the room. When he returned a few minutes later, he carried a large brown envelope under his arm.

He sat down opposite Caldwell and put the envelope on the table.

"You said something about knowing who killed Yoel Tsurnick."

"Not that easy, major."

"What do you mean?"

"I was working with Yoel. I have my own reasons for wanting his killer and the killer of my father-in-law. I know about Ernest Wessel's being in Houston. I want to talk to the man who is taking over this file from Tsurnick. I want to know if we can work together. I need your people's resources. Probably you can use my inside position."

Ravitch was silent. He opened the strings on the file envelope and brought out a thick sheaf of papers.

He thumbed through the file silently for a few moments, then looked up at Chris. The young major's eyes were a brilliant blue.

"I'm taking over this file, Mr. Caldwell. You tell me. Can we work together?"

"Call me Chris and we can start trying."

"Fine, and I'm Paul. Where do we start?"

"Are you familiar with the file? With what Yoel was doing?"

"Yes. I've been project officer on the Red Moon since the file was opened."

"Isn't it unusual for you to take over a field case personally?"

"Yes. It's also unusual to have one of our people murdered."

"More than one," Chris said. "Yoel *and* my father-in-law." He paused, thinking. "My wife, a long time ago."

Ravitch seemed annoyed. "Yoel told me that you didn't know about that."

"I didn't until last night."

"How did you learn?"

"My father-in-law left me a letter. I finally found it. It explained a lot."

"All right," Ravitch said. "I have to tell you, though, Chris. I don't like amateurs off on some kind of vengeance vendetta."

"And I'm not an amateur. I'm a professional who's just come out of retirement. And vengeance isn't the sole province of God or the Israelis."

"Okay, that's fair. I apologize for the cheap shot," Ravitch said.

"Forget it."

"On to cases. What do you know?"

"Police Lieutenant Gomez in San Juan told me that a big burly redheaded man with a wide-brimmed hat was seen in the neighborhood of the restaurant round the time Yoel was killed. I think if you'll check that file, you'll find that Detective Albert Potter fills that description. He's the cop who stopped Yoel and me a few nights ago. He's the one who followed me from the fishing pier where Hirsch died. I think he's the one who killed Yoel. I checked with the police. He's on vacation. I don't know what his connection is, but—"

"He's close to Doyle Blaney. Yoel told you that."

"Yes, but why'd he kill Yoel? I don't know that."

"Ernest Wessel has a way of doing that," Ravitch said.

"Doing what?"

"Getting people to do what he wants, getting them to expose themselves, to take the risks, to court death, while he sits like a spider in the middle of some enormous web vibrating threads."

"You sound like you have a book on Wessel," Chris said.

"Yes. A very ugly book. What are you going to do?"

"Yoel told you about *Morning at Giverny?*"

"Yes," Ravitch said.

"I was wondering if maybe the painting's a fake," Chris said.

"It's not."

"How do you know that?"

"We sent someone to Griffin's ranch to inspect it. The painting is real."

Chris was impressed. "Where did Griffin get it?"

"I don't know," Ravitch said.

"I think it might be a key to all this," Chris said.

"So do I," said the young Israeli.

That afternoon, Caldwell remembered his promise to Dolores McBride and called the law office.

When McBride answered, he said, "Chris, where the hell have you been?"

"Why?"

"I asked Miss Liberal about you and she got all upset. You two have trouble?"

"Nothing important. By the way, I'm quitting."

"Shit. Over a lovers' quarrel?"

"Nothing like that. Susan's got all the work she needs to finish out the SEC application. I've just figured out lawyering's not for me."

"What are you going to do?"

"Clean up Hirsch's place. Then go home. Go swimming."

"And..."

"And what?"

"Nothing," McBride said. "You be sure to call me before you leave."

"You got it, Mac," Chris said as he hung up the phone. He knew what McBride had wanted to say. He wanted to ask, "What about Hirsch's so-called murder? You just going to forget about that?" No, Mac, he thought, I'm not.

250

But enough friends have died, and it's best that you forget it as soon as you can. The killers belong to me.

Caldwell's telephone rang later in the day and Ravitch asked, "Are you in for a pound or just for a penny?"

"In up to my lungs," Chris said.

"Meet me downstairs in ten minutes."

Ravitch was driving a three-year-old black Chevrolet, and as soon as Chris got in, the Israeli pulled smoothly into the early-evening traffic.

"I want you to know that I would expect a rational man to reject what I'm about to suggest," he said.

"Agreed. What is it?" Chris asked.

"I think we should go to Potter's apartment and see if we can find anything that will put him in Puerto Rico two nights ago."

"I do too," Chris said.

"I don't suppose there's any chance of finding the gun," Ravitch said.

Chris shook his head. "Not a chance. All cops have what they call 'clean' guns that can't be traced to them. Chances are he took one down to Puerto Rico—they don't x-ray the luggage for the hold of the plane. He used it, and then when he was done tossed it in the ocean. It's too risky to try to bring a gun back to the States, because they inspect your luggage leaving the island. We going to his house?"

"Yes. His apartment."

"Is he out?"

"Not yet," Ravitch said. "But he stopped for a drink today at Corey's Tavern near his apartment. He made a date with one of the waitresses. He is going to pick her up at seven and take her to the movies."

"All right," Chris said. "Inside or outside?"

"Which do you prefer?"

"Inside," Chris said.

The Israeli major nodded. "It is probably best. He might recognize you, but he doesn't know me."

They parked across the street from a three-story brick apartment building in the northern corner of the city.

"He has no wife?" Chris asked.

"He lives alone," Ravitch said. "He was divorced three

years ago. The waitress at Corey's seemed to know all about it."

"All right."

Ravitch handed Chris a small black plastic box about the size of a pack of cigarettes.

"Keep this in your pocket," he said. "If he heads back here, I'll signal you. I'll try to give you at least five minutes."

"Okay," Chris said.

It was seven minutes after seven before Detective Albert Potter, wearing a tan-colored three-piece suit and a broad-brimmed hat, stepped out the front door of his building. He looked around, then walked to his parked yellow car at a fast pace.

"That's his personal car," Chris said.

"How do you know?"

"The night he stopped Yoel and me he said he was on duty. But he was driving that car. The day he followed me from the fishing pier too."

"All right," Ravitch said. "I'll take him. We'll meet at your apartment at nine o'clock. His apartment is number 310. Sure you can handle it?"

"With luck," Chris said.

"Here is some hardware if you need it," Ravitch said. He handed over a slim plastic envelope containing four shiny metal tools. "You know how to use these?"

"I was educated in the very finest schools," Chris said.

"Okay, go. He's leaving. When you get out of this building, don't take a cab nearby. Walk a few blocks. We don't want him to make you by checking local cabdrivers. Do you have a gun?"

"No. I had to leave Yoel's in San Juan."

"Take this one," Ravitch said. Keeping his hand low and out of sight of passersby, he handed Chris a lightweight .32 caliber revolver. "Use it if you must. Go."

"Stay on his tail," Chris said. He stepped out of the car, and Ravitch pulled away, following Potter's yellow Chrysler.

Chris was pleased to find that the entrance to Apartment 310 was in a small alcove at the end of the hallway, where no one would see him fumbling with the lock.

He took a thin, L-shaped piece of steel from the package Ravitch had given him and was able to slip it into the doorframe alongside the lock. He worked the piece of steel upward until the inside corner of the L engaged the lock bolt. Then he pulled it toward him. The steel pressed against the beveled side of the bolt, pressing it into the lock housing. With his left hand, he pushed against the door and it slid open into the apartment.

The window blinds were open and there was still enough daylight left so Caldwell did not have to risk turning on a light that might be seen from outside.

He felt Ravitch's pistol in his pocket, and the cold metal in his hand gave him reassurance.

Chris walked directly into the bedroom, where he saw a tan vinyl suitcase on the littered floor next to the bed. The luggage was still zipped up. He crouched down next to the luggage. On the handle was an airline identification tag with the large inch-high letters HOU. Houston. He had flown back to Houston. Across the zipper of his bag was a thin green strip that certified that the contents had been inspected and approved by the U.S. Department of Agriculture. Chris nodded. It was the kind of strip that was put on U.S. mainland-bound luggage at the San Juan airport in Puerto Rico. He didn't bother to open the bag. There would be no gun in it. If Potter had somehow managed to bring back his gun in his luggage, he would not have left it inside the bag. Instead he would have taken it out and hidden it in the apartment, wherever he hid his other guns. The unbroken green USDA strip across the bag's zipper proved that he hadn't opened the bag since returning to Houston.

Chris stood up and looked around the bedroom.

A pair of tan slacks and a dark-maroon flowered shirt were tossed carelessly over the back of a chair. The pockets of the trousers were empty, but in the shirt pocket Chris found an airline-ticket folder. Handwitten on the inside flap was an itinerary for "Mr. Potter Alberts." Mr. Potter Alberts had flown to San Juan two nights ago, arriving at 6:00 P.M. He had returned from San Juan nine hours later.

Bingo.

Chris stuck the ticket folder into his jacket pocket. Suddenly there was a beeping sound as the pager in his pocket went off. Startled, Chris pressed the button that silenced the unit.

He went back into the living room and stood at the front door for a moment, looking around to make sure he had left no signs of his presence. The small apartment looked undisturbed.

He slipped back out into the hallway, pulling the door tightly shut behind him.

He walked down the two long flights of stairs to the main floor, then paused inside the fire-exit door, looking through the wire-glass window toward the main entrance. It might be risky to walk out and run the chance of bumping into Potter. He would wait until the detective returned, and then he would slip out when Potter got into the elevator.

Three minutes later, Potter walked in the front door of the building. He was accompanied by a young woman wearing a light-green dress and matching shoes with ankle straps. She was chewing gum.

They walked to the elevator. Potter pressed the up button. Chris pressed against the wall, out of sight of the two people.

After twenty seconds, Potter pressed the elevator button again.

With the lobby empty, he stood close to the young woman and put his right hand on her buttocks. She smiled at him and kissed him lightly.

He jabbed the button one more time, almost angrily, then growled something, took the young woman's elbow, and began walking to the stairway.

Chris glanced out the door just in time to see them coming toward him. The stairway did not go down to the basement. Chris ran up the steps to the second-floor landing. He could hear the door open downstairs and Potter's raspy voice.

"Frigging elevator's always screwed up."

"Little walking's good for you," the girl said. "Builds up the appetite."

"Nothing wrong with my appetite, woman," Potter said. The girl giggled.

254

Chris darted out the door into the second-floor hallway. He walked quickly to the far end of the building, his back toward the doorway to the stairs. After a few moments, he came walking back, opened the stairwell door, and listened. All was quiet.

He walked downstairs, into the lobby, and out the front door. He turned left, away from the side of the building that housed Potter's apartment, and walked quickly away.

Darkness had not yet fallen over the city. He strolled six blocks before he stopped a cab on the street and rode back to his apartment. All the while, he held his hand around Ravitch's revolver in his pocket.

When Caldwell opened the door for Ravitch at nine, the Israeli asked immediately, "Did you get anything?"

"Enough."

"Any trouble?" Ravitch asked.

"No."

"I'm sorry you didn't have much time, but I guess their lust exceeded their love of cinema. They went straight to his apartment."

"No matter," Chris said. "I had time enough."

He went to his jacket, hanging up in the closet just inside the front door, took out the airline-ticket folder, and gave it to Ravitch.

"The times are right," Chris said as Ravitch looked at the folder. "And he did make the trip, because his luggage still has markers on it."

"And nobody goes on vacation for less than a day and travels under a name that isn't his," Ravitch said. He folded up the ticket envelope, nodded his head, and put the folder in his pocket. "This will do. I must leave."

"What's next?" Chris asked, as he walked with Ravitch to the door.

"I will keep you informed," Ravitch said.

Chris opened the door, and Susan Millard stood there. She saw Chris and the man standing next to him.

"I'm sorry," she said. "I..."

"That's all right," Chris said. "He's just leaving."

Ravitch slipped past the tall blonde.

"Good night, Chris. Miss."

Chris said, "Call me tomorrow."

"I will."

Chris looked at Susan as Ravitch walked down the hallway. "Come on in," he said.

As soon as she was inside the door, Susan said, "I'm sorry, but I couldn't just let things end this way."

There was hurt in the young woman's voice, and Chris felt a sudden surge of warmth toward her, an impulse to take her in his arms and comfort her. The unfamiliar emotions confused him, and he took Susan's arm and led her to the couch.

"You sit there," he said. "It's my turn to make you coffee."

"Mr. McBride told me you were leaving."

"Yeah. I am," Chris said as he walked into the kitchen. As he poured water into a saucepan, he heard her voice call after him.

"When?"

"Pretty soon," he called back. "As soon as I clean up this apartment."

He put the water on the stove to boil and went back inside and sat alongside Susan on the sofa.

What was going on? He wanted to reach out and take her hand in his. He wanted to stroke her cheek with his fingertips. What was happening?

"I don't want you to leave," she said.

"It doesn't have to be forever," he said, and then he leaned forward, put his arms around her, and pulled her to him.

She spoke softly alongside his throat. "I meant what I said yesterday, Chris. I love you."

Love? Was that what it was? Was that what he was feeling? It had been so long. Why now? he asked himself.

And then he realized why. He had been freed, freed by Hirsch's letter to him. He had loved Zhava and she had been killed and he had taken the blame on himself. If that was what he did to people he loved, then he would not love again. But Hirsch's letter had changed that. Zhava had not died because of the husband who loved her. She had died because of the work she did. He was free again. And it came back to him in a flood of memories. The conversations with Hirsch. How many times had his father-in-law told him that he should not blame himself for his wife's

256

and daughter's death? But Chris had never listened until he found the letter.

He squeezed his arms tightly about Susan.

"I love you too," he said, and meant it.

"Your water's boiling away," she said.

"Screw it. There's more where that came from," he said as he lowered his face to hers and kissed her gently on the lips.

She pulled her face away from his. A small smile played about her lips. "Are you going to work your wicked will on me? Are we going to make love again?"

Chris shook his head. "We didn't make love the other night. We had sex. Tonight, I'm going to make love to you . . . for the first time."

Suddenly, she pulled away from him and stood up. "I'll turn off that water in the kitchen."

"Go ahead. I guess I won't get any rest until you do."

She walked into the kitchen and pulled the door closed behind her. After she had been gone for a full minute, he called out, "Hey. You turn off the water by turning the knob on the stove."

Then the kitchen door opened and Susan stood in the doorway, naked.

"I didn't want you to change your mind," she said.

Chris stood up, walked to her, and then picked her up in his arms to carry her inside his bedroom.

"There wasn't any chance of that," he said thickly.

Chris gently kissed her breasts, then pulled Susan toward him, kissing the side of her neck, then pressed his lips to hers.

She responded needily. In a moment, their tongues were caressing. He ran his hand slowly up and down her side, then put his hand on her hip and gently moved her onto her back. Leaning over her, his lips still on hers, he let his fingertips circle her stomach with a feathery touch. She responded with a shudder. His hand dipped lower, gently parted her legs, and touched her. She moaned in the base of her throat, then tore her lips from his to begin throwing her head back and forth. Her hips began moving against his hand, then Susan stiffened and a shuddering cry broke from her throat.

257

He held his hand in place for a moment, then pulled her body against his. She clung to him. "Oh, Chris," she said hoarsely.

"Save your applause until the end, please," he said, then moved both his legs within hers. She gasped again at the touch of his body against her, then reached behind him and pulled him into her.

"Make love to me, Chris."

"Yes," he said.

"It's the first time for us, isn't it?"

"Yes," he said.

"But not the last," Susan said.

Chris blew lazy plumes of cigarette smoke toward the ceiling and finally came to a decision. He would tell Susan nothing, because in ignorance there would be safety for her.

Involuntarily he reached out his left hand and rested it on her bare thigh. He heard her inhale a sip of air.

After a moment, she said, "Chris, we ought to talk."

"If we're going to spend the rest of our lives together, you'd better learn that I hate to talk after making love. *You* talk for a while."

"All right," she said.

"Why did Brooks ask you to keep an eye on me?" Chris said.

"It was after I came down here to work with McBride. Otto told me that Gus Griffin had gotten word that somebody would be trying to dig up dirt on him to blackmail him. He asked me to watch Mr. Hirschfeld and let him know of anything suspicious. I didn't find out anything, but later Otto told me that Mr. Hirschfeld definitely was involved in some kind of blackmail scheme. When he died, and you came in, he told me that you were probably involved too, because you were his son-in-law."

"Did you tell him about Hirsch mentioning the Red Moon to you?"

"Yes," Susan said. "It was no big thing, just a remark Mr. Hirschfeld dropped along the way."

For a moment, Chris thought, No big thing but it got Hirsch killed. But he shook that out of his mind. Hirsch had mentioned the Red Moon to others. He would have been killed if Susan had not said a word. His death was not on her hands.

"And did you believe that Hirsch and I were blackmailers?"

He could feel her body move slightly as she shook her head in the dark.

"I didn't know anything about you," she said. "But I couldn't believe it about Mr. Hirschfeld, not that nice, gentle old man."

"Well, just to set your mind at rest, it wasn't true," Chris said. "It was never true, not about Hirsch, not about me."

"Is Otto involved in something?" she asked.

Chris tried to form an answer that would be clever and guileful and sound believable, and finally settled on "I don't know."

"What is this all about, Chris?" Susan asked. "What is this Red Moon business?"

Chris rolled toward her and touched her breast with his right hand.

"Susan, I want you to listen carefully. I'm going to go away for a few days to clean up some personal business. I don't want you to know anything about what's going on. If you know something, you might be hurt, and I don't want you hurt. I just want you to forget everything."

"But you're not going to forget it, are you?" she asked. When Chris did not answer, she said, "That man I met coming in here tonight. He's got something to do with all this, doesn't he?"

"Paul? He's just a friend," Chris said.

"You don't have any friends in Houston," she said.

"He's a friend *of* a friend."

"What friend?"

"An old friend from Israel," Chris said. "Anyway, it doesn't matter. He's dead now."

He lit another cigarette and handed it to her for a drag. "Susan, I love you. Trust me," he said.

She inhaled deeply on the cigarette before answering.

"I don't want to. But I will. For a while."

CHAPTER THREE

Susan made a pot of coffee before she left in the morning, and Chris drank half of it before calling Ravitch.

"Paul," he said, "I'm going to Venezuela. I've decided to check on that old well."

"Why?"

"I was thinking last night about something Yoel told me. He said that Wessel was involved in using art treasures to buy supplies for the Nazis. Suppose that explains how Griffin got to own *Morning at Giverny?*"

Ravitch was silent momentarily. "Interesting," he finally said.

"I want to see for myself to check it out," Chris said.

"When will you leave?"

"Probably tonight."

"Catch the earliest plane you can," Ravitch said.

"Why?"

"It just seems a good idea," Ravitch said casually. "And be careful. You cannot take my ... er, supplies with you."

"I know. I'll figure out something," Chris said.

"If you need me, our embassy in Caracas can contact me immediately at any hour. Just be careful."

"What do we do about Potter?" Chris asked.

"There is nothing for you to do in this matter. It is in my hands," Ravitch said coldly.

"Okay," Chris said. "And Paul?"

"Yes?"

"You be careful too."

"Thank you. *Shalom.*"

Caldwell found the name of a travel agent in the yellow pages of the phone book, and arranged for a flight early that evening to Caracas on Viasa, the Venezuelan national airline, and for hotel accommodations in Caracas.

He was told he could pick his tickets up at the airport.

Detective Albert Potter shared the one great blessing of policemen everywhere. From his earliest days on the force, working shifts around the clock, a cop learned to sleep whenever he wanted to. Potter could get his eight hours if he went to bed at noon or at four in the morning, as he did the night before, after the little waitress from Corey's finally left.

It was almost exactly noon when Potter woke up. He lay in bed, smoking a cigarette. He looked at his suitcase on the floor and decided he would empty it out today. His body felt good, relaxed and rested, with the warm glow that a night of lovemaking always left him. If he lived to be a hundred, he would never understand women like Laura.

Why always game-playing? Laura had known he was going to take her to bed. He had known he was going to take her to bed. But if he had said to her, "Come on to my house tonight and let's make love," she would have said no. First he had to invite her to a movie. That made it right. After the invitation, it was easy to change plans and come right back to the apartment. It didn't make any sense.

He thought of last night, and his groin began to respond to his memories. He stubbed out his cigarette and with his toe fished his shorts out from under the covers. Maybe again tonight, he thought. A pretty young woman.

He padded out into the living room of the small apartment, then froze in place. A man sat in a chair, facing his bedroom doorway. He was a slim man, well tanned, with sun-streaked blond hair. He held a gun in his hand.

"Good morning, Mr. Potter," he said.

Potter thought about lunging back into his bedroom for his gun, hanging on the bedpost.

"Don't try it, detective," the man said.

Some kind of Englishman, Potter thought.

"What do you want here?" he demanded.

"You."

"Well, sucker, you got me. What is this gun shit?"

Paul Ravitch stood up. "I'm bringing you greetings from Puerto Rico," he said.

It was just after noon when Chris Caldwell picked up his phone and called a northern Virginia number he knew by heart.

261

"Ben Lucco, please," he told the operator. He told the same thing to the woman who answered the telephone in Lucco's office. "Tell him it's Chris Caldwell calling."

He received a pleasant but guarded welcome from his former superior. Caldwell came to the point right away.

"Ben, I'm taking a trip down to Venezuela. I want to know how to make contact down there."

"Why?"

"It's a long story and I don't want to go into it, because it's too vague and iffy so far. But if anything solid develops, you'd want to know about it. I want to know how to get to our people if I need information. Or help."

"They're not *your* people anymore, Chris. You changed all that when you resigned. You're just an ordinary American citizen now."

"An American citizen, Ben, but I'm not ordinary and you know it. Do you think I'd be asking you this if I thought it was stupid or unnecessary?"

"You've done stupid things before," Lucco said. "You quit a good job and became a beach bum, for one thing."

"Best thing that ever happened to you, Ben. You know if I'd hung around another three years I would have been director and I would have fired your ass."

"Chris, is it really important?"

"I think it is, Ben. Really important."

"Give me a clue. I've got to have something to hang my hat on, in case people start jumping on me. You know what this jungle is like."

"I know," Chris said. "That's one reason I got out. I'll give you one word, Ben. Oil."

There was a pause. "That's a pretty heavy word. Want to add a few more words to it?"

"Iran. And that's all, Ben. I promise you—if I find anything out, it's yours."

"You're putting me out on a limb, Chris."

"I know and you know I know."

"There's a cultural attaché in our embassy in Caracas. His name is Frank Stanley. He can always reach me."

"Thanks, Ben," Caldwell said and hung up.

After packing, Caldwell called McBride at his office. He had thought it through and decided to tell McBride the

262

truth about where he was going.

"What the hell you going to Venezuela for?" McBride asked.

"Just some things I've got to do," Chris said blandly.

"Okay, if that's the way you want it."

"Mac, please keep this under your hat. I'm not the most popular man in Houston, and I wouldn't want a sendoff— or a welcoming committee."

"I won't say a word, pardner," McBride said.

"Especially to Susan. That girl is talky. And one last thing. If for some reason I don't come back, take care of Hirsch's apartment, will you? Clean it out. I don't want just people messing with his stuff."

"If you don't come back? What kind of talk is that?"

"Well, you know. Planes crash. Just do what I say."

"Okay, Chris, you got it. Anything else I can do?"

"No."

"Stay well, kid," McBride said.

"You too, Mac."

After he had hung up, Chris was satisfied. Someone should know where he was, and a good solid friend like McBride filled the bill. Let Susan think he had gone to Puerto Rico. He trusted her now, but the less she knew, the better. Too much knowledge might put her in danger from the other side.

Susan Millard was reading the final draft of the application to the Securities and Exchange Commission when Doyle Blaney called.

"Hello, Susie. How are you?"

"Busy, Doyle. What is it?"

"Adam wants to know the status of our application."

"He'll have it there for his signature tomorrow. It'll be filed right after he signs it."

"That'll make him feel better. He's got ants in his pants. How about dinner?"

"Sorry, Doyle, I'm booked up."

"Your loss. Hey, I heard that Caldwell left the firm. What happened?"

"Nothing happened. His work here was done and he decided to go back to Puerto Rico. Doyle, I'm really busy on this application. Let's talk some other time."

"Sure, Susie, I've got time."

A few minutes later, Susan began to wonder how Doyle had learned so quickly that Chris had left the firm. What other interesting things might Blaney know? She decided she had been too quick to turn down the dinner invitation, and she looked up and called Blaney's office number, but there was no answer.

"Dammit," she swore softly. She decided to call him that evening at his apartment. Chris had said his business in Puerto Rico would take only a few days, and it would be nice to surprise him, when he came back, by being able to hand him some information he didn't have. She didn't know what kind of information. That was the infuriating part; she understood so little of what was going on, but she knew deep down in her bones that Chris was on the right side. And that was her side. She had made her decision, but still she wondered how Otto Brooks might react when he found out his willing spy in McBride's office was not willing to be a spy anymore. Was Chris right? Had Brooks proposed marriage to her just to move her out of Chris's orbit? Was he that much of a user and manipulator? He had seemed honestly hurt when she had asked for time to consider his proposal. She had been surprised and flattered, and she had not wanted to hurt his feelings by rejecting the marriage offer out of hand. Had he been using her? And was that proposal just the final grotesque display of it?

So many things that she didn't know. Perhaps dinner with Blaney might start to answer some questions.

Doyle Blaney had left his office and walked to Adam Griffin's.

"The application's on its way," he told Adam.

"About damned time, too. When Dad told me that that new guy Caldwell had quit, I thought we'd be waiting again forever."

"No, it's in the bag now, Adam," Blaney said.

After leaving Adam, Blaney began to wonder how Gus Griffin had found out so quickly about Caldwell's resignation. A few minutes later, he wandered down the hall to Gus's office. Gus's secretary, Velma, was at her desk wearing a tight white sweater and, Blaney noted, a bra.

"I liked you better the old way," Blaney said, squeezing the shoulder of her sweater to tweak her brassiere strap.

"I know. What a drag," she said. She sighed. "Got to go with the flow."

"You could flow with me anytime," Blaney said. "Boss in?"

"No, he left. Said he wouldn't be back for the day."

"Okay. I've got to get some papers."

Blaney let himself into the office and clicked the lock behind him. He went quickly to Gus's desk, knelt behind it, and reached down for the small cassette recorder.

The recorder wasn't there.

He fumbled around, confused, then bent all the way over to look under the big mahogany desk. Nothing. It had been removed.

"You make a mighty tempting target, Doyle," a voice drawled out from behind him.

Blaney froze for a moment. Then he pushed himself to his knees, stood, and turned around. Gus Griffin was standing inside the door of the office. He held a pistol in his hand.

"I sorta figured it was you," he said with a twisted grin. "I kept wondering how that Nazi knew everything I was up to."

Blaney shrugged. "Nazi? I don't know what you're talking about, Gus. And would you mind pointing that gun off to the side? Sometimes those things go off, you know."

"I know. Don't think it's not tempting."

"Tough to explain though, boss."

"Oh, I don't know," Griffin said. "'Officer, I found this man Blaney had been robbing me blind. When I told him I was going to send him to jail, he attacked me. So I shot the dirty bastard.'"

"Not too strong, Gus."

"How's this? 'Well, judge, I noticed that my wife was acting kind of funny lately. When I asked her about it, she broke down and told me that Doyle Blaney, my own right-hand man, had done gone and raped her. So I shot the dirty bastard, just like you would do.'"

"What would Sherry say to that?"

"She hates you and she's afraid of me," Griffin said. "She'd go along."

Blaney tried to keep his eyes on Griffin's face, but they kept returning involuntarily to the gun trained so unwaveringly on him. "Gus, I know you well enough to know if you were going to pull that trigger, you'd have done it by now. So what is it?"

"You and I are going to take a ride."

"Gus, you know I wouldn't do anything to hurt you," Blaney said, frightened at the ominous sound in Griffin's voice.

"You're going to have a chance to prove that," Gus said. "We're going to meet your pal Frederick Kirchner."

Chris wrapped Paul Ravitch's gun in a plastic bread bag, knotted the top of the bag tightly, put a wire tie around it, then dropped it into the back of the toilet tank.

At the airport, his ticket was waiting for him, but he had more than thirty minutes to wait till boarding. Habit sent him to the cocktail lounge and bar. At the last moment, he remembered, and ordered Perrier water.

The television set was on, tuned to the local news.

Chris sat in the corner, near the television, his eyes watching the door to the lounge. A man next to him, dressed in a blue corduroy cowboy suit, wanted to talk to him about the Houston Astros. Chris tuned him out by pretending to pay attention to the television set.

"This just in," the announcer said. "A Houston detective was found shot to death late this afternoon in his apartment."

Chris stared at the set.

"The Astros, boy, this year they're—"

"Shut up," Chris growled.

"The body of Detective Albert Potter was found slumped in a chair in the living room of his apartment. His service revolver lay on the floor next to the chair. A single shot had been fired through his head.

"Police said the death was an apparent suicide but that they were continuing to investigate. Detective Potter, who had been divorced from his wife, had been on the Houston force for fifteen years. At one time, he served as liaison between the department and federal law-enforcement agencies. Police said they had no reason to believe that Potter had been despondent."

The camera angle changed from a medium shot to a close-up and the announcer said: "And in Austin today..."

Chris rose and paid his bar check. The cowboy was still trying to jaw at him, but Chris ignored him. That was what Paul Ravitch had meant when he told Chris that Potter was in their hands now. An eye for an eye, a tooth for a tooth, a life for a life. The Old Testament Code of Moses still lived.

Walking down the carpeted pathway toward the plane gate, Caldwell felt somehow better about Potter's death. It was another death, but the man had been a murderer and deserved it. Still, Chris knew it was more than just a feeling for justice. Potter's death was one for his side for a change. After killings and attempted killings and Nazis and double-dealing, Caldwell's side had struck back.

CHAPTER FOUR

Occasionally, Houston oilmen needed a private place to make deals or assignations, and so the Spread, the private club to which Gus Griffin belonged, made special facilities available to them.

Upon notice, at any hour of the day or night, a member could enter the parking lot of the ornate three-story Victorian building through a rear driveway, avoiding the valet parking. The member could park his own car in a dark far corner of the lot, and through a rear door walk directly into a private room to which no one else would have access, while it was in use.

The private room was furnished with everything necessary for anything from large conferences to small love affairs. Drinks and meals could be ordered by a private telephone, but when they were ready, they were placed from outside the room onto a revolving tray built into the wall. The tray was then rotated into the room. No waiter or waitress entered; no one had any reason to see who was inside the room or what they were doing.

In a city in which secrecy was often money, providing that secrecy was the ultimate service offered by a private club.

Blaney had been to the hidden conference room only once, nine years before, when he was first thinking of coming to work for Gus Griffin. At Gus's direction now, he drove his golden Thunderbird into the rear parking lot and pulled up close to the darkened rear of the building. He and Gus got out of the car and walked to the unmarked door.

Gus opened the door with a key, and the two men stepped inside. Gus flipped on a light switch and double-locked the door. He motioned to Blaney to sit in a suede leather chair, then through the house telephone ordered up a bottle of tequila and ice.

Two minutes later, a bell tinkled just once as the revolving service tray rotated into the room. Gus made the drinks and had handed one to Blaney when the back bell rang softly.

Gus opened a panel, exposing one-way glass, and looked outside, then unlocked the door, and Frederick Kirchner stepped inside.

"Mr. Griffin," he said. "Blaney."

The man was wearing a white suit. He looked tired, Blaney thought. Blaney realized how uncomfortable he was. He had the feeling that these men were somehow going to decide his future, and that he would have precious little to say in the matter. And he didn't like it.

"You want a drink, Kirchner?" Griffin asked.

"No," the man said curtly.

"I want you to know that I think it was shit for you to have this asshole tapping my phones for you."

"It was necessary," Kirchner said blandly. With an unmistakable edge in his voice, he nodded to Griffin and said, "Sit down. We are not here to listen to you moan and whine."

Blaney had never heard anyone talk to Gus Griffin that way, and he was not ready for what happened next either. Griffin meekly sat down in an armchair, facing Blaney. Kirchner sat at the other end along a matching leather sofa.

"You will be interested in this," Kirchner said to Blaney. "Detective Potter is dead."

"How?" asked Blaney.

"Murdered. With his own gun."

"That fucking Caldwell," Blaney said.

"It was not Caldwell who killed him," said Kirchner.

"Who then?"

"Three nights ago, Potter carried out an assignment for me in Puerto Rico. You knew about the assignment, Griffin, but you didn't know who was performing it. Apparently he was careless. He was killed today by an Israeli agent."

Blaney listened in hopeless confusion.. What assignment in Puerto Rico? Why the Israelis?

Griffin asked Kirchner, "You sure of that?"

"Yes. You mentioned before certain tapes Mr. Blaney has been making for me. Potter was the man who delivered them to me. Before he died, he must have told the Israeli where I could be found, because he came looking for me. I was fortunate to escape."

"Will somebody tell me what is going on?" Blaney said.

"Shut up," Griffin snarled.

"In due time," Kirchner said softly.

"I don't like this Israeli shit," Griffin said.

"It is not for you to worry about," Kirchner said. "The Israelis are not interested in you or even your oil company. They are interested in me. The day I leave will be the day they lose all interest in Houston and the Griffin Oil Company."

"Then leave, for Christ's sake," Gus said.

"Not just yet. There is still some unfinished business. There is Christopher Caldwell."

"What's he got to do with anything?" Gus said. "Why is he involved?"

"Simply for revenge," Kirchner said. "But as long as he is alive, he is a danger to us."

Blaney still did not understand, but he said, "I hate that fucking Caldwell."

"Good," said Kirchner with a light smile.

"He's in Puerto Rico now," Blaney said.

Griffin shook his head. "Wrong. He's in Venezuela." He looked at Kirchner sharply. "I guess he's looking for the Red Moon."

"Good," said Kirchner. "Venezuela will be a good place for him to die. Don't you agree, Blaney?"

"Any place is a good place for him to die."

"I'm glad you think that way. Because you are going to kill him."

Gus Griffin growled that he would not be home for dinner. Sherry had just hung up the telephone when her daughter, Tina, pulled her lithe young body out of the swimming pool and walked toward her mother, who sat on the patio.

Sherry felt a warm glow just looking at the beautiful blond girl. Although only fifteen, Tina was already taller than her mother. Her hair was a natural honey-dipped gold, and her body, while it would never be as voluptuous as Sherry's, would be long and vibrantly beautiful.

Sherry recognized the warm glow as pride. She was proud of her daughter and proud of what she had been able to do for her. Tina would never know the grinding terror of being totally without money, of being friendless in strange cities, of knowing that you were only a step away from selling your body for rent money or food money.

She would never be at anybody's mercy. Sherry had seen to that. Unless something went wrong.

"What's the matter, Mom?"

"Why do you ask?" Sherry said.

"You've got this long sour puss on," Tina said with a smile of bright white teeth.

"Oh, Gus called. He won't be home for dinner."

"The way he's been acting lately, who cares?" Tina said.

"What do you mean, Teenie?" Sherry asked.

"You know. He's always grumbling or grousing about something. Say something to him and he snaps your head off. He's changing, Mom."

"Ah, you have to understand, he's under a lot of heavy business pressure lately. He'll snap out of it."

Tina was obviously not convinced. "If you say so," she said with a smile. She tossed a towel over her shoulders and walked toward the house. Just as she was about to open the sliding glass doors, Sherry called her.

"Tina. You know that music camp you wanted to go to?"

"Yes?"

"I've been thinking about it. I think you ought to go."

"When, Mom?"

"Well, if your busy schedule permits, how about tomorrow? Stay a couple of weeks."

"Wow. Mother, you are loved," Tina said, and her honest smile was all the reward Sherry wanted or needed.

When the girl went indoors, Sherry's own smile faded. Even Tina had noticed that Gus was growing progressively crazier. Two weeks ago, she had thought the possibility of Gus's murdering her was too slim even to be considered, but now she was not so sure.

He didn't even have to kill her, though. Suppose he just divorced her. He could twist her around until she was left with nothing. And Tina—what would happen to her chance to lead the good life?

271

All of a sudden, Sherry's decision to sell that voting option on her stock looked like a better and better idea. No matter what happened, she and Tina would have something, something that Gus couldn't take away.

But would it be enough?

She got up from the patio and walked around the house. She wandered into Gus's study and looked for the tenth time in the past three days at the paintings on the walls. Caldwell had said that the big one alone was worth over a million dollars. A million dollars, hanging on a wall, never looked at.

She had not spoken to her foster brother Frank since he had handed her up by turning her stock option over to Adam. But she had no one else. It was time to call Frank again.

Susan Millard finally reached Doyle Blaney in his apartment at 9:00 P.M.

"My date fell through," she said. "That dinner date still open?"

"Oh, Susie, I'm sorry," Blaney said. "I'm just packing. I've got to go out of town for a few days."

"Too bad," she said, then added casually, "Where you going?"

"Hush-hush company business," he said.

"Hiding things from your own lawyer?" she said. "Shame, shame."

"No," Blaney said uncomfortably. "It's just that . . . well, Gus is crazy about secrecy."

"I won't tell a soul."

"You don't know how Gus is," Blaney said. "Let's have dinner when I get back."

"We'll see. Give me a call," Susan said, and after she hung up, she wondered where Blaney was going in such a hurry and if it had anything to do with Chris's suddenly leaving town.

The flight from Houston to Caracas took nearly seven hours, including a long, boring stopover at Miami, and with the time difference from Houston, the sky was beginning to lighten when Caldwell's plane finally arrived.

As he picked up his single suitcase in the baggage-claim

272

area and waited for a customs inspection, he had the uneasy feeling that someone was watching him. He turned around quickly. There was a man sitting on a molded plastic lounge chair near the door, looking down at a newspaper in his lap. The man was short and fat and wore a dark-brown suit. As Chris stared at him, the man glanced up, met Chris's eyes, and immediately looked down again at the newspaper.

Chris retrieved his bag and, instead of walking out the main door of the terminal building, walked to the far end before exiting into the street outside.

There he turned and on the outside of the building retraced his steps toward the center of the terminal. When he glanced through the large plate-glass windows at the lounge chairs, the fat man was gone.

Chris hopped into the first cab in line.

"La Mimosa Hotel, *por favor*," he said.

The hotel was a small three-story building on the far side of the business district. Caracas, cupped within a ring of mountains, was a huge city. Tall buildings, bold and modern, towered over small drab utilitarian structures and buildings of traditional Spanish architecture. Although it was still early in the day, a torrent of traffic poured through the streets, and on every block there seemed to be a new skyscraper under construction.

Chris sat sideways in the rear seat, so he could watch to see if his cab was being followed, but he saw no recurring pattern of headlights.

Chris had not yet changed any of his American cash into bolivars, but the cab driver was pleased to accept ten dollars for the ride. Caldwell did not know if he was being ripped off or not, but he was prepared to settle for a ten-dollar ripoff. In Puerto Rico and in the States, particularly in New York, foreigners were often ripped off by cabbies with bills of a hundred dollars or more.

In fluent Spanish, Chris told the courteous desk clerk that he did not know how long he would be staying, and he was given a second-floor room on an inner courtyard overlooking the hotel's small, plain pool.

As he waited for the bellhop to appear to carry up his bag, Chris glanced toward the door. Standing outside, near one of the front windows, he again saw the short fat man.

273

Already it had started.

Chris told the clerk, "I'll take up my own bag," took the key from the counter, and walked quickly up the broad flight of stairs to the right of the lobby.

In the second-floor hallway, Chris ran to his room, opened the door, and tossed his bag inside. Across from his room was a doorway leading to outside steps that went down to the hotel's pool.

Chris wedged that door open with a matchbook, then waited on the metal steps. The sun was rising now, and already the air had grown warm and humid.

Five minutes later, Chris was almost ready to come back into the hallway and reenter his room when the short fat man came down the hall and stopped in front of Chris's room.

Chris ducked down under the glass panel in the door and moved over to the other side, where the doorknob was located.

He pulled open the door, jumped across the hall, and before the small man had a chance to turn, locked his right forearm around the man's throat. The man gasped.

In Spanish, Chris said, "I'll break your neck if you move." With his left hand, he reached out and unlocked his room door, then marched the man inside. The man still gasped and choked. The morning light illuminated the room enough for Chris to find the light switch.

He walked the man over to a chair near the window, and pushed him into it.

"If you want to live, put your hands on top of your head," he said.

The fat man complied. Chris, standing sideways, could see that the door to the room had not closed fully, but it would have to wait.

"All right," he said. "Who are you and what do you want?"

"I was looking for you, Señor Caldwell. A mutual friend sent me."

"Who?"

"Paul Ravitch. He asked me to bring you something." The short man tried smiling.

"What?" Chris asked.

"It is in my pocket. May I lower my hands?"

274

"No. What pocket?"

"My inside jacket pocket. My left side."

Chris stepped alongside the man, out of reach of a sudden kick, and slid his hand into the man's inside pocket. He felt a gun and pulled it out. It was another .32 caliber revolver.

"There are shells in my side pocket," the man said. "Paul thought you might need this."

Chris quickly checked the gun. It was loaded.

"May I lower my hands now?"

"Yes. Of course." Paul Ravitch had told Chris not to try to bring Ravitch's gun to Venezuela, but he had made sure that Chris would not be unarmed.

The fat man smiled again.

"I saw you at the airport," Chris said. "Why didn't you talk to me then?"

"Major Ravitch wanted me to be sure that you were not followed."

"Very dangerous," Chris said.

"Not really," the man said. He snapped his fingers. The front door of Chris's room slammed open and a young man with dark hair and fierce black eyes jumped into the room with a pistol aimed at Caldwell's stomach.

"No," the fat man said sharply. The young man lowered the pistol.

"Señor Caldwell, this is my son, Julio. I am Amelio Guerado. *Shalom.*"

"*Shalom,*" said Chris.

"Here are your bullets," Guerado said. To his son, he barked, "Close the door, Julio. Do you live in a barn?"

CHAPTER FIVE

At Amelio Guerado's insistence, Chris went to sleep. Julio would guard Caldwell's door. Chris tried to explain that this was not necessary, since only two persons, both friends, knew that he was in Venezuela, but Guerado would not have it any other way.

At noon, Julio drove Caldwell to the Altamira Restaurant, near Centro Bolívar, the towering skyscraper-filled governmental heart of Caracas. When he asked inside the restaurant for Señor Guerado, Caldwell was shown to a large rear table in a far corner of the large room, hidden from view of the door by small palm trees growing in the sunlight from a central skylight that dominated the restaurant's roof.

The little man jumped to his feet as Chris approached the table and insisted that Chris sit down before he resumed his place at the table.

"Will Julio not join us?" Chris asked.

Guerado shook his head. "He is young, and the young seem never to need food, at least not when served at a table. They like to eat standing up, these children."

Chris had assumed that Guerado was an official at the Israeli embassy, but the small Latin-looking man was not. He explained that he was a Polish Jew who had lived in Caracas for over thirty years.

"Your Spanish is excellent, that of a native," Chris said.

"My appearance too. My thought was that since I looked like a Venezuelan, a scarce commodity in Poland, I might as well come here and *be* a Venezuelan."

"And your connection with Major Ravitch?" Chris asked.

"I am active in the import-export business and from time to time I have been able to help the major and others do things that they could not do through normal channels."

"Like providing me with that gift this morning in my room?"

"Exactly. It is one of the things I do very well," Guerado said.

"I hope I ask you only for things you do well," Chris said. "Do you know what I am looking for here in Venezuela?"

"Yes. An oil well." The little man shrugged and spread his hands wide. "There are so many oil wells in Venezuela."

"I learned from reports that this well would have been in the east of this country, rather than around Lake Maracaibo. I saw a reference to Monagas and the Gulf of Paria. Is Monagas a city?"

"No. It is a state, Señor Caldwell. Its eastern boundary is the Gulf of Paria, and it is an oil region, that is correct."

"Then that's where I'll start looking."

"It is not so simple, señor. Monagas is large. Finding one oil well there would be like finding one building in your New York."

"I am open for suggestions," Caldwell said.

"I have a number of friends who work in the state petroleum corporation," Guerado said. "They are seeking records of any property once held by this Griffin Oil Company. I suggest you go to the city of Maturín—that is in the center of Monagas—and await my call there. It is some five hundred kilometers."

"I will leave today," Caldwell said. "I am anxious to begin. Can you call me a cab to get me back to my hotel?"

"That will not be necessary, Señor Caldwell," Guerado said. He snapped his fingers, and a second later Julio was standing alongside his father.

"Julio, you will take Señor Caldwell back to his hotel, and then arrange for a car rental for him."

"Yes, Father," the young man said.

Guerado turned again to Caldwell. "I heard from Major Ravitch this morning, and he gave me a message for you. He said to tell you that your white-haired friend is using the name of Frederick Kirchner. He said further that he almost had him yesterday but luck was not with him."

Chris nodded, and Guerado said, "This matter you are involved in, it is very important?"

"Yes, señor. Very important."

"Then go with God, Señor Caldwell," said Guerado, rising to his feet to shake Caldwell's hand. *"Shalom."*

The highway system was better than Caldwell had expected, and he reached Maturín early that evening, before the last rays of the sun had died. He found La Inglesa, the small commercial hotel Julio had directed him to, just off the main business district of the city. Maturín looked more to him like the Venezuela he had expected. Caracas had been a big unwieldy metropolis, but Maturín seemed a Venezuelan town. The streets were shared by automobiles and pack mules. The Spanish-style buildings with their red-tiled roofs stretched out in long rows. Women carried baskets on their heads, and Chris saw policemen on horseback.

His reservation was waiting for him at the small hotel along with a message to call Señor Guerado right away.

As soon as he got into the small room—Latins seemed not inclined to waste space on places meant just for sleeping—he called the number Guerado had left.

"We have found it," Guerado announced exultantly. "The well is located near the town of Pedernales, on the mouth of the Manamo River. The Griffin Oil Company bought it in 1939 and sold it to another company in 1947 after it began to produce oil in greater quantity."

"Good work. How did you find it?"

"Julio's fiancée works in the federal tax offices. She searched through old records."

"Did the records show anything else I should know?"

"The well was drilled by others in 1937 but produced no oil. Griffin took it over in 1939, and it produced about four barrels a day through 1943, then increased production to over a hundred barrels a day for the next several years. The Griffin Company sold it and the well went dry in about 1963."

Chris frowned. "Why did the well suddenly begin producing more oil?"

"I don't know, señor. Perhaps more efficient machinery?"

"Perhaps," Caldwell said.

"What will you do now?" Guerado asked.

"Go to Pedernales. I want to see that well with my own eyes."

"Pedernales is barely an hour's drive, señor."

"Yes."

"Please call every night," Guerado said.

Gus Griffin had one booted foot carelessly upon his large mahogany desk. Doyle Blaney sat cautiously in the leather armchair before the desk. He had often sprawled there casually over the years, receiving instructions and reporting on various projects, but now he felt shaken and tentative. He gripped the arms of the chair and stared at Griffin, who lit a long thin cigar and inhaled deeply before fixing Blaney with his sole good eye.

"Well?" Gus said, spitting out a shred of tobacco and glowering at Blaney from beneath his bushy eyebrows.

"I told Adam I'll have to take a few days off for some personal business," Blaney said. "Kirchner and I are meeting at the airport in an hour." He glanced over toward his luggage.

Griffin looked at Blaney and shook his head in mock sadness.

"You were just too goddam cute for your own good, Doyle," he said. "You really blew it."

"I never meant any harm," Blaney said. "I just thought Adam was right. Then Kirchner came and started talking to me, and it was his idea to get Sherry's stock."

"Last night, I finally figured that all out," Griffin said. "Tell you the truth, I never thought you were smart enough to work it out, and I sure as hell knew Adam wasn't. But if you hadn't been cute, none of this would have happened. If you had come to me right away, instead of trying to feather your own nest, we could have worked it out. And you wouldn't be on your way to Venezuela to murder a man."

Blaney looked around the room uncomfortably, and Griffin laughed.

"Don't worry. The office isn't bugged. Not anymore. If you had just come to me, we could have taken care of Kirchner and that would have been that."

"How did I know that?"

279

Griffin ignored the question. "I'll tell you something you might want to know, you greedy bastard. I was planning to retire and make you president of this company."

Blaney stared at him.

"That's right. You think I was going to give this company to that harebrained son of mine? Or my neurotic wife? Bullshit, Blaney. It was going to be you."

"You should have told me," Blaney said.

"Promise you a reward to keep you honest? I always thought you were honest. At least honest enough. And on my side. I didn't know you were busy double-banking me."

"I'm sorry, Gus."

"I am too. We could've taken care of Kirchner ourselves and no one would have been the wiser. I would have done it myself, but he always seemed to know too much. He knew who I was talking to, what I was doing. I never thought that you were the pipeline."

"I still don't know why I have to go to Venezuela," Blaney said.

"Because Kirchner only saw Caldwell once in a car going a hundred miles an hour. And besides, I want *you* to pull the trigger."

"Why?"

"Because then I'll feel a lot easier about having you around, boy. Remember, I didn't ask you into this game. You pulled up a chair and sat down all by yourself."

"I know."

"You better get moving," Griffin said coldly.

Blaney got up and walked to the door, relieved at being dismissed.

He stopped at the door and said, "You haven't told me yet what it is that you and Kirchner are up to."

"That's right," Griffin said with a sour grin. "Do this job right and maybe you'll find out in time."

"I have to. I've got too much invested now to back out."

"You sure do, Blaney. You sure do."

Caldwell arrived at the tiny port town of Pedernales early the next morning and checked his bag into the Star of Wonder Hotel, a two-story six-room building that was the town's only hotel and whose owner-manager seemed to regard Chris's arrival as a reason to go to church and light a candle to the Holy Mother.

The room he was given was small and dingy, but he was indifferent to his surroundings. His light-tan suit was sweaty and wrinkled, and he promised himself that he would stop and buy some fresh clothing as soon as he found a store. There was no store on the main street of Pedernales. There was a police station, and Chris went inside, where a lone officer, wearing a uniform shirt and blue jeans, slept in a chair with his feet atop a desk.

Caldwell cleared his throat, and the man jumped to his feet. *"Sí, señor,"* he said.

"I am looking for an oil well near here."

"Ah, *sí*. So are we all. All of us hope, one day, we find the oil well and we retire from this business. You find this oil well, I hope you find two and are generous enough to give me one. You will find me a man who will wear his wealth very graciously."

After a few moments, Chris managed to make the policeman understand that he was looking for a well that had been shut down almost twenty years before.

"I have been here only five years, señor," the policeman said sadly. "Perhaps the editor of the newspaper down the street? He is very old and would know."

"Thank you," Chris said. As he walked toward the door and the blistering sunlight beyond, the policeman called after him, "If you find two wells, señor, my offer remains intact. But only for the next fifty years until I steal enough money to retire to my mansion in Caracas."

The newspaper office was closed, but a sign in the door directed Chris to a tavern on the corner, where he asked for the editor and was directed to a small courtyard behind the tavern, where one old man was watching two elderly cronies play dominoes.

"I seek the editor," Chris said.

The kibitzer turned to him. "I am Alonzo Inca. It is my misfortune to hold the job you describe and my incredible good luck that I have been found today by a rich American."

"Perhaps it is a day of good luck for both of us," Chris said. "I am looking for an old oil well, once owned by the Griffin Oil Company."

"Sure. I know that well," the man said, apparently as-

281

tonished that anyone would speak of it after so many years. "I worked there for a long time as a truck driver."

Alonzo Inca, who was delighted to be hired as Chris's guide, moved with alacrity down the block to the parked rental car.

"Don Miguel had the well drilled," he said. "Or was it his son, Don Alfredo? No, it was Don Miguel. We all thought he was crazy, but he was right, there was oil in the ground."

He got into the car alongside Caldwell and pointed him down the main road of the town.

"We had a festival when the well struck oil, because we thought there would be many wells and we would all be rich. But this poor well was the barren bitch of all wells and produced only nine or ten barrels before it died. Finally Don Miguel sold it to the tall American, Greefeen.

"No, it was Don Alfredo who sold it to the American. Don Miguel had died from the fever. Or the lung disease?" Alonzo thought for a moment about the impermanence of human life. "Anyway, up there ahead is a road on the right side. You must take that road, señor."

"When did the American buy the well from Don Alfredo?" asked Chris patiently.

"I *think* it was Don Alfredo, señor, but that was long ago. It may have been Don Miguel."

"God rest his soul," Caldwell said.

"And ours when we go to join him," Alonzo Inca said, folding his hands in his lap.

"When did the American buy the Red Moon?"

"The what, señor?"

"The Red Moon."

"I am sorry, señor, we are talking about an oil well, not a moon."

"I thought that was the name of the well, the Red Moon," Caldwell said.

"Maybe in America where they give names to sandwiches and denim pants, perhaps it is called a red moon, but not here, señor, not ever." He seemed offended.

"All right, Señor Inca, I'm sorry," Chris said. "When did the American buy the well?"

"It was before the World War, señor, but not long before, I think."

282

"And what did he do?"

"You turn up this gravel road, señor. Oh, how many times I made that turn in my truck. Once I made the turn too tightly and my rear wheels almost went into that little ditch. If they had, I would have turned over and it would have been very bad for me. I felt the truck hang in the air for a moment and I prayed to the Good Lady to have mercy on me and then the wheels came down again and I was safe.

"I lighted a candle to her that Sunday in the church, señor, and do you know the very next month I won some money in the lottery...and there is the well, señor. Ah, how many years it has been since I last saw it."

Caldwell saw only a waist-high box of weathered wood in the middle of a field that was growing a scraggly crop of corn.

"That's it? That's all of it?" Caldwell said.

"Sí, señor. They took away the pumping machinery when the well closed down. The storage tank was down by the water of the river, and I would truck the oil down each day. Maybe someday they may all come back again and pump more oil out of this well, but I suppose I am too old now to drive the truck full of oil. They would have a younger man do it," he said sadly. "So I will live out my days as editor of a newspaper."

Caldwell smiled, turned the car around, and started back. He felt a bitter sense of letdown. Hirschfeld and Tsurnick had been killed because of this relic of an oil well in the middle of a field of corn? He gave a bark of laughter, because if he didn't laugh, he might cry.

The old man looked at him with curiosity but politely said nothing.

"Why do you suppose the American bought the well if it produced very little oil?" asked Chris.

"Perhaps it was the best he could afford, señor. Perhaps he had very little money." He paused, then corrected himself. "No, señor, wait. He must have had some money, because after he bought the well, he brought down some men and machinery and he drilled the well deeper and after that it began producing much more oil. Soon I was making two trips a day, instead of one trip a week. Sometimes they would even hire another truck."

"How big was your truck?" Caldwell asked.

"It held one hundred barrels, señor. That is four thousand gallons. I was a very good driver. I never lost a tank. Even Greefeen once told me that."

"And when did this well start to produce so much oil?"

"That was right after the American bought the well. So I think maybe he had money after all. It was simply that he knew there was more oil farther down and Don Alfredo did not."

"And neither did Don Miguel," Caldwell said, turning off the gravel road and onto the wider dirt road.

"That is correct, señor."

Caldwell frowned. "Forgive me, Señor Inca, but I want to be sure I understand. You say the American bought this well and promptly drilled it deeper and was able to get more oil?"

"Much more oil, señor."

"And that was in 1941?"

"It may have been then, señor. Or it might have been before that. It was long ago and I cannot remember every detail. But it was right after Greefeen bought the well that it started to produce more oil."

"And how long did it continue to produce more oil?"

"You turn to the left up ahead, señor." He pointed. "The well continued in good health for maybe eight or ten years, but then it grew tired, like a mother's breast, and began giving less and less oil. The American had sold it to another company by then, a company owned by Venezuelans. They were better to work for in some ways than the American, but they did not pay as well. But we did not have to be afraid that the managers would hit us, as the American sometimes did. Instead, they would have a guard hit us. Only the guard used a stick, instead of his hands. One of the guards broke Pedro Jimenez's shoulder bone one time, hitting him with a stick. That was not a good thing to do."

"That was not the American?"

"No, he had gone by then. I was told much later that he was a filthy capitalist exploiter of the poor, but he paid us better wages than the Venezuelans who bought the well from him. Here is the main road, señor."

Caldwell drove silently, thinking, until they reached

the small tavern again. He paid the man ten dollars instead of the five dollars agreed upon and offered to buy him a beer. Inside, they sat at a table, Alonzo Inca with a beer and Caldwell with a foully sweet Malta India, an alcohol-free malt beverage that tasted like molasses filtered through mudwater.

"Where did you take the oil that came from the well?" Caldwell asked.

"A mile up the river, out of town, there is a storage tank and a pier, señor. The water is deeper there and a small tanker can tie up and have the oil put into it by hoses that lead from the storage tank."

He looked proud, and Caldwell nodded gravely and said, "That is very clever. And ships would come and take the oil away to the refinery?"

"They never told me where they took it, señor," Alonzo Inca said. "One ship would come every few months. It would take just a little oil. We would fill up two hundred barrels and leave them on the pier and this ship would take them on board and empty them into its tanks and then put back the empty barrels. I remember that because the ship was always guarded by one of your United States navy boats that anchored out there near Serpent's Mouth to watch, and then the two ships would leave together."

"But there were other ships?" Caldwell said.

"Yes. They were always different and they came at different times and they took much more oil."

"These ships came alone? Without a navy escort?"

"That is correct, señor. It came through Serpent's Mouth at night and loaded at night and left at dawn. And always before the navy escort one came. It took on much oil, because after it had left, the big storage tank back in the trees was empty, and it held over twenty-five thousand barrels. Once one of those ships sank. Torpedoes. Everyone died. All except one man. A fishing boat found him and brought him back here." Alonzo Inca tapped his right temple. "But he was not all together anymore."

"He was the only survivor?" Caldwell asked.

"Sí, señor. Dr. Delgado saved his life if not his mind. I remember he came from a town up the coast, on the peninsula."

"What town?"

285

"I do not remember."

"What was his name?"

The old man thought. "Pedro?" he said hesitantly. "It might have been Pedro, señor. I can't remember his last name. That was a long time ago, you know. I must be honest with you, señor. His name may *not* have been Pedro."

"You are a very honest man, señor," Caldwell told him. "And you have an excellent memory."

"Was his name Pancho?" the old man wondered.

"I don't know. Would you like another beer?"

"Very much," the old man said. "Thank you, señor. You are a very generous man."

"I am honored to have met you," said Caldwell, preparing to leave.

"But it might have been Pedro," the old man called to him as he was leaving the tavern.

His name was Pedro. Pedro Lorca from the town of Irapa, on the peninsula fifty miles across the Gulf of Paria.

Chris found this out five minutes later when he was driving out of Pedernales and happened to glance to the roadside and saw a sign advertising the residence and services of Hector Delgado, doctor of medicine.

Dr. Delgado was sitting in a rocking chair on the front porch. He was eighty-five years old and his face was as lined as wrinkled waxpaper.

Caldwell said that he was interested in finding a sailor who had been saved by a fishing boat sometime, perhaps in 1944. A question of insurance, and perhaps the doctor might...

"It was December 24, 1943," the doctor said. "Poor man's brain never worked right again. He stayed around here for a while after I treated him, but then he went home to his village."

"Would you have records of his name? Of his village?"

"I have all my records in here, young man," the doctor said, tapping the top of his head with a gnarled index finger. "Pedro Lorca. From the town of Irapa. I remember it well. It was an open file, no one knowing his name or his address, and then one day one of his townspeople passed through here and recognized him and took him home. Pedro Lorca. From the village of Irapa."

"Thank you, doctor, thank you," Chris said.

"You say this is an insurance matter?" the doctor asked.

"Yes, sir."

"Will Señor Lorca collect any money?"

"Probably."

"Remind him he owes me four bolivars," Dr. Delgado said.

"Is that how you remembered him?" Chris asked.

The doctor nodded. "Always check the open files," he said.

"Would you accept my payment now, in advance of the insurance settlement?" Caldwell asked.

"No, young man. It is Lorca's account. He must pay it by his own hand."

"I'll see that he does."

"Tell him he is almost forty years late and even my patience has its limits."

CHAPTER SIX

While the distance from Pedernales to Irapa was only fifty miles as the crow flies, driving it required going west, inland, then snaking one's way up the coastline to the Paria Peninsula at the northeastern tip of Venezuela, then driving out along the southern shore of the narrow finger of land.

The road was bumpy, packed earth, carved out of dense tropical growth, and Caldwell had the feeling that if for just one week no vehicles used the road, the brush and trees and plants would totally consume it, reclaiming it for the jungle, and it would vanish without a trace.

The drive took three hours, but Chris welcomed the chance it gave him to think.

Four barrels a day. That's what Griffin claimed the old well had produced. But Alonzo Inca had often been carrying 150 barrels a day by truck down to the waterside to dump into the holding tank.

Back in Houston, Chris had begun to suspect that perhaps Griffin was selling oil to the Nazis all during the war. He had claimed his well was pumping four barrels a day, but the old man had told Chris it was pumping 150 or 200 barrels. One hundred and fifty barrels a day was over 4,000 barrels a month. In six months, perhaps 30,000 barrels. And at thirty or forty gallons a barrel, a million gallons. A sizable contribution to the Nazis of raw fuel. A sizable contribution to Gus Griffin's pocket.

His mind kept returning to Griffin's claim. Four barrels a day. Four B. He slowed and pulled off to the side of the road for a moment.

Of course. Hirsch's notes. They had mentioned Brooks, 100K, and 4B. The old man had understood. How had Gus Griffin been able to contribute $100,000 to Otto Brooks's first Senate campaign when he claimed his only well was producing a mere four barrels a day?

The money had come from the Nazis. It had come to

Gus Griffin for trying to sabotage America, and he had probably moved it back into America through the law firm of Otto Brooks. And when Brooks ran for the Senate and needed the money, the Nazi payoff had gone right into the pocket of the man who would become the Lone Star Liberal of the United States Supreme Court. And Hirsch had figured it out.

It explained too why *Morning at Giverny* hung in Griffin's study. It had been used by the Nazis to pay him, and he could not show it publicly without having to answer more questions than he wanted to.

And why was Griffin now cooperating with Ernest Wessel in a plan to have Iran take over the small oil company? Because Ernest Wessel had worked on the Nazi procurement program. Tsurnick had explained that. And he had probably dealt directly with Griffin, and then, like a haunting voice from the past, had showed up in Houston one day to blackmail the oilman with threat of exposure.

Griffin took the oil from the well and trucked it every day to the giant holding tank, hidden back in the stand of trees off Pedernales. When he knew the American oil ship was coming, he would fill the few barrels and stand them at dockside. The Americans would hoist the barrels on ship, empty them into their oil tanks, and return the barrels and steam off. In the meantime, the major hoard of Griffin's oil remained back in the woods, untouched, waiting for the Nazis to come and pump it out through the underwater pipe.

Chris drove off onto the roadway again.

He had it now. He was sure of it. But try to prove it?

And what was the Red Moon?

It was midafternoon when Chris pulled into the heart of Irapa. Twenty or thirty years before, the town might have been the mirror image of Pedernales, a sleepy fishing village, but the discovery of good oilfields along the Paria Peninsula had pushed the town into a forced growth.

New buildings were under construction throughout the town. New roads paralleled the main street, and houses stretched back block after block. He realized dejectedly that finding one man named Pedro Lorca here might be more difficult than finding one talkative man in Pedernales had been.

The telephone book was no help. There were no listings for Lorca. The druggist from whom he bought two packs of cigarettes had never heard of such a man, señor, and my deepest apologies.

Off to the right, several hundred yards away, Chris could see the water and the masts of sailing ships, and he drove down there. He walked around the docks, talking to fishing boats just back from their day's run, but it was several hours before he found a grizzled seaman who knew Pedro Lorca.

"Sure—Chololoco," the man said. Chris looked puzzled, and the man translated. "The crazy half-breed. He used to work around here, señor, fixing nets and cleaning fish. He would work long enough to get money to drink and then he would stop working until he ran out of money. But he got old and he does not come here anymore, señor."

"He might be seventy or seventy-five now," Chris said agreeably.

"That is a good age," solemnly said the seaman, who looked to be 175. "Not many live that long."

"Do you know where his home might be?" Chris asked.

The seaman did not answer. He turned instead to a young man working on his boat and began shouting a torrent of high-speed Spanish that Chris could not follow. Occasionally, he heard a word that sounded like "loose." Chris knew they were speaking in a seaman's jargon, a vernacular that insulated them and their conversations from the outside world, that being anyone who did not take to the sea for a living.

After twenty seconds, the seaman turned back.

He pointed off to the right. "You go down this road, señor, until you see La Tigra Tavern on the corner. Turn left there. Pedro's house is up two blocks on the right-hand side. It is a green house. You will know it because it is the only house with curtains in the windows."

"Thank you, captain," Chris said. He offered the man money, but the seaman gruffly refused.

It was a small house on an unpaved road with few neighbors. The sea apparently had given Pedro Lorca very little.

Chris's knock on the frame of the screen door was answered by a tall woman whom he could see dimly through the screen.

"Who is it?" she called out.

"A man of peace," Chris responded in the traditional Venezuelan greeting.

"Then come right in," she answered. When she opened the door, for a split-second he could not speak. Not since he had first seen Zhava had a woman's beauty hit him with such effect. The woman was tall and had long shining ebony hair halfway down her back. Her eyes were dark and far apart, her nose elegantly straight, her full lips a natural rose color in her tan face.

She looked at him quizzically.

"I wish to speak to Señor Pedro Lorca. I was told he lives here."

"Yes, he does. But he is not at home at this moment. I am his daughter. May I help you?"

"I doubt it," Chris said. "I wish to talk to your father about a ship he was on that sank back in 1943. Long before you were born, señorita."

The woman laughed at the flattery. "Not that long before, I am afraid. What is it you wish to know?"

"I am a writer," Chris improvised. "I am doing research for a book on the naval history of World War II and I thought it might be interesting to have the firsthand account of a survivor of a sinking. I would pay your father for his time and trouble, of course."

"Please come in. Father will be back shortly if you wish to wait. He has gone for a stroll."

Caldwell entered the neat living room and sat on a hard sofa covered with slick plastic fabric. A three-year-old girl appeared in the doorway leading to the rest of the house. She leaned timidly against the wall, one finger in her mouth, the other hand playing nervously with the hem of her faded but clean dress.

"My daughter, Elena," the woman said, smiling toward the child. The woman sat on a chair across the room from Caldwell and the child rushed to her, burying her head on her mother's lap.

"A lovely name for a lovely child," Chris said politely. "She is very shy, I see."

"If you are to spend any time here, she will wind up in

291

your lap, chattering like a monkey in a tree." She stroked the child's head affectionately.

There was a moment of silence. A beautiful woman with a beautiful daughter. Just as his Zhava and Shoshana had been.

"It is possible that I am causing you an inconvenience, Señora Lorca?" he asked. "Perhaps I should wait in my automobile until your father's return?"

"No, you may not do that. You will join us for dinner when Father returns. And I am Señora Losada, not Lorca."

"I am Christopher Caldwell, señora."

"Do you know anything of my father?"

"No, señora, just his name," Chris said, and then thought of the fisherman's nickname for Pedro Lorca. El Chololoco. The crazy half-breed. It came back to him what the doctor had said in Pedernales. Something about the poor man's brain never working right again.

His fear was confirmed by the woman. "I am afraid you have come a great distance for nothing, señor. Since that accident so many years ago, my father's mind does not function well. He does not remember what happened to him."

"Nothing?" Chris asked.

"Very little," she said. "And that little comes and goes." She paused. "Like the wind," she said sadly.

Suddenly the little girl pulled away from her mother's lap and ran from the room. A moment later, a door slapped shut at the rear of the house and a voice called, "Luz?"

"In here, Papa," she called back. "We have a guest."

Pedro Lorca appeared in the doorway. He was a stocky gnarled man with a long sad Indian face and alert black eyes. He moved stiffly but vigorously.

"This is Señor Caldwell, Papa," the woman said. "He has come to talk to you."

Caldwell rose and stepped toward the man, ready to shake his hand if a hand was offered. None was.

Instead Pedro Lorca was staring at Luz Losada. "You are in my chair," he said accusingly.

"But now it is free for you, Papa," she said as she stood up. "I warmed it for you."

"My good Luz," he said, smiling. He sat down and looked at Caldwell.

292

"Señor Caldwell," the woman said, "I have forgotten my manners. I will make you a drink. Rum perhaps?"

"Just fruit juice, señora, would be fine."

"And you may speak with my father as you wish," she said.

She went into the kitchen, and Chris sat back on the couch looking at the old seaman. Lorca seemed content to sit quietly, staring at Chris. Finally, Caldwell said, "Señor, I wish to speak to you about your shipwreck."

"The weather is very nice now," Lorca said. "This is my favorite time of year. Sometimes I get chilly."

"Your shipwreck?" Caldwell repeated. "After leaving Pedernales?"

"Do you like to fish, señor? They say the fish are running very good now. I like to fish. Once I worked on the boats, repairing the nets, but now I am old. I work no more."

Little Elena stopped in the doorway of the room and looked at Caldwell. He smiled at her, and she turned and fled.

"In 1943, Señor Lorca, you were aboard a ship that went down after picking up oil near Pedernales. I wanted to talk to you about it."

Pedro Lorca shuffled himself stiffly around in the soft chair.

"They say the fish are running very good now, but they always say that. I think the fish ran better when I was young," he said.

Doyle Blaney and Frederick Kirchner sat side by side in the back seat of the large sedan. The two men in the front had met them at the airport in Caracas. They were swarthy and hawk-nosed, wiry of build, with the same air of latent, explosive hostility about them. They had the look of men who would kill swiftly and unhesitatingly when ordered to do so.

They both spoke Spanish fluently, but Blaney was sure they were not Latin Americans, because they spoke an entirely different language with Kirchner, one he had never heard before. They had not spoken one word to Blaney since meeting the two men at the airport.

"Who are these two?" Blaney finally asked Kirchner.

"They will be our interpreters," Kirchner said with a faint, cold smile. It was one of the few things he had said to Blaney in the more than two thousand miles since they had left Houston.

Kirchner's longest speech came in the back of the car when one of the men gave him a leather bag. Kirchner had opened it and presented Blaney with a small flat automatic. He had carefully explained the weapon's workings, showing him how to load it and how to release the safety catch.

"It is reasonably accurate up to fifteen or twenty feet, and it has the great advantage of being lightweight and able to be carried in your coat pocket without being noticeable. The bullets are special and very effective."

"What's special about them?" Blaney asked.

Kirchner's lips parted slightly in his cold smile. "They do not conform in every detail to the specifications laid down in the Geneva Convention," he said. "They are quite lethal."

They were probably dum-dums, made to fragment on impact, Blaney realized. They might be poisoned as well.

He felt the unaccustomed weight of the weapon in the side pocket of his jacket. It was concrete evidence that the strange events of the last thirty-six hours were not some wild dream. He had been wrenched from his comfortable office in Houston and hurled through the sky to Venezuela, and soon—perhaps in days, perhaps in just hours—he was going to have to shoot a man to death.

The prospect of killing another man had not frightened him when he had joined the FBI. Possibly it had been one of the attractions that organization held for him. He had always enjoyed the legal violence of football in high school and in college, and he had had more than his share of fights as a boy and even as an adult. With the bureau, several times he had come close to trouble by being overzealous in punishing prisoners.

In a way, he regretted that he would be using a gun on Christopher Caldwell. He would have preferred to simply beat him to death with his fists—no getting suckered like the last time—or with a rock or a club if that proved more convenient. But he was glad that it would be Caldwell who was his target in any case.

In the gathering dusk, Kirchner strained to look at a road sign.

"We'll be entering a town called Pedernales in another ten minutes," he said.

"That's our destination?" Blaney asked.

Kirchner nodded.

"What makes you think Caldwell is there?"

"If he has not been here yet, he will be," Kirchner said.

"How do you know?"

Kirchner glanced at him, then stared stolidly ahead. Without turning, he said, "When we enter town, begin using your eyes but try not to show your face."

Blaney obediently leaned forward and began looking around, holding one hand over the lower part of his face with his elbow on the seat ahead as if propping up his chin. The effort was unnecessary. There was no sign of Caldwell.

They stopped at the Star of Wonder Hotel, and one of the two swarthy men went inside. He came back out in a few minutes and spoke rapidly in the strange tongue to Kirchner, who tightened his lips in annoyance. "Caldwell was here today," he informed Blaney. "But only for a few hours, and then left."

"Where do you suppose he went?"

Kirchner pondered the question. "They will try to find out," he decided. "And we will stay here for the night."

The four men registered and took two rooms, each with twin beds. Blaney glanced down at the register as the two dark-skinned men signed in. The driver's name was Abdul something. He could not read the other name.

Kirchner ordered the hotel owner to send food to their room, and the owner, convinced that Pedernales was on the threshold of becoming a major tourist attraction, readily agreed. He produced a pot of *sancocho,* a thick seafood stew that Blaney and Kirchner ate in their room. The other two men had gone out to look around the town.

"My Spanish is not fluent enough now to be useful for this task," Kirchner explained to Blaney. "I spoke the language fairly well at one time, but that was many years ago and I have forgotten too much of it."

The rest of the evening passed in dreary boredom. There were no books to read, no television to watch, not even a radio in the small room. Kirchner showed no inclination to make small talk. For lack of anything else to do, Blaney sat by the window and stared out at the street, hoping to see Caldwell, or a pretty girl, or anything interesting. There was almost no traffic on the dimly lit main street, and Blaney finally gave up and went to bed, even though he was too keyed up to sleep.

Kirchner had lain quietly atop his own bed the entire time, staring at the ceiling, thinking private thoughts, and ignoring Blaney's attempt to start a conversation. He was still lying there when Blaney finally fell asleep.

Pedro Lorca was a native of Puerto La Cruz, 120 miles west along the northern coast of Venezuela. He had gone to sea as a boy, and while his lack of education had made it impossible for him to rise above the rank of seaman, he was a good sailor, well respected, always able to find work. He had married a young woman from the village of Irapa and had moved there because it was his goal to own his own fishing boat one day. He had fathered a son, Miguel, and a daughter, Luz. Miguel was dead. Luz was twenty-nine. Four years before, she had married an oil worker, Enrique Losada, and three weeks after their wedding, he had been killed in an accident. She had returned home to her father, already pregnant with Elena.

Luz told this to Caldwell as the four of them sat in the neat kitchen of Lorca's small home eating a dinner of *hallacas,* a small cornmeal pie filled with chicken and pork and eggs, reeking with garlic.

Elena knelt on a chair, feeding herself neatly with fork and spoon. She kept stealing glances at Caldwell but hurriedly looking away whenever Chris gave her a smile. Luz, as she spoke, watched the interplay with fond amusement. Pedro Lorca sat at the head of the table, head down, intent on his food. He might have been dining alone for all the attention he paid.

"May I speak, señora?"

"Please," Luz said.

"Without offending your father?"

"No offense is possible, Señor Caldwell. My father lives in a different time and place from us. He does not know we are here. Tomorrow he will not remember your visit, and if you should see him every day for the rest of his life, he will look at you each day as a stranger he has never seen before. You will not offend him."

"He has been like this since the accident? Almost forty years ago?"

"That is correct."

"And he never speaks of the accident?"

"No. Sometimes he dreams of it and cries out in his sleep. Sometimes a thought, a memory, will come into his mind, and he will say something that almost makes sense, and for the first dozen times, you hope that at last he is recovering and will soon be the man he once was, but it passes, and nothing changes and he is the same."

"It has been very difficult on you," Chris said.

"Many have it more difficult, señor."

"You are twenty-nine years old?"

"*Si.*"

"Then you were..." Chris stopped in confusion, embarrassed at the question he had been about to ask.

Luz Losada merely laughed. "That is correct, señor. I was born after my father became this way. Unfortunately, perhaps, a man does not need a brain to create a baby." She looked at Chris, and he glanced down toward his plate.

"But you know very little of what happened to your father's ship," Chris said.

"Very little," she agreed. "It was an oil ship. It picked up oil and went to Tenerife, which is in Spain and where there is a refinery. My mother told me this because she always wanted Papa to bring her home something from Spain. He never did. On his last trip to Spain, the ship was destroyed by torpedoes. Or mines. Some escaped on a life raft, but what happened to them no one knows. Only my father was found. He dreams, señor. He screams of the sharks. He screams of the moon."

"The moon? Does he ever mention the Red Moon?" Chris asked.

Pedro Lorca's head jerked up as if on a string. His eyes were bright and flintlike. "Ah, the *Red Moon*," he said. He looked about to say more, then he dropped his head onto his arms and wept.

Chris did not know what to do. He looked at Luz. "I am sorry, señora," he said. "I did not..."

297

"Do not concern yourself. It is not the first time it has happened; it will not be the last."

She stood from her seat and walked alongside her father. Gently she assisted him to his feet and said, "Papa, it is time for bed." Obediently, he followed her from the room. Despite himself, Chris could not help but watch her walk away. She was a big-bodied woman with a full chest and long muscular legs. The smooth roundness of her buttocks through her thin blue dress caused him to swallow. He forced himself to look away. Elena was staring at him.

"My mama is pretty," she said.

Chris smiled. "She is very beautiful," he said. "And you are a very wise child."

"Thank you, señor."

When Luz returned a few moments later, she asked Chris what he had found to talk about with Elena.

"It is our secret, señora," he said.

Luz served coffee, and Elena left the room. Chris sighed and said, "I guess then there's no way of ever learning where your father's ship went down."

Luz looked up at him brightly. "Oh?" she said. "I did not know you were interested in that."

"Well, yes," Chris said cautiously.

"I think I know the location," Luz said. "Or can find it."

"But how?" Chris asked. "It was before you were born."

"Five years ago, before the arthritis made my father suddenly old, he would occasionally go out on the fishing boats as a helper. He was out one day with Álvaro Oropeza, whose boat is the *Blue Shadow*. They were out in the ocean, past Dragon's Mouth, perhaps twenty-five miles, when some of their lines snagged on something underwater. My father tried to free them, but was not able to. Álvaro attempted to help him. Somehow, Álvaro told my father their location. He told me later that my father screamed and wept like a baby. He crawled into a corner of the boat, wrapping his arms around himself like a baby, whimpering. Álvaro told me that he thought it was probable that my father's ship had gone down there and my father remembered the...the..."

"Coordinates?" Chris offered.

"Yes. Coordinates."

"Do you think this Oropeza could find that place again?"

Luz shrugged. "He is a very good captain, señor, with a very good boat. It is equipped with sonar and radar. He is meticulous about keeping charts and logs. If anyone could find it, Captain Oropeza could," she said.

Caldwell smiled at the beautiful woman, a rising flush of excitement tingling within him.

"Señora Losada, I would greatly appreciate it if you would introduce me to your friend Captain Oropeza."

When he finally checked into the Sabana Hotel that evening, Chris thought about Luz Losada and realized that in a way, the lovely Venezuelan woman reminded him of Susan Millard. They looked nothing like each other, except that both were beautiful, but they were both proud women and honest, and they wore their obvious intelligence like badges of honor.

He missed Susan and wished he were back in Houston. It had taken him all these years to be able to say "I love you" to someone, and he wanted to get on with it.

But first, he would finish his business in Venezuela. Chris called Amelio Guerado in Caracas, told him where he was and where he intended to go the next day.

"Diving alone is dangerous, is it not, señor?" Guerado said.

"It can be," Chris agreed, "but I'm an expert."

"Yes, and even experts drown. My son, Julio, knows how to dive. He will accompany you."

"I plan to leave very early," Chris said.

"And I do not plan to have to tell Major Ravitch that I ignored his instructions and did not take every precaution with your safety. What is your hotel?"

"The Sabana."

"Julio will leave now. He will be there before daylight, señor."

There was no point in arguing, Chris knew. Instead he said, "Thank you, señor."

"*De nada*. And good fishing."

CHAPTER SEVEN

When Blaney woke the next morning, he was alone in the room. He dressed, went to the men's bathroom at the end of the hall, and was shaving at the washbasin in the room when Kirchner returned.

"Our two friends are out," Kirchner said. "We will have breakfast." They ate in a small restaurant a hundred yards down the street from the hotel. The food was ample, but the eggs tasted tinny and metallic and the coffee was so strong that Blaney kept adding milk to dilute it.

"Do not be seen," Kirchner ordered him as they left the restaurant. "Caldwell may be back."

Kirchner was gone for three hours, and Blaney hung around his hotel room. After the tall white-haired man returned, they sat quietly waiting.

Late that afternoon, there was a knock on the door.

The two swarthy men entered, escorting a small elderly man with wire-rimmed glasses.

The one who had registered as Abdul spoke to Kirchner. "This is Señor Alonzo Inca," he said. "He has much knowledge of the man Caldwell."

Kirchner eyed the man with interest and motioned for him to sit in one of the room's two plain chairs. "Ask him to tell us what he can about Caldwell," he told Abdul. "Translate into English so that our friend here also will know what has happened."

Sentence by translated sentence, Blaney heard the story of how Alonzo Inca, newspaper editor and former oil-truck driver, had agreed to guide Christopher Caldwell to the abandoned Griffin oil well and the information he had given Caldwell concerning the history of the well. The old man seemed proud that he was able to recall the entire conversation almost word for word, and Kirchner listened patiently and attentively.

He frowned but said nothing when the old man began speaking of the oil ship that was torpedoed and sank, but when Inca mentioned that there had been a survivor, Kirchner's eyes widened and he leaned forward attentively, listening to each word.

Inca finished and looked at Kirchner as if awaiting questions.

"Ask him if Caldwell seemed interested in the ship," Kirchner told Abdul.

"Those were the last questions Caldwell asked," Kirchner was informed. "He was also talking about a red moon, but Señor Inca did not understand what he was talking about. Caldwell asked the name of the survivor of the ship."

"And all Señor Inca was able to recall was Pedro?" Kirchner pressed.

After a brief interchange, Abdul said, "He told Caldwell he thought it *might* be Pedro, but it might also be Pancho. He couldn't remember."

Kirchner nodded, reached into his pocket, and pulled out a roll of bills. He peeled off three and said, "Give these to Señor Inca with our thanks for his services. Tell him he has a very good memory, one that he can be proud of."

The old man's eyes danced as he accepted the money with a gracious nod of his head. Then he spoke rapidly to the interpreter.

"He says he has been thinking since talking to Caldwell and this morning when he woke he remembered that the seaman's name *was* Pedro after all."

Kirchner nodded again. *"Muchas gracias, señor,"* he told the old man directly.

"Pedro Lorca," the man added, grinning widely.

Kirchner's eyes widened.

"From the village of Irapa," yipped Inca, almost capering in his excitement.

Kirchner stared at him. Then a smile spread slowly across his face and he reached out to shake the old man's hand. "Tell him that he has an *excellent* memory," he instructed Abdul. "Then get him out of here. We are leaving right away."

As Alonzo Inca left the room, he turned to make a final statement.

"He says that if we should meet his old friend Pedro Lorca to give him his best regards."

301

Kirchner nodded and bared his teeth.

"Tell him that we look forward to doing so," he said.

When Chris Caldwell left his room before daybreak, Julio Guerado was sitting, back against the wall, across from the door of his room. He nodded to Chris and scrambled to his feet to follow the taller American from the small hotel.

"Your father says you know how to dive?" Chris said.

"*Sí, señor*," Julio said. Chris realized those were the first words he had ever heard the young man speak directly to him.

But if Chris had been annoyed at the youth's presence, the annoyance vanished when they went to the docks to meet Álvaro Oropeza, skipper of the *Blue Shadow*. Oropeza seemed inclined to spend three-quarters of the day negotiating price with Caldwell, until Julio stepped in. He began talking machine-gun Spanish to Oropeza, almost too fast for Chris to follow. He heard the youth mention his father's name, Amelio Guerado, several times. The two members of Oropeza's boat stood back, watching, smiles wreathing their faces. Julio finally turned back to Caldwell.

"It is settled, señor," he said. "What else do you need?"

There was no air compressor available, so Chris rented six filled tanks of air. Caldwell doubted that Julio would be experienced enough to make a deep dive to a wreck. But he could hover near the surface on the end of an emergency line. If something went wrong, he might be able to get down and help Chris.

As the *Blue Shadow* pulled away from the dock and the sun was just beginning to peek over the horizon, Julio said, "I do not understand, Señor Caldwell. What is it that you will be expecting to find on this old ship?"

"In truth, Julio, I don't know. It's a shot in the dark. Somehow I think this ship might be involved with something I'm looking into."

Julio Guerado shrugged. "I hope so, señor," he said politely.

The forty-foot boat had two powerful diesel engines and ripped across the surface of the ocean at a full twenty knots. Occasionally, Oropeza would look back with curi-

302

osity at the two men and the equipment they had rented, but he said nothing. The money was good, it was guaranteed by Amelio Guerado, who was a very large man in the life of Venezuela, and the fishing was not all that good, despite the stories of wonderful catches made, told every night in the little port's taverns.

It was almost noon when they reached the spot Oropeza had been looking for. He cut back the throttles and called Chris up to the flying bridge.

"This is the spot, señor," he said. "I remember it because whenever I reach an obstruction in the fishing grounds, I chart the location. To save myself trouble in the future. This is where we were when El Chololoco became ill."

"Will you be able to locate the exact spot again?" Chris asked.

"With the help of the sonar and the radar and God, perhaps, señor," Oropeza said.

Chris went back onto the deck and began putting on the diving gear. Then he helped Julio with his.

After fifteen minutes of crawling around in slow circles, Oropeza shut the engines.

"Señor, I think we have it," he yelled. He turned to look at Chris. "There is something down there," he said, "but I cannot tell if it is a ship. It might be only rocks. But the depth finder indicates there is something, and this is generally a level bottom."

"How deep is it, captain?" Chris asked.

"Only about a hundred feet," Oropeza said.

Chris frowned. It might be "only" one hundred feet deep to a fisherman, but to a diver each added foot of depth meant that his air supply was depleted that much sooner. And it meant less work time on the bottom because a diver needed to spend a longer time decompressing on the way back up, getting rid of the tiny bubbles of nitrogen that the heavy pressure would force from his air into his bloodstream. If he skimped on his decompression—the gradual climbing back to the surface—a diver risked a painful, crippling, perhaps lethal attack of the bends.

Caldwell put it out of his mind. He had dived many times in the past to a hundred feet or more. It was risky, but it was a risk he was prepared to take. Except that all those previous deep dives—in fact, almost every dive he made, even to the shallowest levels—had been made with at least one companion by his side. He was violating the cardinal rule of simple swimming, much less underwater diving, by going below without a companion.

Oropeza brought the fishing boat around until it was directly over the obstruction on the bottom and dropped anchor.

"I hope you have not cost me an anchor, señor," he lamented to Caldwell.

Julio snapped, "If we have, you will be paid for it, captain."

Caldwell asked one of the mates for two hundred feet of thin line. He tied a large loop in one end of it, then he and Julio entered the water.

Chris said, "You keep feeding this line to me. If I get into any trouble, I'll yank hard. You come down for me as fast as you can. Just follow the line. And remember, don't waste your air by staying under the surface all the time. Just hang by the side of the boat. If I need you, I'll pull."

The young man nodded seriously, fumbling with his mouthpiece.

"Vaya con dios, señor," he said.

Caldwell smiled, winked cheerfully, then sank below the surface.

Ten feet under the surface, Chris again checked his equipment, then swam to the bow of the boat and found the anchor line. He used it to pull himself rapidly downward, using it both as a guide and for assistance in reaching the bottom rapidly. Every minute saved could be important, and there was no problem in descending as rapidly as one could. It was only a too-rapid ascent that was dangerous.

The water was reasonably warm, but it was clouded with salt, and the sunlight faded rapidly. It would be very dark on the bottom; he wished that he had been able to obtain a stronger underwater light. He would have to make do, however.

His trophy bag of tough filmy white mesh trailed behind from one wrist. Each time he saw it from the corner of his eye, he flinched slightly. He had not told Julio, but he was mildly concerned about the possibility of sharks hanging around the wreck.

The end of the anchor line came upon him quickly, and then the ocean bottom. Chris felt a surge of disappointment. The wreck, if there was one, was not even in sight. He let go of the anchor line and began swimming in a widening circle, cursing the waste of time and energy.

Then ahead of him suddenly loomed a dark rise. As he swam closer, it took on form in the ghostly flicker of his light. He swam to it and touched it. It was metal. It was a ship. The old man, Pedro Lorca, locked in the room of his mind with the terrible memories, had been right. It was half buried in silt, and it flickered with waving sea growth. Chris could hardly make out any details.

He swam the length of the hulk. It was lying on its side. It had apparently broken in two, possibly from the impact when it hit the bottom. The two main sections were separated by a distance of about ten feet. The stern of the ship was lying on its right side, the bow of the ship on its left.

Chris saw a group of fish diving fearfully from the light of his torch into a gaping hole near the keel of the ship. Swimming closer, he saw that the torn metal had been pushed inward, obviously from an explosion.

One of the torpedoes must have struck here.

As he continued along the back half of the ship, his torch, weaving constantly back and forth, picked up a protuberance from which a long green streamer of sea growth waved gently back and forth in the shifting ocean currents. He swam closer to investigate, putting his face mask only inches from the round lump jutting from the ship.

Then he froze in horror as he realized it was an unexploded bomb of some kind.

Instinct propelled him instantly away from the object, but he caught himself and returned slowly. He reached out cautiously to touch the device, but hurriedly changed his mind. He had heard too many tales of how torpedoes, shells, limpet mines, and other explosive devices had gone off after decades dormant. Sometimes the slightest jar could be enough to trigger the deadly mechanism.

He wished he could remove it and bring it to the surface for close study, but instead he swam away. He might run that risk later if it was necessary, and he would do it in the proper fashion, carefully attaching a line from above,

305

then swimming well away from the area before any attempt was made to wrench it loose from the side of the ship.

At this depth, if the device should explode, the force of the blast in the water would either kill him instantly or knock him out with a concussion, and an unconscious man would drown in moments under the ocean.

He swam back along the side of the ship toward the bow. The deck made an angle of about forty-five degrees with the ocean floor. Quickly he scooted down under the side of the ship, knowing that a sudden shift or collapse in the ocean floor would let tons of dead old steel fall on him and crush him to death. There were two more holes, implosion holes just like the one he had seen in the stern of the vessel, the metal ripped inward by the force of an exterior explosion.

He knew one thing. The ship had not been brought down by torpedoes. It had been mined.

He came out from under the ship, grateful to be still alive. Farther ahead, he saw the twisted remains of the ship's bridge, almost torn from the ship by the shock of hitting the bottom. The captain's cabin was probably located within that structure, he knew.

He looked at his wristwatch in the light of his lamp. He had been here almost thirty minutes.

He wanted to go into the captain's cabin, but it would be better to wait, to come down with fresh tanks and to get right into it from the beginning of his dive.

He took the lifeline to Julio from his shoulder and gently, so that he would not alarm the young man on the other end of the rope, tied it to a piece of the ship's railing. He would be able to find the ship again when he came down merely by following the rope.

Then he slowly went up the line, staying below his bubbles, stopping every five feet for a full minute to allow his body to purge itself of the nitrogen it had absorbed. It was the worst part of any dive, that waiting in the water, wondering if some large shark might decide to investigate this strange invader of its domain. It rarely happened, and on the few occasions when Caldwell had seen sharks of any size they had warily remained at a decent distance. But sharks were unpredictable at best, and while a

306

hundred might pass a potential meal without giving it even a look, it was no guarantee that the hundred and first would not swoop into it in a mad frenzy of biting and tearing.

Twenty minutes later, he was only ten feet below the surface, and Julio swam down anxiously to look at him. Caldwell gave him a confident thumbs-up gesture and waved him back to the surface, where he joined him five minutes later.

As he broke the water, Chris hollered, "Tie that line to the boat. I've got it tied to the ship."

"You found it? What was it like?" asked Julio, too impatient to wait to climb on board before asking questions. He was rewarded by a random wave that slapped water into his face, causing him to sputter and gasp.

The two divers clambered out of the water onto the boat. Oropeza shook Caldwell's hand formally. "You found your ship? I found the right location?"

"Yes, captain. An excellent job of navigation."

Oropeza smiled broadly and threw a look of pride at both the boat's hands. "We know our business," he said with an innocent lack of humility. "If we didn't, we would starve. But my father, God rest his soul, could have found this spot without the use of depth finders or other modern equipment. He was a sailor, he was."

The younger mate nodded respectfully, but the older man had a twinkle in his eye. "We all know that you are not the man your father was, Álvaro," he agreed cheerfully.

"What did you find?" Julio asked Chris.

"Nothing yet, my friend," Caldwell said, wearily unzipping his wet suit. "I spent too much time looking the ship over. I'm going down again to see if I can get into the bridge. But first I need some hot soup. This is thirsty business, swimming around on the bottom of the ocean."

The sailors laughed. "Soup in ten minutes," the younger one said.

"I'll wait," Caldwell promised.

In Irapa, the four men found the home of Pedro Lorca without much trouble. The heavy sedan coasted quietly to a stop and they sat inside, looking at the small green

307

house for a while. Then Kirchner grunted something to the two men seated in front.

The two men slid quietly from the car and approached the house cautiously. One sidled up to peer through a front window while the other circled around the back. After a few minutes, Abdul returned to the car and leaned in the open window to speak to Kirchner.

"He says the old man is sitting in the front room with a young woman and a small child," Kirchner informed Blaney.

"So what do we do now?"

"We go in and talk with Señor Lorca. We inform him that we are the police. We ask him if he has seen this Christopher Caldwell, who is being sought by the police of his own country—that means you, Blaney. Then we thank him nicely for his assistance and we go away, unless there is reason to think that Caldwell may return here, in which case we shall remain to await him."

"Makes sense," Blaney said.

Kirchner opened the door and walked toward the house, talking quickly to Abdul. The fourth man appeared from around the back of the house, reported briefly, was given instructions, and vanished toward the back of the house again.

Abdul pulled open the screen door and marched in without bothering to knock, Kirchner and Blaney close on his heels.

"*Policía,*" said Abdul, holding up what looked to be some kind of badge in a holder. The three people in the room looked up, startled.

Kirchner eyed the two adults coldly as Abdul spoke rapidly to them in a firm tone of voice. Blaney heard the name Caldwell repeated several times. He also heard "FBI" with a nod in his direction. He tried to look stern and imposing, but he found it hard to do anything but look lustfully at the beautiful dark-haired woman. Her eyes flashed and she looked defiantly at the intruders, her hand reaching down to pat reassuringly the young child who had rushed to her side.

The old man looked at the three of them, Blaney realized, as if an invasion of his house by policemen was so

308

common an occurrence that it was not worth more than a few seconds of his time.

He did not speak. Nor did the woman.

"Tell her she can answer our questions here or at our headquarters. She will not like our headquarters. Nor will her child," Kirchner instructed Abdul.

Abdul spoke to the woman, and she answered him. Blaney heard the name Caldwell.

"She says that Caldwell was here yesterday but he left," Abdul translated.

"Where did he go? Will he be back?" Kirchner demanded.

Abdul repeated the questions in Spanish. Blaney could see the young woman visibly thinking, trying to frame an answer. Finally she spoke.

Abdul translated. "He said that he was going fishing."

Kirchner was about to speak again when the old man looked up for the first time and his eyes focused on the German. The old man rose and advanced several steps, then his eyes widened and a look of astonishment crossed his face.

"You killer," he screamed in Spanish. "You were on my ship."

Kirchner eyed him stonily, then turned to Blaney, still lingering near the front door.

"Shoot him," he said.

"What?"

"You heard me. He knows me from long ago and cannot be allowed to live. Shoot him!"

Blaney felt as if he were sitting in a theater seat, watching action unfold before him on the stage. But it was his own hand that was reaching into the side pocket of his jacket and pulling out the small flat gun. He saw the old man's eyes widen in disbelief and fear at the sight of the weapon.

Then it was out, pointed in front of him, aimed at the old man's chest, and he felt his finger squeeze, heard the sharp splat of sound, and saw the man's chest explode.

The pistol followed the old man as he sank, clutching his chest, and Blaney felt his finger squeeze again. The old man jerked with the impact, then lay still on the floor.

309

Blaney felt remote and uninvolved in what had just happened. He needed no mirror to know that his face was calm and expressionless. It was as if he were standing behind the man who had just fired that gun with such deadly effect.

He was surprised to hear a shrill, anguished scream from the woman. She came rushing forward, her hands raised like claws, as if to attack the three men confronting her. Kirchner barked a brief order, and Abdul stepped forward, his arm swinging in a long arc that ended at the side of the woman's head. She crumpled in a heap atop her father, and Blaney saw the blackjack that the swarthy man had pulled from his pocket.

The child ran to her mother's side, crying, "Mama, Mama!" Kirchner nodded again, Abdul's arm swung again, and his fist thudded against the child's skull and she fell too.

Blaney felt disgust at Abdul's viciousness, a shock he had not himself felt seconds before when he had murdered the old seaman.

There was complete silence in the room, until Kirchner cursed under his breath. "Unfortunate, and a complication I had not expected," he said in an annoyed tone of voice. "I never dreamed that the old man might recognize me after all these years."

"Recognized you from where?" asked Blaney. He could not take his eyes off the unmoving body of the man.

"Never mind. That was long ago. We have a problem to consider now."

"What problem?" asked Blaney, as Abdul's partner entered the room from the kitchen.

"She said Caldwell went fishing," Kirchner said.

"She was lying."

"No. She was telling enough truth so that we would have no reason to punish her child. I know what Caldwell is fishing for."

He thought for a moment, then gave instructions to Abdul.

The woman on the floor gave a moan, rolled over on her side, then got groggily to her knees, holding one hand to the side of her head. Her legs were long and smooth, Blaney noticed.

310

Kirchner was talking to him. "These two will stay here and wait for Caldwell. If he returns here, they will kill him and rejoin us in town. We will go to the docks and try to find out what boat Caldwell is on and if it has returned yet. If it has not, you and I will await Caldwell there and when he comes in, we will conclude our mission."

He turned to leave. Belatedly, Blaney realized he was still holding the weapon in his hand. He replaced it in the pocket of his jacket, then instinctively wiped the palm of his hand on the side of his trousers.

Luz gave a sob of despair and threw herself on her father's body. Abdul eyed her speculatively, then rattled off a query to Kirchner. The latter paused, shrugged, and nodded. He strode from the house with Blaney on his heels.

Blaney heard the woman give a muffled scream of outrage. He glanced back through the screen door and saw one of the men holding her from behind with one hand over her mouth and the other groping down the front of her dress.

Abdul walked to close the inside door, and Blaney could see no more.

"What's going on in there?" he asked Kirchner.

"They want to have some fun with her while they are waiting for our friend Caldwell. I told them to go ahead. It doesn't matter. They have to kill her anyway, before they leave."

He jumped into the driver's seat and impatiently started the engine while Blaney hurried around to the other door. A moment later, they were speeding back along the road toward the waterfront.

Blaney found his thoughts drifting back to the house they had just left, rather than looking ahead to the coming showdown with Caldwell.

He could picture the woman clearly in his mind. He could see the two men tearing her clothes from her body and forcing her legs apart.

He found the image arousing his body, and he crossed his legs and stared down the long dirt street as Kirchner drove off.

311

CHAPTER EIGHT

After a forty-minute rest, Chris entered the water again with two fresh air tanks on his back. He raced down the safety line to the bottom, and when he had reached the sunken ship, untied the rope from the railing and again tied it around his shoulder.

Then he swam directly to the bridge structure of the ship and hung there, considering his course of action.

His greatest concern was not encountering a shark but bumping up against a moray eel in the dark confines of the ship. It was a natural habitat for the strong, savage predators. He reminded himself to be careful not to cut himself against any of the jagged pieces of metal that would be around him. The cut would cause no pain in the cool water, but a trail of blood could invite shark attack.

He entered the shattered bridge slowly and carefully, shining his light around. He thought he caught a glimpse of a snaky body sliding away out of sight, but he could not be sure. It was probably his imagination.

There was a pile of sodden debris against what had once been the wall of the chart room, covered with a layer of silt and muck. Chris looked at it in despair, then moved away to approach a stairwell that led down. Somewhere below was the captain's cabin.

He floated slowly forward, chiding himself for breathing more rapidly than necessary. He moved his torch constantly from side to side. Was it glowing more dimly now?

No matter. He was spending only a few minutes anyway. He had no intention of becoming trapped inside this rusting ruin.

He reached what had once been the bottom of a set of stairs and flashed his light into the pit of a doorway that opened beneath him. He could see a jumble of furniture below. A flicker of motion caught his attention, and the beam of his light flashed to a corner of the room. There,

Two eyes glittered coldly at him for a moment, then slid backward out of sight under an overhang.

As he turned away to retrace his path, the flash of his light saw something else in the corner. A skull. A man's skull and pieces of his skeleton. How good he had died before he had been devoured. There was something else there, near the skull. It was metallic. He fought back his urge to flee and tried to fix his eyes on the object in the dimming light from his torch. It was a small box, the size of a large dictionary. It glinted dull-gray in the flickering light. He remembered how some ships kept their logs in waterproof boxes.

Could that skeleton be the captain? Could that box contain the log of this death ship?

Chris felt his heart pounding, his breath noisily hissing out of the exhaust valve behind his neck. He tried not to hold his breath. He said a quick prayer, then with a lunge he pushed himself into the room. He covered the ten feet to the skeleton in a split second and snatched up the box in his left hand. He turned, shining the light up into the corner where he had seen the eel's eyes. They were there again, glinting at him. He waved his arms about his body, trying to make himself appear bigger in the water than he was. Then, trying to hold the bright light into the eel's beady eyes, he pushed his way back across the room and into the stairway. He swam as rapidly as he could along his path, afraid to look back, afraid not to. In the chart room he stooped and turned, fearful of seeing a long snaky form gliding toward him from the companionway, and he breathed deeply when he saw nothing except the dust and sand and silt his rapid movements had kicked up into the water.

Caldwell held his wrist almost against his faceplate to make out the time. He had only a few minutes left and then he must leave. Inside the rubber cap, he could hear his temples pounding.

He turned carefully and swam upward to where two spokes of the ship's steering wheel could be seen, adorned with a light growth of vegetation. His torch flashed about, and in its flickering light he saw the ship's bell.

He quickly worked the metal box into his trophy bag, then reached for the bell with both hands. The torch floated

313

off on its lanyard, its beam dancing crazily about the ghost of the ship's bridge.

He braced himself, then wrenched at the bell. He felt the time-weakened mount give, resist him, then break loose. He stuffed it into the bag also.

Time to go up. He swam out through one of the window openings of the bridge, into the sea, and looked upward. There was not even a glimmer of sunlight to be seen overhead. He started up, two small strokes, then stopped.

There was one more thing.

He swam to the front of the ship and then darted underneath the starboard side. He looked up at the smooth metal hull. He could make out some of the letters of the ship's name because, as on many old ships, the letters were cast separately and bolted to the ship's hull.

Gently, he moved far to the left, trying not to disturb the sand only a few feet below his floating form, so it would not cloud the water.

He made out each letter from left to right, tracing with his fingers the huge foot-high raised metal letters stretching across ten feet of the prow.

L-A L-U-N-A R-O-J-A.

He spelled it to himself once before he understood it.

La Luna Roja.

The *Red Moon.*

He had found the Red Moon.

CHAPTER NINE

It was after dark when Captain Oropeza eased the *Blue Shadow* into the mouth of the narrow inlet leading to the long Irapa waterfront. As he neared the docks, he began to swear, long strings of Spanish cursewords involving goats and chickens, people's mothers and vegetables from a garden.

"What's the matter?" Chris asked one of the hands.

"It is Rico Sapiro again. He has taken our slip. He does it every night when he thinks we will be out overnight, and every time he does it Captain Oropeza goes and punches his face." He rubbed his hands together and smiled.

Oropeza veered the *Blue Shadow* off from its course and powered it down to the far end of the docks, where he found an open slip. Expertly he maneuvered the boat into it.

Still tired from the day's work, Chris was sitting in the small lower cabin, holding his trophy bag containing the bell and the metal box that he hoped contained the *Red Moon*'s log.

Julio, who had sat quietly next to him during most of the trip back, jumped to his feet. "I will bring the auto, Chris," he said.

Caldwell nodded, and as the *Blue Shadow* moved close to the dock, Julio hopped onto the thin wooden finger pier and walked quickly down toward the center of the boating area where he had parked his car that morning.

Caldwell was shaking Oropeza's hand warmly when Julio drove back. "You are a fine sailor, captain. Indeed you are your father's son." He smiled at the older mate, who grinned back a snaggle-toothed appreciation of his earlier jibe at the captain.

Oropeza flushed with pleasure. "Thank you, señor," he said gravely. "I hope that what you have found is what you sought, and I wish you well for the future. But I must tell you, señor, that not for many dollars would I do what you did today. The ocean is for sailing, not for walking on its bottom."

Chris shrugged. "You know gringos, captain. We are all crazy."

"*Sí*. You are crazy but you are *muy valiente,* very brave. You may sail with me anytime."

"I would sail with you through the gates of hell, captain," Chris said formally. He took his leave when he noticed Julio waving at him from inside the waiting car.

Julio handed him a note. "This was in the car," he said. "It's from my father."

The note read: "Señor Caldwell. Paul advises that Blaney, and perhaps Whitehair, have come to Venezuela. Advises caution. Guerado."

Chris read the note again. If Blaney and Wessel were in Venezuela, they had come for him. But how had they known where he was? He had told no one but Ravitch. And, he remembered, Eustace McBride. He would not mind meeting up with them, but now that he had found out the secret of the *Red Moon,* he wanted that meeting to be back in Houston. Not here.

It was time to leave Venezuela.

"Take me to Señora Losada's house," Chris said. "I want to thank her." He also wanted to tell her what the *Red Moon* was, so that she would understand when her father cried out in his sleep. Perhaps that knowledge would make her life easier.

Julio drove quickly to the lonely street on which Lorca lived and parked across the street from the small house.

"I'll be out in just a moment," Chris promised. On an impulse, he took the stained and corroded brass bell of the ship from the trophy bag between his feet. Luz might find it of interest, and as a sea relic it might be of some economic value to her.

"Take your time," Julio said, leaning back in his seat. "I may nap until your return."

Chris crossed the road, walked up to the front door, and was about to knock when he paused. Some sense told him that something was wrong. The house was too quiet. Looking inside, he could see that the living room was empty, even though the single lamp in the room was lit.

Chris opened the door and entered slowly. He frowned as he noticed that the colorful hooked rug which had been in the center of the floor was lying crumpled to one side. He walked forward hesitantly toward the kitchen. He was halfway across the room when a man stepped suddenly into the doorway of the kitchen. He saw Chris, recoiled in shock, then his hand went to a gun tucked into the belt of his trousers.

"Señor Caldwell," he said.

Acting on instinct, Chris hurled the heavy brass bell at the man, who threw up his other hand in defense. The bell thudded against the man's chest, knocking him backward. His gun went off, but the bullet dug harmlessly into the floor beside Caldwell. Chris turned to his right, took two long strides, and hurled himself at the screened window, folding his hands over his head. The glass window was up, and he crashed easily through the flimsy screen. His shins rapped painfully on the bottom edge of the window. As he landed on the bare dirt below the window, he tucked one shoulder under and made a half-roll, landing on his hands and knees.

He scrambled back toward the house, rolling against the side of the building, then crouched just to the right of the window, the bottom of which was at the height of his chest.

He emitted a groan, the sound, he hoped, of a man injured and only semiconscious.

From inside the house, he heard a man snarl something in a foreign language. He recognized the language. It was Parsi. Iranian. His heart skipped. He heard another man's voice call out from the back of the house. A woman's voice gave a choked scream that broke off abruptly.

Chris groaned again.

The light streaming out from the living-room window suddenly was shadowed as the man with the gun appeared and leaned out, peering into the darkness outside, looking for Chris.

Caldwell lunged up, seized the man's right wrist in his left hand, and yanked hard, pulling him outward. He felt the wrist tendons contract as the gun went off again. He stabbed at the man's eyes with the stiffened fingers of his right hand.

317

The man screamed in anguish as one of Caldwell's fingers poked into a jellylike firmness.

As the man instinctively clapped his left hand to the ruined eyeball, Caldwell stabbed again at his throat, then at his solar plexus. The screaming stopped with a grunt, and the man doubled over in agony.

Chris heard footsteps thudding loudly into the room.

Caldwell clamped his free hand above the elbow of the other man's gun arm, turned his back, and gave a downward pull. The man was yanked through the ripped screen and slammed down upon the ground so hard that he bounced up into a sitting position.

Chris kicked him as hard as he could in the throat, then dove for the gun that had skittered from the man's hand when he hit the ground.

Scooping up the weapon, Chris rolled over on his back and looked up to see a second man putting his head out the window. He too was carrying a gun.

Caldwell began squeezing the trigger as fast as he could pull it. The other man recoiled, then vanished from sight. Chris realized he had emptied the weapon. Rolling over again, he scrambled to his feet and dashed into the darkness at the front of the house, dropping the gun as he ran.

He saw that the inside light of their car was on. Julio was coming across the street at a run, a pistol in his hand.

Chris ran to him and snatched the gun from his hand. "Take cover," he ordered.

"Sí," Julio said.

A dog down the road was barking. A voice called from a distance, *"Qué pasa? Qué pasa?"*

Chris glanced back. The man lying beside the house did not move.

He thought he heard a groan again. A woman's groan.

He ran toward the front door, dove through the screen, and hit the floor inside, rolling toward the side, toward the protective shield of a large stuffed chair. He stopped and waited a moment. There was no sound.

Then he heard Luz give a faint shuddering moan from the back of the house.

He stood and moved cautiously toward the doorway at the back of the living room. He glanced down at the man

318

on the floor inside the window and felt his stomach clench.

He had blown the man's head to pieces.

He stopped, listening intently for any sound in the kitchen or in the two small bedrooms on the left side of the house. He heard Luz moan again. There was a thud, then the sound of stumbling footsteps.

Luz staggered into view. She was naked. Her face was bruised and reddened, and blood flowed down her upper thigh. She stared dazedly into the kitchen from her bedroom door, then turned her head and saw Caldwell and froze in horror.

Chris lowered the gun, stepped forward, and reached out to steady the woman with his left hand.

"How many were here?" he hissed.

She looked at him blankly.

"How many men were here?" he said again, shaking her by the shoulder.

"Four," she mumbled almost unintelligibly.

"Where are the other two?" he said.

"They left. They shot Papa, then they left. Just two stayed behind. They did...they did this to me." She stopped, then pulled away from Chris. "Elena. Where is Elena?"

Caldwell followed her into one of the small bedrooms in the back of the house. Pedro Lorca was lying on the floor. Elena was huddled in a corner of the room, her thumb in her mouth, rocking back and forth, making moaning sounds. Luz rushed to her and lifted the child into her arms.

Caldwell knelt and felt for the old man's pulse, then saw the gaping bullet wounds in his chest and knew there would be no pulse. The body already had the odor of death.

He turned and saw Elena huddled in her mother's arms, whimpering. There was a tiny trickle of dried blood on her face.

"What happened to her?" Caldwell asked.

"One of them hit her." Her voice was anguished, filled with pain. "They warned me not to fight or they would hurt her badly. They had me in the other room."

Chris went to a small closet. Inside he found a bathrobe, and he went to Luz and put it over her shoulders. "Here,

319

put this on," he said. "Let's get you both to a doctor."

Chris took the baby from her arms, and she fumbled her way into the robe. As they walked out, Julio was in the living room, staring down at the second gunman. He looked up at Chris with wide eyes.

"The one outside is dead too, señor," he said.

"Good for the rotten bastard," Chris said. "Help the woman. She and the child have been hurt. We have to get them to a doctor."

"Papa," screamed Luz. "Oh, Papa!"

"He's dead," Chris told Julio. "Help the woman. Carry her if you have to."

He hurried out of the house and across the dirt road to his car, placing the child tenderly on the rear seat. He climbed into the driver's seat as Julio came toward him, half-carrying and half-dragging Luz. "Papa," the woman cried again, struggling feebly and gazing back toward the house.

"Get in the back with her and help her hold the child," Caldwell instructed. "This may be a rough ride."

He drove swiftly but carefully, trying to avoid holes and bumps in the ill-kept roads. As they entered the heart of town, Luz whispered directions for reaching the small community hospital. She held the child tightly in her arms, with Julio bracing her on the bumps and sharp turns.

Caldwell almost hit another car as he went through a stop sign and around a corner too fast. He cursed as he fought the wheel, wishing he were driving Susan Millard's Porsche, which was built for fast maneuvering.

The hospital was a small two-story brick building with no emergency entrance, only a large double set of front doors. Caldwell jumped from behind the wheel, yanked open the rear door, and reached for the child. "You help Luz into the hospital," he told Julio. Suddenly he remembered the gun stuck roughly into his belt and said to Julio, "Take the gun."

He ran to the hospital carrying his frail burden. Julio and Luz were close behind him.

A young doctor took the woman and child away, and when the nurse behind the desk heard Caldwell's brief explanation of their injuries—assault and rape—she pushed a button beside her telephone three times. An elderly unarmed guard in a sloppy uniform appeared a few minutes later and looked at Chris and Julio suspiciously.

"Have you called the police yet?" Caldwell asked the admitting nurse.

"Yes, I have," she admitted reluctantly, apparently afraid that the answer might cause the two men to try to escape.

"Good," he told her. "I need to use your telephone."

"That would not be proper, señor."

"This is a police emergency," he said. She hesitated, her hand still clamped over the top of the telephone.

"Julio," Chris barked. The young man stepped forward and ordered the woman to release the phone in the name of his honored father, Amelio Guerado, who could buy and sell this entire hospital's staff and seven generations of their family and who would personally vouch for Señor Caldwell, who was a great man, an important man in the United States.

The nurse's hand came off the phone.

He snatched up the telephone and gave the operator Amelio Guerado's number. When the man answered, Chris outlined the situation in a few terse sentences. "Julio is all right. He is not injured," he quickly reassured Guerado. Then he added, "I'm calling in the CIA."

Guerado was silent for a moment. "I understand," he said. "How much will we be involved?"

"Are you known to my people?" Chris asked.

"We have had dealings," Guerado said.

"I will try to keep you out. For what it's worth, you are a friend of a friend who has been making me feel welcome in Venezuela. *Adiós.*"

He laughed bitterly as he depressed the receiver button. Some welcome.

The next call was to Frank Stanley in the American embassy in Caracas.

It took three line switches before Stanley came on the telephone, noncommittally quiet-voiced.

"This is Chris Caldwell. Do you know who I am?"

"I've heard the name."

"Good. I'm in the Irapa hospital. A Venezuelan national

321

has been killed. I've killed the two men who did it. It's a mess, and it concerns you people. The police will be here any minute and they're going to be asking a lot of questions I'll find hard to answer."

"We'll keep an eye on the situation, Mr. Caldwell," the voice said coolly.

"You'll do a hell of a lot more than that, and you'll do it right away," Caldwell snapped. "I think there's a good chance that those two men I killed tonight are Iranians. What kind of headlines do you think that's going to make?"

Chris glanced at the nurse and the guard. He was talking in rapid-fire English, and it was obvious that they did not understand the language.

"You're coming at me a little fast, friend," Stanley said.

"And the local police are coming at me even faster," Chris said. "I hear their sirens."

"What do you suggest, Caldwell?"

"Take the closest man you've got to here and get his ass moving here right away. Then call Ben Lucco in Langley and follow his goddam instructions. Tell him the crap is going to hit the fan unless you guys pull the right strings in a hurry. Tell him that—"

He broke off at the nurse's sudden sigh of relief. Following her eyes, he saw three armed policemen enter the hospital door. One carried a rifle.

"That's it," Chris said. "The fuzz are here, loaded for bear. Goodbye." He hung up, nodded pleasantly at the nurse, and said, "Thank you very much."

He walked toward the police officers, his hands in front of him, in plain view. "I am unarmed, gentlemen," he said. "I killed two men a little while ago."

"May we see your identification, señor?"

He turned so that the officers could see his hand was reaching into his pocket only for his wallet. He withdrew it and handed it to them. The police officer began looking through the papers and cards inside as Chris began a stripped-down explanation of the night's lethal action.

He stopped as a young doctor walked out through the swinging doors of the emergency room. When he saw Caldwell, he nodded. "Both will be all right," he said. "The woman has been abused but will recover. The child was more frightened than anything else."

"Thank God," Chris said. When he turned to continue talking to the police, he noticed that Julio had gone.

Kirchner and Blaney had waited for three hours at the Irapa fishing docks, watching the empty slip where they were told the *Blue Shadow* always tied up. Kirchner had not spoken a word in the car while they waited, and Blaney found his mind wandering back to the small house of Luz Losada, thinking about the woman, wondering what was going on and wishing he were there.

When a boat pulled into the *Blue Shadow*'s slip, they got out of the car, Kirchner told Blaney to wait and be ready. He had gone toward the edge of the dock and watched and waited, but no American stepped off the boat, only a burly tattooed seaman wearing a yachting cap and a young boy who was obviously his mate. As Blaney watched, he saw Kirchner talk to them in a guttural halting Spanish.

After a few minutes' conversation, Kirchner returned to the car. "That is not the *Blue Shadow*," he said. "That fisherman says the *Blue Shadow* will probably be out all night."

"What do we do now?" Blaney asked.

"We wait. We wait as long as we have to."

Boats came in as night fell, filling up all the slips on the long waterfront. They waited and watched but saw no sign of Christopher Caldwell.

Once they saw a young Latin-looking man walk by them, gaze at them curiously, then get into a car and drive to the far end of the pier area. Later, they saw his car's lights moving away.

Fifteen minutes later, Kirchner said he was going to walk the line of boats to make sure the *Blue Shadow* had not slipped in without their noticing it. Five minutes later, he was running back to the car.

"It's in," he said. "Docked down at the end. It's empty."

He started the engine as Blaney said, "It may have been there for hours, for Christ's sakes."

"No. The engines are still warm," Kirchner said. He pulled the car away from their parking spot and sped down the street, toward the house of Pedro Lorca.

They had gone only a few blocks when they were nearly

sideswiped by a speeding car that roared through a stop sign and around a corner, almost skidding into them.

"Stupid Latins," Kirchner snapped, veering toward the curb.

"That's him," Blaney yelled, grabbing Kirchner's arm. "That was Caldwell driving that car."

Kirchner looked at him with a startled expression, then started to make a U-turn to follow the other vehicle, but by the time he had turned around, Caldwell's car was out of sight.

Kirchner stomped on the gas pedal. "Did he see you?" he demanded of Blaney. "Do you think he recognized you?"

"He couldn't have. He was too busy wrestling with the wheel. Where the hell's he going-in such a hurry?"

"We will find out. Is your weapon ready?"

"Right here."

As they approached a corner, Kirchner glanced into the side street. Far ahead, he saw a pair of taillights racing away from him. He spun the wheel and skidded into the street.

A block later, he had lost Caldwell's car again. Kirchner swore and methodically began driving back and forth through each of the streets. Ten minutes passed before they drove by the small hospital.

"That's the car," Blaney said, pointing to Julio Guerado's black sedan, parked in the hospital's entrance drive.

Kirchner stopped and parked fifteen yards away from the other vehicle. As he did, a siren became audible, and moments later a police jeep pulled up to the hospital entrance.

Kirchner uttered a guttural German oath. "They have beaten us here," he spat.

"I think we ought to haul ass out of here," Blaney said. It suddenly occurred to him that Caldwell, in the hospital, might at any moment begin telling the police a story that would make Blaney wanted for murder.

"And I do not care what you think," Kirchner snarled, as three policemen jumped from the jeep and ran into the hospital. One of them carried a rifle.

They sat silently in the car for a few minutes, until a nurse left the small one-story building. Kirchner jumped from the car and walked over to the woman. Blaney could hear him talking to the nurse in Spanish. Finally, she walked away and Kirchner returned to the car.

"What's going on?" Blaney asked.

"Caldwell is telling the police about killing two men who killed Pedro Lorca and raped his daughter." He put the car in gear and began to drive away. "There is nothing for us here. Caldwell is beyond our reach. For the moment."

"I think we should get out of here as fast as we can," Blaney said.

"First we must visit the Lorca residence again. Your Mr. Caldwell is causing me more and more problems. I am looking forward to the time when I can repay him for them."

Blaney decided that he was riding with a maniac, a fanatic. And he had put first his future and now his life in the man's hands. They drove in silence until they turned into the street of the Lorca home. There were no police cars in view. Kirchner muttered in an annoyed voice: "I *knew* I should have had the woman killed right away."

Julio and Caldwell were at police headquarters, weary of having told their story several times to three different policemen. One of them had not been too bad, Caldwell had thought with idle professional appraisal.

When Julio had mentioned his father's name to the police and explained that Caldwell was a vacationing friend of the family, the police had treated them with great deference and respect. It had made it easier for Chris to lie.

He had told them that he had been in Venezuela to visit his old friend Amelio Guerado, and that he and Julio had decided to do some diving to see if they could locate an old wreck. Pedro Lorca had given them the location of the wreck. When they returned after diving, they had gone back to Lorca's house and found him dead, his granddaughter hurt, Luz Losada raped. Two men were there. Caldwell had killed them after they attacked him. It was not the full truth, but it was enough.

The ranking officer of the police unit walked into the
325

room, followed by two men Caldwell had not seen before. But they were Americans, and he decided that the CIA had arrived.

"It is very strange, Señor Caldwell," the police commander commented, sitting on the edge of a desk with one leg swinging idly. "Your story checks out in almost every detail. Señora Losada insists that neither of you was among the men who invaded her home and did unspeakable things to her. Captain Oropeza swears that until just a few hours ago, both of you were with him. We found the brass bell that you mentioned, and Captain Oropeza has identified it. The window screen was broken in the manner you described, and there is evidence of shots having been fired. There are traces of blood on the living-room floor, and the body of Señor Lorca was in the rear bedroom as you told us."

"Then what is strange?" Chris asked.

"We cannot find the bodies of the two men you have confessed to killing, señor."

Caldwell blinked. "They were gone?"

"That is correct, señor."

"They were dead," Chris said. "Someone must have come and removed them. Perhaps the other two men Luz spoke of."

"We have come to that same conclusion, Señor Caldwell," the police officer said with a short polite bow.

"You have no description of these men?" Caldwell asked.

"Alas, no. Señora Losada is in no condition to speak at length on such matters. We have put out an alert, but..." He spread his hands expressively. "You do not know who they are?"

"No, commander, I do not," Chris said. But it was Wessel and Blaney. He knew it. But how had they followed Chris to Venezuela? How had they known? He looked at the officer again. "What about us? Do we have to stay here or are we free to go now?"

The two Americans were still standing inside the door, quietly listening.

"The young man may leave anytime," the police officer said. "His father, Señor Guerado, is well known to us and has assured us that if we need him, his son will be available

326

for further questioning. Also, he has had but a limited role in tonight's activities. Normally, Señor Caldwell, we would detain you, even though I would have difficulty in telling you what kind of crime you might have committed. However, these gentlemen have vouched for you." He nodded toward the two Americans at the door. "They have promised also to make you available if needed. So you may go also."

"I'll be around a little while anyway," Chris said. "I want to talk to Señora Losada. She deserves an explanation of what has happened. If she is in financial difficulty, perhaps I can assist her."

"That is gracious of you, señor," the policeman said. He left the desk to shake hands with Chris. "Go with God, señor. I hope that you find quieter ways of spending the rest of your vacation in Venezuela."

"No more devoutly than do I," Chris said. "You have been very kind and very professional in a very difficult time."

"Thank you."

Outside the small police station, Chris asked the two CIA men to wait and took Julio aside.

"The metal box from the *Red Moon*—is it still in the car?"

"That is why I vanished those few moments from the hospital," Julio said. "Urchins here will steal anything. I have it locked safely in my trunk."

"Good going, Julio. Will you be able to drive back to Caracas safely?"

"No, señor. I have spoken to my father. He has directed me to stay with you until you no longer have need of my services."

"Thank your gracious father for me, Julio. He is quite a man, and I hope you are as proud of him as he should be of you." The youth flushed under the compliment. "But I have already managed to get you almost killed tonight. I have no further need for you. Go home."

"If it is your wish, Señor Chris," Julio said.

Chris clapped a hand around the youth's arm. "Julio, one day I'll get back here and we'll remember all this over drinks. But I'm on my own now."

"Then I will drive back tonight."

Chris lowered his voice. "Drive to my hotel first. My car is parked in front. The keys are in the glove compartment. Lock the metal box in the trunk and then give the keys to the clerk to hold for me."

"It is done."

"And my thanks to your father."

"For what, señor? He has done nothing."

"For having raised such a son. He has done much."

"Is this almost a wrap?" one of the CIA agents called to Chris.

Caldwell ignored him and shook hands with Julio Guerado. "Go now."

He turned back to the agents. He had made up his mind what he would tell them.

Nothing.

They had served their purpose in clearing the way for him to get out of police custody. But he was not now about to give them Ernest Wessel or Gus Griffin or Otto Brooks or Doyle Blaney or any of the other bastards that might be involved in this.

They all belonged to Chris. If there were any leftovers, they belonged to Major Paul Ravitch of the Israelis. The CIA could hold its hand on its corporate collective ass.

As he got into the CIA agents' car, one said, "We want it all, Caldwell. Don't hold anything back."

"You'll get what I give you," Chris said. "I'll make a full report to Ben Lucco when I get back to the States."

"Maybe," the man said.

"And don't get snide," Caldwell said. "I'm in no mood for your horseshit. I killed two men tonight, and that's something I promised myself I'd never do again. And an innocent old man got killed and a woman and her baby got messed up, so don't give me any static, because I'd just as soon hit you as look at you. I'll talk to Lucco. Nobody else."

CHAPTER TEN

Before he went to his room, Christopher Caldwell opened the trunk of his car and removed the gray metal box he had recovered from the *Red Moon*. He carried it upstairs with him and stared at it under the dim light of a forty-watt lamp.

The box was built like a strongbox, its hinged top fitting flush into the four sides. There was a lock on the side. The box looked sturdy enough, and Chris knew they were designed to be waterproof. But after almost forty years?

He held the heavy box near his ear and shook it gently. He heard no sound of water inside it. He wanted desperately to open it, but he was afraid to. If whatever the box contained was delicate, fragile, sudden exposure to warmth or light might destroy it. It was a job for an expert—most likely the kind of expert that Major Paul Ravitch would have access to.

His bones ached. In the frenzy of the night he had forgotten how tired he had been from his exhausting dives during the day, but now the fatigue washed over him in waves.

Before he went to bed, he took the gun that Amelio Cuorado had given him from his luggage. He put the metal box that might contain the *Red Moon*'s log under the blanket next to him and placed the gun under the pillow. He locked the door carefully and placed a chair under the doorknob. He was asleep within three minutes after his head hit the pillow.

And awake in ten.

He remembered what Yoel Tsurnick had told him. "The big question is still: What is the Red Moon? . . . We just have to figure out how that piece goes in to complete the puzzle."

They had thought they had that piece when Brooks and then Gus Griffin had said the Red Moon was the name of Griffin's first well. But it was a lie. The *Red Moon* was a ship. It was an oil tanker, and as he lay in bed, the pieces of the puzzle began to flow around in his mind, and slowly they began to line themselves up, making edges, making corners, filling in the centers. Chris realized he had been right. Gus Griffin had been running a little gold mine of an oil well in Venezuela at the start of World War II. It was pumping over 150 barrels a day and he was selling all but a few drops of it to the Nazis. That was why he had been able in 1942 to contribute a hundred thousand dollars to Otto Brooks's Senate campaign, even though Gus claimed at the time that the well was producing only four barrels of oil a day. Hirsch had recognized the significance of that immediately. It explained the notes he had written down. Brooks. 100K. 4B. He had known what it meant, but he had probably mentioned the Red Moon to the wrong person and before he could follow through on it, he was killed.

Late in the war when the Nazis were running short of gold, they had probably started to pay Gus Griffin with stolen art. It was probably at that time that he had met Ernest Wessel, who now called himself Frederick Kirchner. Maybe Wessel had recruited Griffin to help the Nazi cause. And maybe when the Nazis stopped paying him in gold and Gus saw the tide of war changing, flowing against the Nazis, he panicked and decided to do away with the people who could inform on him. Wessel and the crew of the *Red Moon,* the oil ship. He had planted those mines on the ship, probably timed to go off when the ship was far out to sea.

But two men had survived. Wessel and Pedro Lorca. Lorca had finally gotten back to his own village and would have lived out a peaceful, witless, unmemoried life there, dying of old age, if Chris Caldwell hadn't shown up. And Wessel? Wessel had gone on, through the Middle East, still fighting Jews. And probably when the new government took over in Iran, he had offered them, as the price for letting him live, control of an American oil company. How long had he kept Gus Griffin's secret, waiting for just the right moment? And then one day, he must have shown up in Houston and told Griffin that he knew about all the men Griffin had killed trying to cover up his dealings with the Nazis, and he had presented his bill. What else could explain Gus Griffin's sudden decision not to fight Adam's plans to make the company a public one?

It should have been simple. But a nameless Israeli spy had heard something, and before dying he had whispered the words "Red Moon." And that had brought Tsurnick to Houston. And it had involved Hirsch in the matter. And they were dead. Just as Pedro Lorca was now dead.

And Caldwell lived to avenge them as he had never been able to bring himself to avenge his own wife and daughter.

There was still one more question running around in his mind. Blaney and Wessel had come to Venezuela; they had obviously picked up his trail. But how had they known where he was? Only two people had known where he was going—Ravitch and Eustace McBride.

He tried to put the question out of his head, to try to avoid drawing the obvious conclusion. He concentrated instead on thinking of Susan Millard, and he finally fell into a sound sleep.

He was up shortly after dawn. He stuffed the ship's log into his suitcase and put his revolver into the rear waistband of his trousers. He slipped on a light khaki jacket and carried his suitcase down to the trunk of his car. He drove several blocks until he found a small restaurant and parked directly in front where he could watch his car from inside.

He was on his second cup of thick Venezuelan coffee, ready to order his breakfast, when one of the CIA agents he had met the night before came into the small café.

He sat across from Caldwell and signaled the fat little waitress for a cup of coffee.

"I talked to Lucco in Langley this morning," he said.

"It's still night there," Chris said. "Ben's working late."

"We're all working late, thanks to you. Lucco wants you to get your ass out of Venezuela and back to the States right away. He'll talk to you when you get there."

"All right," Chris said. He was in no mood to be combative.

"You're a menace," the agent said. "Killing fucking Iranians. Fucking oil deals. Fucking Nazis. Fucking Israelis."

"What Nazis? What Israelis?" Chris asked.

"Lucco's been checking, so don't be cute. He knows you're involved with the Mossad, chasing down some Nazi bastard who might be hiding out in Houston. He says too many people have been killed. I knew you were a bad one, Caldwell, but I didn't think you had gone over to the Israelis."

"I thought you and they were on the same side," Chris said.

"Only when they want to be. You know them. You've been stationed over there. They play their own hand their own way."

The agent sipped his coffee, laced heavily with cream, put it down, and stared at Caldwell, shaking his head. "I have this feeling that the world would be a better place if I could find a dungeon to lock you in."

"I'll give you the next best thing," Chris said. "I'm leaving."

"When?"

"Right away."

"Good."

"And thanks for last night," Chris said.

"Call it a farewell gift," the agent said.

Luz Losada was red-eyed but composed when they admitted Chris to her room at noon. There were lines in her face he had not seen before, but she was still beautiful. She looked at Chris calmly, and he wondered if she was still under sedation.

"It is good of you to see me, Señora Losada," he said, putting a small vase of tiny white flowers on the table beside her bed and sitting down. "How is your little girl?"

"Elena is fine," Luz said. "She was in here only minutes ago and already she is telling me what we will cook for dinner. She has forgotten already and will forget more. The young are so lucky."

"I cannot tell you how sorry I am for you," Chris said. "How my heart aches for you."

Her eyes filled, but she fought back the tears and reached over to put her hand on his arm. "Thank you, señor," she said in her throaty voice. "I am glad you came so that I could thank you for saving my life last night. And most of all, for saving my daughter's."

332

She dabbed briefly at her eyes with a facial tissue.

"I am responsible for your tragedy," he said. "If I had not come to talk with your father, this terrible thing would not have happened."

She squeezed his arm. Her grip was surprisingly strong.

"No, señor. I do not know why those men did what they did to us, but no good man is responsible for the actions of animals. Last night was a nightmare, but I know that you did not kill my father. And I know that you killed two of those beasts," she said with grim satisfaction, her dark eyes flashing. "I bless you for that. They were going to kill us, those men. They spoke openly of it. You saved our lives."

"You know now that I am not writing a book about sea accidents," he said, and the woman nodded.

He went on, "I am searching for some evil men, following a trail that goes back to your father's youth. I just do not know how they followed me here."

Luz frowned. "There was something...something my father said just before he was shot. He looked at one of the men...one of the two that you did not kill...and said that he remembered him. He said the man had been on his ship when it was sunk. That was when my father was killed."

"Was that man tall? With white hair?" Chris asked.

"Yes."

"What else was said?"

"Nothing that I remember. I screamed and rushed forward, and then I felt a pain in my head. One of them must have hit me. I was unconscious for a while. The man who did the shooting and the man who ordered it were leaving when I woke. Some were talking in American, some in a language I never heard. Then the two men they left behind..."

She shuddered and did not finish the sentence.

"The man who shot your father—what did he look like?"

"I did not see him well, señor. He stood behind the man with the white hair. But he was big and he spoke American. They said he was with your FBI," she said.

A nurse put her head in the room, pointed to the watch on her wrist, and shook her head.

Caldwell sighed. Luz was still holding his arm. "They

want me to leave, señora, so you may rest."

"No, they want you to leave so that they may poke at me like some sort of dinner fowl," she said.

He stood and patted her hand. "Eat now, take your medicine, do what the doctors say. Become strong again for Elena."

"I will always be that strong, señor," she said. When he reached the doorway, she called his name.

"Señor Caldwell."

He turned.

"Perhaps one day we will meet under happier circumstances."

"I hope so," Chris said.

"Will you find those men who killed my father?"

"Or die trying," Chris said.

Caldwell went to the hospital office and made arrangements to pay for the woman's medical charges, then went to the hotel to settle up his bill. It was time to leave Venezuela.

"So what the hell did you accomplish?" Gus Griffin growled at Kirchner and Blaney. "Some greaseballs dead and you still didn't get Caldwell and we don't even know what he found out."

"Pedro Lorca had to die," Kirchner said. "He recognized me. He might have been able to recognize you."

"Who cares? What the hell would some spic know? But you're the one, Kirchner, who missed Caldwell when you had the chance."

"We couldn't stay any longer. They would be looking for us. But we'll get Caldwell. We would have had him this time if those fools, those fanatics who run Iran, had sent us someone competent. But we'll get him. He will be back."

"Yeah," said Griffin sourly. "Probably with the CIA, the FBI, and a goddam Marine division. Mistake after mistake."

"You made your mistake years ago when you failed to kill me," Kirchner said.

"I've sure as hell paid for it."

"Caldwell will bring no one," Kirchner said confidently.

"He is a free lance and he desires to slay his dragon by himself."

"Well, I want to know when he's back," Griffin said. He turned toward Blaney. "You've got the hots for that Millard girl, so get close to her. Pump her and make sure we find out if and when she hears from Caldwell."

"Doesn't she always tell Brooks everything?" Blaney asked.

"Lately she's been dodging him," Griffin said. "She may be more hooked up with Caldwell than we know. So you find out."

"Okay," Blaney said. He knew he was getting in deeper and deeper and he still didn't know fully what was going on, but he didn't think anyone would tie him in with the killing of Pedro Lorca. But if Caldwell came back to Houston, he would take pleasure in snapping that last possible incriminating link. And meanwhile, he would look forward with pleasure to getting close to Susan Millard.

CHAPTER ELEVEN

By telephone, Caldwell explained to Amelio Guerado in Caracas that he would be catching an early-evening flight back to Houston but would like to return Paul Ravitch's gift.

Guerado understood immediately. He asked for the flight number and told Chris that Julio would be at the airport to meet him.

After checking his suitcase at the United Airlines ticket counter, Chris found Julio watching him from across the lobby.

"It's okay, Chris," he said. "You aren't being followed. I've been watching."

"Good." He went with Julio into a men's room and there gave Julio the pistol that Amelio Guerado had given him. Julio slipped it into an empty shoulder holster inside his jacket. Chris nodded approvingly. The boy was prepared and he always had his wits about him. His father could be very proud of him.

"I haven't forgotten," the youth said. "Someday, you'll come back on a real vacation."

"Believe it," Chris said.

"And we'll go out to that sunken ship for fun," Julio said.

"That one or another one," Chris said. Somehow, diving to the *Red Moon* would never be fun for Chris.

His plane raced the sun westward across the sky, constantly falling farther behind, and when the plane swooped in to land in Houston, night had fallen.

Chris picked up his luggage from the carousel and was met by a uniformed airport officer.

"Mr. Caldwell?"

Chris nodded.

"It's been arranged that you don't have to go through a customs check. You can just leave through that door over there."

"Thank you," Chris said.

Just outside the door, he was met by a young man with a mustache, who wore a flowered shirt and white jeans.

"Caldwell, my name's Brian Anthony," he said. "We once worked for the same company."

"Yes," Chris said.

"Our mutual friend, Ben, wants you to call him now."

Chris followed the CIA agent to a bank of public phones. The agent dialed a number, gave a credit-card identification, and then handed the phone to Chris.

"Yeah, Ben," said Chris.

"When are we going to talk?" Lucco asked.

"I just arrived," Chris said. "Your man met me, and he knows what he's doing. I'm going back to my father-in-law's apartment tonight. All right to talk to you in the morning?"

"First thing," Lucco said.

"You got it," Chris said.

After he hung up, he thanked the agent, Brian Anthony. He had obviously overheard the compliment Chris had paid him to Lucco, because he said, "If you need anything, call. We're on Rusk Street, and, God help us, our number's in the phone book."

"The joys of living in a democracy," Chris said.

Chris flicked on the light switch in Hirsch's apartment, looked around, then closed the door behind him and bolted into the bathroom. He lifted the lid of the toilet tank and pulled out the plastic bread bag containing the .32 caliber revolver Ravitch had given him.

He ripped the bag open. The gun was still dry. With it cold against his hand, he prowled through the apartment, checking every closet, every corner, even under the bed, everywhere a man could hide. When he was satisfied the apartment was empty, he called Yoel Tsurnick's old telephone number. There was a new message, in Paul Ravitch's voice. It said simply, "At the signal, leave your message, please."

"This is Chris. I'm back. Call right away."

He hung up and walked to the kitchen to make coffee, but before he could even fill the pot with water, the telephone rang. It was Ravitch.

337

"Welcome home," he said. "I understand you had some excitement."

"Yes. You have some fine people there," Chris said.

"Glad we could help."

"Can you come over here?" Chris said.

"Immediately," Ravitch said.

He was there inside fifteen minutes. Over coffee in the kitchen, Chris said, "You know what went down in Venezuela?"

"Yes. Amelio filled me in."

"The old man recognized Wessel. Tall, white-haired man, the daughter said. Blaney pulled the trigger. How did you know that they were on their way to Venezuela?"

"Score one for your girlfriend," Ravitch said.

"Who? Susan?"

"Yes. The lady I met in the hall here one night. She found out somehow that Blaney was on his way to Venezuela, and she tracked me down like a bloodhound to tell me that. She didn't know you were in Venezuela."

"I didn't tell her," Chris said.

"But she guessed. At any rate, after she told me about Blaney, I checked and found out that a man answering his description and another man who sounded like Wessel had flown to Caracas. It was too late to intercept them, but I wanted you to know they were there."

"It might have saved my life," Chris said, remembering his caution when he had entered the Lorca house where the two Iranians waited for him.

"Thank her, not me," Ravitch said. He sipped his coffee and said, "The *Red Moon* a ship. We never would have found that out."

"And it was mined. I think Griffin did it to get rid of anybody who could tie him in to working with the Nazis."

"Probably."

"And so I've got a present for you," Chris said.

"Oh?"

Chris brought out the metal log box.

"What is that?"

"I took it off the *Red Moon*. I think it's the captain's log," Chris said.

Ravitch lifted the box, hefted it in his hands, and then

338

placed it down on the table. "You didn't open it?"

"I was afraid to. I thought whatever's in it might just disintegrate in the air."

"Good."

"I thought you might have some people who could—"

"Yes, we do and they can," Ravitch said. "Tell me, though, why didn't you just give this to the CIA?"

"Because this isn't their operation," Chris said. "It's ours. Yours and mine."

"The CIA has been interested in you and me," Ravitch said. "We've heard from Langley. What are you going to tell them?"

"As little as I have to."

Ravitch shrugged. "We're about at the point where my superiors are going to insist we turn this over to your government."

"So they can do what? Hold a goddam Congressional hearing on Arab infiltration of the domestic oil market? Bullshit. We'll wait six months and nothing will happen."

"What do you want to happen, Chris?" asked Ravitch.

"The same as you. I want Wessel, because he's behind all this. Once we've got him, I don't mind turning everything over to the CIA or the FBI or the Houston Park Police, for that matter, and let them deal with Blaney and Griffin and oil companies and Iran and do whatever the hell they want. I want Wessel. He killed Hirsch."

"Revenge is a bad motive," Ravitch said.

"Yeah? And what's your motive for wanting Wessel?"

"All right," Ravitch said. "We can probably hold off the CIA another day or two." He rose to leave, and Chris followed him toward the door.

"That was a good job, by the way, on Potter," Chris said.

Ravitch smiled, a boyish grin on his young unlined face. "What job? I read in the papers that he committed suicide."

"Yes, of course. A great American tragedy," Chris said.

"An even greater one is that I learned where Wessel was, in a small motel near Arcola. But he eluded me."

"There's always a next time."

"Yes, there is," Ravitch said as he left, with the log box from the *Red Moon* securely under his arm.

Susan Millard's voice was thick with sleep when she

answered Chris's telephone call.

"Oh, Chris, I'm so glad you're back. You're back, aren't you?"

"Yes. I understand I owe you one," he said.

"Well, get over here and pay up. If there's anything I can't stand, it's a deadbeat."

"Be there in fifteen minutes."

Chris tucked his revolver into the back of his waistband when he left the apartment. Downstairs, he realized he had been foolish to leave his rented car parked out in front of the apartment building; it would be too easy to spot and he could not take the chance that no one was looking for him yet.

He paused inside the front entrance to the apartment building, letting his eyes grow accustomed to the darkness, before he stepped out onto the sidewalk. He scanned the street in both directions but saw no pedestrians, no one slumped inside a parked car. He walked quickly to his car, started it, and pulled from the parking space. He drove two blocks without lights before deciding no one was following him, then turned on his lights and drove directly the three miles to Susan Millard's apartment building. He parked around the corner from her building's main entrance, then stood on the corner, watching the building and street for five minutes, before determining that no one had the place staked out.

Riding upstairs in the elevator, he made up his mind that he was going to tell Susan everything. Her early warning might have saved his life in Venezuela, and he owed her the truth. The grim thought nibbled at his mind that maybe he wanted to tell someone the whole story, just in case something happened to him. He had no illusions about Paul Ravitch. Once the Israeli major got Ernest Wessel, he would walk away from the whole case as if he had never heard of it. Chris wanted someone else to know, someone who would care.

Susan was wearing a cocoa-brown silk robe when she answered the door. As Chris stepped inside, she said, "You haven't been followed, have you?"

Sharply, worried, he said, "No, why?"

Susan said, "Too bad. I wanted an audience to see what I'm going to do to you," and then she threw her arms

340

around him and pressed her lips to his. His hands trailed down her back, and he responded to her. They stood there for long moments, and then Susan's hands clasped behind his back and pressed against the revolver in his belt. He felt her body tense for a split second before she stepped back away from him.

"I'm sorry," Chris said. He took the gun from his belt and put it on a small table in the living room.

"No, *I'm* sorry," Susan said, "but I guess I'll never get used to things like that." Her face brightened. "Can I make you a drink? Coffee or something?"

"No," Chris said as he came back and took her in his arms again. "I only want you."

Later, lying in bed, Chris told her the whole story. About Hirsch and Zhava and their work for the Mossad, about Wessel and Griffin and the *Red Moon,* about Blaney's murder of Pedro Lorca, about the paintings in Griffin's study and what they meant, about Luz Losada and her rape and about the men he had killed. He omitted only what he knew about the death of Detective Albert Potter; for some reason, it was important to him that she not consider him someone who took death lightly, someone who might be no better than the men he was hunting.

"That's incredible," she said. She was lying, half turned toward him, her head on his bare shoulder. His left hand idly stroked her soft blond hair. "Incredible."

"But it's true," he said. "All of it. I've got enough now to knock the hell out of this Iranian oil deal, but I want more than that."

"What do you want? What are you going to do?" she asked.

"I don't know. A week ago, I could have told you honestly that I'd be glad to track them down, one by one, and blow them away on the street. But I don't feel like that anymore. There's been just too much killing, too many deaths. I want to make sure that Wessel doesn't get away. The rest of them, let the law handle." He leaned over and kissed her on the forehead. "You've made a piece of cheese out of me."

"No," Susan said. "I've civilized you."

"If you believe that, wait until you see what I do to you

in five more minutes. Have you heard from Brooks?"

"The day after you left. He called and I told him I wouldn't marry him. He sounded relieved."

"Can't blame a man for sounding relieved at being saved from a fate worse than death," he said.

"You'll pay for that, wise-ass," Susan said and pulled the short hairs on his stomach.

"Brooks probably knew I was on my way to Venezuela and that they were coming after me. I guess he figured that the problem with me would soon be cleared up. How'd you find out they were coming after me, anyway?"

"I delivered the SEC application to Adam Griffin and we walked down to Blaney's office—I don't know why, he wanted to talk or something. Blaney wasn't in there, but he had a piece of paper on his desk. I could read it and it was a schedule of flights on Viasa Airlines, some notes he had made. I could see the words 'Houston' and 'Caracas' and a lot of times. I think then I realized that you had lied to me when you said you were going to Puerto Rico. What a pain in the ass you are."

"How'd you notify me?" Chris asked.

"I remembered that man I met in your apartment that night. You told me his name was Paul and he was an Israeli. The more I got thinking, the more I thought that he was probably connected with the government somehow, probably working on this case with you. I called the consulate, described him and his name, and they put me through. We fenced for a while, and then I realized he was the right man. He came to meet me at my apartment and I told him what I thought."

"Did he tell you I had gone to Venezuela?" Chris asked.

"Him? That's a laugh. He wouldn't tell me it was raining if my convertible top was down. Why didn't you tell me the truth? Didn't you trust me?"

"I didn't want you involved," Chris said. "I thought it might be dangerous."

"If you didn't tell anybody, how did they know you went to Venezuela?" Susan asked.

"Mac," Chris said coldly. "McBride is one of them."

"Oh," she said. After a pause, she asked, "Why'd you tell me all this now?"

"Because I know what it's like not knowing the truth," Chris said. "Accusing yourself and living with the hurt because you didn't know something *wasn't* your fault. I've been there. I didn't want you there."

CHAPTER TWELVE

Sherry Griffin was wearing large owl-eyed sun-glasses as she waited inside the small motel room near the airport. Fifteen minutes after she arrived, she heard a knock on the door. When she opened it, Frank Everts stepped inside and smiled at the blond woman.

"Hi, sis," he said. "You can take those shades off. I know who you are."

"Did you find out?" she asked.

"Yeah. It's worth even more than you thought. It could be sold privately for maybe two million dollars."

Everts moved his arm to put it around her shoulders, but Sherry stepped away, went to the far side of the room, and sat in one of the two armchairs, next to a round table with a high pole lamp built into it.

"You sit over there," she said, pointing to the bed.

"Jesus, you really got a bug up your ass, don't you?" Everts said.

"And how else am I supposed to treat the loving brother who handed me up and started all this mess?"

"I told you, sis, they took me too. I didn't know that that lawyer in L.A. was using me. I was as surprised as you were."

Frank was lying, and Sherry knew he was lying. If he had not been part and parcel of the scheme to get her stock option to Adam Griffin, how had all the papers she had signed wound up in Adam's hands an hour after she signed them? But it wasn't worth worrying about anymore. Not now.

"We'll let that slide, Frank," she said crisply. "Now this is how it goes down."

"I'm all ears," he said.

"No, Frank, you're all mouth. But this time try to be a little bit brain, please. Gus and that creepy Kraut who's been living at the ranch are going to be out tonight. Gus already told me. Tina's at music camp and the maid is off.

344

You come at nine o'clock." She fished into her purse and tossed him a key across the ten feet that separated them. Everts tried to catch it, but missed and the key fell to the floor. He picked it up.

"You come at nine," she repeated. "That opens the side door to Gus's office. Get in, get the painting, and get the hell out. Break the lock so it looks like a robbery. Then go back to L.A. and wait for word from me."

"It sounds simple enough," Everts said.

"It should be," Sherry said. "The only problem will come if you try to get smart with me. Then I'll let Gus know it was you and he'll come after you and kill you."

"Hey, sis. You and me. Together like always." He tried a smile, but it was not answered. He said, "What makes you think Gus won't suspect me?"

"I know who he'll suspect," Sherry said.

"Who's that?"

"Some guy named Caldwell."

Sherry rose to leave, and Everts followed her to the door.

"One question," he said. "What brought all this on, anyway?"

For answer, Sherry lowered her sunglasses. While she was wearing heavy makeup, it was obvious that both eyes had been blackened. She had faint bruises over her cheekbones.

"'Cause he's gone crazy. Ever since that Kraut started hanging around, Gus is nuts. He got drunk and beat me up the other night. If I stay much longer, he's going to kill me. And I ain't about to be killed." She pushed the glasses back up her face. "Don't screw this up, Frank, or you're a dead man."

He smiled again. "Stop worrying, sis. You can count on me."

Without answering, she left the room. Everts stood there, looking at the closed door, the same half-smile on his face.

"Sure, sis," he said softly. "You can count on me."

Susan had agreed to call in sick, and take the day off and stay in her apartment.

"That's ridiculous," she had said.

"It's what I want," Chris said. "Things are going to start to happen, and I don't want you in the way."

"You're not...you're not..."

"No," Chris said. "I'm not going out playing Wyatt Earp or anything like that. I don't know what I'm going to do; probably just ask a few more questions and then turn things over to the authorities."

She had accepted that, and Chris had left her apartment before daylight, knowing however that he was going to do a lot more than ask a few questions.

He fell asleep on the sofa in Hirsch's apartment, but napped only fitfully, waiting for the telephone to ring. When it did ring, it was the cool, lightly accented voice of Paul Ravitch.

"Sorry, Chris," he said.

"What happened?"

"The ship's log was in the box. But there had been water in there too. The ink just washed off the pages. There's nothing but a blue smear."

"Back to square one," Chris said bitterly.

"Hold it," Ravitch said. "Remember, my people are the ones who put together the Dead Sea Scrolls after two thousand years and after they were torn into postage-stamp-size bits by Bedouins. Eventually, we can reconstruct that book and everything in it."

"We don't have time to wait for 'eventually,'" Chris said. "We can blow this oil deal out of the water, if we want. Maybe even get the police interested in these bastards. But that log would have made it a lot easier."

"I know," Ravitch said. He sounded as dismal and forlorn to Chris as Chris sounded to himself.

The two men were silent for long seconds, thinking. Then Chris said, "I've got an idea. Maybe we can flush them out in the open."

"Start talking," Ravitch said.

Chris called the number in Langley, Virginia, and was quickly connected to Ben Lucco.

"It's about time," Lucco snapped. "You said this morning."

"Christ, you're grumpy. It still is this morning," Chris said.

346

"Just barely."

"Can you come down here tonight?" Chris asked.

"What the hell for?"

"Because I can put everything in your hands tonight. The whole ball of wax."

"I don't even know what the ball of wax is," Lucco said.

"You'll find out tonight."

"Caldwell, you're getting to be a number-one pain in the ass."

"It's part of my native charm," Chris said.

"Yeah? Well, native-charm this. What the hell was the director doing asking about you a week or so ago? What the hell are you doing with the Israelis? What—"

"What'd the director want?" Chris asked.

"He had your personnel file pulled. He was obviously checking on who the hell you were."

Chris thought that it was Brooks. He was the only person involved in this who was high-level enough to be able to talk to the CIA director. He had probably checked out Caldwell for Gus Griffin.

"My fame is spreading far and wide," Chris said lightly.

"Yeah. Even to Israeli cables. We picked up some of them and there's a reference to a Caldwell and a Red Moon and a painting and I don't know what the hell they mean, and sure as shit pretty soon somebody's going to ask me. Particularly if they get wind of your fucking murderous rampage in Venezuela."

"Tonight, Ben. I'll tell you everything tonight."

"And I think that Ravitch is involved in this somehow, and I don't like that son of a bitch. He just lost an agent in Puerto Rico, and that kind of unhinges those Israelis."

"His hinges are all in order," Chris said. "Tonight, Ben. Come down and check into the airport Holiday Inn and wait there. I'll call you by ten P.M."

"I don't think I have any choice," Lucco said. Chris could imagine him, sitting in his office, sleeves rolled above his elbows, his mouth working furiously on an unlit cigar, convinced that everything that happened anywhere in the world happened solely to make his life miserable. It was the right attitude for a spy, and Lucco was a good one.

"No, you don't, Ben. No choice. I'll see you tonight."

I hope, Chris thought after he hung up.

And in Langley, Ben Lucco said to himself, Bullshit. There are always choices.

The package from Ravitch arrived in midafternoon by messenger. It was an envelope inside an envelope, and Chris was required to show his driver's license before the messenger would surrender it to him.

He took it to the table in the living room and ripped open the package. There was a single sheet inside the inner envelope, and Chris examined it carefully.

Beautiful. It was a Xerox copy of an apparent page from a ship's log. The original page had obviously been waterstained, and the ink was smudged in places.

It was written in Spanish.

"Log of the *Red Moon,* December 23, 1943, Luis Garcia, Captain. Took on this day 30,000 barrels of oil at Pedernales from offshore connection with inland tank. American who provides oil is named Griffin. He uses another name but German passenger, Wessel, has told me his true name. Will leave with morning light for Tenerife Refinery in Spain."

Chris read it again and smiled. It was a beautiful forgery, beautiful enough to trap a traitor.

He picked up the telephone and dialed a familiar number. Eustace McBride seemed surprised to hear his voice, but he recovered quickly and asked casually, "How was Venezuela, kid?"

"Uneventful," Chris lied. "Listen, Mac, I need a favor. A big one."

"Just name it."

"I don't want you to ask me a lot of questions about this," Chris said, "but I've got to go to Griffin's ranch tonight. There's something I've got to find there. Can you call him to an emergency meeting or something, just to get him away from the place? Say, at nine o'clock?"

McBride hesitated, thinking.

"Yeah, I think so," he said. "There's always some diddle-daddle with this SEC application. I can tell him we can square it away over dinner. Let me try to reach him and I'll call you back."

348

An alarm bell sounded in Chris's head. "No," he said. "I'm not at the apartment. I'll call you in half an hour. And, Mac...don't tell Griffin I'm back in town."

"Okay," McBride said.

"Hold on," Gus Griffin said and pressed the hold button on his telephone. He looked across his desk at Frederick Kirchner.

"Caldwell is back. He asked McBride to get me away from the ranch at nine o'clock tonight."

"Good," Kirchner said. "We will arrange a welcome for him."

Griffin clicked the telephone back on and said, "Okay. If anybody asks, you and I are meeting for dinner tonight at the Spread. Thanks."

Griffin hung up. "What the hell could he want at the ranch?" he asked Kirchner, but the German was staring off into space, the corners of his eyes pulled down in an expression of puzzlement.

"I don't trust Caldwell," he finally said, still staring out the window. "I think we should be ready for a surprise and perhaps have a surprise of our own for him."

"Gus, you're home."

Sherry was in the living room of the ranch house, large tinted glasses covering the bruises around her eyes. She could not hide her surprise when her husband came through the front door.

"Of course I'm home. It's my fucking house, isn't it? Where's Gloria?"

"You said you weren't coming home, so I gave her the night off."

"Good," he said and walked toward the rear of the house and his private office.

She called after him, "Should I make something for dinner? Will your friend Frederick be here too?"

"He'll come later. Forget dinner. Go to the movies or something."

Sherry sat for a moment, stunned. Then she ran toward the stairs leading to her bedroom. She hoped she could reach Frank before he left the motel to come to the ranch.

There was no answer in his motel room, and Sherry felt a sinking sensation in her stomach. Things were going wrong again.

Night was gathering in the air when Major Paul Ravitch left the building just off Greenway Plaza and walked quickly toward the underground garage where his private automobile was parked.

As he was getting into the car, two men rushed up from behind him. He could feel a pistol barrel stuck into his back. Ravitch was pushed into the car and slid across into the passenger's seat. One of the other men got behind the wheel and the second man entered the back seat.

"What is this all about?" Ravitch asked calmly.

CIA agent Brian Anthony looked over from the driver's seat. "There's someone coming down from Langley. We're taking you to meet him."

"This is a very foolish stunt," Ravitch said.

"Tell it to Ben Lucco," Anthony said as he drove away.

"Hello, Susie," drawled Doyle Blaney's voice over the telephone.

"Oh. Hello, Doyle."

"How've you been? Haven't seen you in a while."

"I've been busy," Susan said.

"Hear anything from Caldwell?"

"No. Why?"

"Well, I thought if he got back, he'd be sure to call you."

"Then I guess he hasn't gotten back," Susan said. "Is that why you called?"

"No. I know it's a little late and all to be calling, but I thought you might like to sneak out for some dinner."

"Sorry, Doyle. I don't really feel up to it."

"What's the matter? You not well?"

"I took off today. I wasn't really feeling top-notch. In fact, I was just getting ready for bed."

"Well, I'm sorry about that. Maybe some other time."

"Yeah, Doyle. We'll see," Susan said.

When she hung up the telephone, Susan was satisfied. She thought she had been convincing about not hearing from Chris, and even though she didn't like it, she was going to stay home for the evening, as he had told her to. He seemed to have had his reasons.

When he hung up the telephone, Doyle Blaney was satisfied too. Susan Millard was home; the rest of it would be easy.

"Gus Griffin," he snapped into the telephone.

"Sherry, Gus."

"Where the hell are you?" Griffin demanded.

"Upstairs."

"I thought I told you to go out," Griffin said.

"I didn't feel like going out."

"And I don't give a good goddam what you feel like," Griffin snarled. He looked at his wristwatch. It was almost nine o'clock. "I want you to stay in that room and not come out."

"Bullshit," Sherry snapped. "I'll do whatever I goddam please."

"Oh, you will, will you?"

Gus Griffin slammed down the telephone and stomped from his desk toward the door that led to the main section of the house. Sherry had been asking for it, and it was time to teach her a lesson.

A real lesson.

CHAPTER THIRTEEN

Frank Everts checked his luminous wristwatch again. It was one minute until nine. He listened again at the outside door to Griffin's office. He heard nothing.

Sherry had better not have screwed it up, he thought, as he quietly eased the key into the lock and opened the office door. He listened again, heard nothing, and stepped into the office.

The lights were on and the office door leading to the main part of the house was open. Everts walked to the door and closed it, then locked it. He saw the big painting on the wall near the sofa, and despite his worrying about time he stopped to look at it a moment. He shook his head. How the hell could something that ugly be worth two million dollars?

But it was. And when he got out of here with it he was going to be that much richer. And Sherry? Well, if Sherry outlived Gus, she would be a very wealthy woman. What would she need with another two million dollars?

Lying on her bed in the darkened room, Sherry felt her heart pound as she heard Gus's footsteps stomping down the hallway toward her door.

He slammed the door open.

"You in here?"

"In bed, Gus. Close the door."

Griffin left the door open and walked to the bed. As his eyes adjusted to the dim light entering from the hallway, he could see Sherry lying naked on the bedspread. As it always did, her seeming vulnerability started to defuse his anger.

"I told you to get the hell out tonight," he said.

"Why, Gus? I thought we could spend an evening together. Like we used to." She reached up her arms toward him, but he roughly slapped them away.

"Because I told you to get out, that's why. Any more

why doesn't concern you. You just do what I tell you."

She grabbed his wrist and pulled him down onto the bed.

"I don't want you to hit me anymore, Gus," she said.

"You should have thought about that a long time ago," he said.

Morning at Giverny was anchored at both lower corners by bolts installed into the wall, and Everts cursed as he slowly worked the bolts loose with a small pair of pliers he carried in his pocket.

The bolt on the left side unscrewed easily enough, but the one on the right seemed to be frozen solid. Finally, he freed it with a healthy yank and began unscrewing it. To reach it, he had to hold the painting away from the wall. When the bolt came loose, it began to fall. Instinctively he reached for the bolt to catch it. His left hand released the heavy-framed painting and it hit against the wooden wall with a thump.

He paused for a moment, but heard nothing. There was another bolt at the top of the painting, and he began to loosen that.

Thump.

"What the hell was that?" Griffin growled. He stood up.

Sherry pulled at his hand. "Who cares, Gus? It was nothing. Come here."

"Somebody's down there," he said.

"Who cares, Gus? Stay with me."

Griffin fumbled in the end table for a pistol he had Sherry keep in there. He had it in his hand as he turned toward the door. Sherry grabbed his wrist again, and he viciously backhanded her across the face.

"Treacherous bitch," he snarled. "You come out of this room tonight and I'll put a bullet in your face." He ran out the door and toward the steps leading downstairs as Sherry fell back on the bed.

Everts had freed the painting. He had his tools back in his pocket and was just about to lift the painting from its mounting wires when he heard a sound outside the door.

He ran to the door leading outside and fled into the darkness. He was gone before Gus Griffin opened the door to the outside walk, stepped into the warm night, and looked around. He saw nothing. Shaking his head, he stepped back inside his office. Nothing seemed touched or moved.

It must have been his imagination, he thought. It had not been Caldwell. There was nothing in the office that Caldwell could want.

Upstairs, Sherry waited, dreading the moment when she would hear shots in the house. But there were no shots. Had Frank done it? Had he gotten away with the painting?

Chris had waited until five minutes after nine. Ravitch by now should be in place. He had seen no cars turning off Route 59 onto the road leading to Gus's ranch. He checked his gun carefully one more time, stuck it into the back of his belt, and drove back onto the roadway from the small stand of trees where he had been concealed.

He parked in the driveway in front of the ranch house and took the manila envelope from the passenger's seat, then walked up to the house and rang the front doorbell.

There was no answer, and he rang again. His throat was dry and he could feel perspiration coating his body. He had to be careful now. Wessel was the big fish, and he didn't want him out of his net.

The door was pulled open, and Gus Griffin stood there. For a moment, Chris could see the look of surprise on Griffin's face, and then the big oilman lifted his hand and was pointing a revolver at Caldwell's stomach.

Gus smiled. "Come on in, son. I've been expecting you."

He waggled the gun in his hand toward Caldwell, and Chris walked inside. Griffin closed the door behind him, then pushed the gun into his back and herded him through the front rooms toward his office in the back of the house.

"I thought you were going to be out," Chris said.

"I know. Can't trust anybody these days, can you?"

Inside his office, he pushed Chris toward the sofa.

"Sit there and keep your hands on top of your head," he ordered. Chris complied, raising the manila envelope up above his head, and Gus stepped forward and yanked the envelope away roughly.

"It's yours," Chris said. "It's from the *Red Moon*." He was beginning to worry. Where the hell was Wessel?

"So you found it? I thought you probably would," Griffin said.

"Yeah, I found it. Right where you sank it with those mines."

Gus perched on the edge of the desk and looked to make sure Chris's hands were still on his head. Then he reached into the envelope and pulled out the single sheet. He glanced down and read it quickly.

"How'd you get this?" he asked.

"The captain's log was in a waterproof box. I found it in the ship. The log was still readable. It made you out a traitor, Griffin."

"Wessel," Gus said softly. "So that's his real name."

"That's right. You know him as Kirchner, don't you?"

Gus tossed the sheet of paper behind him onto the desk. "Yeah."

"And he was the Nazi you dealt with when you were selling them oil, and now he's helping you turn your company over to the Iranians."

"You're pretty well informed. Tell me, why does somebody so smart do something so stupid as come here?"

"I didn't know you'd be here," Chris lied. He stretched his hands above his head, and they touched the corner of the frame of the large painting. It moved slightly to his touch.

"That was how I knew," Chris said. "The painting. I knew it had to come from the Nazis. I guess you had to sell them a lot of oil to get it."

"The bastards," said Griffin. "They were running out of gold. When they started to pay in paintings, that's when I quit."

"It was that Nazi gold that sent Brooks to the Senate, wasn't it?"

"Sure. 'Course, he didn't know about it until later. Old McBride knew. He was my friend, and he knew everything. He convinced me that it'd be good for us to have a Senator in Washington. Brooks is just a fool. He didn't know anything."

"Is that how you got Mac to hand me up?" Chris said.

"The boy was shocked. He always thought his daddy was Oliver Wendell Holmes. When I told him that if I went under his father's reputation went under too, he saw

355

the light. Tradition counts for a lot around here."

Chris looked toward the door to the hallway. He could see nothing out in the darkness, but Ravitch should be out there, ready to move at any moment. But where was Wessel?

"I'm surprised you're alone," Chris said. "I figured your Nazi buddy would be here with you."

"I am," came a voice from the doorway. Chris looked over to see Ernest Wessel step inside, a pistol in his hand. Chris stared. The man was tall, and his snow-white hair was combed immaculately back. His face had the hint of a sneer around the lips. This was the man who had killed Hirschfeld, the man he had been seeking since coming to Houston. Chris wanted to jump up from the couch and rip the man's throat out with his hands. He felt the gun inside his belt press insistently against his back.

Chris forced himself to stay in his seat. Wessel gave a brief, ironic bow, accompanied by a slight but distinct heel click.

"At last we meet," he said.

"You Nazi bastard," Chris said.

"He had this," Griffin said. He held out the Xeroxed page of the ship's log to Wessel, who came over and read it, then crumpled it and tossed it onto the desk.

"That's just a copy," Chris said. "The original's safe." But even as he said it, he could see a cruel, patronizing smile on Wessel's face. He knew. He knew it was a forgery. Perhaps there had been no possible way the *Red Moon*'s captain could have known Griffin's name, or even Wessel's name.

But Griffin spoke.

"We thought you might have something like that, Caldwell. We came prepared to deal."

"Not a chance," Chris said. He had to play out the bluff.

"You don't know what we've got to offer."

"And I don't care," Chris said.

"Try Susan Millard," Griffin said. Chris stared at him, and Griffin nodded. "That's right. Blaney's bringing her here now."

"Enough talk," Wessel said. "Have you searched him?"

"No," Griffin said. "I didn't have time."

"Fool. Stand up," Wessel barked to Caldwell.

356

Chris got slowly to his feet.

"Turn around," Wessel said.

Chris obeyed and then felt the top of his head explode. His last thought as he slipped into unconsciousness was, Where is Paul Ravitch?

Sherry could hear nothing but a dull mumble of voices from downstairs. Even standing on the balcony outside her bedroom, she could not tell what was going on in Gus's office.

She had heard the doorbell ring but had been afraid to leave her room to see who it was. Who was downstairs? Who was Gus talking to?

Frank had failed to get the painting. She knew it. Gus was no fool. If Frank had gotten away with the painting, Gus would have remembered how Sherry had tried to keep him in her room. He would have been back to talk to her.

But Gus had his gun. Had he captured Frank? Was Frank, even now, telling him how Sherry had put him up to stealing the painting?

Sherry went back inside her room and started to dress. She was getting out while she was still able.

Paul Ravitch washed his hands in the bathroom of the small airport hotel for the third time. Quickly, he ripped down the two shower curtains alongside the tub. He tied their ends together in a rough knot, then took one end of the long sheet of plastic and shoved it into the control panel of the small air-conditioner-heater built into the wall below the window. He closed the top of the small metallic lid to the control panel, pressing down hard, so that the plastic would not slip out too easily. It did not have to work; it only had to look authentic.

He quietly unlocked the bathroom door. He removed a wooden drawer from the small vanity under the sink and held it in his right hand. He took a deep breath and slammed the wooden drawer against the window of the fourth-floor room, shattering it outward. With his left hand, he threw the strung-together shower curtains through the hole in the glass so that they dropped outside. He jumped back behind the bathroom door and prayed that the agents were well trained.

357

He heard a thump on the door, and then a heavy kick and the door flew open, bumping against his body.

He could not see but he knew the agent must have seen the broken window and the phony escape rope trailing through it, because the man cursed and ran past him toward the window. The other agent waited outside the bathroom as he should. As Ravitch hoped he would.

Ravitch pushed the door closed behind him and jumped onto the back of the agent who was approaching the window. He slammed his hand against the side of the man's throat, and before the man could recover and turn, the Israeli had wrenched the automatic from his hand. The man stopped struggling when he felt the gun leave his hand, and Ravitch moved around behind him and locked his arm around the man's throat. He held the gun to his head and hissed: "Walk forward and open that door slowly. Tell your man it's you coming out."

At the door, the agent yelled: "Anthony. It's me. Don't fire."

He pulled the door open, and the two men walked into the room.

Agent Anthony's eyes opened window-wide when he saw Ravitch with the gun at the other agent's temple.

"Put down your gun, please," Ravitch said.

Quietly, Anthony complied.

"Move to the other side of the room," Ravitch said. Anthony hesitated, and the Israeli major barked, "Hurry."

The agent moved away, and Ravitch hurried over to pick up his gun.

"All right," he said. "I want you both in that closet." He pointed with the gun toward a large clothes closet in the far corner of the room. As they got in, he said, "What I told you before is true. This is a matter of life and death. When Lucco comes, tell him I will contact him later and answer any questions he may have. Now you two sit quietly in there while I make some telephone calls. And hope I will be in time."

He closed the closet door and walked toward the telephone. The closet door slid open slightly, and he pointed his gun in that direction. "Back in there," he barked, "until I tell you it's safe to come out." The door slid closed. Quickly

358

Ravitch removed the clips from both automatics, then put the guns on the floor under the bed and set the clips atop the dresser.

"Yes, operator, I'll wait," he said loudly.

He walked quietly to the front door of the room and let himself out. Then he ran down the hall to the exit steps. He hoped he would be in time.

There was no sound from Gus's office as Sherry sneaked quietly down the steps to the first floor. She noticed the front door was ajar. Someone might be out there. So she walked quickly across the deep-piled carpet toward the kitchen on the side of the house away from her husband's study.

She didn't know what had happened with Frank and the painting, but right now she didn't care. Whatever had gone down had gone down wrong, she told herself, and all she wanted to do was leave—leave the house, leave her lunatic husband. If he was planning to kill her, let him tell her about it by telephone.

She opened the side kitchen door and stepped out into the breezeless night. Crickets raised a din in the open fields that sloped away from the house.

She turned and had begun to walk stealthily toward the front of the ranch when suddenly an arm was thrown about her neck and she felt her right arm twisted up behind her back.

She tried to scream, but the arm across her throat cut off all her attempts at sound.

"Going somewhere, Mrs. Griffin?" a hated voice asked. It was that German, that fish-eyed robot who had been hanging around their house for the past week.

She managed a groan, and the pressure on her throat lightened.

"Goddammit," she hissed. "You're hurting my arm. Let me go."

"We'll let your husband decide that, Mrs. Griffin," Wessel said. He twisted the arm even higher up behind her, then pushed her back toward the kitchen steps.

When he shoved her roughly into Griffin's office, Sherry saw a young man lying face down on the floor.

359

"Frank," she said involuntarily and ran over to kneel by the body.

"It's not Frank," Griffin snarled. "Not your beloved stepbrother." He glanced up at Wessel, his face questioning.

"I found her trying to sneak from the house through the side door," Wessel said.

"I'll take care of her," Griffin said.

"And I will again wait outside," Wessel said. He took his revolver from his pocket and turned back toward the front door of the house.

Sherry saw that the body lying on the floor was Caldwell's. She could see his back rising and falling with his breathing. He was alive.

"Frank, huh?" said Griffin. "Tell me, Sherry, why did you think it was Frank?"

She looked at him blankly from her kneeling position on the floor, but she did not answer.

"Were you expecting your little brother here?" Griffin said. "Maybe that's what that noise was that we heard before." Involuntarily, Sherry glanced over toward the paintings on the walls. *Morning at Giverny* was still there. Frank had not gotten it. "Is that why you expected that to be Frank? Maybe you knew he was supposed to come here?"

Sherry could think of nothing to say, nothing that might appease the white-haired man sitting on the desk before her, idly slapping a revolver from hand to hand.

He shook his head in disgust. "I thought I told you to stay in your room," he said.

She shrugged. "I was just trying to get out of here, Gus. Go to a movie or something. Just like you wanted."

There was no understanding on Gus's face, no expression of agreement. "I don't know what I'm going to do with you," he said. "But I'll think of something."

Sherry was sure of that. He would think of something, and she was sure it would be bad.

As Chris struggled back to consciousness, the first thing he was aware of was a woman's perfume. He squinted his eyes tightly to lessen the pain of opening them, then looked

360

to his side, expecting to see Susan. Instead, Sherry knelt by his side.

His head throbbed where he had been hit by Wessel. As he tried to raise himself to his feet, he groaned.

"Easy," Sherry said. "Just take it easy."

He got to his knees and saw Griffin leaning against the desk. The man looked blurry, far away.

"The girl," Chris gasped. "Where's the girl?"

"She's on her way," Griffin said. "Then I think maybe we'll get some answers out of you." He waved toward Chris with his revolver. "Get over against that wall," he said. "Sit against it."

Chris complied, and Griffin ordered Sherry, "Sit on that couch and don't move and don't talk unless I tell you to."

"Yes, Gus," she said meekly.

His head was clearing now and the focus was coming back to his eyes. There were only three people in the office. Wessel was not there. Suddenly, Chris remembered the look he had seen on Wessel's face when the Nazi had inspected the fake page from the log of the *Red Moon*. He had known it was a forgery. But he hadn't told Gus. Otherwise Gus would not be talking about getting answers out of Chris.

Why hadn't Wessel talked?

And then, as quickly as he posed the question to himself, Chris knew the answer.

"Where's Wessel?" Chris asked.

"Outside, looking around. Waiting for Blaney."

"We've got to talk before he comes back," Chris said.

"Talk," Griffin said. "Nobody's stopping you."

"That page from the *Red Moon*'s log? It's a fake," Chris said. "And Wessel knows it."

"Good try, son," Griffin said. "But when your girlfriend gets here, we'll find out about that."

Chris shook his head, but the sudden movement sent sharp sparks of pain through his skull.

"Dammit, listen to me," he said. "Wessel knows the thing's a fake. I don't know how he knows, but he knows. But he didn't tell you that, did he?"

Griffin was staring at Chris.

"Go on," he said.

361

"Well, this is why he didn't tell you. Griffin, this whole thing has been blown to hell. Iran's not getting your oil company. There's not a chance anymore; too much has happened. Wessel knows that. But he's waiting for Blaney and the girl to come, just as if it were important that they be here. He doesn't need them. If he thought I knew anything that he needed, goddammit, don't you think he'd be able to get it out of me? The Nazis were good at that."

Griffin said, "What are you talking about?"

Chris had the sinking feeling that he wasn't making sense; he wasn't getting through to the oilman.

"He's waiting for everybody to get here so he can kill the whole bunch of you. He doesn't want to leave anybody behind who can talk, who can hand him up, who can stop him from getting out of the country." Chris was talking faster now, trying to get it all in, trying to convince Griffin just by his intensity. "When the cops find all our bodies, it's going to take them so long to sort things out that Wessel will be gone. Safe, somewhere else. And we'll all be dead."

Griffin pushed himself away from the desk and walked toward Chris.

"I don't think so," he said.

"Six people have been killed already," Chris said. "You think a few more are going to matter to him? When's the killing going to end? You know you're going to have to kill me. If you bring Susan here, you'll have to kill her. Sherry will know; she'll have to go. And how long do you think you'll be able to trust Blaney? The Israelis are after you. You going to keep killing them? They'll just keep coming at you. My friends in the CIA know what's up. This deal's dead, Gus. All you can do is cut your losses."

"How do I do that?" Griffin was standing in front of Chris, his back to Sherry.

The woman had watched Chris as he was talking, and she knew he was telling the truth. *Listen, Gus,* she wanted to shout. *Listen to him. It's true. I can tell truth.*

"You can cut your losses by staying alive," Chris said. "We don't want you. Screw you. We want that Nazi. That's all." Where the hell was Ravitch? Chris wondered. He should have been there long before. Was it possible that Wessel had intercepted the young Israeli?

362

Gus shook his head again. "I don't think so," he said.

Chris looked past him toward Sherry.

"Sherry, can't you talk to him? You're going to be dead. We're all going to be dead."

"Gus," she started. "Listen to—"

Gus snarled at her, without turning. "You just shut your face," he ordered. "Nothing would have happened if it hadn't been for you. You've done enough already. We'll just wait for the girl to get here."

But it was true. Sherry knew it. She could see it on Caldwell's face. That creepy Nazi would kill them all without blinking an eye. Well, maybe Gus didn't mind dying, and if he wanted, he could take everybody with him. But not her. Not her.

Sherry reached her hands over her head, and they touched the bottom of the frame of *Morning at Giverny*. She pushed with her hands and felt the painting move. Frank must have been interrupted before he could finish the job, but he had loosened the painting. It moved. She clasped her fingers along the bottom of the painting's heavy ornate wooden frame and slowly began pushing upward. The weight resisted her effort for a moment. Then, with a slight jerk, the painting began sliding up the wall.

Chris kept his eyes riveted to Griffin's face, willing with his mind that the old man keep looking at him.

The painting wavered over Sherry's head for a moment, then she moved it forward and it began swinging toward Griffin's head.

Chris glanced suddenly to the side of the room away from Sherry and allowed a look of shock to cross his face. Griffin involuntarily flicked his glance in that direction, just as the heavy painting slammed forward against the top of his head. There was a sickening thud, and then Griffin crumpled slowly before Chris's eyes and sank to the floor.

He dropped his gun to the carpet, and Chris jumped to it. The painting fell from Sherry's hands on top of Griffin's legs.

"Good girl," Chris told Sherry. "Come on, let's get out of here."

"Did I kill him?"

"I don't know. I promise, we'll come back for him." He

rose to his feet and looked down at the oilman. "Too bad, Gus," he said. "I was telling you the truth."

Major Paul Ravitch, cursing the CIA, skidded his car off the exit ramp from Route 59 and onto the narrow access road that led toward the Griffin ranch. He had been steadily gaining on a car that had been far ahead of him, but now the car's taillights had vanished. He hoped Caldwell was still alive.

Caldwell grabbed Sherry's arm and led her through the side door to the outside walk.

"You take off," he told her when they were outside. "Go off into those fields and get lost for a while."

"In a pig's eye," Sherry said. "I'm staying with you."

"I've got to find Susan," he said.

"And I'll be with you," Sherry said.

"Okay," Chris said. "But if there's any trouble, you split, you hear?"

"Fine. Let's go."

Holding her by the elbow, Chris led her quietly around the house, toward the pool area near the front. As they neared, he noticed that the patio lights were on, and that getting to the front of the house to intercept Blaney's car would mean having to cross the lighted area.

He hung back for a moment, saw no one, then led Sherry at a sprint around the far side of the pool.

Suddenly a voice rang out.

"Hold it right there, Caldwell."

Chris looked across the pool. Blaney stepped out of the shadows near the front of the garage. Susan was with him. Her mouth was gagged, and Blaney's arm was around her throat. His other hand held a pistol, and it was pointed at Susan's temple.

"I said stop, or she gets it," Blaney said coldly.

Chris froze in position, and Blaney said, "All right. Toss that gun away. Far away."

In the light from the overhead lamps, Chris could see the glinting fear in Susan's eyes. Without turning, he tossed the gun behind him. It landed in the grass, beyond the paved deck of the patio.

"What are you doing with him, Sherry?" Blaney asked.

"Where the hell is everybody?"

Before Sherry could speak, Chris said, "In the back. In Griffin's study." If he could get out of the lights of the patio area, back into the dark alongside the house, he might have a chance.

"Back away from that gun, Caldwell," Blaney said. He grabbed Susan roughly by the arm and yanked her with him as he walked around the end of the pool, past the diving board, his pistol trained on Caldwell's stomach. Her hands were tied behind her.

"Are you all right, Susan?" Caldwell asked.

She nodded, and Blaney said, "All righter than you're going to be, sucker." He was smiling. Had he smiled like that when he shot the old man in Venezuela? Chris was seized with a flaming hatred, and only by an effort of will was he able to resist his urge to spring forward and throw his body on Blaney.

"Let's go. Get moving," Blaney said. "Let's see what Gus says before I put you away, CIA man."

Blaney was only five feet from Chris, the gun still aimed at Caldwell's stomach. The smile was locked onto Blaney's face as if it had been painted. He had let go of Susan's arm and she stood quietly next to him, but her eyes flashed a message to Chris. She was trying to tell him something, but what?

Caldwell started to turn, but as he did Susan slammed herself against Blaney. The big man shouted, teetered for a moment, then fell into the swimming pool. As he went under, Chris could see the revolver still in his hand. When he came up, it would be firing.

Chris took one step and launched himself into a flat dive into the pool.

Ernest Wessel was prowling the ranch grounds on the far side of the house when he heard the sound of voices coming from the pool. He moved stealthily in that direction, keeping himself hidden in the shadows. He hoped it was Blaney and the woman; he wanted to tie up all his loose ends at once.

With a groan, Gus Griffin came to on the floor of his office. He lay there for a moment, then remembered what had happened. He raised himself to his knees and looked around. The office was empty.

"Son of a bitch," he snarled as he struggled to his feet and walked unsteadily toward his desk, where he kept a loaded .44 Magnum.

Paul Ravitch stopped his car at the end of Griffin's driveway, turned off the key, and ran to the cover of the trees bordering one side of the drive. He checked his gun, then began moving toward the house.

CHAPTER FOURTEEN

Caldwell caught Blaney just as the big man was about to reemerge from the water. He squeezed Blaney's right wrist with his left hand, and as they both broke the surface of the water, he filled his lungs with air.

Just over his head he heard the explosive sound of the pistol firing, then he put his hand on Blaney's right shoulder and with a powerful kick of his legs pushed both of them down underwater.

As they neared the bottom of the pool, Chris switched his grip on Blaney's right wrist and dug his fingertips deep into the tendons and ligaments on the inside of the other man's arm, and the gun dropped from Blaney's hand.

Blaney's face was only inches from Chris's, and Chris could see the fright and shock in the other man's eyes in the bright illumination from the underwater lights built into the pool's sides. Bubbles trickled from the sides of Blaney's mouth as he tried to punch out at Chris, but the water so slowed his movements that the blow never reached Chris's face. Chris again pushed down on the other man's shoulders, pressing him down again deeper into the water and then flipping behind him, where he wrapped his right arm around Blaney's throat and nipped the man's waist between his knees.

Blaney tried to reach behind him to claw at Chris's face, to drive him off, but Caldwell just moved his head out of reach. He felt power surging through the arm that locked Blaney's neck, a power born of hate, of an urge to kill. Slowly the two men moved toward the surface of the pool, but before they could break the water, Chris reached up with his left arm, found the underside of the low-level diving board, and pushed against it, and the two men plummeted again down to the bottom.

367

Blaney's arms were flailing and he tried desperately to turn in Chris's grip so he could face his tormentor, but Caldwell only squeezed harder. There was a sudden burst of air expelled from the big man's mouth, noisily bubbling its way to the surface. His air gone, Blaney began to claw and kick desperately, trying to fight loose. For an instant, Chris felt his grip loosen, but he tightened up his arm again and squeezed harder. Blaney's hair floated in front of his face like the shimmering shafts of some underwater plant growth. Then Blaney's arms stopped struggling and slowly settled down toward his sides. His body went limp in Chris's arms, and Chris released him. Blaney's body seemed to hover in the water for a moment before rising slowly toward the surface. Chris kicked his feet and propelled himself upward, breaking the water, gulping a chestful of air into his tortured lungs and then, in one smooth movement, hoisting himself up over the wall of the pool and onto the cement walkway.

Sherry had released Susan from her bonds, and she ran to Chris and threw her arms around him.

"You all right?" he asked.

She nodded. Over her shoulder, he could see Blaney's body floating, face down, his arms spread out wide to his sides. He had started over to pull him out, to see if the man could be revived, when the first shot rang out. He threw his arm around Susan and drove his legs toward the sodded lawn on the far side of the cement-and-stone pool deck. With his other hand, he grabbed Sherry's wrist and pulled her with them, and all three hit the grass. Another shot sounded and Chris heard the slug rip into the wooden fence behind him.

When the shot fired by Blaney had rung out, Ernest Wessel had changed his mind. A shot that he had not ordered meant resistance, disturbance. Perhaps Caldwell had reinforcements and they had arrived. It would have been nice to eliminate all of them, but it was more important to survive. He veered away from the house and ran toward his car parked in the driveway.

Still moving alongside the trees, Ravitch ran toward the house. He saw lights on in the pool area and ran across the drive. Then he heard a motor start and a car pull away from the curb.

In the light from the carriage lanterns that lined the drive, he could see the man's snow-white hair. It was Ernest Wessel. Then the headlights of Wessel's car came on and he sped toward Ravitch.

The Israeli, clearly outlined in the headlights, took careful aim at a spot on the windshield directly in front of the driver, then fired.

The windshield splintered, but the car kept bearing straight toward him. At the last second, Ravitch jumped to safety behind another car, and Wessel's car turned out of the driveway and onto the access road leading from the ranch.

For a second, Ravitch looked at the car's speeding taillights. He could catch Wessel on the open road. His car was faster and he was younger. Probably a better driver.

Ernest Wessel. A man with the mutilation of millions of Jews on his hands.

Then, in rapid succession, he heard two shots coming from near the pool.

He sighed and made a decision for the living over the dead.

Ravitch turned away from the sight of Wessel's car and ran toward the house.

He ran past the garage as another shot rang out. When he turned the corner, he was on the lighted edge of the patio. There was a body floating in the pool. At the far end of the patio, Gus Griffin stood, firing past the pool, and Ravitch could see Caldwell and two women, rolling, tumbling through the grass, trying to escape Griffin's shots.

Ravitch stepped into the open.

"Drop that gun," he called out.

Griffin wheeled and fired a shot at Ravitch.

The Israeli major dropped into a crouch, squeezed his trigger, and Griffin staggered backward. His gun flew from his hand and a small red dot appeared on his forehead, growing larger as he fell to the ground. He lay still.

Caldwell rose to his feet, still holding the two women's hands.

He looked at the Israeli major and said, "You're late."

"Sorry, old boy. Unavoidably detained," Ravitch said,

as he turned and looked disconsolately along the road where he had last seen Ernest Wessel's car.

Ravitch was calming down the two women in the living room of the house, while Chris called the airport motel where the Israeli had been held prisoner. When he got the room, he said, "Let me talk to Ben. This is Caldwell."

Lucco came on the line screaming.

"If you're with your friend Ravitch, you tell him his ass is grass in this country. And so is yours, buddy."

"When you're ready to listen, let me know," Chris said.

"Talk, prick."

Chris gave him directions to the Griffin ranch and said, "Come right out."

"What's the problem now?" Lucco said.

"No problem, exactly. Except there's as many dead bodies lying around here as there were at the Alamo."

"Shit," said Lucco.

"Could be worse," Chris said. "I'm alive."

"Only until I get my hands on you. Is Ravitch there?"

"Yes."

"Make sure he stays there."

"He said he loves you too, Ben. Hurry on out," Chris said.

It took an hour for Caldwell to tell the entire story. He laid it all out for Lucco, who sat with him and Ravitch in the kitchen of the ranch house, leaving out only the circumstances of the death of Detective Albert Potter, who had killed Yoel Tsurnick in Puerto Rico. "He committed suicide when he found out we were on to him," Chris said.

When he was done with the story, Chris made his suggestion, but Lucco laughed aloud.

"Cover up? Cover this up? Are you kidding?"

"Makes sense to me," Ravitch said.

"I don't care what makes sense to you. You know your days in this country are numbered anyway, Ravitch," said Lucco.

"Next year in Jerusalem," Ravitch said mildly.

"Think about it for a minute, Ben," Caldwell said. "You've got Iranian agents messing around in this country. Trying to take over an oil company no less. You've got some of them getting killed. You've got some of them killing other people. One of those goddam spies was a Nazi, for Christ's sakes. You've got them wandering around Venezuela, killing innocent civilians. You've got a respected Houston oilman who worked for the Nazis in World War II and killed a shipload of people to cover his tracks. Tell me, you want any one of those things in the papers? If all this crap gets out, do you think America will have one friend left in the world? Who isn't laughing in our faces, that is?"

"It still won't wash, Chris," Lucco said. "We can't just go around covering up killings. We're not even supposed to be working domestically at all."

"Yeah, yeah, yeah, I know that. I read the rulebook once too. There's one other reason. The best one yet."

"What's that?"

"Your director. He was involved. He was leaking information to Brooks, who was leaking it to Griffin, who was passing it along to Ernest Wessel, former Nazi and now spy for Iran. That could be a pretty convincing argument upstairs," Chris said. "Particularly when they know the alternative is police and press and trials, and you can bet I'll tell everything at a trial that I've told you tonight."

Lucco looked dejectedly down at the table.

"It won't work," he said finally. "It's a fucking conspiracy, and you know how conspiracies are. More than two people involved and it'll be on the six-o'clock news tomorrow night."

"No," Chris said. "You're talking about another world. Who are the only two people who could talk? Sherry? Her husband tried to kill her and now she's going to inherit his oil company. She'll be happy to have tonight written off."

"And the other broad?" asked Lucco.

"Susan'll be with me," Chris said.

Lucco shook his head again. "It's fucking midnight," he said. "I don't have time."

"You've got all night," Chris said. "I think you ought to get on that phone."

371

CHAPTER FIFTEEN

Susan Millard's long, tan body erupted from the water with the grace of a dolphin. She held a shell aloft, waving it toward Ravitch and Caldwell, who sat on the beach behind his Puerto Rico home, looking quietly out toward the sea.

Chris raised his hands high above his head and applauded silently. Susan nodded and dove back under water.

"It's all over," Ravitch said. "It was in the paper this morning that Otto Brooks has decided to pass up appointment as Chief Justice and retire from the Supreme Court. He said it's a time for younger men."

"Good," Chris said. "And Sherry's got her millions and Adam's got his oil company and poor Griffin and Blaney were both lost at sea in that terrible boating accident, and it's all done. In a pig's ass. You should have gotten Wessel that night."

"Don't think I haven't told myself that," Ravitch said. "But I'm satisfied. And you should be too. You even got a chance to punch McBride in the nose."

"He never understood what was going on," Chris said. "He still doesn't. Any word on Wessel?"

"No," Ravitch said. "But he's back in Iran by now. Don't worry, Chris. We will get him. Time is on our side." He looked out at Susan splashing happily through the water. "Time is on our side," he repeated.

They sat silently as Susan came in to shore, then walked up and sat on a towel next to Chris.

"What are you going to do now?" Ravitch asked him.

Chris leaned over and kissed Susan. "I don't know," he said. "Maybe be a beach bum and live off my wealthy wife."

"He's going to take his bar exam and practice law," Susan said firmly.

"Oh, I am?" Chris said.

"Yes, you are," she said.

He turned to Ravitch and said, "I'm going to take my bar exam and practice law."

"I'll try to direct some business your way."

"Your business I don't need," Chris said. He got up quickly and walked across the dry powdery sand toward his house. A few moments later, he was back. He dropped a paper bag in front of Ravitch. The Israeli opened it and saw it contained a pistol.

"That was Yoel's," Chris said. "I won't need it any more."

"I'm happy for you," Ravitch said as he stood and threw the weapon far out into the cool blue waters. "Be happy for yourself."

EPILOGUE

Hossan Mahedi gazed curiously at the white-haired man with the erect carriage and the cold blue eyes who stood stiffly in front of his desk.

"A very interesting project that you and my predecessor were working on," he said mildly.

"It was my concept," Ernest Wessel said fluently in the formal Parsi language. "It would have worked were it not for the filthy Israelis. And it might work yet."

The new head of the Islamic Revolutionary Security Forces shook his head sadly.

"No, my friend, I am afraid it was not meant to be. It was ingenious and it was bold, but I am afraid your *Red Moon* has sunk. It is over."

"I will think of something else," Wessel said confidently.

"Yes. I am afraid you will. That is quite the problem. You will continue to think of grand schemes until you run out of Iranians to die for you. I am sorry, Mr. Wessel, but for you, World War II has just ended."

He pressed the button on his desk twice. The door behind Wessel opened to admit a uniformed officer and two burly guards.

"You may take our friend away," the official said. "Be sure to give him a Koran to read."

Wessel began to shout as the guards seized his arms and bound his hands behind his back. The Iranian stood, took a prayer rug from a shelf, spread it on the floor, and knelt, facing Mecca. He bowed deeply and began reciting his prayers as the German was dragged from his office.

Wessel was hustled quickly through the corridors and down into a small bare cell in the basement of the former Savak building.

"You are making a mistake, you pigs," Wessel yelled as the cell door slammed shut. "You are in league with the Jews."

374

He was dozing when the cell door swung open with a clang early the next morning. The guards entered and swiftly stripped his outer clothes from him, replacing them with a loose, coarsely woven robe. His hands were again bound behind his back and he was hurried out of the building and into a black van. There were three women sitting in the van, along with half a dozen guards.

"Who are these women?" Wessel asked the guard on his right as the vehicle moved away.

"Prostitutes," the guard said curtly. "No further talking."

One of the women began to wail. The guard beside her slammed his elbow into her ribs, and she gasped and fell silent, except for muffled sobbing.

Ten minutes later, the vehicle came to a stop. The side door opened and Wessel saw they were in what appeared to be a small vacant city lot. A large number of people were standing around the edges of the field, shivering in the early-morning chill.

Then a hood was placed over his head, blotting out the scene.

Two guards seized his arms and half-dragged, half-lifted him out of the van and led him across the field in a stumbling run. Suddenly his feet were swinging in space. The guards released their grip and he fell, in a standing position, into a deep, narrow pit in the ground. He heard the women screaming and wailing. The crowd buzzed excitedly.

Dirt began raining down around his feet. Within moments, he was buried to his knees...to his waist...to his chest. His composure broke and he howled an oath in German as he realized he was being buried alive.

But then the dirt stopped cascading about him. His head was still above ground. He could still breathe. He tried to rub his itching nose against his shoulder but could not reach it. He could hear a voice rattling off a long religious pronouncement dealing with the sin of prostitution and the duty of the faithful to stamp out the evils of a decadent society. The crowd yelled loudly in agreement.

There was a pause.

Then the first stone struck him.

"Jewish swine," he yelled. "The Russians will eat you

for breakfast." His voice inside the hood reverberated in his own ears.

He could hear one woman screaming methodically, over and over again. Then she fell silent, but the crowd kept roaring. He could hear the sacred name of Allah, shouted often with exultation and fervor.

The stones, although softened by the hood, were hitting him regularly now. He felt his nose break. The impacts were growing stronger and stronger.

Then an especially savage blow sent a sunburst of blazing pain through his head. He seemed to be staring again at that blazing sun in the tropical sky half a lifetime ago, with the big black fins silently circling the frail raft.

Then there was nothing.

By the time the guards unearthed his torso and removed the hood nearly an hour later, his head was a bloody featureless lump. The bullet through the back of the skull was an empty formality.

About the Author

Warren Murphy is the author of one of the world's leading action series, *The Destroyer*—a tongue-in-cheek men's adventure series that has sold millions of copies around the world. He is a full-time writer and lives in New Jersey. Watch for the movie, *The Red Moon*, coming soon from Davis/Panzer Productions.